Mike Lawson served for years as a senior civilian executive for the United States Navy. He lives in the Pacific Northwest. *The Inside Ring* is his debut novel.

THE INSIDE RING

Days before an assassin's bullet winged the president, General Andrew Banks, the Secretary of Homeland Security, had received a note which read: *Eagle One is in danger. Cancel Chattooga River. The inside ring has been compromised. This is not a joke.* When Banks showed the note to Secret Service Director Patrick Donnelly, he ignored it. The supposed assassin is found dead, but Banks resolves to dig deeper. He turns to Speaker of the House, John Fitzpatrick Mahoney, who has the perfect guy: Joe DeMarco, a lawyer who owes his career to the Speaker. It's a tall order for DeMarco, but Mahoney is determined that Donnelly should be taken down, and sets DeMarco on a twisting trail through the Secret Service, the FBI, and the Department of Homeland Security.

MIKE LAWSON

THE INSIDE RING

Complete and Unabridged

CHARNWOOD
Leicester

First published in Great Britain in 2005 by
HarperCollins*Publishers*
London

First Charnwood Edition
published 2006
by arrangement with
HarperCollins*Publishers*
London

British Library CIP Data

Lawson, Michael, *1948 –*
    The inside ring.—Large print ed.—
    Charnwood library series
    1. Presidents—Assassination attempts—
    United states—Fiction
    2. Political corruption—United states—Fiction
    3. Suspense fiction 4. Large type books
    I. Title
    813.6 [F]

    ISBN 1–84617–464–3

Published by
F. A. Thorpe (Publishing)
Anstey, Leicestershire

Set by Words & Graphics Ltd.
Anstey, Leicestershire
Printed and bound in Great Britain by
T. J. International Ltd., Padstow, Cornwall

This book is printed on acid-free paper

For my father
Bernard Norman Lawson
1924 – 2004

Acknowledgments

I am deeply indebted to a number of people for their help in publishing this novel.

At the Gernert Company, Matt Williams for his hard work on all the contracts, Tracy Howell for her expertise on foreign rights, and Karen Rudnicki for her help and her patience with all my phone calls and questions.

I want to thank Abner Stein, Andrew Nurnberg, and their associates for getting the book published in so many countries overseas. Talk about European allies! One day I hope to meet all of you in person so I can thank you properly.

At Doubleday, my editor, Stacy Creamer, for the improvements she made to the manuscript, particularly the twist she added at the end. Also at Doubleday, Karla Eoff, for her outstanding work in finding all the typos, misspellings, and broken English; and Tracy Zupancis, for all her assistance to a beginner.

The person I am most grateful to is my agent, David Gernert, for agreeing to represent a new author, for his boundless enthusiasm, for the time he took to help me improve the manuscript, and for his phenomenal ability to convince others that it was a book worth publishing. David, thanks to you, I'm now doing what I've always wanted to do.

Prologue

The video begins with the President walking toward a marine helicopter.

The rapids of the Chattooga River are visible behind the helicopter, and beyond the river is a dense pine forest, the ground rising sharply to a bluff overlooking the river. The President is dressed in khaki pants, a blue T-shirt, and hiking boots. Over the T-shirt he wears a lightweight fishing vest with multiple pockets for storing tackle. He appears relaxed, his pace is unhurried. He smiles and waves once in the direction of the camera, and then ignores it. In the third year of his first term he's comfortable with the mantle of power, undaunted by the media's ever present eye.

There are two Secret Service agents in front of the President and two behind him. The agents wear identical dark-blue Windbreakers and all have on sunglasses. A puff of wind exposes the automatic weapon one agent carries on a sling beneath his Windbreaker.

Walking next to the President, on his right, is the writer Philip Montgomery. Montgomery also wears outdoor clothing, though his outfit has a more lived-in look than the President's. Montgomery is talking to the President as he walks, then looks toward the camera and holds his hands apart as if describing a good-size fish. The President shakes his head and mutters something, his lips barely moving. Montgomery throws back his head and laughs.

As the group of men nears the helicopter they pass into the shadow created by the bluff across the river. A Secret Service agent in front of the President, the agent on his right-hand side, takes off his sunglasses. He folds them quickly and attempts to pocket them in his Windbreaker, but he misses the pocket and the sunglasses fall to the ground. The agent quickly bends at the waist to scoop up the glasses but Philip Montgomery, who is still talking to the President and looking to his left instead of forward, bumps into the agent's rump as he's reaching for the glasses. The agent pitches forward, almost falling, and the collision throws Montgomery off balance and he stumbles into the President.

This chain reaction of gaucherie would have been slightly amusing, something for the anchormen to chuckle about on the evening news, except it ends with Philip Montgomery's brains exploding out the back of his skull. A second later a spray of blood spurts dark red from the President's right shoulder.

With the second shot the President's security detail reacts. A Secret Service agent shoves the President hard to the ground then lies on top of him, covering him with his own body. The other three agents form a protective triangle around the President's prone form. The agent who had dropped his sunglasses stands directly in front of the President's head, and between this agent's spread legs can be seen the President's face. His eyes are white-blue saucers of panic and pain.

The picture spins: a slice of blue sky, a fuzzy

2

wedge of green forest, the whirring blades of the helicopter. When the camera refocuses, the agents have weapons in their hands and are frantically searching the area for a target. One of the agents suddenly points upward, at the bluff, and his weapon begins to spit bullets into the air. At the same time the agent fires, the assassin fires a third time. His bullet hits the forehead of the agent who is lying on the President, missing the President's face by less than two inches. Experts later testify that the bullet passed between the legs of the agent who was standing in front of the President.

The last images frozen on the screen are Montgomery's body, limbs bent at awkward angles, and then a close-up of the President's face: a crimson mask created by the blood pouring down from the forehead of the agent who died protecting him.

WASHINGTON, D.C.

CHATTOOGA RIVER ASSASSIN FOUND DEAD
Probable Suicide Victim

By Sharon Mathison
The Washington Post

Last night police in Landover, Maryland, found the body of the man believed to be responsible for the attempted assassination of the President and the deaths of author Philip Montgomery and Secret Service Agent Robert James.

At 10:30 p.m. on July 19th, a 911 caller reported hearing a single gunshot at the home of Harold Mark Edwards. Landover police responding to the call entered the house and found Mr Edwards's body.

According to FBI spokesperson Marilyn Peters, Edwards died from what appeared to be a self-inflicted gunshot wound from a .45 caliber automatic pistol. Ms Peters said that in a suicide note, written in what appears to be the victim's handwriting, Edwards confessed to attempting to assassinate the President on July 17th. In this same note, Edwards stated that he had acted alone.

Edwards was an unemployed machinist who

was laid off sixteen months ago when his job was outsourced to Thailand. The FBI spokesperson said the Secret Service was in possession of two letters written by Edwards earlier this year in which he blamed the President for losing his job. In one of those letters, Edwards threatened the President's life.

Also found in Edwards's home were two rifles. Preliminary ballistics tests conducted by the FBI indicated that one of the rifles was the weapon used during the assassination attempt.

Mr Edwards was a prior member of the Army Reserve and was classified as an expert marksman. His neighbors said that he was an avid hunter and also said that he had been despondent over his inability to find work.

Still unanswered is how Edwards could have penetrated the President's security at Chattooga River, Georgia, the morning of July 17th. When asked to comment, Secret Service spokesperson Clark Brunson would only say that the Secret Service does not discuss procedures used to protect the President.

1

The receptionist — Boston-bred, fiftysomething, hard and bright as stainless steel — arched a disapproving eyebrow at DeMarco as he entered Mahoney's offices.

'You're late,' she said. 'And he's in a mood today.'

'So since I'm late I guess that means I can go right in,' DeMarco said.

The receptionist was married to a successful accountant, a very nice man, very slim and neat and considerate. On those rare occasions they made love she fantasized about burly Italian construction workers. She used to fantasize about black men with washboard abs and shaved heads but the last few months it had been men who looked like DeMarco: dark hair, blue eyes, a Travolta dimple in his chin — and arms and shoulders made for wife-beater undershirts. However, fantasy man or not, she didn't approve of tardiness — or flippancy.

'No, you can take a seat,' the receptionist said, flashing a brittle smile, 'and in a few minutes, after I finish my tea, I'll tell him you're here. Then he'll make you wait twenty more minutes while he talks to *important* people on the phone.'

DeMarco knew better than to protest. He took a seat as directed and pulled a copy of *People* magazine from the stack on the coffee table in front of him. He was addicted to Hollywood gossip but would have died under torture before admitting it.

Thirty minutes later he entered Mahoney's office. Mahoney was on the phone wrapping up a one-sided conversation. 'Don't fuck with me, son,' Mahoney was saying. 'You get contrary on this thing, this time next year, the only way you'll see the Capitol will be from one of them double-decker buses. Now vote like I told ya and quit telling me about promises you never shoulda made in the first place.'

Mahoney slammed down the phone, muttered 'Dipshit,' then aimed his watery blue eyes at DeMarco.

'You see Flattery?' Mahoney asked.

DeMarco took an unmarked envelope from the inside breast pocket of his suit and handed it to Mahoney. DeMarco didn't know what was in the envelope; he made a point of not knowing what was in the envelopes he brought Mahoney. Mahoney sliced open the envelope and took out a piece of paper the size and shape of a check. He glanced at the paper, grunted in either annoyance or satisfaction, and shoved the paper into the middle drawer of his desk.

'And the Whittacker broad?' Mahoney asked.

'She'll testify at the hearing.'

'What did you have to give her?'

'My word that I wouldn't tell her husband who she's been sleeping with.'

'That's all it took?'

'She signed a prenup.'

'Ah,' Mahoney said. Greed never surprised him — nor did any other human frailty. 'So those

8

bastards at Stock Options R Us will spend eighteen months in a country club prison, the guys who lost their pensions will eat Hamburger Helper for the rest of their lives, and her, she'll get her fuckin' picture on *Time* as whistle-blower of the year. Jesus.'

DeMarco shrugged. There was only so much you could do.

'You need anything else?' he asked Mahoney.

'Yeah, I want you to . . . ' Mahoney stopped speaking, derailed by his addictions. He reignited a half-smoked cigar then reached for a large Stanley thermos on the credenza behind his desk. The thermos was battered and scarred and covered with stick-on labels from labor unions. Mahoney poured from the thermos and the smell of fresh coffee and old bourbon filled the room.

As Mahoney sipped his morning toddy DeMarco studied the bundle of contradictions that sat large before him. Mahoney was an alcoholic but a highly functional one; few people accomplished sober what he had managed in his cups. He was a serial adulterer yet deeply in love with his wife of forty years. He stretched soft-money laws like rubber bands and took tribute from lobbyists as his royal due, and yet he was the best friend the common man had on Capitol Hill. John Fitzpatrick Mahoney was Speaker of the House of Representatives and only the vice president stood between him and the Oval Office should the President fall. DeMarco doubted the authors had Mahoney in mind when they penned the Twenty-fifth Amendment.

The Speaker was DeMarco's height, almost six feet, but DeMarco always felt small standing next to him. Mahoney had a heavy chest and a heavier gut, and created the impression of a man perfectly balanced, impossible to rush, fluster, or inflame. His hair was white and very full, his complexion ruddy red, and his eyes sky blue, the whites perpetually veined with red. His features were all large and well formed: strong nose, jutting jaw, full lips, broad forehead. It was a face that projected strength, dignity, and intelligence — it was a face that got a man elected to a national office every two years.

Mahoney swallowed his laced coffee and said, 'I want you to go see Andy Banks.'

'The Homeland Security guy?'

'Yeah. He needs help with something.'

'What?'

'I dunno. We were at this thing last night and he said he had a problem. Something personal. He says somebody told him I had a guy who could look into things.'

DeMarco nodded. That was him: a guy who looked into things.

'Go see him this morning. He's expecting you.'

'What about that problem in Trenton?'

'It'll wait. Go see Banks.'

2

Andrew Banks, secretary of Homeland Security, was a retired marine three-star general. He was fifty-nine years old, tall and flat-bellied, and his brown suit and olive-green tie resembled the uniform he had worn for thirty-three years. He had a prominent nose, a gray crew cut, and a mouth that was a slash above a thrusting chin. DeMarco noticed that his eyes, magnified slightly by wire-rimmed glasses, were the color of roofing nails.

Behind Banks's desk, framed by two American flags, was a large pre-9/11 photograph of the World Trade Center. The twin towers had been shot looking up from ground level, and they rose, seemingly forever, white and pristine, into a flawless blue sky. The photograph was a vivid, silent reminder of Banks's responsibilities.

DeMarco sat in one of three chairs arranged in a semicircle before Banks's desk. The chair was so uncomfortable that DeMarco wondered if it had seen prior duty in an interrogation room at Guantánamo Bay.

'John Hastings, Congressman Hastings, told me about you,' Banks said. 'He said he was being flexed by someone to influence his vote. He wouldn't tell me who or how, but he said he went to Mahoney for help and the next thing he knows, there you are, prying things off his back. He said you're some sorta troubleshooter.'

Banks stopped as if expecting a response from DeMarco, but DeMarco, like a good witness in court, hadn't heard a question so he said nothing.

'Well I have a problem, maybe a big one, and I don't want a lotta people knowin' about it. I was wondering what to do when I saw Mahoney at this function last night. I asked him what he could tell me about this guy DeMarco I'd heard about. And Mahoney, that prick, you know what he says to me? He says, 'I don't know any DeMarco but he'll be at your office tomorrow morning.' Then he walks away and starts chattin' up some gal half his age.'

She was probably one-third his age, DeMarco thought.

'The thing is, I don't know zip about you.'

'I'm a lawyer,' DeMarco said.

'A lawyer?' Banks said. The D.C. lawyers he knew looked smooth and sophisticated, slick enough to slide under airtight doors. This DeMarco looked like a kneecapper for an Italian bookie.

'But you're also an investigator, aren't you?' Banks said.

'Yeah, sometimes,' DeMarco said, and shifted his butt in the uncomfortable chair. 'General, are you going to get around, anytime soon, to telling me what your problem is so I can tell you whether I can help or not?'

Banks smiled. It was a smile that said it'd be a distinct pleasure to take DeMarco out into the parking lot and beat him bloody with his fists and feet.

'Mister, I'm trying to decide if I want to hire you and you're not helping yourself, sittin' there saying nothing.'

'General, I'm not here for a job interview and you're not hiring me. The federal government pays my salary. I'm here because the Speaker told me to come see you.'

Banks opened his mouth to give DeMarco an old-fashioned, Parris Island tongue-lashing, then remembered he wasn't addressing a buck private. He shook his head and muttered, 'This fucking town.'

DeMarco could sympathize with the man's frustration. He didn't like D.C. himself most days.

Banks rose from his seat and walked over to a window. He turned his back to DeMarco, shoved his hands into his pockets, and stared down at the traffic on Nebraska Avenue. He pondered his options less than thirty seconds — officers are trained to make decisions — and turned back to face DeMarco.

'Hell, I have to get on with this,' he said. 'I have too much on my plate as it is and I can't take the time to find someone else. And Hastings did recommend you. Hastings was in the corp, you know.'

Semper fi, DeMarco almost said, but controlled his wit. 'I didn't know that,' he said instead and shifted again in the chair. It felt like the damn thing didn't have a seat cushion, just a thin layer of cloth stretched over the hardest wood on the planet. Or maybe it wasn't wood, maybe it was metal or that stuff that rhino horns are made of.

'Okay,' Banks said, 'but you have to promise me something. You have to promise that you'll keep everything I'm about to tell you completely to yourself, that you won't tell another living soul. You promise?'

'I do,' DeMarco said. He considered raising his right hand when he responded but decided that would be a bit much.

Banks studied DeMarco's face, looking for twitchy-eyed indicators of falsehood, but DeMarco, journeyman liar that he was, gave up nothing. And DeMarco was lying.

'You better be tellin' the truth, bud, or I'll rip off your head and shit down your neck.'

DeMarco looked at his watch. He suspected Banks's problem was a family thing: one of his kids was in trouble or his wife was having an affair with someone human.

'Okay,' Banks said again, and he took in a lungful of air through his big nose as if preparing to dive into deep waters. 'I want you to investigate a Secret Service agent named Billy Ray Mattis.'

'An agent?'

'Yeah.'

The name rang a bell.

'Investigate how?' DeMarco said.

'I want you to . . . ' Banks stopped.

'Yes,' DeMarco said. It was like trying to get a virgin's knickers off, getting this guy to say whatever was on his mind. Finally the dam broke.

'I want you to see if Mattis was an accomplice in the assassination attempt on the President.'

14

'Whoa!' DeMarco said, half rising out of his chair. 'Stop right there. Do not say another word.' DeMarco shook his head in disbelief at what he had just heard. 'And anyway,' he said, 'I thought the guy who shot the President acted alone.'

'Yeah,' Banks said, 'he probably did.'

This was ridiculous, DeMarco was thinking. 'Look, General,' he said, 'you wanted to know about my background. Well, I'll tell you. I'm a lawyer who does odd jobs for Congress. That's it. If a constituent turns into a stalker, I make him go sit in a corner. If a congressman thinks his kid is doing drugs, I find out before the kid becomes a liability. If a politician thinks his wife is cheating on him, I make sure she's not screwing a journalist. That's the kind of stuff I do, sir. Little stuff. Small stuff. Assassinations are out of my league. Way out of my league. So if you really believe this agent was involved in the assassination attempt, you need to talk to the FBI.'

'I don't want to do that,' Banks said. 'At least not yet.'

'But why not?'

Banks didn't answer him. He just stood there looking simultaneously guilty, stubborn, and annoyed.

In the four days since the assassination attempt Banks and Patrick Donnelly, head of the Secret Service, had been interviewed by the FBI. The press had camped out on their doorsteps screaming questions at them, and Congress, in a rare and rapid bipartisan gesture, had slapped together a nosy panel that had grilled both men for hours on how the President's security had been so disastrously penetrated. Banks had had multiple opportunities to tell people he suspected a Secret Service agent of involvement in the assassination attempt — yet here he was, telling DeMarco he couldn't.

DeMarco knew he should leave. Just get his ass out of this fuckin' chair, walk out, and never look back. He also knew if he left before finding out what was going on, Mahoney would flay him.

Before DeMarco could decide one way or the other, Banks picked up an index card lying on the blotter in the center of his desk. He held it gingerly, by one corner, as if it was coated with anthrax, and handed it to DeMarco.

'This is what started it all,' Banks said. 'That's not the original but that's what it said, verbatim. I sent the original to . . . Never mind. Just read it.'

DeMarco read: 'Eagle One is in danger. Cancel Chattooga River. The inside ring has been compromised. This is not a joke.' The note was signed: 'An agent in the wrong place.'

3

The Speaker had recently taken to walking at lunchtime in a futile attempt to prevent the heart attack that was certain to kill him. He had told DeMarco to meet him at the Taft Memorial at noon. DeMarco had arrived at twelve fifteen and it was now twelve thirty.

At the Taft Memorial stands a ten-foot bronze statue of Senator Robert A. Taft and behind his statue is a carillon made from white Tennessee marble that rises one hundred feet into the air. The twenty-seven bells in the carillon were cast in Annecy, France, and the largest bell weighed seven tons. What Senator Taft had done to deserve such tribute had faded from memory — at least from DeMarco's memory — but he was grateful that the memorial was located in a pleasant urban park close to the Capitol. It was a good place to wait for his boss.

DeMarco took a seat on a wooden bench facing the memorial. He closed his eyes to nap and enjoy the sun on his face but he was soon denied this simple pleasure by two noisy squirrels. One animal was frantically chasing the other across the lawn, around bushes, up and down tree trunks. Whenever the chaser would finally corner the chasee, the trapped one would back up, feign desperation, then escape with a death-defying leap to a thin limb which seemed out of reach and incapable of bearing its weight. DeMarco didn't know if the chase was a mating ritual or just plain fun, but there was no end to it. He wished one of the critters would miss when it jumped but the vivid image of a bushy-tailed little body, spread-eagled on the ground, a ribbon of blood oozing from its bucktoothed mouth made him change his mind.

DeMarco was so busy fantasizing the demise of tree-dwelling rodents that he was startled when Mahoney sat down heavily on the park bench. He was even more startled by the sight of Mahoney in athletic togs: size XXX-large blue sweatshirt, blue sweatpants with white trim, and squeaky new Nikes the size of canoes.

'I saw General Banks this morning,' DeMarco said.

'And?' Mahoney said, still trying to catch his breath.

'Well, sir,' DeMarco said, 'Banks wants me to investigate the recent assassination attempt on the President.'

'You?' Mahoney said.

Mahoney's reaction may have been appropriate but DeMarco was mildly offended.

'Yes, sir. The General is concerned that a Secret Service agent may have had some part in the assassination attempt.'

'Ah, that's horseshit,' Mahoney said and looked at his watch, bored already by Banks's silliness. 'And anyway, if he's really worried he oughta be talkin' to the Bureau.'

'I agree and that's what I told him,' DeMarco said, 'but the part I thought you might find interesting is that both Banks and Patrick

Donnelly are withholding evidence from the FBI, and — '

'Donnelly?' the Speaker said, turning his magnificent head to look at DeMarco for the first time.

'Yes,' DeMarco said.

'Donnelly,' the Speaker said again, then he grinned, his teeth yellow and strong, and DeMarco was reminded of a large rumpled bear, one that has just spotted its lunch walking toward him.

Oh God, DeMarco prayed, please don't let this happen.

'Tell me what Banks said, Joe,' Mahoney said. 'Don't leave out a thing.'

DeMarco did and when he finished Mahoney just sat there, a small smile on his lips, a contented look on his broad Irish face. In an attempt to head off the disaster he feared was coming, DeMarco said, 'Sir, it's pretty unlikely this agent's guilty of anything — even Banks admits that — but in case he is, the right thing to do is to tell the Bureau. Or the press.'

Mahoney nodded as if agreeing with DeMarco but there was a gleam in his eye. It was the gleam of a man who has sighted a sail on the horizon and knows that it's his ship that's coming in.

DeMarco played his last card. 'If the FBI catches me fooling around in this, it could lead back to you. You don't want — '

The Speaker rose slowly from the bench.

'Help Banks out, Joe,' he said. 'Do whatever the man wants.'

Mahoney patted DeMarco affectionately on

19

the shoulder. As he walked away there was a spring in his step caused by more than his new tennis shoes. He was a few paces up the sidewalk when DeMarco heard him bark a laugh and say, 'Donnelly. I fuckin' love it.'

4

'Do you like chamber music, Joe?'

'No. I like rock and roll. I like jazz. I like Ella singin' the — '

'That's nice, dear. A quartet is playing Mozart in the National Art Gallery cafeteria today. Meet me there at three. And don't be late.'

'Do you know someone in the quartet, Emma?'

The phone was silent. 'The cello player,' Emma finally said, and then she laughed. 'I'm becoming predictable in my dotage. I hate that.'

'The last thing you'll ever be is predictable, Emma, but what I have to tell you can't be told in front of the cello player.'

'I'll send her shopping. Just be on time, Joe.'

★ ★ ★

The cafeteria was crowded and a number of spectators were standing, yet Emma sat alone at a table for four. DeMarco could imagine music lovers approaching, asking politely if they might sit, and Emma backing them off with a glance and a growl, like a lioness protecting a bloody haunch from a flock of timid vultures. At present, the lioness was serenely drinking a glass of white wine while tapping a manicured nail in time to the music.

Emma was tall and slim. Her features were

patrician, her complexion flawless. Her hair, cut short and chic, was neither gray nor blonde but some mysterious shade in between. She was beautiful in an austere way and with her ice-blue eyes she reminded DeMarco of the actress Charlotte Rampling. He suspected that she was somewhere between fifty and sixty, not because she looked it, but because of what little he knew of her history.

The operative word with Emma was always 'suspected.' She refused to discuss herself, past or present. She would drop hints — tantalizing, inconsistent tidbits — but would never explain when asked to clarify. She admitted to having once worked for the government, but she wouldn't say in what capacity or for which department. She claimed to be retired but was often out of town for extended periods and never returned with a tan. She lived expensively and owned a home in pricey McLean, Virginia — property that did not seem affordable on a civil servant's pension. She was gay but something she had once said made DeMarco think she had been married and might have a child. But he wasn't certain; he was never certain.

DeMarco knew that Emma was at times enigmatic because she chose to be, because it suited her contrary nature. But he also knew that she was sometimes elusive because she had to be.

As he walked toward her table, DeMarco glanced over at the musicians and noted, as he had expected, that the cello player was a beauty:

a tall, willowy, Viking blonde — with legs to die for, spread erotically for her cello.

DeMarco pulled back a chair to take a seat next to Emma. She heard the chair scrape the floor and said without looking, 'That seat's taken. So are the other two.'

'Liar,' DeMarco said.

'Takes one to know one,' Emma muttered.

Pointing his chin at the cello player, DeMarco said, 'She's a hottie, all right.'

'A hottie? God, Joe.'

As DeMarco listened to the quartet he wondered why all these people were here. Did they really enjoy this music or was it something they forced themselves to endure, a self-prescribed dose of sophistication, the cultural equivalent of swallowing a carrot smoothie for one's health.

'When will this end, Emma?' DeMarco said. 'I'll slip into a coma if it goes on much longer.'

'Sit there and be quiet,' Emma said. 'It's time you learned to appreciate something other than the Dixie Chicks.'

The quartet finally finished and the cello player handed her instrument to a pimply-faced volunteer. She wagged a finger at him in a stern you-be-careful-with-that gesture, then moved toward Emma's table, blonde mane flying behind her, long thoroughbred legs flashing. Had Emma not been his friend DeMarco would have been jealous. Hell, he was jealous.

Seeing DeMarco, the cello player hesitated when she reached the table but Emma said, 'It's all right, Christine, sit down. Christine, this is

Joe. Joe's a bagman for a corrupt politician.'

'Jesus, Emma,' DeMarco said.

'Which one?' pretty Christine asked.

Thankfully, Emma ignored her question and said, 'Joe, be a good bagman and fetch Christine a glass of white wine.'

'Yes, ma'am,' DeMarco said.

DeMarco returned with Christine's wine and a Pepsi for himself. Emma was complimenting Christine on her playing, gushing how the third movement had almost moved her to tears. DeMarco rolled his eyes when he heard this; bamboo splinters jammed under her toenails wouldn't move Emma to tears. To his relief Emma finally said, 'Dear, I have some business with Joe. Something tedious. Would you mind if I met you at your suite in an hour? I'll bring some of that champagne you like.'

'And strawberries?' Christine asked.

'Strawberries too,' Emma said.

As Christine walked away, Emma shook her head and muttered, 'Strawberries and champagne. What a cliché.' Turning to DeMarco, she said, 'So, Joseph, what's the problem? Might I assume that shit Mahoney has once again dropped you in the soup?'

'The Speaker was at a dinner the other night, drunk as a Lord, when he decided to loan me to Andy Banks.'

'Homeland Security?'

'Yeah. So I meet with General Banks this morning and he tells me he has a small problem.'

'Joe, I have a lovely friend waiting for me.'

'Banks thinks a Secret Service agent may have

24

been an accomplice in the assassination attempt on the President, and both Banks and Patrick Donnelly are withholding information from the FBI.'

'Well! You do know how to get a girl's attention.' Then Emma said exactly what Mahoney had said: 'Tell me what Banks told you, Joe. Don't leave out a thing.'

5

Philip Montgomery and the President had been roommates at Harvard. Montgomery was the best man at the President's wedding, and the President had returned the favor for two of Montgomery's three nuptials.

The President went on to become governor of his home state, then U.S. senator, then President. He was a bright man, though not a brilliant one, and felt he was dodging his responsibilities if he worked less than sixteen hours a day. Montgomery, the President's opposite in temperament, was a literary genius who drank like Tennessee Williams and played and fought and fucked like Hemingway. He was a master of the twelve-hundred-page epic that blended fact and fiction so artfully that it was difficult to tell which parts were which, not that his readers particularly cared.

Every year, for more than twenty years, the President and Montgomery got together for three or four days to enjoy various pastimes: skiing, hunting, fishing, river rafting — and a lot of drinking. This annual holiday with Montgomery, an event that was highly publicized, was the only time the President appeared to let his hair down. As for Montgomery, his hair was always down. After being elected to the highest office in the land, the President continued to enjoy his reunions with Montgomery and insisted that his Secret Service detail be as small as possible. The reason for this was to minimize the number of people seeing him and a Pulitzer Prize winner behaving like drunken fools. Like the time they threw empty whiskey bottles into the Bitterroot River and blasted them to bits with automatic weapons borrowed from the President's bodyguards; hardly an activity he wanted reported to either the environmentalists or the gun-control crowd.

This year Montgomery and the President had decided to do a little fishing in Georgia, on the Chattooga River. The dates of the trip — July 14 to July 17 — had been established long in advance as is necessary with a president's schedule, but according to Banks the location of the trip wasn't finalized until late May. Naturally, a host of people knew about the trip and the number of potential leaks was almost infinite.

Banks had received the warning letter four days before the President was scheduled to depart for Georgia and the first thing he did was call Patrick Donnelly, director of the Secret Service. Donnelly told Banks it was damn unlikely that an agent had sent the letter. In fact, he found it amusing that Banks had given the letter any credibility at all — not an attitude the general appreciated.

Banks pointed out to Donnelly that the letter had been printed on Secret Service letterhead, placed in a Secret Service business envelope, but most important, it had been delivered via the department pouch. The pouch was a mailbag delivered by armed courier and used to transport classified documents between Secret Service headquarters on H Street and Banks's office on Nebraska Avenue. Only personnel inside Secret Service headquarters, a secure facility, had access to the pouch and it was delivered directly to Banks's executive assistant.

Then there was the jargon in the note: Eagle One and the inside ring. 'Eagle One' was the President's code name. The 'inside ring' was those agents closest to the President whenever he was on the move. The outside ring was the agents guarding the perimeter: agents in the crowd, on rooftops, manning strategic control points. If the outside ring was penetrated, the inside ring was to die protecting the Man.

Donnelly still claimed the letter was a hoax. Maybe an agent *had* sent it — a lot of his people weren't happy with changes Banks had made since taking over Homeland Security — but that still didn't mean there was any truth to the letter. Then Donnelly, a master of the bureaucratic full nelson, dared Banks to call up the President and ruin his long-awaited vacation based on an unsigned note that claimed he was at risk from his own bodyguards. Banks didn't make the call, but he did keep the warning letter.

Seven days later Philip Montgomery and a Secret Service agent were killed and the President was wounded. After the assassination attempt, Banks was racked with guilt, terrified the note had been authentic and that he had failed to act upon it. He called Donnelly and told him that he was sending him the warning letter. He wanted it analyzed for fingerprints and

DNA in saliva on the envelope seal, and for Donnelly to make an effort to find out who had put it in the pouch.

Donnelly tried his best to talk Banks out of having the letter analyzed. He told him if he sent the letter to a lab and started questioning people, the contents of the letter would be leaked to the media within hours. Absolutely the last thing they needed, Donnelly said, was to give birth to a preposterous theory that the Secret Service could have been involved in the assassination attempt. But Banks insisted. Donnelly may have been a presidential appointee but Banks was still his boss.

The next day Donnelly came to see Banks. Although he categorically dismissed the possibility of Secret Service complicity, he did take steps to convince Banks that the warning letter was bogus. First, he told Banks, in accordance with standard Secret Service procedures for incidents like this, all the agents at Chattooga River were given polygraphs to see if they were involved. All the agents had passed as would be expected. And if this wasn't good enough, there was the timing of the note and its relationship to the men assigned to the inside ring.

At Chattooga River the outside ring consisted of more than sixty agents. The cabin where the President had stayed was selected not only because it was located near several good fishing holes but also because it was in an isolated area with limited access. Three days before the President's arrival the Secret Service sent a large advance team to the area, drew an imaginary circle five miles in diameter around the cabin, then blocked off all roads and trails into the area and manned these entry points with agents. Following this, they searched the area inside the circle by air and on foot to make sure no one was there. All people entering the area before the President's arrival were escorted through to make sure they left, and after the President arrived, people were not allowed to enter at all. Periodic surveillances of the area were conducted by helicopter during the entire time the President was visiting.

Confident the perimeter was secure, and in keeping with the President's explicit direction to minimize the number of on-site guards, the inside ring at Chattooga River consisted of only four agents: Billy Mattis, Robert James — the agent who was killed while covering the President with his own body — Richard Matthews, and Stephen Preston.

The inside ring had been selected on July 5th and the warning note was sent to Banks five days later, July 10th. At the time the letter was sent agents Matthews and Preston had not been assigned to the Chattooga River detail. Two other agents had been assigned but those two men, who carpooled together, were in a traffic accident on the Beltway on July 12th and Matthews and Preston were last-minute substitutes. Thus, explained Donnelly, whoever wrote the note couldn't have been referring to Matthews or Preston. Banks argued that maybe one of the two agents who had been originally assigned had compromised the President's security *before* the traffic accident, and that the accident had been a ruse to avoid being at Chattooga River the day of the shooting. Donnelly said this was damned unlikely since the accident had involved a head-on collision with a cement mixer.

The third agent was the man who was killed: Agent James. Donnelly ruled him out based on his distinguished record, the fact that he had served the Secret Service for twenty-five spotless years — and that he died saving the President's life. Banks, however, countered Donnelly's logic, suggesting that maybe the assassin had shot Agent James to silence him. Donnelly said that idea was absurd; it was clear from the video of the shooting that the first shot hit Montgomery by accident, the second shot winged the President but didn't kill him, and the third shot had been aimed at the President but missed and hit the agent. Banks had to agree with him.

This left a single agent: Billy Ray Mattis. Mattis also had an impressive record, but since he hadn't been killed like Agent James or assigned after the warning letter had been sent like the other two agents, Donnelly couldn't rule him out as definitively as the other three men. But the main problem with Mattis, Banks told DeMarco, was that he looked hinky on the video. Hinky.

The next day, while Banks was still stewing over what to do about the warning letter, the body of Harold Edwards was found along with the suicide note that said he'd acted alone. Donnelly called Banks shortly after the discovery of Edwards's body and said that the lab had drawn a blank on the warning letter: no finger-prints, fibers, saliva, anything. He also said that he'd personally talked to the courier who'd delivered the pouch to Banks's office and the courier had no recollection of any agent giving him a letter for delivery to Banks.

But Banks still wasn't happy.

6

Most people had left the art gallery cafeteria immediately after Christine's quartet finished playing. A cleanup crew was now stacking chairs and clearing off tables, and the man in charge was giving Emma and DeMarco looks encouraging them to leave. Emma was impervious to the looks.

'I don't get it,' Emma said. 'What exactly does Banks want you to do?'

'He says he wants me to see if there's a link, no matter how remote, between Mattis and the assassination attempt,' DeMarco said. 'He's not convinced Mattis is guilty of anything, and at the same time he's not a hundred percent positive he's innocent either. All he wants me to do is check out Mattis and then he says he can rest with a clear conscience.'

'A politician striving for a clear conscience,' Emma said, 'is like Sir Percival searching for the Grail.'

'Aside from that medieval insight, Emma, what do you think?'

'Joe, sweetie, we're in Washington, D.C. Here live the fine people who brought you the Bay of Pigs, Watergate, Iran-Contra, and invisible weapons of mass destruction. Do I think it feasible that a government agency — particularly one headed by a weasel like Patrick Donnelly — could be involved in an attempt to kill a

33

president? The answer is yes. Do I think it *likely*? The answer is no.'

Emma took a sip of her wine. 'And the reason Banks wants you to investigate Mattis is because he looks 'hinky' on this video?'

'I guess. Banks says he's a big believer in listenin' to his gut, and his gut's tellin' him there's something wrong with Mattis. By the way, the agent in the video, the one who dropped his sunglasses? That was Billy Ray Mattis.'

'Is that why Banks is suspicious of him?' Emma said.

'I don't know, but Mattis was also the agent who stood directly in front of the President after the shooting started. That last bullet the sniper fired, the one that killed that other agent, went right between his legs. Missed his johnson by an inch.'

'Small target,' Emma muttered. 'Who took the video, by the way?'

'A local station out of Gainsville. The President thought it would be a treat for them to get an exclusive of him and Montgomery flying off in the helicopter. They were given about four hours' notice.'

A member of the cleaning crew stopped at their table, a dignified-looking Hispanic. He asked Emma politely if she'd be leaving soon so his crew could finish cleaning up. Emma just stared at the poor guy until he backed away, bowing, making apologies in two languages.

'And there's something else that's bothering Banks,' DeMarco said.

'Oh?' Emma said.

'Yeah. Patrick Donnelly. He says Donnelly's response to the warning note was out of character. I don't know how long Donnelly has been director of the Secret Service but — '

'A long time,' Emma said.

' — but according to Banks he doesn't have a reputation as a guy who goes out on a limb and he certainly doesn't go out on a limb for his agents. Banks said he was surprised that Donnelly didn't try to get the Chattooga River trip canceled just to cover his ass. At a minimum, he should have switched out the agents assigned to the inside ring, but he didn't do that either.'

'I agree,' Emma said. 'So why didn't he?'

'Banks doesn't know, but it's just one more thing that's making him nervous.'

'I'll tell you another thing that would make me nervous if I was Banks,' Emma said.

'What's that?'

'Why didn't the person who wrote that letter send it to Donnelly, the guy directly in charge of the Secret Service, instead of Banks?'

'I hadn't thought of that,' DeMarco said.

Emma was silent for a moment before saying, 'So why doesn't Banks just call up the FBI, tell 'em about the warning letter, and let them investigate?'

'He says he's not willing to unleash a media hurricane about Secret Service involvement in the assassination attempt based solely on his gut feeling. And he's particularly not willing to do that now that they've got Edwards's suicide note.'

'So he wants you looking into this instead of the Bureau?'

'Yeah. At least I won't leak the story to the *Post*. Well, maybe not.'

'I guess you're better than nothing,' Emma muttered.

'Thanks for that vote of confidence, Ms Emma, but frankly I agree with you and that's what I told Mahoney. But once I told him Donnelly was acting weird on this thing, he insisted I get involved.'

'What's Mahoney have against Donnelly?'

'I don't know. And there's one other thing: Banks doesn't think Donnelly really had that note analyzed.'

'He thinks Donnelly lied to him?' Emma said.

'Yeah. Banks doesn't think there was enough time to check the letter out, not if they analyzed for DNA and questioned people and stuff like that. And when I told Mahoney that, his big ears really perked up.'

'From what I've heard about Donnelly,' Emma said, 'I suppose anything's possible.' She ran a hand through her short hair as she thought over everything DeMarco had told her. 'Tell me something, Joseph,' she said. 'That note said the inside ring had been 'compromised,' whatever the hell that means. Exactly *how* could any of those four agents guarding the President that morning have compromised his security?'

'Good question, Emma, and I don't know. They certainly protected him when the shooting started, and the dates and location of the trip were hardly state secrets. And if the FBI had

36

found some major hole in the Service's security procedures, that would have been all over the news by now. So far no one is blaming the Secret Service for misconduct, dereliction of duty, or anything else. Not yet, anyway.'

'Well,' Emma said, gathering up her purse, 'this is all very interesting, Joe, but as I said earlier, I have a lovely friend waiting for me. Is there anything else you wanted?'

'Yeah. How 'bout asking your buddies to do a records check on Mattis? See if he knew Harold Edwards. Check out his finances, his history, that sorta thing.'

'He's a Secret Service agent, sweetie. I doubt the data-bases will be revealing.'

'We gotta look.'

'We?'

DeMarco shook his head in despair. 'Why in the *hell* would Mahoney want me fooling around with something like this, Emma? I mean, Jesus. If he wants to cause Donnelly a problem all he has to do is leak this shit to the *Post*.'

'Honey, I think the Speaker is playing a zillion-to-one long shot. I don't think he believes there's a snowball's chance in hell that Mattis or anyone else in the Secret Service was involved in the assassination attempt. But he *hopes* they were. And if they were, he can destroy Patrick Donnelly — not just annoy him with some unflattering press.'

'That damn Mahoney,' DeMarco said.

'Come on, Joe, quit whinin' and let's get crackin'. You have to take me someplace where they sell fresh strawberries.'

37

7

DeMarco passed under the Capitol's Grand Rotunda without an upward glance. To reach the stairway leading to his office he had to excuse his way through a cluster of tourists, their sunburned necks straining skyward as they gazed reverently at the painted ceiling above them. The tourists irritated him. He was in a bad mood already because of this nonsense with Banks, but it bugged him, every day when he went to work, these rubberneckers in their baggy shorts blocking the way.

He descended two flights of stairs. Marble floors changed to linoleum. Art on the ceiling was replaced by water stains on acoustic tile. The working folk dwelled on DeMarco's floor. Here clattered the machines of the congressional printing office and directly across from his office was the emergency diesel generator room. The diesels would periodically roar to life when they tested them, scaring the bejesus out of DeMarco every time they did. And just down the hall from him were shops occupied by the Capitol's maintenance personnel. Considering what DeMarco did some days, being located near the janitors seemed appropriate.

The faded gilt lettering on the frosted glass of DeMarco's office door read COUNSEL PRO TEM FOR LIAISON AFFAIRS, J. DEMARCO. The title was Mahoney's invention and completely meaningless. DeMarco entered his office, took off his jacket, loosened his tie, and checked the thermostat to make sure it was set on low. Adjusting the thermostat was something he did from force of habit, for his psychological well-being; he knew from experience that twisting the little knurled knob had absolutely no effect on the temperature in the room. He could call his neighbors, the janitors, to complain but knew he would rank low on their priority list. Who was he kidding? A guy with an office in the sub-basement didn't make the list.

In his office squatted an ancient wooden desk from the Carter era and two mismatched chairs, one behind his desk and one in front of it for his rare visitor. A metal file cabinet stood against one wall, the cabinet empty except for phone books and an emergency bottle of Hennessy. DeMarco didn't believe in keeping written, subpoenable records. On his desk was an imitation Tiffany lamp — a redundant appliance as strips of harsh, fluorescent lights provided all the illumination needed — and on the black-and-white tile floor was a small Oriental rug, the predominant colors being maroon and green. On the wall opposite his desk were two Degas prints of dancing ballerinas. His ex-wife had given him the faux-Tiffany lamp, the rug, and the ballerinas — a futile effort on her part to 'warm the place up.' Only an arsonist, DeMarco had concluded long ago, could give his office any warmth.

DeMarco took to the chair behind his desk.

He put his feet up, laced his hands behind his head, and closed his eyes. What to do about Billy Ray? He doubted the agent was guilty of anything. It was just as Emma had said: Mahoney was playing a long shot and using DeMarco's career for chips. He was hoping DeMarco would get lucky and find out Billy Mattis was dirty, in which case Donnelly's failure to properly investigate the warning letter could be used to nail his slippery hide to the wall. DeMarco didn't know why the Speaker disliked Patrick Donnelly but it was obvious he did. The bear wanted to gobble him up.

So since the bear wanted his snack, DeMarco was stuck. He couldn't disobey a direct order from Mahoney yet he could do nothing that would come to the attention of the Secret Service or the FBI. If they discovered he was mucking about in their business they'd stomp him to death with their wing-tipped shoes — and when the stomping began the Speaker would pretend he'd never heard the name Joe DeMarco. So he would investigate Billy Ray as ordered, but carefully. Invisibly. Discreetly. And investigating Billy meant making a gigantic leap of logic: he had to assume Mattis was guilty. To think otherwise left him nothing to do.

DeMarco's investigation began with the warning note. He took the index card Banks had given him and reread the words. The signature was interesting: 'An agent in the wrong place.' It sounded as if the author was being coerced or had knowledge he didn't wish to have. It was a . . . *reluctant* signature. So if the note was legitimate and if the Secret Service was somehow involved in the assassination attempt, maybe Billy Mattis was the one who sent the note. He knew the assassination was going to take place, didn't want any part of it, but could do nothing to stop it.

A second possibility was that the note referred to Mattis and he had intentionally dropped his sunglasses to give the shooter a clear shot at the President. A third and more likely possibility was that the note was a prank and Mattis was innocent. Possibilities and could bes and ifs. He was skipping down a yellow brick road of nonsense in a political land of Oz.

Banks had also given DeMarco a copy of Mattis's personnel file, so he put aside the index card to shine the bright light of his intellect on that thin document. He would learn all there was to know about his quarry; he would study the jackal's past.

According to the file, the jackal was as American as grits and moonshine. He was born in Uptonville, Georgia, wherever the hell that was, and had lived there until he enlisted in the army at age eighteen. He spent fourteen uneventful months in South Korea and after the service joined the Army Reserve and spent a couple of years at a community college. Following college, the Secret Service hired him and he'd been with the agency for six years.

There were two noteworthy incidents in Billy Ray's file. Billy's Army Reserve unit had been activated for eight months in the get-Saddam war and he had performed some unspecified act

41

of heroism worthy of a Purple Heart and a Bronze Star. The second incident had occurred two years earlier and closer to home.

While Billy was standing on a street corner in Gary, Indiana, waiting for the President's motorcade to pass, a bank robber decided the President's visit would provide perfect cover for a robbery. It never occurred to the robber, who had the IQ of a rabbit, that the President's route was saturated with both uniformed and undercover cops. As the robber exited the bank, alarms sounded. A nearby cop turned toward the noise, drew his weapon, and the robber shot at the cop. The crowd scattered, screaming civilians running in every direction like chickens from a hawk, and at that moment the President's limousine turned the corner. Billy, the closest agent to the robber, was afraid to fire his weapon for fear he would hit the civilians, yet at the same time he had to make sure the robber didn't shoot bullets in the President's direction. Billy charged the robber. His body armor deflected the robber's first shot; he caught the second with his left bicep before he tackled the robber and disarmed him.

Billy Mattis may not have been the brightest guy on the block but he was a brave man. He had been scarred twice in the service of his country. He was a Secret Service agent and a decorated veteran. He had willingly put himself in harm's way at Chattooga River. Could there possibly be an individual less likely to attempt to kill a president?

One thing DeMarco did notice while reviewing Mattis's personnel file was that until two and a half months ago Mattis had never had any of the glamour jobs. He was often a perimeter guard at the White House or Camp David, and frequently one of the anonymous agents standing on the street whenever the President graced Middle America with his presence, but he had never been a personal bodyguard to the President or the President's family. DeMarco couldn't tell from the file if Billy had been assigned to the praetorian guard on May 15th because of his previous heroism or if he just had enough seniority in the Service to automatically get the detail. He needed someone with the inside skinny on the Secret Service to tell him more about Billy's promotion. The fact that he'd *recently* been assigned to the President's security detail struck DeMarco as intriguing — well, intriguing if you liked conspiracy theories.

DeMarco put Billy's file and the index card in the top drawer of his desk and locked the drawer. Leaving his office, he walked down the hall to the maintenance shop. He knocked, waited patiently until he heard a deep voice say 'Yo,' and opened the door. Three black men dressed in dark-blue coveralls were seated at a table playing pinochle. A fourth man, also black, also wearing coveralls, was working on an air-conditioning unit on the shop bench. When the cardplayers saw DeMarco he was greeted by the now expected chorus: 'It's the I-talian stallion.' 'The wop who don't stop.' 'The guinea wit da skinny.'

'Jesus,' DeMarco said, 'do we have to go through this every damn time?'

'Yeah,' the man at the workbench said. 'We

43

have to go through this every damn time because they're idiots and because you look like Sonny fuckin' Corleone.' Then the man wiped his right hand on the leg of his coveralls, walked over, and shook hands with DeMarco.

'How's your boy, Curtis?' DeMarco asked. Curtis Jackson's oldest son played catcher for the Mets' triple-A team. Last week he had blocked the plate when a first baseman the size of New Jersey slid into home. He didn't drop the ball but he was out cold for two innings.

'He's okay. Got a head like his mother. He'll be back playin' next week.'

'That's good.'

'Hey, Dee-Mar-ko,' one of the cardplayers said. 'You noticed you the only white guy in the building got an office in the basement?'

'He ain't white,' cardplayer number two said, 'he's I-talian. He darker than you, Clark, he got a tan.'

'You oughta join a union, DeMarco,' cardplayer one said. 'That way you get seniority, you get an upstairs office.'

'Hell, no,' DeMarco said. 'If I joined a union, I'd have to wear them ugly coveralls and get my name sewn on the pocket.'

'DeMarco, you fool,' cardplayer two said, 'you never sews your *own* name on your pocket.'

'Yeah,' said cardplayer three, 'I got *your* name on my shirts, DeMarco, and one of these days they gonna fire your lazy ass.'

As the cardplayers whooped and high-fived each other, DeMarco said to Curtis, 'Why aren't those guys working?'

44

'Not that it's any of your business but their shift doesn't start for an hour. They come early to play cards and get away from their wives. You need something, Joe?'

'Yeah. Can I borrow your TV and VCR?'

'Sure,' Curtis said, 'but bring 'em back before tomorrow afternoon. The Skins got an exhibition game.'

This prompted a fifteen-minute discussion between DeMarco, a die-hard Redskins fan, and the cardplayers. The cardplayers, unhampered by sentiment or geographic loyalty, ran down the coach, the defensive line, the offensive line, and a fullback who they said ran like a fat girl. They were unanimous, however, in their support of the cheerleaders.

Back in his own office, DeMarco popped a borrowed copy of the assassination tape into the VCR. He tapped the play button on the remote then sat back, finger poised to pause the tape. He was ready to assess the hinkiness of Billy Ray Mattis.

The television commentators and their hired experts had, for the last four days, endlessly discussed the fact that Mattis had dropped his sunglasses before the first shot. And they had all reached the same conclusion: Mattis's fumble was a clear sign that God was a Democrat. Had Mattis not dropped his sunglasses, Montgomery would not have bumped into Mattis's ass, and, in turn, Montgomery would not have bumped into the President — in which case the first bullet would have blown the President's head apart. The lads and lasses at the FBI didn't disagree with this interpretation of events, yet neither they nor the journalists had seen the warning note.

As DeMarco watched the tape this time he thought that Mattis was *maybe* more nervous than the other agents. And as the President's group approached the helicopter, right before the first shot, Mattis *seemed* to scrunch his head down into his Windbreaker, like a turtle trying to make its head disappear. Yet, DeMarco noticed, Mattis moved quickly and without hesitation to protect the President and he had fired his weapon before any of the other agents.

There was nothing conclusive about the film yet DeMarco now understood what Banks meant. Mattis did look different than the other agents but it was difficult to articulate how and there was nothing you could point to with any certainty. More important, DeMarco knew that by now the FBI had positively Zaprudered the video: they had taken it apart pixel by pixel, blown up every frame, and built 3-D computer simulations. If the FBI and its legions of white-coated techies had found nothing suspicious on the tape there was no way that DeMarco's naked eyeball would find a smoking gun. After watching the video five times, DeMarco gave up; the tape either showed a very alert agent acting as he'd been trained or a very nervous agent with fore-knowledge of a shooting that was about to occur.

DeMarco looked at his watch. It was four p.m. The sun was over the yardarm — at least in the mid-Atlantic it was — and that was close enough for DeMarco. He called Alice.

8

The Monocle was a historic drinking establishment on the senate side of the Capitol, a block from Union Station. The walls were covered with photographs of smiling, glassy-eyed politicians. Mahoney's own picture was displayed prominently near the entrance, a thick arm around the neck of a rival who looked decidedly uncomfortable.

DeMarco liked the place. The kitchen served an adequate meal, the bar an excellent martini, and from his favorite stool he could watch the young ladies who worked on the Hill fast-walk by in their tight skirts as they hustled to catch the Metro at Union Station.

Mr William, the Monocle's afternoon bartender, brought DeMarco his martini, the expression on his face as solemn as if he were bearing the Eucharistic wine. Mr William was in his sixties, black, skinny, and six foot six. He had inherited from his forebears the dignified, mournful face of an undertaker — a face which belied a filthy, adolescent mind.

'You watch the Birds against Seattle last night, Joe?' Mr William asked.

'We have discussed this before, sir,' DeMarco said, 'and you know my feelings on this subject. I will watch the Orioles only when the Senators return to Washington.'

In 1971 the Washington Senators left D.C. and

moved to Texas to become the Texas Rangers, and all good D.C. baseball fans mourned the team's departure as if their sainted mothers had expired. For years Washingtonians had lobbied to return a major league team to the capital but the owner of the Baltimore Orioles blocked every effort, rightfully concluding that a team in D.C. would take butts out of the seats at Camden Yards. It appeared that Washington might finally prevail in the coming year, but only by giving major financial concessions to the Orioles' owner, a man DeMarco had come to loathe with a passion that could only be understood by other baseball fanatics.

'Then you didn't see Rodriguez's triple play followed by Rodriguez's inside-the-park home run?' Mr William said.

Shit. Either a triple play or an inside-the-park home run was as rare as dinosaur droppings. And he'd missed 'em both. Fuckin' Orioles. Their owner was an avaricious spoiler, their front office cheaper than Scrooge's offspring, and their pitchers not fit to play at the highschool level — but they had Alonzo Rodriguez, currently the best player in either league. But DeMarco would not lift his embargo. Ever.

'Screw Rodriguez and his triple play,' DeMarco said, trying to act as if he meant it.

'You're a stubborn man, Joe.'

He was. DeMarco sipped from his martini, nodded his gratitude to the martini's creator, and said, 'Excellent, Mr William. May I use your phone please?'

'You don't have a cell phone, like all the other

yahoos who come in here?'

'Yeah, but I don't want to use up my minutes. Come on, gimme the phone. It's not like you pay the bill.'

DeMarco dialed. 'It's Joe,' he said when Emma answered.

'Say it ain't so, Joe,' Emma said.

'You sound cheery, Emma.'

'I'm healthy, wealthy, and wise — and unlike you, I have an active sex life. Why shouldn't I be cheery? So what do you want? I'm doing my nails.'

'I'd like to borrow one of your associates for surveillance duty.'

'The Mattis thing?'

'Yeah.'

'Goin' whole hog, are you?'

'What's an investigation without surveillance, Em? I'll have your man tail Billy for a day or two then I'll report back to Banks that he's as pure as the fallen snow.'

'The fallen snow is black from pollutants, Joe. Anyway, what will you be doing while my guy's tailing Billy?'

DeMarco told her.

'I think Mike's free,' she said. 'I'll have him call you.'

'Is this the same Mike you loaned me in February?'

'Yes.'

'Good. He's an okay guy. By the way, Emma, what's his background?' DeMarco rolled his eyes when he asked the question, knowing he was wasting his breath — but as Mr William had observed, he was a stubborn man.

'Oh, the usual,' Emma said. 'Navy SEAL, licensed to kill, that sort of thing.' Emma hung up.

The truth was Mike could be licensed to kill. DeMarco had discovered in the years he had known her that Emma had access to a wide variety of talented people: ex-cops, ex-soldiers, and, he suspected, ex-criminals. She knew wiretap experts, document forgers, and computer hackers. They were all competent and for reasons he was sure he would never know, completely loyal to Emma.

DeMarco had met Emma by giving her a ride. He had just dropped off a friend at Reagan National. He was parked ahead of the cab lane, checking traffic on his left, ready to pull out, when his passenger door opened and a woman entered his car. She was attractive, middle aged, and dressed in an elegant white pantsuit that was rumpled from travel. She was also out of breath, and it didn't look as if she'd slept for a while. The only thing she was carrying was a purse.

DeMarco said, 'Hey, what — '

'In about ten seconds,' the woman said, 'two men are going to come out of the terminal. They're armed and they're going to try to kill me. They'll probably kill you too since you're with me. Now drive. Please.'

The woman was desperate, DeMarco could tell, but not panicking.

'Hey, look — ' DeMarco said.

'You now have less than five seconds. I work for the government and I'm not lying.'

DeMarco almost said 'I've heard that line before' but he didn't. He was starting to get scared. He looked intently at the woman. She could be someone running from the cops or a mule hauling drugs. But he didn't think so. She didn't have a particularly kind face but it seemed to be one you could trust.

DeMarco glanced into his rearview mirror at that moment and saw two dark-complexioned men run out of the terminal. They looked frantically up and down the sidewalk in front of the terminal, and then one of them pointed at DeMarco's car.

'Shit,' he said, and he stepped on the gas and pulled into the arriving airport traffic. 'Why didn't you just take a damn cab?' he said to the woman.

'Did you see the line at the cabstand?' she answered. She looked behind her. 'Damnit, they had a car waiting.'

DeMarco checked his rearview mirror. The two men were getting into a black Mercedes sedan.

'What's going — '

'Just get me to the Pentagon,' the woman said. 'And if a cop tries to pull you over, don't stop.'

'Wait a — '

'You'll get the cop killed. Now drive. Fast.'

The woman checked the traffic behind them. The Mercedes was gaining on them. She pulled a cell phone out of her purse.

'It's me,' she said into the phone. 'I just got in from Cairo. I've got the sample but they were waiting for me at baggage claim. That wasn't supposed to happen, you moron!' She was silent for a moment. 'No, I don't have a gun. How the hell was I supposed to get a gun on the plane? Look ... Shut up. Listen to me. I'm with a civilian. We're in a 19 ... ' She looked over at DeMarco.

'Ninety-four,' he said.

'A 1994 Volvo, maroon in color. We're just leaving National and headed for the GW Parkway. You'll be able to tell it's us because we'll be going a hundred miles an hour with a Mercedes on our tail. Now scramble someone. Fast!' She closed the cell phone.

'What's your name?' she said to DeMarco.

'Joe,' he said.

'Well, Joe, you need to put the pedal to the metal. A wreck is the least of your problems at this point.'

The Mercedes was directly behind them now but it wasn't trying to pass or cut them off.

The woman glanced back at the other car. 'They're going to wait until you're on the parkway, then I'm guessing one of those guys is going to pull out an automatic weapon and shred your tires.'

'Jesus!' DeMarco said. 'Why don't you just throw whatever the fuck they want outta the window?'

The woman laughed, apparently not realizing that DeMarco hadn't been joking.

DeMarco reached the George Washington Parkway with the Mercedes fifty yards behind him. He was soon going ninety miles an hour and was thankful that traffic was light. He looked in his rearview mirror and saw one of the guys in the Mercedes stick half his body out the passenger-side window. Then he saw flashes of orange light erupt from the end of the man's arm — he didn't hear any shots being fired — then he saw sparks, about a dozen of them, fly up from the asphalt next to the Volvo.

'Son of a bitch!' DeMarco screamed. He jammed his foot down on the gas pedal, but it didn't move. The Volvo couldn't go any faster.

Then it was over.

A helicopter, a big black one, was suddenly above the Mercedes shining a spotlight down on it and DeMarco could see a guy hanging out of the helicopter holding a rifle. Where the helicopter came from, DeMarco didn't know. The Mercedes slowed down slightly, apparently looking for an exit or a turnaround. DeMarco didn't slow down; he kept the gas pedal jammed to the floor. A minute later he saw red-and-blue lights from five or six cars flashing in his rearview mirror and the Mercedes was surrounded.

'You can pull over now,' the woman said.

DeMarco kept going.

'It's okay,' the woman said. 'Calm down. Pull over.'

DeMarco did and when the car stopped he put his head on the steering wheel for a moment and closed his eyes. Without raising his head he said, 'Would you mind telling me — '

'Sorry, Joe, but I can't.'

The damn woman would never let him finish a sentence.

A white van with government plates pulled up behind DeMarco's Volvo. The woman got out but before she closed the door she said, 'By the way, I'm Emma. And thank you.' Then she got back into the van and took off.

The next morning DeMarco was sitting in his office, flipping through the paper to see if last night's incident had made the news. It hadn't. A moment later there was a knock on his door, which surprised him as people rarely visited his office. He opened the door. It was Emma.

'How did you . . .'

DeMarco had started to say 'How did you find me,' then realized that would have been a very silly question.

'I just wanted to thank you properly for what you did last night,' Emma said. She entered DeMarco's office without being asked, raised an eyebrow at the decor, then handed DeMarco an envelope. 'Two seats for the Wizards for tomorrow night, right behind the players' bench. I've heard you're a sports fan.'

'Jeez, thanks,' DeMarco said. The tickets must have cost about five hundred bucks. 'I appreciate the tickets but I'd still like to know what happened last night.'

'I'm sorry, Joe, I can't tell you. But as they say in the funnies, you have the thanks of a grateful nation. And, Joe, here's my phone number.' She handed DeMarco a card that had nothing on it but a phone number with a 703 area code.

'If you ever need help — with anything — give me a call,' Emma said.

54

'Well,' DeMarco said, thinking about his current assignment from Mahoney, 'you wouldn't by any chance know a guy who can crack a safe, would you?'

That had been the beginning of a long, often bizarre, relationship which DeMarco had never regretted.

DeMarco did know one small thing about Emma. He had asked the Speaker to run a background check on her shortly after he met her. DeMarco was guessing she was CIA, something Mahoney should be able to confirm easily. Or so DeMarco had thought.

When the Speaker got back to DeMarco, he was as flustered as DeMarco had ever seen him.

'She's ex-*DIA*,' Mahoney said.

The Defense Intelligence Agency was formed by Secretary of Defense Robert McNamara after the debacle at the Bay of Pigs in 1961. Some said it was the organization the CIA wanted to be when it grew up. Not only was it so competent that it rarely made the papers but it was involved in military operations so sensitive and so vital that even ranking politicians feared to challenge them.

'When I asked about her, my buddy said he'd get back to me. Next thing I know I got two guys in my office so fuckin' scary I almost soiled my britches. They wanted to know how I knew her name and why *I* was askin'. Me. The Speaker. Anyway, after I do a song-and-dance routine like goddamn Fred and Ginger, they finally tell me she's ex-DIA — and I think the ex part might even be bullshit.'

55

No kiddin', DeMarco had thought.

'But that's all they'd tell me, Joe,' Mahoney said. 'Whatever she used to do for them is something they wanna keep buried until the Potomac dries up.'

But that was enough for DeMarco: to know the one thing about Emma that explained why Emma never explained.

The sound of a dump truck landing on the bar next to DeMarco's right elbow startled him from his reverie. It turned out not to be a dump truck but Alice's purse, fifteen cubic feet of fake leather filled, apparently, with everything she owned.

Without acknowledging DeMarco, Alice signaled to Mr William. He approached tentatively. Mr William was a gregarious person who enjoyed his patrons; Alice was the rare exception.

'Black Jack on the rocks, string bean, and make it snappy,' Alice said.

'Yes, ma'am,' Mr William said. It's difficult for a man six foot six to cower but Mr William managed.

'You know,' Alice said to DeMarco, 'since you knew I was coming and you know what I drink, you coulda had my drink waitin' for me.'

'Like your liver would shut down if you got your evening booster shot five minutes late.'

'Don't be a smart ass.'

Mr William delivered her drink then backed away like Michael Jackson doing his moonwalk.

'Hey,' Alice yelled at him. 'No peanuts? None of them little goldfish things?'

'I'll get you some, ma'am,' Mr William said,

his face wooden, his eyes bright buttons that warned of impending homicide.

Alice was fifty, with dyed blonde big hair, too much makeup, and twenty pounds she didn't need. She had a husband she referred to as 'that asshole' and a son she called 'that little jerk.' Alice lived for only one thing: the slot machines in Atlantic City, a mecca she pilgrimaged to every weekend. She worked for AT&T.

Alice slugged down half her drink and then began to rummage through her bottomless purse. 'Here,' she said, dropping six wrinkled pages on the bar in front of DeMarco: Billy Mattis's phone records for the last three months.

Assuming Billy was actually involved in the shooting, he had at least one accomplice — the guy who pulled the trigger. And if you have an accomplice, DeMarco reasoned, you have to communicate with him. Ergo, one looks at phone bills to see who Billy has been blabbing with lately.

DeMarco realized that if Billy Ray was a professional hit man or an undercover agent for a foreign government, his methods of communication would be more sophisticated than the kitchen telephone. But just looking at Billy Ray's file, DeMarco was positive the man was not a mole the Russians had trained from birth, then parachuted into rural Georgia to work his way into the confidences of the American elite.

'You know, it was a lot of work to get those records,' Alice said to DeMarco as she stuffed peanuts in her mouth. To Mr William she yelled, 'Hey, stilts! If it ain't too much trouble, how 'bout another one here.'

'Alice,' DeMarco said, 'who are you kidding? You hit maybe three keys on your keyboard to get this stuff.'

'How would you know?' Alice said. 'You work for the phone company too, Mr Big Shot? Anyway, I'm a little short this month.'

Alice was a little short every month. DeMarco suspected the only thing keeping the loan shark's bat from her wrinkled kneecaps was the monthly retainer he paid her.

As Alice droned on about the state of the economy in general and her personal finances in particular, DeMarco looked at Billy Mattis's phone records. Alice's computer had provided names and addresses of people and businesses Billy had called from his home phone and using his calling card. DeMarco would have Emma's people check out the names to see if anyone was noteworthy, but nothing leaped out at him: no calls to businesses that made spotting scopes or sniper rifles — and most important, no calls to the late Harold Edwards.

The only strange thing he did find was that in June Billy had called a Jillian Mattis twenty times in a two-week period. Jillian Mattis, DeMarco remembered from Billy's personnel file, was Billy's mother. He looked at the previous month's bill and saw that Billy had only called his mother four times. The high number of calls began two weeks after he had been assigned to the President's security detail. DeMarco realized that Billy's increased phone calls to his mother during this period could have a number of mundane explanations. Maybe she'd been sick around that time and he was just checking on her. Or maybe Billy was planning to visit her and was finalizing his plans. Or maybe Billy was a closet mama's boy.

'Well,' Alice said.

'Well what?' DeMarco said. He hadn't heard a word she'd said for the last five minutes.

'Can you give me an advance?'

'Yeah,' DeMarco said. Giving in to Alice was easier than haggling with Alice. And Lord knows Trump could use the money.

9

Middleburg, Virginia, was fifty miles west of the capital, a picture-postcard of a town surrounded by rolling green hills that were once Civil War battlefields. The battlefields were now white-fenced pastures where well-bred horses pranced. Wealthy Washingtonians bought land near Middleburg, and on weekends attended steeple-chases and pretended they were country squires.

Frank Engles was not a country squire; he owned a bed-and-breakfast. His establishment was a multihued Victorian with leaded-glass windows and sun-catching dormers and was as romantic as a bouquet of roses. It was the sort of place DeMarco might have chosen to take a girlfriend to spend a fall weekend — if he had a girlfriend.

DeMarco had told General Banks he needed to talk to someone who knew Billy and understood the Secret Service's promotion practices. Banks had his people contact the Service's human resources department and they very fortunately came up with Frank Engles. The very fortunate part was that just before he retired Engles had supervised Billy.

A plump, white-haired woman wearing an apron dusted with flour answered the doorbell. She told DeMarco he would find Engles behind the house doing some chores. He walked around the house as directed and saw a man in the backyard splitting wood. The man's back was to DeMarco. Lying on the ground near the man was a dog.

DeMarco liked dogs that were cuddly and came only to his knee. The dog he was now looking at was a German shepherd the size of a Shetland pony and as cuddly as a polar bear. The beast's head swiveled toward DeMarco like a gun turret, and then it gave a single yelp and charged. DeMarco, in turn, did what he always did when confronted by a hundred-and-twenty-pound canine moving in his direction with its teeth exposed: he stood completely still, tried to look unthreatening, and wished like hell he was armed.

Engles finally noticed the tableau behind him: DeMarco frozen in mid-stride, trying not to quiver like a flushed quail, and his four-legged monster in a ready-to-lunge position. The retired agent came trotting over to DeMarco and with a little chuckle said what dog owners always say: 'Hey, don't worry about Ol' Bullet. He's just bein' friendly.'

Engles was in his early sixties. He wore faded jeans and a yellow T-shirt with I ♥ VIRGINIA on it. He had wary-looking gray eyes, a nose that had been broken more than once, and there was a bald spot on the back of his head that looked like a monk's tonsure. The tonsure, combined with his broken nose, gave him the appearance of a priest who didn't turn the other cheek.

Since DeMarco wanted Engles's cooperation he didn't tell him he should keep his pet wolf shackled to a short chain and muzzled. Instead

he said, 'Yeah, looks like a really friendly pooch.'
The dog was now sniffing DeMarco's groin.

'Mr Engles,' DeMarco said, trying to ignore the damn dog, 'I'm Joe DeMarco. I work for Congress.' DeMarco flipped open a leather half wallet and showed Engles his congressional security pass.

'Congress?' Engles said, glancing down at DeMarco's credentials then back up at De-Marco's face. DeMarco was willing to bet that Engles had just memorized every word on his security pass.

'Yes, sir,' DeMarco said. 'I'm here concerning the recent assassination attempt on the President. As you may have heard, there's a committee taking a hard look at the President's security. I'd just like to ask you a few questions.'

'Seems to me Congress oughta do their own damn job,' Engles grumbled, 'and let the experts take care of security.'

DeMarco gave him an embarrassed half smile, and said, 'Confidentially, I agree with you, sir, but when my boss says ride, I hop on my horse.'

The I'm-just-a-working-stiff routine worked.

'Yeah, sure,' Engles said. 'Come on up to the house. I'll buy you a cup of coffee and you can ask your questions. Bullet! Get off that man's suit. Dog's so darn friendly he'd just lick a robber to death.'

Dog owners always say that too.

Engles took DeMarco to a kitchen that smelled of apples and cinnamon and had a fireplace big enough for a Yule log. It was a comfortable, cheery room and he could imagine generations of grandkids licking the spoon from the icing bowl. Engles poured coffee into two large mugs and they took seats at a sturdy wooden table. Ol' Bullet flopped down on the floor near Engles's chair.

'So what do you need from me?' Engles asked as he added cream to his coffee. 'I'm retired, you know.'

'We're taking a look at agent-selection procedures, Mr Engles. We're particularly interested in how the inside ring is picked. You know: experience requirements, qualification criteria, that sort of thing.'

The 'we's were for Engles's benefit. DeMarco was hoping he'd imagine an army of marching gray bureaucrats, the full and ponderous weight of government behind his mission.

'What's goin' on here?' Engles said. 'You can get all that stuff right from the department's personnel office. They have write-ups about training programs, selection guidelines, qualification criteria, all that crap. You didn't drive down here for that. Why are you really here?'

So much for the ponderous weight of government.

'Yeah, you're right,' DeMarco said, feeling like he'd been caught trying to hold up Santa Claus. 'We're curious about one agent who was at Chattooga River. A man you supervised before you retired.'

'Who is it?' asked Engles.

'Billy Ray Mattis.'

'You think Mattis shouldn't have been

assigned to that detail? Is that what this is all about?'

'Not necessarily, but he was the youngest and least-experienced agent on duty that morning.'

DeMarco knew Billy was the youngest agent based on the video; he was guessing he was the least experienced.

'You guys know Mattis took a bullet for the President in Indiana?' Engles asked.

'Yeah, I've seen his record. Is that why you selected him, because of Indiana?'

Engles went silent, his hands betraying his nervousness as they squeezed the coffee mug in front of him. Ol' Bullet sensed the change in his master's mood. The mutt's eyes locked onto DeMarco's jugular and from his throat came a low, rumbling sound. Engles reached down and ruffled the fur on the dog's thick neck, calming it, while he thought about DeMarco's question.

When Engles still didn't respond, DeMarco said, 'Look, I'm not trying to pin a rose on Billy Mattis. I just want to know why he was picked for the most sensitive assignment in the Service.'

'Maybe it's me you're trying to pin the rose on,' Engles said.

'Mr Engles, you retired before the assassination attempt. There's no way you can be held culpable for anything.'

'Yeah, right,' he said.

His voice oozing false sincerity, DeMarco said, 'All we want to do, sir, is make sure the President continues to have the best security in the world — the kind of security men like you have always provided.' He hoped Ol' Bullet

64

couldn't smell the bullshit in the air.

Engles looked at DeMarco, looked away, and then looked back. He cleared his throat.

'I didn't select Mattis,' he said. 'Every other man who worked for me, I handpicked. But with Mattis, one day I just get word he's being moved into my unit. When I asked why, I was told not to make waves. Somebody doing a favor for somebody. Happens all the time.'

'What do you mean?'

'I mean the Secret Service is like any other big company. People get transferred around. Bosses make deals with other bosses to help their fair-haired boys. Or a guy's having problems in one division so they move him somewhere else to see if he'll do better.'

'Is that what happened in this case?'

Engles shrugged. 'I don't know.'

'So who moved him into your unit?'

Engles hesitated. 'Well, I heard it was Little Pat, hisself. Now I don't know that for a fact; it's just what I heard.'

'Patrick Donnelly *personally* moved him into your unit?' DeMarco was unable to keep the shock from registering in his voice.

'Like I said, that's what came out of the rumor mill.'

'Why would the director of the Secret Service take an interest in the career of Billy Mattis?'

'Hell, I don't know. I also don't see what the big deal is here. Mattis passed all the qualification boards, and when I got to know him, I liked him. Quiet guy. Serious about his work. Mind always on the job. Not one of those guys who gets bored and starts watching skirts in the crowd.'

'So you didn't complain about the assignment?'

'No. I was pissed because I didn't have a say in it, but there was no reason to make a stink. I would have, had he been a fuckup, but he wasn't.' Shaking his head, he added, 'Poor Reynolds.'

'Reynolds?'

'Guy who replaced me. He must be catching hell right now, lettin' that guy Edwards get into position that morning. I saw him the other day leaving his house, fuckin' newsies shovin' microphones in his face.'

'Yeah,' DeMarco said, feigning sympathy for poor Reynolds. 'But what about Mattis? How much hell do you think he's catching right now?'

'For what?' Engles asked.

'You must have seen the video of the shooting. How Mattis dropped his sunglasses right before the first shot was fired.'

'Is that what this is all about?' Engles said, eyes blazing. 'Look, any man in that unit could have dropped something, or tripped, or moved the wrong way. Just because Mattis did doesn't have a damn thing to do with his experience or the selection procedures or who assigned him or any other fuckin' thing.'

'Yeah, you're probably right,' DeMarco said, sounding unconvinced. 'But tell me, how did you rate Mattis's performance when he worked for you, Mr Engles?'

Engles, still fuming, took a breath to regain his composure.

'Let me put it this way,' he said. 'I had two kinds of good people who worked for me. I also had a few bad ones over the years but we won't waste our time talking about those. The first kind, the kind who eventually move up through the ranks, were the guys who figured things out on their own. They didn't always do exactly what you told them, but they did what you really wanted done. You understand what I'm sayin' here?'

DeMarco nodded.

'The second kind of good guy,' Engles said, 'was Billy Mattis. He just plain followed orders. Every organization needs people like him, people you can always rely on to do what they're told, but Billy's rank and file, a frontline grunt, and he always will be.'

'What about his personality?'

'I already told you: quiet, easygoin'. Raised proper, taught to respect his mama and love his country. He didn't have any close friends in the unit but he got along with everybody. He was a likable guy. I liked him.'

'How 'bout his politics?'

'I honest to God don't remember him ever expressing a political opinion about anything. I couldn't tell you if he voted Republican or Democrat, or if he voted at all.' Engles frowned. 'Why are you asking about Mattis's politics? You people think he actually had something to do with the shooting?'

Yikes. 'Of course not,' DeMarco said.

'I sure as hell hope not. That boy would no more be involved in something like that than Ol'

Bullet here would turn himself into a cat. Ain't that right, Bullet,' Engles said, tugging on the dog's collar.

DeMarco thought he saw Ol' Bullet smile but the dog may have been choking.

DeMarco schmoozed around with Frank Engles another fifteen minutes trying to get him to remember nasty things about Billy Mattis. Nada. Billy Ray was the Muffin Man, Mr Goodwrench, sugar and spice and everything nice. And he probably was.

As DeMarco was driving back to Washington, picking dog hairs off his trousers, his cell phone rang. It was Banks.

'Be in my office at one,' Banks said. 'The FBI has something new on the assassination attempt and they're sending someone over to brief me.'

10

The FBI briefing consisted of a single agent equipped with a spiral-bound notebook, and DeMarco could see that Banks was disappointed. The retired general had obviously been expecting a Pentagon PowerPoint presentation with multicolored charts showing maps, shooting angles, and enlarged copies of lab reports.

The agent, one Gregory Prudom, was a man of medium height with regular features. His hair was short and brown. His blue suit, white shirt, and red-and-gold striped tie were bureaucratic camouflage. He was so nondescript that his own mother couldn't have picked him out of a lineup. At the same time, he had the air of a man who would hold the line if commanded, never giving an inch until directed to retreat. A titanium cookie cutter down at Quantico stamped out men like Agent Prudom.

Prudom started the briefing by glancing at DeMarco and saying, 'General Banks, I was told to extend to you the courtesy of a progress report but I was of the understanding you would be alone. May I ask who this gentleman is?'

'Courtesy, my eye,' Banks said. 'I run Homeland Security. I have a need to know.'

'You do, sir, but does this gentleman?'

'Yeah. He's one of my assistants.'

Turning to DeMarco, Prudom said, 'May I see some identification, sir?' DeMarco smiled at

Prudom but didn't reach for his wallet. This son of a bitch didn't look like anybody's assistant, Prudom was thinking; he looked like guys he'd brought up on racketeering charges.

'You don't need to see his ID, Mr Prudom,' Banks said. 'You'll take my word that he's properly cleared and with a need to know. Now get on with it.'

Prudom sat a second pondering his options, looking Banks directly in the eye. He wasn't intimidated; he was just trying to figure out if bucking Banks was in the Bureau's best interest.

'Yes, sir,' he said at last, and opened his notebook. He flipped to a page with a few notes scribbled on it and said, 'We finally figured out how Edwards pulled it off.'

'That's great,' Banks said, but DeMarco thought he looked nervous.

'The day the President was shot,' Prudom said, 'the agents never saw the shooter; they weren't even sure where he fired from.'

'Then what the hell were they shooting at?' Banks asked.

'The bluff above the river,' Prudom said. 'It was the only place that provided any cover so they saturated it with bullets in an attempt to keep the shooter from firing again. They were unsuccessful, as you know, because the shooter fired a third shot after the agents opened fire, killing Agent James, the agent who was lying on top of the President.

'After the third shot, the shooting stopped but no one could get up to the bluff right away to go after the assassin. The remaining Secret Service agents had to get the President into the helicopter so he could be evacuated to the nearest hospital, and two of the three agents accompanied the President in the helicopter. The third agent stayed at the site and — '

'Who was the agent that stayed?' Banks asked.

Prudom consulted his notes again. 'Agent Preston. Anyway, as soon as the helicopter lifted off, the agent, Preston, called the agents guarding the five-mile perimeter around the cabin and told them to start moving in toward the shooting site. After that Preston went up the bluff by himself to go after the shooter. It took him half an hour to climb to the top and by the time he got there the shooter was gone. Or so he thought.'

'What's that m — ' Banks started to say but Prudom raised a finger silencing him.

'Our forensic people arrived on scene four hours after the shooting but they couldn't find a thing: no brass, no footprints, no areas where the grass had been trampled down. Everyone figured Edwards had to have fired from the bluff, it was the only thing that made sense, but the Secret Service was adamant they would have spotted the guy. They said they'd patrolled the bluff right up until it was time for the President to leave, and the helicopter that was taking the President back to Washington had been hovering above the bluff until just prior to the President's departure. Everybody figured Edwards must have done one helluva camouflage job not to be seen on top of that bluff before the shooting, either that or he was the fuckin' Invisible Man. Excuse me, sir,'

71

Prudom added for his blue language.

'Go on,' Banks said.

'From the beginning,' Prudom said, 'one of the guys in our lab said the shooting angles didn't make sense. He did a bunch of computer simulations, and kept saying that in order for the angles to make sense, the shooter would have to have been about three feet *below* the top of the bluff. Everybody blew the tech off, figuring his calculations were screwed up. Yesterday this tech got permission to fly down to Georgia, and he finds a hole in the *side* of the bluff, three feet *below* the top.

'You see,' Prudom said, excited now, 'Edwards had burrowed this hole — it was about six feet long and three feet in diameter — into the side of the bluff sometime before the President arrived at Chattooga River. He camouflaged the opening so you couldn't see it unless you were about two inches away, looking straight at it.'

'Jesus,' Banks said.

'Yeah,' Prudom said, abandoning any attempt at formality, 'this bastard lowered himself over the side of the bluff, probably suspended from a rope, and dug a damn shooting blind into the side of a hill. Based on the timing of the President's trip, the arrival of the Secret Service's advance team at Chattooga River to secure the area, and patrols performed while the President was there, we think he dug the blind at least a week before the President arrived. Then, just before the President arrived, the son of a bitch snuck in at night, right past the guys guarding the perimeter, and entered the blind.

He hid in the blind the two days the President was fishing on the river with Montgomery and then — and this is the really amazing part — he stayed in that damn hole for at least a day *after* the shooting. He got away the second night when all the evidence techs had knocked off for the day, and he went right by the FBI's perimeter guards. It's the only way he could have gotten off that bluff.'

'I saw pictures of this guy Edwards in the *Post*,' DeMarco said. 'He didn't look all that athletic. You know, kinda hefty.'

It was the first time DeMarco had spoken, and Banks gave him a look that said assistants should be seen and not heard. DeMarco pretended not to notice.

Prudom shrugged. 'He was small enough to fit in the blind. We measured. And every chubby guy you see isn't out of shape either. Plus this guy was a hunter and he was in the reserve, which brings me to the next thing,' Prudom said. 'The rifle he used was a Remington 700 with a Leupold Mark 4 tactical scope. We traced the serial numbers and found out it was stolen a month ago from an Army Reserve armory.'

Banks looked over at DeMarco. Billy Ray Mattis was a member of the Army Reserve.

'Which reserve unit was it stolen from?' DeMarco asked.

'Edwards's old unit. The one over at Fort Meade in Maryland,' Prudom said.

DeMarco remembered from Billy's file that his Army Reserve unit was based in Richmond, Virginia.

'I thought Edwards was a hunter,' DeMarco said. 'Why didn't he use one of his own guns?'

'He hocked 'em,' Prudom said, 'because he'd been off work so long. All he had in his house were a couple of shotguns.'

'And I suppose the Bureau is investigating the armory theft?' DeMarco said.

Prudom nodded impatiently. 'Of course, along with army CID, but we haven't come up with anything that ties it directly to Edwards — other than the fact that all the weapons that were stolen were in his damn house. The .45 he killed himself with? It came from the armory.'

'Is the rifle the only physical evidence you have?' Banks asked.

'You mean besides the suicide note?' Prudom said.

'Yeah,' Banks said.

'Well, we found a receipt in his car from a gas station about thirty miles from Chattooga River. But the guy left nothing in the shooting blind, and when you think about it, that's also amazing. He was in that hole digging, eating, shitting, pissing, and shooting — and he managed not to leave any trace. He took all his garbage with him when he left and while he was in there he must have been covered head to foot in some kinda suit because he didn't leave any hair or skin or anything else we could get DNA from. We didn't find the suit in his house, by the way.'

Prudom closed his notebook. 'The good news, General, is that this helps the Secret Service. I mean it's not like their procedures were sloppy or they were goofin' off on the job. This guy Edwards may have been a whack job — but he

74

was good. Really good.'

'But how did he plan this thing?' DeMarco asked. Banks almost gave himself whiplash as his head spun toward DeMarco.

'What do you mean?' Prudom said.

'You said Edwards went down to Georgia the week before the Secret Service's advance team arrived at Chattooga River, and that's when he dug the shooting blind. How'd he know when to go?'

'We're not sure, but this thing the President did every year with Montgomery always got plenty of ink. And obviously lots of people here in D.C. knew when the President was leaving and where he was going. The other thing is, we found out the other day that when Montgomery was at some book signing he talked about going down to Georgia to do some fishing with the President. We got that from his publicist. So to answer your question, we don't know exactly how Edwards figured out the President's schedule but we do know that planning for the trip wasn't controlled like the Manhattan Project.'

After Prudom left, Banks and DeMarco sat together in silence a moment thinking about what Prudom had told them.

'You know,' Banks said, 'Mattis being in the reserve, same as Edwards, you need to follow up on that armory break in.'

'If the FBI can't find anything, I doubt I'll be able to.'

'Yeah, but you gotta check it out.'

'Sure,' DeMarco said.

He had no intention of checking it out.

11

The man sitting at the bus stop across from Secret Service headquarters wore a blue polo shirt, chinos, and sandals with white socks. He was in his sixties, had iron-gray hair, and a face that DeMarco could envision, for some reason, behind the plastic face shield of a riot helmet. This was Emma's man Mike, last name unknown.

'Hi,' DeMarco said as he sat down next to Mike on the bench.

'Hey, Joe,' Mike responded, but he didn't look at DeMarco. His eyes continued to scan the building across the street, moving from exit to exit, and occasionally over to a nearby parking lot. When you got a guy from Emma, you got a pro.

'How's it going?' DeMarco asked.

'Like watchin' paint dry,' Mike replied. 'He leaves his house at six thirty and gets here at eight — 395 was a fuckin' parking lot this morning. He goes directly to this building where he stays all morning. What he's doin' in there, I don't know. At twelve he comes outside, grabs a burrito from a street vendor, takes a walk around the Mall, then goes back inside the building.'

'Did Mattis see you tailing him?'

Now Mike looked at DeMarco; his stare answered DeMarco's question.

'And I take it no one approached him while he

76

was taking his lunchtime walk.'

'You take it right,' Mike said.

They sat in silence for a while, Mike watching the building, DeMarco watching the women walk by. As he sat there, DeMarco thought back to the FBI briefing. What Edwards had done fascinated him. He couldn't imagine a man lying in a dark, claustrophobic space for two days waiting for the opportunity to take a shot and then having the balls to stay in the shooting blind while the FBI scoured the bluff above him for evidence.

Which made DeMarco think of something else: Why did he take the shot he took? There must have been an easier shot Edwards could have taken while the President was fishing. Instead he waited until the day the President was departing, surrounded by his bodyguards. Then he remembered that Prudom had said that while the President was on the river the Secret Service had patrolled the bluff, so maybe that's what had prevented Edwards from shooting earlier.

The skill it had taken to sneak into and out of the area was also remarkable. Prior to the shooting Edwards had to get past a Secret Service cordon to get to the shooting blind he had previously dug. After the FBI's forensic people arrived on-site, Prudom said they worked sixteen hours a day, and when they weren't there, the area had been patrolled to keep out sightseers and protect the crime scene. Yet the assassin had left the shooting blind, probably the day after the shooting, reconcealed the blind, and either climbed back up to the top of the bluff or down the bluff to the river, carrying his waste and all his gear with him. Then he waltzed past all the people guarding the site.

The rifle also intrigued DeMarco. Why would Edwards have taken the assassination weapon back to his house? Why didn't he just dump it the first chance he got? It was almost as if . . .

'You ever seen pictures of Mickey Mantle, Joe?' Mike said. 'I don't mean right before he died of cancer, but when he was playing.'

'Sure,' DeMarco said.

'Well that's who this kid looks like. He looks like the Mick, ol' number seven. Why am I tailing a guy who works for the Secret Service and looks like Mickey Mantle, Joe?'

DeMarco rose from the bench. 'I'll check in with you again tomorrow, Mike. Thanks for helping out on this.'

'Sure, Joe,' Mike said, 'but if I gotta spend another day sittin' in the sun on a concrete bench, I'm gonna go crazy. And when I do, you're gonna be the first person I kill.'

* * *

DeMarco lived in a small town house in Georgetown, on P Street. The town house, a carbon copy of several others on the block, was a narrow two-story affair made of white-painted brick. Wrought-iron grillwork covered the windows; ivy clung to the walls; azaleas bloomed in the flowerbeds in the spring. It was a cozy place, and he and his neighbors pretended the artfully twisted black bars barricading their lower-floor windows were installed for aesthetic reasons. He had purchased the house the year he married.

The interior of DeMarco's home looked as if thieves had backed a moving van up to the front door and removed everything of value — which, in a way, is exactly what had happened. A house once filled with fine furniture, Oriental rugs, and pricey artwork now contained only a few haphazardly selected pieces that DeMarco had bought at two yard sales one Saturday morning. The entertainment center in his living room had been replaced with a twenty-four-inch television on a cheap metal stand. A lumpy recliner sat a few feet from the television and on the floor near the recliner was a boom box that served dual purpose as a radio and a place to set his drink when he read or watched TV.

DeMarco tossed his suit coat on the recliner — the antique oak coat stand that had been by the door was gone — and walked toward his kitchen. Each step he took on the bare hardwood floors echoed throughout the house like punctuation marks in a sonnet to loneliness.

When DeMarco's wife left him she decided not to take the house. Her lover had a house. She didn't, however, like her lover's furniture so her lawyer made DeMarco a deal: if he didn't contest the divorce he would pay no alimony and get to keep his pension and a heavily mortgaged house. In return, his wife would get all the furniture and furnishings — and all the money in their joint savings account, the cash value of his insurance policies, and DeMarco's best car.

DeMarco's dinner was two slices of cold pizza

eaten while standing in front of the refrigerator. Dinner the night before had been the same pizza, except hot from the box. DeMarco was a good cook and he enjoyed cooking, but he didn't enjoy cooking for one.

He felt restless after his supper and the pizza sat like a cheese boulder in his gut. He changed into a pair of shorts, a sleeveless Redskins T-shirt, and a pair of scuffed tennis shoes and trudged slowly up the stairs to the second floor of his home. For a brief period, DeMarco's ex had used one of the two upstairs bedrooms as a studio, ruining yards of perfectly good canvas while whining that the windows didn't let in the northern light. This hobby, like others that followed, lasted only a short time before she returned to those activities at which she excelled: shopping and adultery.

Now the bedrooms were empty and the only thing in the upper story of DeMarco's home was a punching bag, a fifty pounder that swung black and lumpy from a ceiling rafter like a short, fat man who had hanged himself. When asked why he had installed the heavy bag he would shrug and say it was for aerobic exercise, but the truth was that he loved to beat the shit out of an inanimate object when the mood struck him.

He put on his gloves, warmed up with a little shadow-boxing, and attacked the bag. The bag took the first round but by the second he was drenched with sweat, pounding leather with a vengeance, imagining his wife's lover's ribs cracking like kindling with each blow. His wife's lover had been his cousin. He was so into violent fantasy that he almost didn't hear the doorbell ring.

Standing on his porch was a compact man in his thirties wearing a gray suit. When DeMarco noticed the pistol in the shoulder holster beneath the man's suit jacket, he gave the stranger his full attention. Behind the man was a black limousine with government plates parked at the curb.

'Are you Joseph DeMarco?' the man asked.

'Yeah,' DeMarco said, still trying to catch his breath. 'How can I help you?' DeMarco thought it prudent to be polite to armed men.

'Patrick Donnelly, director of the Secret Service, would like a word with you, sir. Would you mind joining the director in his car?'

Ah, shit, DeMarco thought. Shit, shit, shit. On the case less than two days and the Secret Service already knew he was involved. He thought of slamming the door in the agent's face and running to hide under his bed.

'Please, sir, would you mind coming with me,' the man prodded.

Dignity prevailed over the ostrich defense. 'You bet,' DeMarco said, his voice sounding more confident than he felt.

Donnelly's driver opened the rear door of the limo for him. Feeling foolish in his shorts and Redskins T-shirt, DeMarco stepped into the car and took his place on the jump seat so he could face Patrick Donnelly. The armed driver closed the door behind DeMarco then remained standing outside the limo, several feet away; apparently Mr Donnelly didn't want his man to hear their conversation.

Lil' Pat Donnelly stared at DeMarco, his eyes projecting his hostility. He was a slender man in his late sixties, no more than five feet six inches tall. His hair was dyed glossy black and parted so precisely on the left side that DeMarco could imagine him using a straightedge to guide his comb. He had small features, close-set ears, and narrow black eyes with drooping lids. His mouth was a cruel slash and his face was covered with a smear of five o'clock shadow. DeMarco thought he looked like a fencer, slim and wiry and nasty — the type who would use real swords if allowed the opportunity.

DeMarco ignored Donnelly's glare and looked casually around the limo, at the leather upholstery, the small TV, the bar inset into the back of the front seat. The jump seat of the limo was more comfortable than his recliner, and he bet Donnelly's TV got better reception than his did.

'Afraid I'm gettin' sweat on your upholstery,' he said to Donnelly. 'I was working out.' *Ya little shit*, he added silently.

'Shut up,' Donnelly said. 'You were in Middleburg today where you interrogated a retired Secret Service agent. What in the *hell* makes you think you have the authority to do such a thing?'

DeMarco gave Donnelly the same line he'd fed John Engles. 'Congress is concerned about the President's security, Mr Donnelly, and — '

'Congress my ass,' Donnelly said. 'You talked to Frank Engles because Banks told you that jackass idea of his about Billy Mattis.'

DeMarco's face gave away nothing but inside his gut was a small mad animal, gnawing at the lining of his stomach. He knew how Donnelly had found out about him: Engles, still loyal to his old outfit, had called some pal and told him about DeMarco and his questions. The word immediately went up the chain of command to Donnelly. Donnelly knew, even if no one else did, about Banks's concern with Mattis. And maybe Donnelly had someone check Banks's appointment calendar and found out that DeMarco had met with him. DeMarco should have used a phony name with Engles.

'What happened at Chattooga River is a matter for the FBI and the Secret Service, mister, and you are going to stay out of it. Do you understand? Not only have they found the guy who did it, there are still three hundred goddamn FBI agents investigating the assassination attempt! Even if you had the authority, what in the fuck do you think you could possibly do that the FBI and my people aren't already doing?'

Before DeMarco could respond, Donnelly said, 'I run the Secret Service, you idiot, which means I can find out anything about anybody. I know, for example, that you're John Mahoney's heavy. If it's something easy, getting a few guys to compromise on some chicken-shit bill, Mahoney sends his chief of staff, that fat guy who wears suspenders. But when he doesn't want to compromise, when he wants to shove his dick up somebody's ass, he sends you.'

'I don't work for the Speaker,' DeMarco said,

'I'm an independent coun — '

'Bullshit. You don't show up on any org chart linking you to Mahoney, but Mahoney set up your position. Counsel Pro Tem. What a crock. You work for Mahoney and I know it.'

But can you prove it? DeMarco wondered.

'I also know *why* Mahoney doesn't want any official connection to you. Your father was Gino DeMarco, a low-life cocksucker who worked for Carmine Taliaferro. Fifteen years ago your daddy wasted three of Taliaferro's rivals before the fourth one got lucky and plugged him. Isn't that right?'

DeMarco said nothing but he felt like ripping Donnelly's tiny ears off for calling his dad a cocksucker.

'The amazing thing,' Donnelly said, 'is that Mahoney hired you when you got out of law school. I don't know *why* he hired you — that's the one mystery I haven't unraveled — but I know he did. And I do know that your father is the reason Mahoney keeps you down in his cellar. He doesn't want to have to explain your dago ass to *anybody*.'

Donnelly leaned forward so his face was closer to DeMarco's and said, 'So let me ask you something, sonny boy. Knowing John Mahoney to be the self-serving son of a bitch that he is, how long do you think you'll keep your job when the press finds out about you and your father and your job with the Speaker?'

'Did you personally assign Billy Mattis to the President's security detail, Mr Donnelly?' DeMarco said.

'Why you . . . ' Donnelly took a breath. 'Now you listen to me and you listen good: my agents are *clean*. They all have outstanding records, particularly Mattis, and they all passed lie detector tests. Banks is a fool to think the Secret Service had any part in this.'

'Then why didn't you have the warning note analyzed?'

'You impertinent son of a bitch!' Donnelly said, his face turning scarlet.

That's it, DeMarco thought. *Have a stroke, you little fuck.*

Donnelly opened his mouth to scream something else but managed to get his emotions under control. He jerked his thumb in the direction of DeMarco's house. 'I'd suggest you put that place on the market,' he said. 'You're not going to be living in this town much longer.'

'Really,' DeMarco said.

Donnelly smiled. His teeth were small and sharp. 'Your job requires a security clearance, smart ass. Guess what agency does the background checks to provide that clearance? Now beat it.'

DeMarco stepped from the limo and closed the door quietly. As he watched the taillights of the limo disappear up the block, he stood quietly in the center of the street, feeling the sweat go cold on his arms and legs.

So Donnelly knew about his father.

12

A woman answered Emma's phone; she sounded like Emma, the same low voice, the same inflections, but the speaker wasn't Emma. The woman, whoever she was, passed the phone to Emma who said, 'If you're a telemarketer, I'm going to hunt you down, burn your house, and kill your dog.' She sounded serious.

'It's Joe, Emma. And wouldn't it be easier to get on one of those do-not-call lists?'

'Those lists are unconstitutional.'

'And house burning and dog killing aren't?'

'Why are you calling at such an ungodly hour?'

'Emma, it's only nine.'

'Oh. So what do you want?'

'Patrick Donnelly just came to my house and threatened me. The other day, when we listened to your friend, the cello player, you seemed to know something about him. I'd like to know what you know.'

'He came to your house?'

'Yeah.'

Emma hesitated then said, 'All right. Come on over.'

Her voice sounded strange. She sounded . . . worried. DeMarco had rarely known Emma to be worried about anything.

Emma answered her door wearing jeans, a white T-shirt, and a blue smock smeared with paint. DeMarco didn't know she painted; just one more thing about her he'd discovered accidentally. She took DeMarco into a living room that could have made the cover of *House Beautiful* and poured them whiskeys. She slugged hers down and immediately poured herself another.

Before DeMarco could say anything a young woman entered the living room. He was immediately struck by her resemblance to Emma. She was tall like Emma and had Emma's nose and Emma's chin, but her hair was dark and her eyes were brown. The young woman looked over at DeMarco, her expression wary.

'Julie, this is Joe DeMarco. A friend of mine.'

No smart-ass cracks tonight, like DeMarco being a bagman. Emma was definitely not herself.

The young woman nodded at Joe then turned back toward Emma.

'I'm tired. Jet lag, I guess. I'm going to hit the sack,' Julie said.

I'm tired, *Mom*. That's what it sounded like to DeMarco. He was sure the young woman was Emma's daughter.

'That's a good idea, hon,' Emma said. 'We'll sort this out in the morning.'

And Emma, DeMarco thought, sounded absolutely, unbelievably maternal. A maternal Emma seemed stranger to DeMarco than snakes cuddling.

After Julie left the room, DeMarco said, 'Is everything okay, Emma?'

Emma shook her head, dismissing DeMarco's question.

'Tell me what Donnelly said to you,' she said.

DeMarco relayed the gist of his one-sided conversation with Donnelly.

'I knew about your father,' Emma said.

DeMarco nodded, not the least surprised. 'I know this is going to sound strange,' he said, 'but he wasn't a bad guy.'

Emma didn't say anything but her eyes widened momentarily in amazement.

'Yeah, I know what you're thinking: he was a killer. How could he not have been a bad guy. But from my perspective, as his son, he was okay. He was a quiet man, not some Mafia big mouth always trying to prove how tough he was. And when my dad wasn't, uh, working, we had dinner together like other families and most of the conversation centered around me, his only child. What I was doing in school, how I was doing at sports, why my grades weren't better. That sorta thing. He was good to my mom and he was good to me. He and I used to go see the Yankees play almost every Saturday they were in town, and Sundays he always made breakfast — pancakes and sausage.'

DeMarco was silent a moment, remembering his father, how he sat in the bleachers with him at Yankee Stadium, an old flat cap on his head, an unlit cigar in his mouth, not cheering much, mostly just watching DeMarco enjoy himself. And he remembered his mother when they got home from the games and how she'd rail at his dad for feeding him so much junk, and his dad standing there, this big guy with arms that could bend rebar, his head hanging contritely while his cap hid the pleasure in his eyes. DeMarco knew one thing for sure: his mother had never feared his father.

'I really didn't know what he did until I was about fifteen,' DeMarco said, 'and even then I had a hard time believing it. I just couldn't imagine him taking some guy out to a marsh in Jersey and putting one into the back of his head.'

'Did you ever talk to him about his job?' Emma asked, her voice soft.

'I tried once, when I was sixteen. I asked some inane question like, 'Is it true, Dad, that you work for Mr Taliaferro?' He knew what I meant. But my dad wasn't much of a talker when it came to personal things.'

'Reminds me of someone else I know,' Emma said, obviously meaning DeMarco.

'Anyway, all he said was something like 'A man can't always choose his life,' then he switched the subject. We never discussed it again.'

'Families,' Emma said, maybe referring to her own.

DeMarco took a sip of his drink, his mind in the past.

'He was the one who talked me into going to law school.' DeMarco smiled. 'I think he figured I could make a good living defending his co-workers.'

'So why *did* Mahoney hire you after you got out of law school?' Emma asked.

DeMarco laughed.

'I have a godmother, a friend of my mom's I call Aunt Connie. She lives in Albany now and works for a labor union, but when she was young she worked in D.C. Today Aunt Connie's a bit broad in the beam, has a mustache, and a face like a sad horse. But when she was young she looked like Sophia Loren. She was an absolute knockout.'

'Ah, I think I can see where this is going,' Emma said.

'I'll bet you can,' DeMarco said. 'Anyway, Aunt Connie — who never married — has a son, a successful fellow who works for a very big bank. And Aunt Connie's Italian, as I believe I've indicated, but her son bears an amazing resemblance to a large Irish fellow I know.'

'Indeed,' Emma said.

'I got my law degree about the time my father was killed. Thanks to my mom, and my father for that matter, I never had a damn thing to do with the Mob. I've never been arrested much less convicted of a crime, but because of my dad I couldn't get a job as a process server. There wasn't a law firm in the Western Hemisphere who wanted Gino DeMarco's kid on its payroll. My mother complained to my godmother and I think she talked to you-know-who. Maybe she threatened him with doing paternity tests on a certain fella who works for a bank. And I believe you-know-who — the happily married father of three legitimate children — succumbed to Aunt Connie's wishes and gave her poor, unemployable godson a job.'

'So she blackmailed him.'

'Maybe, but maybe not. Mahoney might have felt he owed her because of the kid or maybe he still cared for her enough to help me out. I don't know. Whatever the case, neither she nor Mahoney has ever confirmed a word of what I just told you. All I know is I got a call from the Speaker one day, completely out of the blue, and I was offered a job.'

'A job you should quit.'

'And do what, Emma?' They'd had this discussion before.

'Oh, never mind. What will Mahoney do when you tell him Donnelly is thinking of talking to the press about your father?' Emma said.

'I don't know. I'll talk to him tomorrow. Now tell me about Donnelly.'

'Little Pat,' Emma said, 'is a piece of work.'

According to Emma, Donnelly had been with the Secret Service for forty-one years and director for the last fifteen. His reputation was similar to J. Edgar Hoover's: he ran the Service with an iron hand, establishing rules for agent behavior with the whimsy of a king. Also, similar to Hoover, it was rumored that he used the power of his office to pry into the lives of private citizens.

'After the assassination attempt on Reagan back in '81,' Emma said, 'they tried to give him the boot. He was deputy director then and already showing his true colors, but Donnelly burrowed in and let it be known that if he was fired he'd tell the paparazzi where the bones were buried. He survived Reagan's term but with Chattooga River people are clamoring for his head again.'

'Who's doing the clamoring and why?' DeMarco asked.

'Anyone who's been here very long. He's a conniving, manipulative little shit who blackmails politicians to get what he wants.'

'What does he want? Money?' DeMarco asked.

'No. I understand he's fairly wealthy. He wants power. Power over politicians, power to expand the scope of his agency, power to stay in his job until he dies.'

'If he's wealthy why doesn't he just retire?' DeMarco asked. He could not imagine anyone continuing to work for the government once they were eligible for retirement.

'I told you. He loves his job. The Secret Service is his private army and he acts like the dictator of some banana republic. And if the rumors are true about him having the goods on folks here in power town, he may never go.'

'How did he make his money?'

Emma frowned at the question. 'I don't know,' she said and sounded astounded that she didn't. She sat a moment, thinking, then got up from the couch, walked over to the phone, and dialed a number.

'George, it's Emma. I'm fine. How are you?'

She and George — whoever the hell George was — chatted for about five minutes before she got down to business. She asked George what he knew about Patrick Donnelly's finances and then all DeMarco heard on his end was 'uh-huh,' 'oh?,' 'Is that right.' Before she hung up she told George that lunch sometime would be delightful.

'George said — '

'Who's George?' DeMarco asked.

'George said he doesn't know where Donnelly got his money, and if he doesn't know I'm not sure who would. He does know he was raised poor in Pennsylvania so he probably didn't inherit. He's never been married, so he didn't get it that way. And he's never worked in the private sector. Tomorrow I'll call a researcher I know.'

DeMarco suspected 'researcher' was a euphemism for hacker but didn't bother to ask.

Emma finished her drink and walked back to the liquor cabinet. DeMarco had never seen her slamming down drinks like this. Emma poured another and returned to her chair.

'Donnelly's not acting rationally,' she said.

'What do you mean?'

'Donnelly's a good bureaucrat and good bureaucrats don't take chances. It's just like Banks said: when he got that warning letter, Donnelly should have *immediately* pulled the inside ring. And Donnelly wouldn't have given a damn if he'd screwed up the President's vacation with Montgomery. So why didn't he do the safe thing?'

'Maybe — ' DeMarco said.

'And why would he come to see you personally? People in his position don't make threats that can be directly attributed to them. He's not only taking an unusual interest in Billy Mattis, he's exposing himself by doing so. What in the hell could be making him behave this way, Joe? And what on earth could be the connection between a humble agent and the director of the Secret Service, a man who's been in his job

93

longer than God? Donnelly is acting like a man who — '

Before Emma could finish her thought, a muted cry came from one of the back rooms of her home. It sounded like Julie crying out in her sleep.

Emma rose, her face pinched with concern. 'You have to leave now, Joe. I need to take care of . . . of something.'

'What's going on with Julie, Emma? You know I'll help any way I can.'

Emma — always so cool, so aloof from the fray. But not tonight. Tonight she looked like a cornered animal. A very dangerous cornered animal.

'Thanks, Joe, but . . . Good night.'

13

'Sir, did you hear what I just said? Donnelly knows I work for you and he knows about my father. He's threatening to go to the press.'

Mahoney still didn't respond; all his attention was focused on the impressive chest of a nearby waitress. DeMarco knew Mahoney was almost seventy yet the man was more preoccupied with sex than the average teenager. The inventor of Viagra was probably included in his will.

'He may know who your father is,' Mahoney said after the waitress had disappeared from view, 'but he can't prove you work for me.'

'But if he could, you have links to unions, and the unions have links to the Mob, and the Mob has links to me. A possible spin on all that is that the Mob has you in their pocket and I'm their guy on-site to keep an eye on you.'

The Speaker gave DeMarco a calculating look — calculating, it seemed to DeMarco, the benefits of continuing to employ him. After fifteen years of doing backroom skulduggery for John Mahoney, work that rarely had anything to do with the practice of law, DeMarco knew he was less employable than the busty waitress — who at that moment stopped at their table.

'Would you like some more coffee, Mr Speaker?' she said.

'Darlin', you are a ray of sunshine in an old man's dreary day,' Mahoney said.

'Oh, you're not that old, Mr Speaker,' the little darlin' said, knowing her tips depended more on smiles and cleavage than they did on service.

Mahoney waited until the waitress left before taking a flask from the inside pocket of his suit. He tipped an ounce of bourbon into his coffee cup, sipped loudly, then said, 'Donnelly ain't gonna do shit. He knows if he tries something now, I'll leak all this warning-note crap to the media.'

'He also implied he might torpedo my security clearance.'

'Yeah, I guess he could do that. His guys could make you look like Osama's understudy if they put their minds to it.'

'That's just great,' DeMarco said. 'And if he does?'

Mahoney ignored DeMarco's question. He lit a cigar stub sitting cold in the ashtray next to him, blew smoke skyward, and studied the smog he had created. No one seated at nearby tables reminded the Speaker that the restaurant was nonsmoking.

'So what's happenin' with this Mattis guy?' he asked.

DeMarco told him what he'd done to date: records and financial checks under way, the surveillance on Mattis, his discussion with Frank Engles in Middleburg. Mahoney was particularly intrigued by the rumor that Donnelly had personally assigned Mattis to the President's security detail but was otherwise unimpressed by DeMarco's efforts.

'Any connection between Mattis and this guy

Edwards?' Mahoney said.

'Nothing so far but I'm still waiting to hear back from one of Emma's friends.'

Mahoney took another puff on his cigar and brooded, engaging the gears of his Machiavellian mind. 'Donnelly's worried big-time about something,' he said. 'Comin' to visit you was unnecessary, an act of desperation.'

Exactly the conclusion Emma had come to, DeMarco thought.

Mahoney smiled and waved to a White House staffer who was passing by. He muttered 'Little cocksucker' then said to DeMarco, 'Put some pressure on this agent, Joe. Get in his face, as the kids say.'

'Get in his face how?' DeMarco asked.

'I dunno. Think of something.'

14

DeMarco's eyelids felt coated on the inside with a layer of sand and he suspected only the odd-numbered cells in his brain were firing. It was five thirty a.m. He was with Emma in a rented car, a model suitable for a staid law enforcement agency, and they were waiting for Billy Mattis to leave for work. DeMarco concluded, sitting there with his eyes closed, his head braced uncomfortably against the passenger-side window, that only swineherds, milkmaids, and other rural labor should be up at such a ghastly hour.

Emma sat impassively behind the wheel, preoccupied with her own thoughts. Emma's typically aloof, slightly amused view of her fellow human beings was missing again today. It may have been the hour but DeMarco suspected her daughter's troubles were still on her mind.

He was surprised that Emma was here at all; she typically considered surveillance chores beneath her. When he asked why she had come this morning instead of sending Mike, Emma had said, 'Oh, just curious about Billy, I guess.'

And she could have been telling the truth. Emma may have owed DeMarco for saving her life, but he suspected the reason she sometimes helped him was boredom rather than obligation. She loved the thrill of the hunt, even though the game DeMarco hunted was pussycat tame compared to what she had chased in her former life. Then there was the gossip factor. DeMarco's assignments quite often garnered juicy information about the city's elite, information they hoped would never, ever make the morning papers. Not only did Emma take an all too human delight in some of the things DeMarco told her, he also suspected that she fed some tidbits back to her previous employers, the dark, ever watchful gnomes at the DIA. But the real reason he suspected she was here this particular dawn was not curiosity or boredom or gossip — it was patriotism. Emma may have considered herself the nation's preeminent cynic, but if Mattis or anyone else had tried to kill the President, and if she could help stop them from trying again, she felt she had an obligation to do so.

Whatever her motive, DeMarco was glad to have her and he thought she looked perfect for her role. Her lean body was clad in a practical-looking dark pantsuit, a white blouse open at the throat, and shoes made for both creeping and running. To complete her ensemble she had a gun — a very big gun — in a holster on her hip. She looked official, efficient, and deadly.

DeMarco had thought the gun a bit much and had said so. Her response had been: 'I like to have at least as much firepower as the person I'm tailing, particularly when he's a potential accomplice to murder.' DeMarco still didn't think Billy Mattis was an accomplice to anything but it was too early to argue with Emma. Her wit would slice him open like soft fruit. Or she might shoot him.

DeMarco opened one eye and glanced over at Billy's house. They were parked across the street from it, making no attempt to hide. When Billy left for work he would see a Jack-and-Jill team in what appeared to be a government vehicle parked on his doorstep. And when he drove off they would follow, practically touching his bumper.

DeMarco's objective was to comply with the Speaker's command to put some pressure on Billy and see what happened. If Billy had nothing to hide, he should eventually ask them what the hell they were up to. They'd say Billy was confused, that they were just a couple who happened to be going the same direction all day. As plans went, DeMarco realized, this one lacked definition.

At six fifteen, a lean six-footer with short blond hair exited Mattis's house. The man was wearing sunglasses and dressed in a blue suit, a short-sleeved white shirt, and a solid blue tie. The suit jacket was draped over his arm. When he saw DeMarco and Emma parked on the street in front of his house, he stopped and stared at them. He might have thought they were journalists, but he would have quickly dismissed that idea because journalists would have charged across the street to question him.

Mattis stood a minute longer, clearly thinking about coming over to speak to them, then changed his mind and opened the door to his car. After he backed down his driveway, he looked over at Emma and DeMarco one more time before driving away; they both stared straight ahead, pointedly ignoring him.

Emma stayed no more than two car lengths behind Billy all the way from Annandale into the District. When Billy reached the lot where he parked, Emma parked in a position where Billy would see them as he walked to the entrance of his building. Billy again looked over at them as he walked by, and again hesitated, still trying to decide if he should challenge them.

Billy entered his building and Emma directed DeMarco to a spot where he could see two of the building's exits. When DeMarco worked with Emma he noted that she immediately assumed command. Emma took up her post on the other side of the building so she could watch other doors. In the next three and a half hours, DeMarco was asked for spare change five times, cigarettes twice, and directions once. He found it hard to distinguish the tourists from the bums.

A few minutes before noon Billy emerged from his building. He stood on the steps, scanned the area, and immediately saw DeMarco. And as Billy stared at DeMarco, DeMarco stared back and pulled a cell phone from his pocket and called Emma.

Billy descended the steps and began walking in the direction of the National Mall. DeMarco followed and Emma joined DeMarco at the next corner, falling into step beside him.

At Constitution Avenue, the street running parallel to the Mall on its north side, Billy turned left, in the direction of the Capitol. He looked over his shoulder once at the man and woman behind him, but from that point on kept his head rigidly fixed in the direction he was walking.

DeMarco had lived in D.C. more than a decade but continued to be as impressed by the panorama of the Mall as any first-time visitor. It was a vast plain where battles had been waged and history forged. The area between the Capitol and the Lincoln Memorial — almost three miles long and half a mile wide — had been for years the site of people coming together like armies, protesting wars, defending civil rights, rallying against the insensitivity of the ruling class. On both sides of the Mall were majestic buildings housing government agencies and the Smithsonian Institution — inflexible, granite bastions of power standing beside marble sanctuaries of art and history. Unfortunately, the proximity of art and history has little influence on those who govern, and hence the protests.

Billy walked a quarter of a mile before stopping at a street vendor's stand in front of the National Gallery of Art. He ordered a hot dog from the vendor, looking over at Emma and DeMarco again as he waited for his change.

The East Wing of the National Gallery was designed by I. M. Pei and seemed out of place with the more traditional structures surrounding the Mall. Its walls came together at impossibly sharp angles, particularly the southern face, which always made DeMarco think of the bow of a stone ship sailing through a concrete-and-asphalt urban sea.

In the atrium, suspended from the ceiling, was a large Alexander Calder mobile. The mobile was constructed of steel and aluminum and painted black and blue and red. It had a wingspan of nearly eighty feet and weighed almost a thousand pounds. Lying on the ground the mobile would have appeared as aerodynamic as an anvil, but suspended it was an object of the skies, born for flight, and the smallest air currents caused it to flutter and twist. DeMarco could see the mobile gently turning as Billy took his hot dog from the vendor.

As Billy slathered mustard on his hot dog, Emma took up a position under a nearby tree, aiming her cold blue eyes at Billy's broad back. With an imperial jerk of her head she directed DeMarco to another tree twenty feet away. Emma's strategy was to surround Billy psychologically if not physically.

Billy finished putting relish on his hot dog. He walked a few steps, dropped the wrapper from the hot dog in a nearby waste can, and took a seat on a bench a few feet away. From the bench, his head turned first to look at Emma, then over to DeMarco. He took an uncertain bite of the hot dog and chewed it slowly. DeMarco watched Billy's Adam's apple bob; he was so nervous he was having a hard time swallowing.

Emma then made a move that DeMarco thought was both inspired and ridiculous. She walked up to the hot dog vendor, obtained a paper sack from him, and went over to the trash can where Billy had thrown the wrapper from his hot dog. She reached inside the trash can and delicately picked up the wax paper using only two fingers, then looked Billy in the eye as she placed the wrapper in the sack as if she were collecting evidence from a crime scene.

Billy stared at Emma for a moment and attempted to resume his lunch. He raised the hot dog toward his mouth to take a second bite but stopped with it an inch from his lips. Suddenly he threw the hot dog on the ground and strode aggressively toward Emma. DeMarco quickly moved to stand next to his partner.

'Why are you followin' me?' Billy asked. His body was rigid with anger and his fists were clenched. DeMarco could hear the South in his speech and figured that Billy's voice was normally low pitched and gentle. Behind the display of righteous outrage, DeMarco could also sense his fear.

DeMarco had seen Mattis in the video and pictures of him in the papers, but the video and the photos hadn't prepared him for the impression the man made up close and in person. He did look like Mickey Mantle as Mike had said, and the resemblance was more than physical: he projected the same all-American, country-boy innocence that Mantle had at the beginning of his career. Billy's face, his voice, his clear blue eyes all conveyed exactly what he was alleged to be: simple but honest, dutiful son, faithful servant to his nation's masters. He looked exactly like the kind of man who would take a bullet for a politician.

Speaking to Emma, Billy repeated, 'Lady, I asked you: Why are you followin' me?' For some reason Billy assumed Emma was in charge, a small point which annoyed DeMarco.

Emma, uncharacteristically, glanced over at DeMarco to see how he wanted to play it. DeMarco thought of giving Billy the runaround: telling him they weren't following him, while making it apparent he was lying through his teeth — but he didn't.

He didn't know what made him say it. He'd like to claim he had made some gigantic, intuitive leap, but he hadn't. The first thing that popped out of DeMarco's mouth was completely unfiltered by his brain.

'You were just an agent in the wrong place, weren't you, Billy?' DeMarco said softly.

When DeMarco quoted from the warning letter, Billy, who had been staring belligerently at Emma, shut his eyes. He kept his eyes closed for several heartbeats, hoping the two 'agents' would be gone when he opened them, then turned his head slowly to face DeMarco.

'What . . . what the hell's that supposed to mean?' he said.

'I think you know, Billy,' DeMarco said.

'Damnit, who are you guys? FBI?'

'Billy,' Emma said, 'you sent a note to General Banks telling him to cancel the President's trip to Chattooga River. How did you know what was going to happen that day?'

'I don't know what you're talkin' about,' Billy said.

Unlike Patrick Donnelly — or for that matter, Joe DeMarco — Billy Mattis was not a professional liar. He was blinking so rapidly his eyelashes seemed like butterflies trying to reach escape velocity.

'Billy,' DeMarco said gently, 'I think you've been sucked into something ugly. Maybe we can help you.'

'I don't know what you're talking about,' Billy repeated. 'Look, I wanna see some ID from you guys.'

'Why did you duck Billy?'

'Duck?'

'At the river that morning. You dropped your sunglasses to give the shooter a clear shot at the President. You ducked right before the shot was fired. You can see it on the tape.'

Billy's face flushed crimson. He took an aggressive stride toward DeMarco and jabbed him hard in the chest with his index finger. 'That's a goddamn lie,' he said. His anger was genuine and for the first time DeMarco could hear truth ring in the agent's voice and could see it in his face.

'You can see it on the film, Billy,' DeMarco persisted. 'You were as nervous as a cat on a griddle walking toward the helicopter that morning. Your eyes were bouncing all over the place. You — '

'My eyes were moving, damnit, because I was scanning the area like I was supposed to.'

'I don't think so, Billy. I think you knew what was going to happen and at just the right moment you dropped your glasses. Did you give Harold Edwards the President's itinerary, Billy?'

Beads of sweat popped out on Billy's forehead, and DeMarco could see rings of perspiration begin to form in the armpits of his short-sleeved white shirt. Billy opened his mouth to speak, and then shut it, his lips becoming a hard line barricading a tongue he couldn't trust. Finally he said, 'I said I want to see some ID. Now!'

Ignoring the agent's demand again, DeMarco said, 'How did you get by the polygraph, Billy?'

Mattis looked confused. 'What polygraph? Nobody gave me a polygraph.'

Now it was DeMarco's turn to hesitate because again it sounded as if Billy was telling the truth. Then DeMarco remembered it was Patrick Donnelly who had told Banks and the FBI and DeMarco that Billy had been given a polygraph test.

'Then let's talk about how you were assigned to the President's security detail, Billy.'

Shaking his head adamantly, Billy said, 'No. We're not talkin' about anything else. I'm not saying another word to you two.'

He started to walk away, then stopped and turned. There were tears glazing the surface of his blue eyes, making them sparkle like wet gems. 'I did my job that day. I did everything I could to protect him.' His voice caught when he added, 'I would have died for him.'

And DeMarco believed him.

As Billy walked away, DeMarco thought again of Calder's mobile as it slowly turned in the atrium of the museum. Calder's mobile: a substantial object balanced so delicately that the current created by a single door opening could set it in motion.

Like Billy Ray Mattis — one small push and he began to spin.

15

'I'll be damned,' Emma said softly.

'Son of a bitch,' DeMarco said at the same time.

'When you quoted from that note, Joe, I thought that sweet boy was going to lose his lunch.'

'Yeah, he definitely knew about the warning letter. No doubt about it. But when I accused him of ducking during the shooting, he almost took my head off. He was telling the truth when he said he'd die to protect the President.'

'Yes,' Emma said, 'but he's involved and I would certainly like to know how. And I'll tell you something else, Joe: I don't think the FBI or anyone else has really questioned that lad very hard. I think Donnelly's been shielding him, somehow, from the FBI's interrogators.'

'That fuckin' Donnelly. I'm gonna go see Banks. Right now. I've gotta convince that stubborn shit to talk to the Bureau.'

Emma looked at DeMarco in surprise. 'I thought the Speaker said to wait and see what Donnelly does next.'

'Screw the Speaker,' DeMarco said with more conviction than he felt.

Emma smiled, the first sign of humor he'd seen from her all day. 'So what would you like me to do, sweetie, while you're talking to the good secretary?'

'Can you stick with Billy?'
'No, but I'll call someone.'

★ ★ ★

As would be expected, the secretary of Homeland Security was not sitting in his office, twiddling his big thumbs, just waiting for lowly Joe DeMarco to pay him a visit. DeMarco sat in Banks's waiting room for two and a half hours watching important folk come and go. He noticed during that time that all who entered Banks's office were happier when they arrived than when they left, and by five o'clock DeMarco was becoming quite unhappy himself. He'd missed lunch and his stomach was beginning to rumble.

At five thirty he was finally allowed in to see Banks. Taped around the walls of Banks's office were poster-board organizational charts. The general was moving from chart to chart with a red felt-tipped marker making big Xs through rectangles representing divisions or departments. Every time he crossed out a box he would say 'Gotcha' like a man swatting a fly. Now DeMarco could see why those who had visited him had left not smiling.

While continuing to study the charts, Banks said to DeMarco, 'When they formed Homeland Security they jammed twenty-two different agencies together, one hundred eighty thousand people, and each agency already had its own support structure. You know, overhead guys, financial people, admin staff, personnel departments, that sorta thing. But do you think the people that run these agencies would volunteer to combine some of these functions to reduce costs? Hell no, not them. Goddamn rice bowls, they're costing — '

'You need to tell the FBI what you know.'

Banks stopped studying the charts and fixed his hard eyes on DeMarco. 'You found something, didn't you?' he said. It wasn't really a question.

'Maybe,' DeMarco said and proceeded to tell Banks how he had confronted Billy Mattis on the Mall and how the agent had reacted when he had quoted from the note.

Banks threw his red marker at the wall. 'Goddamnit, DeMarco!' he yelled. 'I didn't tell you to question the man. You're about as subtle as an elephant's dick!'

DeMarco couldn't tell Banks about the Speaker's order, so instead he said, 'I was wasting my time, General. I couldn't find a link between Mattis and Edwards, or anything else that incriminates him. I thought the best thing to do was to put some pressure on him and see how he reacted — and I got one hell of a reaction, sir. If you'd been there you'd understand what I'm saying.'

Before Banks could have him flogged for insubordination, DeMarco hurried on to say, 'And the other thing is, Billy denied being given a polygraph. Donnelly could be lying about that too, just like he lied to you about analyzing the warning note.'

Banks started to say something then stopped.

He realized that it was possible that his worst fear had come true: the note had been genuine and he'd failed to act on it.

'It's time to talk to the FBI, General. You need to get them looking at Mattis.'

Banks ignored DeMarco and instead bent to pick up the marking pen he had thrown, and then walked over to his window and looked down at the traffic jam on the street below him. DeMarco wanted to tell him that all that traffic was caused by people who were through working for the day and going home to eat.

'No,' Banks finally said. 'All we've got at this point is your gut feelin' — which isn't any better than my gut feelin'. You stick with it a couple more days and see if you can get something solid.'

'General,' DeMarco said, 'if Mattis is tied to Harold Edwards, the odds of me coming up with anything substantial to prove it are less than remote. Virgin birth is more likely. The longer you wait to talk to the FBI, the colder the trail's going to be and the worse you're going to look in the end.'

Banks shook his head. 'Not yet, bub, not yet.'

DeMarco argued with Banks for ten more minutes but he couldn't sway him. As he turned to leave the secretary's office he heard the marker squeak and Banks say, 'Gotcha.'

16

'Did you tell Mahoney about Billy's reaction yesterday?' Emma asked.

She and DeMarco were driving in the middle lane of I-395, three cars behind Billy Mattis. It was six thirty a.m., the following day.

'No. You're forgetting that the Speaker's only interest in this case is Patrick Donnelly,' DeMarco said. 'If I'd gone to him, he would have said the same thing Banks said: keep at it a couple more days and see what happens. My life's dominated by assholes.'

The freeway was unusually congested, even more so than normal, and drivers were competing for position like NASCAR racers. They had just slipped five cars behind Billy. As they approached the last exit in Virginia, before crossing the Fourteenth Street Bridge into D.C., Billy suddenly cut right, almost hitting the front fender of a van in the next lane. He then cut across a second lane, forcing another car to hit its brakes, and took the off-ramp. If Emma had been caught by surprise, she didn't act like it. She calmly watched as Billy drove out of sight.

'Shit,' DeMarco said, slapping the dashboard. 'What the hell's he doing?'

'Losing us,' Emma said, but she was smiling.

'What's so damn funny?' DeMarco asked irritably.

'He lost us but he didn't lose Sammy.'

'Sammy?'

'An old friend,' Emma said.

Emma and her old friends.

'So what's Sammy doing?' he asked.

'Joe, I've told you before: one car can't follow another car in heavy traffic, particularly when the guy you're tailing knows he's being tailed. You need at least two cars, and you're better off with four. Mike wasn't available today so I called Sammy last night and told him we needed backup. He's been riding in the exit lane ever since we got on the freeway and he followed Billy off the ramp.'

'Damn nice of you to tell me that Sammy was on my payroll,' DeMarco said.

'Oh, quit being so grumpy.'

DeMarco grunted in response; a grunt was better than admitting Emma was right. As usual.

'I hope you didn't tell Sammy *why* we're tailing Mattis.'

Emma arched an eyebrow at DeMarco's impertinence. 'I didn't tell him anything. Just to follow Billy if he shakes us and see if he talks to anybody.'

DeMarco grunted again. They rode in silence a few minutes before he said, 'Maybe we should take the next exit and see if we can locate him.'

'That would be silly,' Emma said. 'We'll go get some coffee, then go to Billy's office. He'll get there eventually and when he does, Sammy will be behind him.'

At eight thirty Billy indeed arrived at his parking lot, locked his car, and walked slowly over to the Secret Service building. His eyes were fixed on the pavement as he walked. At one point, he shook his head as though he might be having a conversation with himself. He didn't see Emma and DeMarco parked at the far end of the lot, although he would have if he had looked up. After Billy went inside his building, Emma and DeMarco stepped out of their car.

'So where's your pal Sammy?' DeMarco asked.

Emma ignored his question and continued to scan the parking lot. When she didn't see Sammy after a few minutes she said, 'I wonder if Billy met someone and Sammy followed the other guy?'

'Yeah, right,' DeMarco said. Mattis, with all his training, had probably ditched this Sammy character five minutes after he exited the freeway.

Twenty minutes later, Emma raised her arm and waved at a small man walking in their direction.

Sammy Wix weighed about a hundred pounds and was short enough to be a jockey's big brother. His homely, long-nosed face was wrinkled, tanned, and leathery; he looked like a sun-worshiping troll. He also had a handshake which made DeMarco wince.

'So what's our Billy been up to, Sammy?' Emma asked.

Sammy spoke in a dense New York dialect, all dems and dises, mangling the English language with his tongue.

'He drives a couple a blocks after he gets offa da freeway, Em, den he circles around like he's trying to make chur nobody's followin' him. Den he stops at a 7-Eleven to use da phone. Da store's got two boots side by side, and since he doan know me from Adam, I bops on over to da boot next to him and listen to him jabber.'

He stopped and smiled. It was a tight little smile, just a twitch of the lips. It was the kind of smile that said people always underestimated Sammy Wix and he liked it when they did.

'He punches lotsa buttons, like he's dialin' long distance and chargin' da call to a card.'

'Did you get the number of the booth he called from?' DeMarco asked.

Sammy looked at DeMarco for the first time and twitched his little smile again. 'Chur,' he said, 'and da time a da call.' His eyes lingered on DeMarco for a moment as if he didn't quite trust him. DeMarco wondered if his face reminded Sammy of guys that used to chase him home from school when he was a kid.

'Anyway,' Sammy said, continuing to address Emma, 'he sounded real excited. He says, 'Uncle Max, sometin's funny, sometin's happenin'.' Den before he can say anyting else, da guy on da other end, dis Uncle Max, starts screamin' at him. I can tell cuz da kid holds da phone away from his ear. Den he says 'Sorry, Uncle Max' a whole buncha times, den he says, 'No, I'm callin' from a phone boot,' den he says, 'I'll call Dale,' den he says he's sorry again, a whole bunch more times. Den he hangs up.'

Sammy stopped, as though he was finished with his story.

'So where's he been since the phone call?'

115

DeMarco asked. 'He's half an hour late for work.'

'I was just gonna tell you dat.' Little gotcha smile. 'After da call he hangs up and calls anudder number. Someone answers. Billy calls him Dale, says dey gotta talk. Da udder guy, dis Dale guy, he jabbers awhile, den Billy hangs up again.'

He paused again, as if he was finished, but this time DeMarco waited. He was wise to the little bastard.

'Den he gets in his car and drives into D.C., near GW University, parks and stands by his car. A few minutes later, dis udder guy shows up, lookin' like maybe he just got outta bed. He walks up to Billy and Billy starts blabbin', all excited, wavin' his arms. I can't hear what dere sayin' cuz I gotta stay in my car, cuz I'm double parked down the block. Can't ever find parkin' in dis fuckin' town. Anyway, da udder guy smacks him.'

'Smacks him?' DeMarco said.

'Yeah. A slap, not a punch. Kind of a getta-grip-on-yourself smack. Den da udder guy jabbers at Billy awhile, puts his arm around his shoulder like he's tryin' to make him feel better, calm him down. Billy nods his head a whole buncha times, blows his nose, like maybe he's cryin', den finally he gets in his car and leaves.'

'I wonder who da udder guy . . . I mean, who the other guy was?' DeMarco said to Emma. Emma just looked over at Sammy.

Sammy's lips twitched. 'As soon as Billy takes off, I slides into his parking space and takes off

116

on foot after da guy Billy was talkin' to. He walks back to an apartment right around da corner, a brownstone on Nineteenth and G. I look at da tenants' names on da mailboxes. Only one name with da first initial D. Someone named D. Estep.'

17

DeMarco called Alice, gave her the phone number of the booth Billy had used, and told her to start tapping her keyboard. He wanted to find out who Uncle Max was.

Alice, sounding distracted, said it was going to be a couple of hours before she could get the information DeMarco needed.

'Alice,' DeMarco said, 'I know it only takes you ten damn minutes to trace a number for me. I need this quick.'

'I was just leavin' for a doctor's appointment when you called. I've been havin' these chest pains lately. I think it's my heart.'

'Alice, you don't have a heart. It's indigestion. Go to the doctor tomorrow.'

'I'm not going to risk a heart attack for you!' Alice said, stung by DeMarco's bedside manner.

'Alice, you know what's worse than having a heart attack?' DeMarco said.

'What?'

'Starving to death — which is likely to be your demise since you feed your paycheck to a slot machine every week. You need that check I send to you, Alice. You are on retainer — just like a lawyer — but if you don't provide the service for which you have been retained I'm going to stop mailing you money, in which case you'll be eating dog food by the end of the month.'

'Listen to me, you insensitive prick,' Alice

hissed. 'I'm going to the doctor. I'll be back in a couple of hours unless he puts me in the hospital, and when I get back, I'll do your damn trace.'

Alice hung up without saying good-bye.

★ ★ ★

D. Estep lived in a three-story apartment building housing a dozen tenants. DeMarco buzzed the door marked 'Manager' and was greeted by a belch, followed by, 'Yeah?'

'Are you the manager?'

'Yeah.'

'I need to talk to you. Buzz me in, please.'

'If you're a salesman, you can fuck off.'

'I'm not a salesman. I'm a government investigator and if you don't let me in, I'm gonna make your life miserable.' And I'll huff and I'll puff and I'll . . .

'My life's already miserable, asshole,' the manager said, but before DeMarco could complete the chorus by saying he would make it more miserable, he heard the click of the door lock being released.

The apartment manager was one of those aesthetic creatures blessed with an enormous belly and no butt. He wore a too-tight green T-shirt and baggy blue jeans, so from the front you were treated to the lovely sight of a roll of fat flopping over his belt, and from the rear, the crack of his rump.

The manager took a seat in a swaybacked recliner then picked up a Budweiser from a

119

nearby end table. There were three empty beer cans on the floor next to the recliner. As he took a drink his eyes drifted toward a television set tuned to a soap opera, seeming to forget DeMarco was in the room. The dingy apartment was hot and smelled of smoke, stale beer, and rapidly ejected stomach gases.

DeMarco walked over to the television set and punched the off button.

'Hey! What'd you do that for? I was watchin' that.'

DeMarco looked around for someplace to sit and concluded that his dry-cleaning bill would be less if he stood.

'I want to talk to you,' DeMarco said, 'and I want your undivided attention.'

'So talk, but make it quick. That's my favorite show.'

'You have a tenant in 2B named D. Estep. I want to know about him.'

'What for?'

'Because I'm investigating him.'

'Yeah, but ain't this invasion of privacy, or a violation of his civil rights, or some such shit?'

'Right now, I'm just invading *his* privacy. How would you like it if I started invading yours? For example, I'll bet you get a few tips at Christmastime or maybe you have another job, one that pays cash. I'll bet you don't report everything you make to the IRS. Am I right?'

'Okay, okay. I get the point. So whaddaya wanna know? I never liked him anyway, the cornpone asshole.'

'Cornpone?'

'He's from way down South. Talks that goofy Southern way.'

'You have a file on him? He must have filled out some paper when he rented the apartment.'

'Yeah, lemme get it.'

With a grunt he heaved himself out of the recliner, made the futile gesture of tugging up his pants, and walked slowly over to a battered olive-green filing cabinet. He rummaged through the cabinet for a few moments and finally pulled out a single, wrinkled sheet of paper.

DeMarco took the paper from him. It was a standard rental agreement and it identified the occupant of apartment 2B as Dale Estep, no middle initial, and gave as a prior residence an address in Folkston, Georgia. DeMarco had no idea where Folkston was. He copied down the address and Estep's social security number. The space for references was blank. Rental terms were for a three-month lease, paid in advance, and a five-hundred-dollar damage deposit.

'Isn't a three-month lease unusual?' DeMarco asked.

'Yeah, but he said I could keep the damage deposit when he moved out.'

'What's he doing that he only needed a place for three months?'

'Beats me. When I asked, just trying to be friendly, he told me to mind my own business.'

'What do you think he does?'

The apartment manager shrugged; the T-shirt rose. 'I don't know,' he said. 'He comes and goes at odd hours, sometimes he's not here three, four days at a time.'

121

'He live alone?'

'Yeah. He's had a few babes over, different one every time. Most of 'em look like hookers.'

'Has he ever had a man over?'

'You mean is he queer?'

'No, I mean is there anyone, male or female, who's a regular visitor?'

The man's brow furrowed as if DeMarco had asked him to define gravity. He finally said, 'There's one guy I seen, maybe three times. Don't know his name. Blond guy. Short hair, like maybe he's military. Young. Neat.'

'Does Estep keep a car here?'

'Yeah. A Vet. Cherry red. It's got Georgia plates, those, you know, vanity plates. His says GATOR.'

* * *

DeMarco threatened the apartment manager with dire federal consequences if he talked to Estep, and drove to his office. There was a message on his answering machine from heart-pained Alice. 'He called a Maxwell Taylor in Folkston, Georgia.' She gave DeMarco Taylor's address. She paused before saying, 'I'm sure you don't give a shit, but the doctor said my heart's okay.'

Indigestion, just like DeMarco had thought.

DeMarco called Emma next. He gave her the Georgia addresses for Maxwell Taylor and Dale Estep, Estep's social security number, the GATOR license plate, and asked her to see what her extended federal family might know about the men.

'We gotta find out who these guys are, Emma,' DeMarco said. 'They just popped up out of the blue. They're obviously connected to Billy but we need to know if they're linked to Harold Edwards in some way. This could have nothing to do with the assassination attempt.'

DeMarco spent the rest of the morning trying to get a line on Maxwell Taylor in his own way. Sammy Wix said Billy had called him *Uncle* Max but a glance at Billy's personnel file showed there was no mention of a relation named Taylor. The file was inconclusive, however, as the only relatives required to be listed on government personnel records are immediate family and family employed by the government — Uncle Sam's airtight method for controlling nepotism.

In going back over Billy's file he did see something he hadn't noticed before: no father. Billy's file had the cryptic initials 'NA' in the block where he was supposed to write his father's name. Unless immaculate conceptions were back in vogue, he doubted 'Not Applicable' was applicable. He knew the Secret Service performed extensive background checks on its employees and would have thought that the absence of paternal information would have raised an eyebrow. But then this was the government, an entity infrequently applauded for accuracy.

Since Billy's personnel file was no help, he called the high school from which Billy had matriculated. The high school was listed in his file even if Billy's sire was not. He spoke to the vice principal, a lady who sounded like Andy Griffith's sister. DeMarco faked a genteel Southern accent and claimed to be a reporter from Atlanta. He told the lady that it had come to his slow-witted editor's attention that a son of ol' Georgia was guarding the President the day that Yankee tried to kill him. He wondered if there was someone there at the school who remembered the man.

The vice principal was delighted to tell DeMarco she knew Billy personally, having worked at the school since reading became a mandatory subject in Georgia. She put him on hold while she found a high-school yearbook, then reeled off a list of Billy's accomplishments, which consisted primarily of lettering in every sport played with a ball. Scholastic achievements were not mentioned.

DeMarco eventually steered the conversation toward Billy's family and asked what she could tell him about Billy's folks. There was a lengthy pause and when the lady finally answered some of the down-home Dixie friendliness was gone from her voice. She suggested DeMarco speak to Billy directly if he wanted to know about his ma and pa. She actually said 'ma' and 'pa.'

It was clear to DeMarco by the tone of the woman's voice and the pauses between her words that she knew more but was going to keep it to herself. DeMarco's final question — did she know Billy's favorite uncle, Max Taylor — got the schoolhouse door slammed on his tongue. He was coldly informed it was against school policy to give out information on former students, and any further questions would have to be submitted in writing to the county school board.

DeMarco slowly put down the phone. He had touched a nerve asking about Billy's lineage but couldn't imagine why.

★ ★ ★

Clyde's was a Georgetown institution, founded, according to the brass plaque near the front door, more than forty years ago, yet it still seemed to be a place in search of an identity. Model planes hung over some tables, palm fronds over others; the menu ranged from chili to French cuisine; old posters of steamships competed with pictures of motorcars and bicycles and busts of athletes from bygone days. On one wall, near the front bar, was a large picture of Custer's last stand that would have seemed more appropriate in a Montana saloon. It was one of DeMarco's favorite places.

He took a seat at a wobbly table near the bar to wait for Emma. A waitress, a pretty young woman with too much blue eye shadow, asked him what he wanted to drink. He hesitated. He really wanted a sweet drink, something like a piña colada, but he could imagine the waitress snickering as she placed his order. So he manfully ordered a vodka martini and when the drink arrived and tasted like cold kerosene, it occurred to him that a man could pay too high a price for manliness.

DeMarco checked his watch; Emma was late,

which was unusual. He sipped his drink and again he grimaced. Maybe when Emma arrived he could convince her to order a piña colada and they could switch drinks.

DeMarco glanced over at the door, and as he did, he noticed a woman sitting at the bar. She had dark hair, an olive complexion, and a very, very nice figure. The woman and DeMarco made eye contact and the woman gave him a soft smile. Not a come-hither smile, DeMarco thought, but a friendly, hello-stranger smile. Or maybe it was a come-hither smile.

Emma arrived. She walked regally over to DeMarco's table then waited until he got up and held her chair for her. She did things like that sometimes.

The waitress asked Emma, 'May I get you something, ma'am?'

'Oh, I don't know,' Emma said, sounding distracted. Then before DeMarco could stop her, she pointed at his martini and said, 'Just give me whatever he's drinking.'

After her drink arrived, Emma said, 'This fellow, Estep. He's a park ranger.'

DeMarco didn't hear her; he was looking at the darkhaired woman sitting at the bar. Emma followed his line of sight and her lips compressed in irritation.

'Joe, did you hear what I just said? Estep is a park ranger.'

'A ranger?'

'Yes. He's in charge of a swamp in Georgia. The Okefenokee Swamp.'

'The Okefenokee?'

126

'Am I going to have to repeat every damn thing I say tonight?'

'Sorry. So why the hell would a park ranger be smacking Billy around?' DeMarco asked.

DeMarco glanced back at the bar again. Another woman, laden with packages from a marathon shopping excursion, joined the dark-haired woman at the bar. The two women hugged like old friends. Damn, DeMarco thought; he had hoped the woman was by herself.

'I don't know,' Emma said, 'but Mr Estep is not your normal nature lover. He's a Vietnam vet with two citations for bravery but who was then given a bad-conduct discharge from the military when he was twenty.'

'Why?'

'I don't know. The DEA had a jacket on him for peddling a truckload of pot across state lines back in the early eighties. He was given a suspended sentence because of his military record.'

'But you said he was given a dishonorable discharge.'

'No, I said it was a bad-conduct discharge, and I also said he had medals. Maybe the judge felt guilty for dodging the draft and went easy on him. I don't know. All I know is what my friend at the DEA had in his machine.'

'And that's all he had?'

'Yes. Just the one arrest twenty years ago and nothing else.'

'And Max Taylor?' DeMarco asked.

'Nothing,' Emma said. 'No criminal record

with anyone. My guy's still looking to see if either he or Estep have connections to Edwards.'

DeMarco watched the dark-haired woman say something to her companion, then both women looked over at DeMarco and the dark-haired woman smiled at him again. Definitely a come-hither smile, DeMarco thought. No doubt about it.

'Oh, for God's sake, Joe,' Emma said. 'Why don't you just go over and say, 'Hi, my name's Joe DeMarco and I'm smitten because you look just like my ex-wife. Are you by any chance a slut too?' '

'She doesn't look like — '

'Yes she does. The same Italian coloring, the same cute little ass — and the same big tits. When on earth are you going to get over that woman?'

DeMarco shrugged.

'How many women have I set you up with, Joe?'

Here we go again, DeMarco thought. But he didn't answer Emma's question.

'Three,' Emma said. 'And all three were lovely. And they all possessed traits your ex-wife didn't have, little things like a sense of humor and compassion and intelligence. And they all, God knows why, liked you. And you didn't call any of them back.'

DeMarco knew she was right. His wife had been vain and spiteful and not all that bright — and she had cheated on him with his own cousin, a shitbag who worked as a bookie for his father's old outfit. His wife used to tell him she

128

was going to New York to see her mother, and then she and his cousin would spend the weekend in Atlantic City. But she had also been the most sensual woman DeMarco had ever known. And it was more than sex; he had fallen in love with her when he was sixteen and she was fourteen. She had been his first everything: the first girl he had held hands with; the first girl he kissed; the first woman he made love to. He wanted to tell Emma that love wasn't logical, but they'd had this discussion before. And the mood Emma was in tonight, she'd shred his heart into thin strips.

'You need to get on with your life, for Christ's sake,' Emma said. 'Buy some damn furniture, get a girlfriend, and join the human race again.'

'Okay, okay,' DeMarco said. And yeah, he guessed the woman did look like his ex.

'So where do you think I should go with this, Emma?'

'Are we talking about your social life or the case?'

'The case.'

'I don't know.'

Emma rarely said 'I don't know.' She sat there for a while, preoccupied with her own thoughts, a long-nailed finger idly tracing the rim of her glass.

'I'm going out of town tonight, Joe. I'll be back tomorrow or the next day. Call Mike if you need something.'

Christ, he'd been so absorbed with his atrophied libido that he'd completely forgotten about Emma's problem. He felt like a selfish shit.

'Emma, is this about the young woman I met at your place the other night? Julie?'

'Yes.'

'Is she your daughter, Emma?'

Emma hesitated. 'Yes,' she finally said.

There was no way DeMarco was going to ask how it was that Emma came to have a daughter. Instead he said, 'Emma, what can I do to help? Tell me.'

Emma took a sip from her drink and studied DeMarco over the rim of the glass.

'My daughter's a brilliant young woman who has terrible taste in men. Two years ago she became involved with a married man. She finally came to her senses and told him that she didn't want to see him anymore but he won't let her go. He's obsessed with her. The last six months he's harassed her relentlessly. E-mails. Midnight phone calls. He's had people follow her. He's tapped her phone. He's opened her mail. A month ago he scared off a man she was dating and last week he caused her to lose her job, which is why she came home. He's ruining her life.'

'So tell his wife.'

'Julie did. His wife is a doormat who has tolerated his affairs for years. And she's probably been abused by this monster and is terrified of him.'

'And the police won't help?'

'He is the police. Actually he's the district attorney in a large western city. He's very rich and very powerful and very well connected. The governor is a personal friend; a U.S. senator is his uncle.'

'What are you going to do?' DeMarco asked.

Her pale blue eyes were as cold and lethal as the polar seas.

'I may kill him,' Emma said.

18

U.S. Army Colonel (Ret.) Byron Moore, was five foot seven, had a slender build, and wore black horn-rimmed glasses. His hair was dark, cut short on the sides, and combed forward on top to compensate for a receding hairline. He also had a slight hunchback and walked with a limp, both conditions caused by wounds incurred in Vietnam. DeMarco always thought of Shakespeare's Richard III when he saw him.

DeMarco met Moore five years ago. The Speaker had been tipped that an aide to a rival politician was using a military connection at the Pentagon to obtain inside information on defense contracts. The man in the Pentagon would find out which company was due for the next infusion of military moola and the congressional staffer would rush out and buy oodles of stock for himself and his cohort. The Speaker was probably jealous that he had not thought of the scheme himself.

During the investigation DeMarco made the mistake of concluding that Byron Moore was the inside man at the Pentagon. One night while he was following Moore, Moore doubled back on him, flipped him on his ass with some sort of judo move, and promised to crush his windpipe with one finger. Moore smiled when he made the threat. Although DeMarco was four inches taller and fifty pounds heavier than the colonel, he didn't have the slightest doubt that Moore was capable of doing exactly what he said.

Moore eventually informed DeMarco that he was working for the military on the same case. He also told DeMarco that he had his head so far up his ass that sunlight was but a memory, that he had everything all wrong, and then told him who the real culprit was. His initial meeting with Byron Moore had been an altogether humbling experience.

DeMarco discovered Moore had been a hell of a soldier: Green Beret, three tours in Vietnam, an expert in unarmed combat and demolitions. He had been forced to retire two years ago when he was passed over for a star. When DeMarco asked why he had not been promoted, Moore gave him a wry smile and said it was pretty simple: the army didn't make generals out of little hunchbacks — it wasn't good for the military's image.

Moore lived alone in a small apartment overlooking Arlington National Cemetery. There was an undeniable, poignant beauty in the endless rows of white markers but it was not a view DeMarco would have wanted to see every day. The colonel's apartment was filled with pictures of friends in uniform and the memorabilia of campaigns the Pentagon would just as soon forget. On a side table, almost hidden by other photos, was a picture of a young Byron Moore: tanned and shirtless, his body straight and well muscled. He was holding an M16 and squinting into a cruel Asian sun. There was also a picture of Moore at his retirement ceremony.

He was in full-dress uniform, his blouse a rainbow of gallantry, a ceremonial saber on his belt. The bitter smile on his lips was as crooked as his spine.

The army had been his life and his love, and Byron Moore ached for it. While he and DeMarco talked he gazed out the window at the white headstones, and DeMarco could imagine him alone — which was almost all the time — anticipating the day his name would be engraved on one of them.

'I hope you're not doing something to make this guy Estep mad, Joe,' Moore said.

'Not yet,' DeMarco said. 'Why? Is he a scary guy?'

'He's a wacko. He joined the army after high school — volunteered, not drafted. He was a hell of a shot and they used him mostly for long-range recon. They'd send him out by himself, three, four days at a time, and he'd scout the territory. If he saw something to kill, he'd kill it.'

'Is that the wacko part?'

'No, that was his job. But he liked the killing a little too much. You've heard about guys who made necklaces out of ears over there?'

DeMarco nodded.

'Estep was a real collector.'

'Is that why he was given the bad-conduct discharge?'

Moore shook his head. 'It took a special kind to work the bush alone. When you could find someone with the balls to do it, you put up with a few eccentricities.' Moore paused a moment.

134

DeMarco sensed he was thinking about himself, not Dale Estep, and he wondered about the colonel's eccentricities.

Moore walked over to his desk and picked up a hand grenade he used for a paper weight. DeMarco knew instinctively that the grenade was still functional and not a harmless souvenir. Squeezing the grenade as if it was one of those spring-loaded hand strengtheners, Moore said, 'One day Estep's on patrol with a squad and they come on a rice paddy. Seven Vietnamese, half of 'em women, tending the plants. The second looie in charge wants to cross the paddy but he can't tell if the farmers are friendlies or Cong. He tells his guys to spread out, sit tight, and watch for a while.

'Well, this one old guy stops work and wanders off a bit from the others to take a crap. He's squatting over a trench when a shot rings out. The old guy stands up, screaming, looking down at the place where his balls used to be.'

DeMarco involuntarily shuddered.

'Estep mows 'em all down before they can get to cover. Never misses. Seven shots, seven slopes — faster than you can blink. The lieutenant goes bananas. Starts screamin' 'Cease-fire' like it's his cousins being killed. Now the lieutenant doesn't give a shit about the gooks, of course — he's thinking My Lai. He sees his career going up in smoke every time a body drops. Later, Estep says he didn't hear the order to stop shooting but he did hear the order, which nobody else heard, to start.'

'And that's what got him discharged.'

135

'Yeah, but the paperwork says he was booted out for 'repeated insubordination.' There's no record of what happened in the rice paddy that day.' The colonel flipped the grenade in the air and caught it in his left hand. Winking at DeMarco, he added, 'Today that lieutenant wears two stars.'

'If there's no record of the incident, how did you find out about it?' DeMarco asked. Moore just stared at him. Stupid question.

'One guy who knew Estep over there,' Moore said, 'said he was the best shot he'd ever seen in his life. He also said Estep just *loved* killing things. People, monkeys, birds. Any fuckin' thing. He liked shootin' and killin' more than baseball and beatin' off.'

Thinking of the shooting blind, DeMarco asked, 'Do you think a guy with his training could hide pretty well? I mean for a couple of days in a place with people all around him?'

Moore laughed. 'Hide pretty well! Let me tell you a little story, Joe. Before my first tour we were running a training exercise against another squad. This squad was trained the same way Estep was, for long-range recon, and their job was to hide from us in an open field and our job was to find them before they killed us with paint balls. The field was two miles long, half a mile wide, and there wasn't much cover. My guys were pretty good. We found three of them. While we were standing there looking for the fourth guy we get hit, all of us, in the back of the head by paint balls. Hurt like shit, I'll tell you. Anyway, the fourth guy, we must have walked right over him. When I turned around to see where he was I still couldn't see him, then all of a sudden the earth opens up and this kid in a gillie suit rises out of the ground. He's grinning from ear to ear even though the side of his face is a mess, a mass of welts, one eye swollen completely shut. Some bug had been biting the shit out of him the whole time we were searching and this guy never moved.'

Moore tossed the hand grenade into the air again.

'Could Estep *hide* for a couple of days? Hell, Joe, a guy like him could hide in your toilet bowl for a week and you wouldn't see him.'

19

Emma had seen Eric Mason's photo on an Internet site, and she was sure he was the man walking toward the black Lexus. He was a handsome six footer with dark hair and a golfer's tan and eyes that twinkled when he smiled. He was wearing a double-breasted gray suit, a blue shirt with a white collar, and a maroon tie. He whistled as he walked, jiggling his car keys in time to the beat. He seemed immensely satisfied with the world and his place in it.

Emma was wearing a short red wig and big sunglasses. She was dressed in jeans, a University of Nevada sweatshirt, and hiking boots. She walked toward Mason, timing her pace so that she met him just as he reached his Lexus.

'Excuse me,' Emma said. 'Aren't you Eric Mason, the district attorney?'

Mason smiled at the woman, flashing white, perfectly capped teeth. 'Yes, I am,' he said. He was anxious to be off to his club where he was meeting his broker for drinks, but it never hurt to be nice to potential voters. And the woman was attractive, though too old for him he realized looking closer.

'Just wanted to make sure,' Emma said, then she swung the sap she had been holding down at the side of her leg and broke Eric Mason's perfect nose. Mason spun around at the force of the blow and Emma swung the sap again, hitting him at the base of his skull. Mason collapsed unconscious to the ground, and Emma picked his car keys up from the concrete where he had dropped them. By the time Emma opened the trunk of Mason's car, another woman was at her side to help place Mason in the trunk.

★ ★ ★

Mason regained consciousness slowly. He was lying on his back; he wasn't bound but he had very little room to move. Reaching up, he felt a hard, smooth surface above him, only four inches from his face. He was in a container of some sort, and the air smelled stale, dank . . . earthy. At that instant he realized he was in a coffin, underground, and he began to scream and beat his hands against the lid.

As he screamed he thought he heard a voice in his ear. The voice was telling him to be quiet. He stopped screaming, his panic barely under control, and realized there was an earpiece in his left ear and that's where the voice was coming from.

'That's better,' the voice said. He recognized the voice of the red-haired woman who had sapped him in the parking garage.

'What the hell are you doing?' Mason yelled. 'Who are you? Let me out of here!'

'What's wrong, Mr Mason. Are you claustrophobic?'

She knew he was; Emma had researched the man carefully.

'Goddamnit, let me the fuck out of here!'

'Mr Mason, the air you're currently breathing is coming in from a one-inch-diameter tube directly over your head. Look up, Mr Mason. I'll shine a light and you'll see.'

Emma shined a small penlight down the breathing tube. She could see Mason's eyes; they were enormous, ready to pop right out of his head.

'The breathing tube is open now, Mr Mason, but since you're being rude I'm going to put a stopper in it.'

'No!' Mason screamed.

'Your air supply will run out in exactly fifteen minutes. I'll talk to you again in sixteen minutes.'

'No,' Mason screamed again and watched in horror as the light disappeared and he heard something being shoved into the opening of the breathing tube. For the next few minutes he screamed and pounded on the coffin lid with his hands and kicked upward with his feet.

The voice in his ear said, 'You're using up your oxygen much too fast, Mr Mason. I don't think it will last fifteen minutes as I said earlier. Maybe thirteen or fourteen minutes. Can you hold your breath for three minutes, Mr Mason? You don't smoke, do you?'

Emma knew that he did.

As Mason lay there in the dark, trying not to breathe, trying not to panic, Emma watched him. Above his head was a small fiber-optic cable connected to a video monitor, the cable itself less than a quarter inch in diameter. Emma could record Mason's demise if she chose to. She shut off the microphone she had been using to communicate with Mason and said to her friend, 'You did a good job on this, Sam.'

Emma and Samantha were seated on plastic lawn chairs. They were in a rented garage two miles from Mason's office. The coffin was lying on the floor at their feet; the earthy odor Mason had smelled upon awakening was caused by a small mound of compost near the breathing tube. Samantha had rigged the coffin with the breathing tube, the video monitor, and the communication system.

'It was pretty simple,' Samantha said. 'I had all the stuff in my shop; I didn't have to buy anything but the box.' Though officially retired from government service Samantha occasionally helped out certain agencies — and old friends — who had special surveillance needs.

'Well, I appreciate it,' Emma said. 'Coffee?' she asked, reaching for the thermos by her feet.

'Love some,' Samantha said.

They were just two gals enjoying each other's company, their pleasure interrupted only occasionally by muffled noises coming from the coffin.

'How's Richard doing these days?' Emma asked. Richard was Samantha's husband.

'He's nuts about fly-fishing at the moment. You know Richard. He becomes absolutely obsessed with whatever his latest hobby is, and we've spent every weekend the last two months on some river or lake or beaver pond.'

'A man can have worse hobbies than fly-fishing,' Emma said.

'Yeah, like this asshole,' Samantha said,

looking down at the coffin.

Emma checked her watch. Ten minutes to go. She glanced at the video monitor to check on Mason. She hoped he didn't have a heart attack.

'And how's your granddaughter doing?' Emma asked.

Samantha had been very precise in her calculation of the volume of air in the coffin, and when Emma checked on Mason ten minutes later he was gasping like a fish out of water and breaking his manicured nails on the lid of the coffin.

Emma pulled the stopper out of the breathing tube and shined the penlight down on Mason's face.

'Mr Mason, are you ready to listen now?'

'Yes, yes,' Mason said. 'Just tell me what you want. Is this about one of my cases?'

'No, Mr Mason. This is about a young woman named Julie Fredericks whom you have been harassing relentlessly the last six months. She can't sleep, she's lost weight, and she's taking antidepressants. She's on the edge of a nervous breakdown — all because you won't take no for an answer.'

'Julie?' Mason said, seeming genuinely puzzled.

'Yes, Julie,' Emma said. 'You are an egomaniac without a conscience, Mr Mason. And you are afraid of nothing because you know the legal system can't touch you. You will continue to harass this young woman until she either kills herself or kills you. And killing you would ruin her life.'

'I'll stop,' Mason said, 'I swear to God I will.'

'It never occurred to you that somebody would ignore the law and attack you physically, did it? That's the kind of thing gangbangers do. You never dreamed it could happen to a powerful man like yourself, and certainly not for something as trivial as stalking a young woman.'

'Please, I promise . . . '

'And it was so easy. I took you out of the parking garage in the building where you work, in a building crawling with law enforcement personnel. Do you still feel invincible, Mr Mason?'

'Who are you?'

'I'll get back to you on that in sixteen minutes, Mr Mason. No, let's make it seventeen minutes this time.'

Emma inserted the stopper back in the breathing tube, cutting off Mason's scream.

'How's Audrey?' Samantha asked.

'She moved to New York.'

'Oh, I'm so sorry, Emma.'

'She had a job offer she couldn't pass up, something she'd wanted for a long time.'

'You couldn't go with her?'

'You know me, Sam. I'm pretty set in my ways. And . . . well, maybe it was for the best.'

Emma waited this time until Mason passed out, then pulled the stopper from the breathing tube. She was afraid for a minute that she might have to open the coffin to resuscitate him but he came to on his own.

'Can you hear me, Mr Mason?' Emma said.

Mason's response was to noisily suck in as much air as he could.

'Now to answer your question: Who am I? Well, I belong to a society that was created to help women like Julie Fredericks, women who are abused and terrorized by men. Women who receive no protection from the law because the law is run by men like you. It is a society of women for women, Mr Mason. A society which saves women like Julie Fredericks from predators like you.'

Emma looked over at Samantha and mugged a face. She sounded like the leather-clad heroine in a comicbook adventure. Samantha grinned back at her and silently mouthed: *You go, girl.*

'I promise I'll leave her alone,' Mason screamed.

'I don't believe you, Mr Mason.'

Emma jammed the stopper back into the breathing tube and Mason began to cry. Claustrophobia combined with the thought of being buried alive, further combined with the very real experience of being suffocated was enough to push a brave man over the edge — and Emma knew Eric Mason was not a brave man.

Sixteen minutes later, Emma pulled the stopper from the breathing tube again. She wrinkled her nose; Mason had soiled his expensive suit. It took several minutes before he calmed down enough for Emma to talk to him.

'Mr Mason,' Emma said, 'do you believe we can get to you anytime we want?'

'Yes!'

'Do you believe that some nice woman who looks like a grandmother could walk up behind you with a silenced gun in a shopping bag and put a bullet in your spine?'

'Yes!'

'Do you believe that a young woman who looks like a secretary could gain access to your building and poison the coffeepot right outside your office?'

'Yes!'

'Do you believe a young mother, a very credible young mother, could run you down while you're jogging and say you tripped and fell under the wheels of her car? Do you believe those things can happen to you now, Mr Mason?'

'Yes, goddamnit, yes. I believe you!' Mason shrieked.

'I hope so, Mr Mason, because one of those things *will* happen to you if you ever bother Julie Fredericks again. Do you understand?'

'Yes, I swear to God I'll never — '

'In ten minutes, Mr Mason, you'll hear an alarm clock ring. When you hear the alarm, push up on the lid of the coffin. If you push up the lid before the alarm sounds, you'll blow off your hands.'

Samantha pressed her hands over her mouth to keep from laughing.

'Your car is parked outside the building you're in, Mr Mason. The keys are under the floor mat on the passenger side. And Mr Mason, after you've changed your shit-stained pants, and after you've spent a few days in your office with your flunkies telling you what a big shot you are, and after your nose has healed and you look in the mirror and become delighted once again

145

with what you see, do *not* start to think that this experience you've just had was some sort of nightmare, that it didn't really happen. We'll be back, Mr Mason, if Julie Fredericks ever hears from you again.'

20

'Hello, Emma.'

'Neil,' Emma said, nodding her head.

'You didn't tell me you'd be bringing a friend, Emma,' Neil said, pointing his chin — or to be accurate, three chins — at DeMarco.

Neil was an immensely fat man in his fifties with a yellow-gray ponytail hanging down the back of his balding head like the tail on an animal with mange. He was dressed in a Hawaiian shirt, baggy shorts, and sandals. His calves were almost as big around as DeMarco's thighs.

The large room he occupied was filled with computers, recording equipment, and a dozen other electronic devices that DeMarco couldn't begin to name. The only illumination in the room was provided by the monitors of the computers. Neil sat on a stool with casters, his buttocks overflowing the seat. The stool allowed him to move quickly and effortlessly between his gadgets. When he wasn't talking, he sucked on a lime-green Popsicle.

'He's all right, Neil,' Emma said. 'Not only is Joe my friend, he's the client.'

DeMarco thought Emma looked tired but she seemed to be her old self again. Maybe she had talked to the man who was bothering her daughter. DeMarco knew Emma could be persuasive.

'Ah, the client,' Neil was saying. 'So he's the one paying the bill?'

'No one's paying, Neil. Tel Aviv. Remember?'

'Emma, my staff and I — '

'Your staff?'

Neil jerked his head in the direction of a young African American man wearing a Washington Wizards sweatshirt. Neither Emma nor DeMarco had noticed him when they entered the dimly lit room. He was in a corner, almost invisible behind the screen of a laptop computer. Rust-colored dreadlocks hung to the young man's shoulders; his body moved in rhythm to whatever sound was coming from the headphones he wore. He was so absorbed in his work and his music, he didn't appear to realize that Neil had visitors.

'Staff isn't good, Neil,' Emma said.

'Neither is bringing unannounced friends, Emma.'

Emma made a gesture with her head acknowledging Neil's point.

'As I was saying, Emma, my staff and I spent more than thirty hours on this project. Thirty hours I could have devoted to paying clients.'

'We'll consider Tel Aviv paid in full, Neil. Okay?'

Neil was silent a moment, then his face broke into a broad smile exposing oddly formed teeth.

'In that case, Emma, let's go into my office where we can be comfortable.'

Emma and DeMarco followed Neil's large backside from the computer room, through a metal door, and entered an adult's playpen.

Every board game imaginable was stacked on shelves. Nintendo and Sega hardware was connected to forty-five-inch plasma television screens hanging on the wall like modern art. A pinball machine, pool table, and foosball table stood all in a row.

Neil gestured Emma and DeMarco to two overstuffed armchairs in front of his cluttered desk and took a seat behind the desk in a chair that must have been specially built to suit his bulk.

'Can I get you and your friend anything, Emma? Popsicle, Nutty Buddy, fudge bar?'

'Oh, good Lord. Get on with it, Neil.'

Neil picked up a laptop from the floor behind his desk. He opened it and tapped a few keys. 'Ah, here we are,' he said.

'First I can find no links between the late Harold Edwards and any of the other players in this Dixieland drama. Mattis has never contacted him by phone or by e-mail. He and Edwards never served in the same Army Reserve unit, nor did they belong to any of the same churches, clubs, or other social institutions. Edwards was ten years older than Mattis and lived exclusively above the Mason-Dixon Line, which would further reduce the chances of them being acquaintances at some prior point in their lives.

'From Edwards's medical records, I noticed that he's slightly over his ideal weight . . . '

DeMarco almost laughed aloud at this. Anyone less than a hundred pounds too heavy would be considered 'slightly' overweight by Neil.

' . . . but is otherwise in good health, and from court records I observed that he's had two DUIs in the last thirty-six months.'

Neil took another slurp from his Popsicle before saying, 'Now for William Raymond Mattis. The lad is a GS-11 and his wife is a hairdresser who makes about five bucks an hour.' Neil looked up from the computer screen to Emma and shook his large head in dismay. 'We really do need a livable minimum wage in this country.'

'Get on with it, Neil,' Emma said again.

'William and his wife live within their means and exactly as would be expected based on their income. Their home has a mortgage that will not be paid off for forty years; they have less than five thousand dollars in their joint savings account; they own two vehicles, both with nigh one hundred thousand miles on the odometer. Thank God for William's civil service pension or these people would be eating Spam three meals a day after they retire. Bottom line: if this lad is an apprentice assassin, the work doesn't pay for shit at the entry level.

'Next we come to the swamp tender, Mr Estep. This one was interesting. He, like William, is a midlevel government worker. Unlike William he has no money in savings. I pulled his tax returns. He has no financial instruments paying interest, at the same time, he pays no interest. Meaning he has no outstanding loans. I concluded initially that Estep took his meager salary, lived within his means, and possibly inherited his home. Then I did something inspired — which is why people other than Emma pay me so well, Joe: I checked his insurance policies.

'The good Mr Estep possesses every toy known to macho man. He has a 1999 Corvette, bought new at the time and top of the line. His house, on which he has no mortgage, is assessed at one hundred and twenty thousand dollars. If he lived somewhere civilized, say Arlington for example, that same house would be worth half a mil. He owns a 2000 Jeep, a 2003 four-wheel drive Ford truck, a bass boat worth thirty thousand, and a Jet Ski worth fifteen thousand. His gun collection is insured for thirty thousand. What do you think of dem apples, Emma and friend?'

'The same as you, Neil,' Emma said. 'He has some source of invisible income, it pays cash, and it pays very well.'

'You could Capone this one if you wanted, Emma. For leverage, I mean.'

'Capone him?' Emma said.

DeMarco spoke for the first time. 'Al Capone was sent to prison for tax evasion, not for being a gangster.'

'I know that,' Emma said. 'I'd just never heard Capone used as a verb before.'

Bet you didn't know, DeMarco was thinking. Emma didn't like it when she wasn't the smartest person in the room.

Neil sucked loudly on his Popsicle and stripped the stick bare. 'And now we come to the really interesting ones,' he said. 'Taylor and Donnelly. These two gentlemen were financially reborn in 1964.'

'What does that mean?' DeMarco said.

'Prior to 1964 both Donnelly and Taylor had lower-middle-class incomes as would be expected considering their professions. Donnelly was a newly hired Secret Service agent and made a GS-5's salary in 1963, about five thousand dollars per annum. Mr Taylor enlisted in the army, rose to the exalted rank of sergeant, and after he was discharged, worked for the state police in Texas. He made, in 1963, less than Donnelly. These young men — Donnelly was twenty-five at the time and Taylor was twenty-seven — had no savings and didn't own real estate. Neither was — nor have ever been — married.

'I let my fingers do the walkin',' Neil said, wiggling pudgy digits. 'Both of these men were raised dirt poor, Taylor at the no-shoe poverty level in rural Georgia and Donnelly not much better in Pennsylvania where his father was a foundry worker.'

'So what happened in 1964?' Emma said.

'I don't know, Emma dear. And that's why my staff and I spent so much time on this request of yours. Do you have any idea how hard it is to get information from forty years ago, prior to the birth of the thinking machine?'

'So what did you find, Neil? And I swear to God if you don't stop dragging this out, I'm going to break parts of your body.'

'You've always been so violent, Emma,' Neil said.

'Luckily for you in Tel Aviv,' Emma muttered. Neil shuddered at the memory.

'We'll start with Donnelly,' Neil said. 'In 1964, he paid income tax on an inheritance of approximately two million dollars.'

'Who did he inherit from?' Emma said.

'I don't know. As I said, this happened in 1964, before our lives were reduced to ones and zeros. But I do know he couldn't have inherited from his no-pot-to-piss-in Pennsylvania relations. It's possible Donnelly had a rich aunt who lived in Singapore and he was her favorite nephew. I just don't know. All I do know is that Donnelly dutifully reported his newfound wealth to the IRS, and, sap that he is, paid an amazing amount of tax for his honesty.

'From that point on he has behaved in such a fiscally conservative manner that it makes my stomach turn. If someone gave me two mil in 1964, I would have casinos next to Trump's in Atlantic City by now. But Donnelly, this boob, sticks his inheritance money and the salary he makes as well-paid civil servant, into savings accounts, CDs, bonds, mutual funds, that sort of thing. Absolutely no imagination, no risk-taking. He is today worth approximately six million, if you include his home.'

A net worth of six million sounded fantastic to DeMarco, but Neil was clearly disdainful.

'I also looked at Donnelly's insurance records since I found Mr Estep's so enlightening. They revealed that Donnelly is a modest collector of Oriental art. He buys a sword or a rice bowl every couple of years. His collection is insured for two hundred thousand but his ability to purchase Eastern trinkets is well within his income.'

153

'But you don't know where his original nut came from,' Emma said.

'No, Emma, for the third fucking time, and I feel very bad about that. May I continue?'

Emma nodded.

'The esteemed Mr Taylor. This good ol' boy is Donnelly's opposite, a financial wunderkind. I take my hat off to him. In 1964 Taylor quit the Texas state police, returned home to the red earth of Georgia, and started buying *everything*. Where he got the money for his original purchases is a complete mystery, the financial equivalent of spontaneous combustion. In part this is because at the same time that he began acquiring things, he also retained the services of the best tax firm in Atlanta.

'Now, Emma, as you know, I'm rather good at following the greenback trail but these boys in Atlanta are absolute wizards at financial obfuscation. Taylor's returns show charitable deductions to every organization but the Klan; enormous business losses; tax shelters in which you could hide a humpback. My best guess at Taylor's current net worth is more than a hundred million, but I could be wrong by a factor of four.'

'But he started in 1964, the same time Donnelly inherited?' Emma asked.

'Oui, but how much he started with and where it came from, I don't know. And it really pisses me off.'

'Could you Capone Taylor?' DeMarco asked.

'No way. The Atlanta tax boys I mentioned. And theoretically, Taylor's fortune could be

154

completely legitimate. Say, for example, he won nine thousand in a poker game in 1964 and he used the money to buy IBM. His money doubles. Then he buys some land and sells it and his money quadruples. And so on. Maybe that's the way it happened and nothing underhanded happened in 1964. I just don't know, Emma.'

'Did their paths ever cross?' DeMarco said.

'Not that I could see. In 1963 Donnelly was stationed in Los Angeles and Taylor, as I said, was in Texas. Between June 1964 and January 1966, Donnelly was stationed in New York and from 1966 until the present he's been in D.C. Taylor left Texas in December of 1963 and moved back to his hometown in Georgia. He's lived in the same house since 1965.'

Emma rose from her chair. She reached out to shake Neil's hand then noticed the sticky green juice stain of his last Popsicle on his fingers. She reached into her pocket for her car keys instead.

'Thank you, Neil,' she said.

'Anything for you, Emma,' Neil said.

21

'Well, Joe,' Senator Maddox said, 'I wish I could hep ya but I just don't know that much about ol' Max, him livin' down there by the swamp, so far out of the mainstream. He's jes a good ol' boy who supports the Party, God bless him, and that's all I know about the man.'

'Senator,' DeMarco said, not bothering to disguise his disbelief, 'Maxwell Taylor's rich enough to buy his own swamp. If I know that much, I know you know one hell of a lot more. It's important for me to get a fix on this man, sir.'

'I'm sorry, Joe, but — '

'How's Mrs Maddox, Senator?' DeMarco said, and both men turned to look at a picture on the corner of Maddox's desk: the senator's wife, a onetime Southern belle turned battle-ax.

J. D. Maddox was the senior senator from Georgia and had been in politics since he wore short pants. The J.D. stood for Jefferson Davis but about the time they gave blacks in Georgia the opportunity to vote he started using his initials instead of his given name. He had an accent as thick as a slab of Alabama ham, snowy white hair, and a Mark Twain mustache. These more attractive features joined a face blotched red from too many juleps and a stomach bloated from free lunches. He had become in his seventies, and possibly because he intended it, a caricature of a Southern politician.

Two years ago, Maddox — married man, father, grandfather, and archenemy of all things unholy — had been dipping his wrinkled old wick into a twenty-nine-year-old staff assistant. An aide to another politician got wind of Maddox's little fling. The aide discovered that whenever he wanted the senator's vote, all he needed to do was give him a wink and a nudge and remark on the sweetness of young Georgia peaches.

The Speaker heard about Maddox's troubles and was naturally sympathetic. DeMarco was dispatched to get the pesky aide out of the senator's hair and did so by discovering that the lad had a penchant for the hookers on Fourteenth Street. The senator was so grateful to DeMarco that he promised his eternal gratitude — two years apparently being the time span of eternity.

Maddox was now seated behind a desk the size of an aircraft-carrier flight deck, twirling one end of his mustache with a liver-spotted hand. He was trying to come up with a nice way to tell DeMarco to go to hell. Maddox may have owed DeMarco a favor but Max Taylor was a member of his constituency. On the other hand, DeMarco's reference to the senator's wife was an unstated threat. Maddox, experienced politician that he was, chose pragmatism over principle.

'Max Taylor's an enigma, Joe. He's got more money than Midas but I'll bet outside the state of Georgia there ain't ten people who know his name. Outside of Charlton County, there ain't fifty people in Georgia who've ever heard of him.

157

But in Charlton County, every man, woman, and large dog knows Max for the simple reason that the man *owns* the whole damn county.'

'Where's Charlton County, Senator? I mean, what major city is it near?'

'It's not near a major city, son. It's near the Okefenokee Swamp.' Rising from his chair with some difficulty, the senator said, 'Come on over here, Yankee, and I'll show you on the map.'

DeMarco joined Maddox near a Georgia state map that took up most of one wall in his office.

'You see right here?' Maddox said, 'This square in the southeast corner, right next to Florida? That's Charlton County, Georgia. All them little green hash marks you see there takin' up the whole western half of the county is swampland — the great Okefenokee. Right here along the eastern rim of the swamp, runnin' along Highway 23, are all these little pissant towns, like Racepond, Uptonville, and St George. The biggest one's Folkston, county seat and home of Maxwell Taylor.'

DeMarco remembered from Billy Mattis's file that he had been raised in Uptonville. According to the senator's map this put Billy's hometown less than a map grid away from Folkston, where both Estep and Taylor lived.

'What do you mean, Senator, when you say he owns the county?' DeMarco asked.

'Ah am speakin' quite literally, son. Max Taylor owns three-quarters of the land in the county and damn near any business bigger than a gas station. He's been buyin' up the place for forty years. It's the man's personal kingdom.'

158

This may have explained Taylor's current financial position but not how he got started.

'Where'd he get the money for his initial purchases, Senator?' DeMarco asked.

Maddox ignored DeMarco's question while he returned to his chair. The chair's springs protested his arrival. He smiled slyly, pumped his eyebrows like a Dixie Groucho, and said, 'That's one of them things that makes Max an enigma.'

'What do you mean, sir?' DeMarco asked. Christ, it was like pulling teeth with this guy.

'Nobody knows where he got his seed money from, is what I mean. Max was raised in a one-room shack, with no indoor plumbing. His father was a sometime miner, a sometime logger, and a full-time drunk. He beat his wife and he beat his kids. And Max has two sisters, one about fifteen years older than the other. I've heard talk the older sister is the younger one's mother and that Max's father was the father. You know what I'm sayin'?'

DeMarco nodded.

'Anyway, it was that kinda family and Max left home when he was sixteen. He spent a few years in the army then got a job with the Texas highway patrol, and in 1964 or so he comes back home and starts buyin' things. But where the money came from — well, it beats the hell out of me, Joe, and that's God's truth. If I had to guess, I'd say Max had more money in 1964 than can be explained by just plain thrift.'

The senator paused to blow his nose loudly into a red bandanna.

While Maddox was inspecting the contents of

159

his handkerchief, DeMarco asked, 'Did you ever hear any rumors about him being involved in anything illegal, Senator?'

'No, Joe, can't say as I ever did. But then Max always struck me as a careful man.'

'What about his politics, Senator?'

The senator flashed dentures as white as toilet-bowl porcelain. 'Let me tell you a story about Max's politics. Max called my office one day a month before an election — this was years ago, keep in mind — and discussed his immense dissatisfaction with my position on some bill affecting one of his investments.'

'What kind of investment, Senator?' DeMarco asked. 'Do you remember?'

'Oh, I remember all right. Offshore oil. Max belonged to some group that wanted to sink a couple of wells in some bird sanctuary off the coast. The tree huggers in the cloakroom voted to block the drillin' and I voted with 'em as a trade-off for a military contract I wanted for a company in Savannah. Max didn't give a rat's ass about them birds, I can tell you that.'

The senator wheezed a laugh in recollection of the event, and the laugh turned into a full-blown coughing fit that changed the color of his face from red to indigo. When his eyes stopped watering, Maddox said, 'Now I'll tell you what he did, Joe. Max called me up and told me his county — I repeat, *his* county — was votin' against me in the next election. Can you imagine the ego it would take to make such a statement? Now I naturally thought he was full o' shit as Charlton County had always voted for the Party in the past, so I blew him off. But come election day, Joe, damn near every registered voter in that county voted for my opponent. Ninety-eight percent of them.

'Now if you think about it, son, that oughta scare the hell out of you. Max either told those people how to vote and they obeyed like a buncha sheep or he controlled the ballot boxes and changed their votes. Either way's scary, if you ask me. I retained my seat by a margin thinner than a gnat's pecker, Joe.'

The senator paused to take a drink from a coffee mug on his desk. To DeMarco, it smelled as if the coffee was made from bourbon beans.

The senator smiled at DeMarco. 'Fortunately, these days I rely more on the good people in the cities than I do the rednecks living by the Okefenokee, so I don't lose as much sleep as I used to when Max is pissed. But I'll tell you that one time he damn near gave me a heart attack.'

DeMarco was silent a moment as he tried to figure out how to ask the next question. He couldn't find a subtle way to do it.

'What are Taylor's feelings about the current administration, the President in particular?'

'The President? Well, I reckon he likes the man. He donated fifty grand to his last campaign.'

'Why would he do that?'

'The President's a big believer in tax reform, Joe — and ol' Max pays a lot of taxes.'

'Has he called lately to complain about anything the President's done?'

'No. Why are you askin' about Max and the President, son?'

22

DeMarco hesitated, then raised his fist and knocked on Billy Mattis's front door. A pretty woman in her late twenties opened the door. She had shoulder-length ash-blonde hair cut in an outdated Farrah Fawcett style and a good figure displayed in shorts and a tank top. DeMarco had the immediate impression of ditsy yet good-natured and likable. He couldn't help but think that there should have been a couple of tow-headed kids tugging on the hem of her shorts.

'Hi,' she said with a smile. 'What can I do for you?'

DeMarco took out his ID wallet and flipped it open and shut before she could read it. 'Federal government, ma'am,' he said in his best Joe Friday voice. 'I need to talk to Mr Mattis.'

'Uh, sure,' she said, momentarily unsettled by DeMarco's seriousness, then she brightened again and added, 'I'm Darcy, Billy's wife. Come on in.'

She was proud to be Billy's wife; DeMarco could tell just by the way she said the words. As he followed her into the house, she said, 'Y'all work with Billy?'

'No, ma'am, I just need to speak to him.'

'Well, you have a seat and I'll go get him.' She left the room yelling cheerfully, 'Honey, there's a fella here to see you.'

DeMarco looked around Mattis's home. He

knew from fat Neil's report that they didn't have much money but he could see that every piece in the house had been selected with care by a discerning eye. The place was warm and comfortable and inviting. He wished he could ask Darcy Mattis to help him decorate his nearly barren home.

Billy entered the room. His short blonde hair was damp, as if he had just stepped from the shower. He was wearing a white T-shirt and blue jeans. His feet were bare. *Barefoot boy with cheek of tan*, DeMarco thought. When Billy saw DeMarco standing in his living room, he rocked back on his heels in surprise and DeMarco could almost see the knot of apprehension forming in his flat stomach.

'What the hell are you doing here?' Billy said.

DeMarco saw Darcy Mattis's eyes go wide. These were polite, decent people and her husband's unexpected hostility shocked her.

When DeMarco didn't answer immediately and Billy continued to glare at him, Darcy Mattis looked toward DeMarco with concern and distrust. Her faith in her husband was unwavering, her loyalty given without question. If Billy didn't like DeMarco, she didn't either.

'What's goin' on Billy?' she asked. 'Who is this man?'

'Billy,' DeMarco said, 'we need to talk. It might be best if we spoke alone.'

Billy looked over at his wife, then back to DeMarco.

'No. We don't need to talk. Get out of my house.'

'Billy, I'm here to help you. Whatever

happened at Chattooga River, whatever you did, I know you were forced into it.'

'Billy, what's he talkin' about?' Darcy Mattis said.

Hearing the alarm in his wife's voice Billy took her hand and said softly, 'He's not talkin' about anything, hon.' His Southern accent was designed to sooth her cares away but this time it didn't work. Looking back at DeMarco, he said, 'And he's leaving. Now.'

'Billy, don't be a fool,' DeMarco said. 'I know about Taylor and Estep.'

Billy's face blanched white. 'Oh, Christ,' he said. The words slipped out before he could stop himself.

'Billy, it's not too late,' DeMarco pleaded. 'Level with me.'

Billy shook his head. DeMarco could tell he was still thinking about Taylor and Estep. He looked so shell-shocked that he reminded DeMarco of a cancer patient who has just been told he has but months to live.

'Billy,' Darcy Mattis said, 'this is scarin' me. What's going on?'

Billy gave his wife's hand another squeeze and said, 'Hush, hon. Everything's all right.' The love that existed between these two people was palpable. It made DeMarco ache to think how Darcy Mattis would be affected if anything happened to her husband. It also made him wonder what it would be like to be loved so unequivocally.

'It's not all right, Billy,' DeMarco said, 'and you know it.'

164

'Get out of here, goddamnit, or I'm gonna hurt you!'

No he wouldn't, DeMarco thought. This man didn't hurt people, he protected them. 'Okay, Billy. I'll leave, but please call me if you change your mind.' He handed Billy a card with his phone numbers on it and when Billy didn't take it from him, he set it down on a nearby end table.

Looking at Darcy Mattis, DeMarco said, 'See if you can talk some sense into your husband, Mrs Mattis.'

'You leave my wife out of this,' Billy said, taking a step toward DeMarco, his hands curling into fists. 'Now get the hell out of my home.'

DeMarco returned to his car and sat there in the darkness doing nothing for an hour. He wanted to see if Billy would run to Estep. He didn't. At ten thirty the lights went out. DeMarco doubted Billy was sleeping soundly.

DeMarco used his cell phone to call Emma's man Mike. He told him that tomorrow morning he wanted Sammy to follow Billy and Mike to stick with Estep.

'And what are you going to be doing?' Mike asked.

'Coordinating your efforts,' DeMarco said.

23

Some days go badly. They begin badly and end badly and in between beginning and ending nothing good happens. DeMarco's first indicator that he was going to have one of those days was when he overslept. He jumped into his car — hair wet and uncombed from his shower, his shirt untucked, his tie undone — and raced down his driveway and knocked the contents of his trash can onto his neighbor's manicured lawn. He smeared tomato sauce on his hands picking up the garbage.

That should have been enough for one morning but a whimsical god decided it wasn't. Driving down the center lane of the Beltway, DeMarco's car decided to eat its own transmission. The majority of the motorists caught in the backup he created before he could push his car to the side of the road, male and female alike, raised one finger in support as they passed him. The two hours he spent waiting for the tow truck gave him ample time to feel sorry for himself, time to think that this day couldn't possibly get any worse.

DeMarco was seated in the waiting room of an overpriced Georgetown garage — the sort of place where they give you Starbucks coffee to compensate for ninety-dollar-an-hour labor charges — when he received a call from Mike.

'Billy went to see Estep again,' Mike said.

'When he left for work this morning he drove around a while to make sure he wasn't being followed but Sammy stuck with him. Sammy's a leech on wheels. He finally ends up at this restaurant on K Street, not too far from Estep's apartment. Estep was at the place when Billy arrived. I tailed him there.'

Mike said Estep did most of the talking while Billy just sat there 'lookin' whipped.'

'Sammy went in and tried to hear what they were talking about, but couldn't get close enough. Estep was clutching Billy's forearm and whispering to him. 'Kinda frantically' is how Sammy put it — like he was trying to convince Billy of something. After they talked, Billy drove to his office with Sammy tailing.'

'What did Estep do after Billy left?' DeMarco asked.

'He sat in the restaurant for half an hour, just smoking cigarettes and drinking coffee. Thinking I guess. Then he gets up and makes a real quick phone call. He sits back down and about ten minutes later the phone in the restaurant rings. He talks for a while then he makes another phone call that lasted about ten minutes.'

'Give me the number of the phone,' DeMarco said, 'and I'll call Alice.'

'I already did. Alice is mad at you. She says you don't care if she dies or not.'

'I don't. So what did Alice find out?'

'Zip. The first call may have been a signal. You know, call and let the phone ring once and hang up, and then the person called goes to another booth and rings Estep back at the restaurant.'

'What about the second call, the one that lasted ten minutes.'

'It went to a bar in Waycross, Georgia.'

'So we don't know who he called?'

'That's what I already told ya.'

Not able to think of anything else to say, DeMarco said, 'Well, stick with Estep.'

'I'll do that,' Mike said.

Christ, he was grumpy today. 'Sammy's got my cell phone number, doesn't he?' DeMarco asked.

'Yeah, and I'm sure he'll call when he needs your advice.' Mike hung up without saying good-bye.

Employee morale seemed to be in a slump. Might have to organize a company picnic, DeMarco thought.

★　★　★

DeMarco took a cab to his appointment at the Marriott; he was, at that point, five hours late. The man he was meeting, George Morris, CFO of a sheet-metal fabricator in the Speaker's district, was not a happy man. Then again, he would have been unhappy if DeMarco had arrived on time.

'We *have* to reduce pension benefits, Joe. We're letting Mahoney know as a courtesy. We're not asking permission.'

'He said no,' DeMarco said. The fact that the Speaker had told DeMarco to help General Banks didn't stop him from giving him other assignments.

'Hey, it's either that or we start laying guys off.'

'You won't lay anybody off. Those two defense contracts you got, there in the fine print, they specify fines for late delivery. Somebody over at the Pentagon is going to start reading the fine print the day you hand out a pink slip.'

'Goddamnit, Joe, we're dying! Our competition's outsourcing everything and our material costs are skyrocketing. We have to do something.'

'George, tell me something. If you guys are dying, how is it that your board gave your CEO a three-million-dollar bonus this year? That's on top of his twelve-million-dollar salary.'

'How did you find — '

'And you, you got one point six million, stock options included.'

'I deserved every penny of that bon — '

'You are not going to cut pension benefits and you are not going to lay people off.'

Morris sat for a moment, fuming, before he said, 'Why the hell did we contribute half a million to his goddamn campaign? You tell me that, DeMarco.'

'You contributed half a million to get two defense contracts worth six hundred million which keeps twelve hundred people employed.'

'But our profit margin — '

DeMarco's cell phone rang.

Sammy Wix's nasal Brooklynese filled his ear. 'Dis guy Mattis. He's sittin' inna bar, like he's waitin' to meet somebody.'

'Great,' DeMarco said. 'Call me when someone shows up.'

169

'Uh, boss, I hafta leave by six. I told Emma, when she hired me for dis gig, I could work every day dis week 'cept tonight. It's my grandkid's birthday. Emma said it wouldn't be a problem.'

Shit. 'Sure, Sammy, I understand. Where are you?'

Sammy told him.

'I gotta go, George. Don't cross Mahoney.'

Then DeMarco remembered that his car was still in intensive care.

Now he would discover the meaning of a bad day.

24

The cab dropped DeMarco off in front of a Greek deli. Sammy Wix was sitting inside at a window table.

'He's in dat bar over dere,' Sammy said, pointing across the street with his narrow chin. 'Guess he needed a snort.'

'Me too, Sammy,' DeMarco said. He thought for a second. 'Sammy, how soon do you have to leave?'

'Not for an hour.'

'Good. Why don't you go into that place and have a drink yourself. See if Mattis is talking to anyone.'

Sammy's tongue flicked out of his mouth like a snake trying to catch a raindrop. 'Chure, I can do dat,' he said.

DeMarco took Sammy's seat in the deli. Thirty minutes later, Sammy came back wearing a smile. Little bastard had a double, DeMarco thought. 'He's just sitting dere by hisself, boss,' Sammy said. 'Drinkin' beer, real slow. Maybe he's not meetin' somebody. Maybe he just feels like gettin' hammered, or he don't wanna go home right away to da old lady.'

DeMarco could understand a man with Billy's problems feeling the need for a few beers, but Billy didn't strike him as a drinker.

'Does the bar have a back exit, Sammy?'

'Yeah, but it's got one of dem fire alarm bars

171

across it.' Sammy shuffled his feet a bit. Finally, he cleared his throat, and said, 'Uh, boss, I gotta get movin'. I don't want to be late for my grandkid's party. He's my favorite, da little fucker.'

'I understand, Sammy. Take off.'

Sammy was a few paces away when DeMarco remembered his car. 'Wait a minute, Sammy,' he called to him. 'I don't have any wheels. My car's in the shop. If this guy takes off I'll be in a bind. Can you take a cab and let me borrow your car? I'll pay for the cab.'

'No sweat, boss. And I'll just take da Metro. It stops right by my daughter's place. Here's da keys to my wagon.'

Sammy pointed to where his car was parked. 'And, boss,' Sammy said, lowering his voice, 'in case ya need it, dere's a rod unda da front seat. A .38. It's loaded and da safety's off.'

'Sammy,' DeMarco said, 'if I find myself anywhere near a situation that requires a gun, I'll call a cop.'

The comment surprised Sammy. DeMarco looked like a guy who would have his own arsenal.

DeMarco hoped Billy would keep drinking long enough for him to have dinner. He ordered a gyro and a beer and settled onto a stool by the window counter to wait. It turned out to be a long wait. He tried talking to the deli owner to pass the time, but the language barrier was insurmountable. The deli guy didn't follow baseball and DeMarco didn't speak restaurant economics. By eight, he had had two more beers

172

and the owner was starting to close down his establishment. When he began mopping directly under the stool on which DeMarco was sitting, DeMarco took the hint and left to loiter in the doorway of a nearby computer store.

At eight thirty, Billy finally emerged from the bar. DeMarco watched as he went over to his car and unlocked the door. For a man who had been drinking since five, Billy was surprisingly steady on his feet. Why would he spend almost four hours alone in a bar and still be sober? DeMarco wondered if he had been waiting for somebody and the person hadn't shown up. Another possibility occurred to him as he became aware of the rapidly fading light: maybe Billy was waiting until dark to meet someone.

Sammy's car was a 1986 Plymouth station wagon that was longer than a limo. DeMarco was worried he wouldn't be able to keep up with Billy until he turned the key in the ignition. The wagon may have belonged in an automotive museum but the motor sounded as if it came from an Indy racer. Now if he could just find the gizmo to get the seat back before his knees were permanently disabled.

DeMarco expected Billy to drive toward the Beltway and back toward Annandale where he lived, but instead he headed in the opposite direction. The longer DeMarco followed him the more puzzled he became. Instead of vectoring toward any of the arterials leaving the city, Billy was heading directly into the southeast segment of the District.

Southeast D.C. is an urban combat zone, a

social experiment gone badly awry. It's a region of drive-by shootings, gang violence, and crack-induced mayhem. Driving through the area you keep your doors locked and pray you don't run out of gas. DeMarco couldn't imagine why Billy Mattis had decided to run this inner-city gauntlet.

Billy crossed the John Philip Sousa Bridge and stopped near Minnesota Avenue. There was a bank with an ATM on one corner and a Rite Aid drugstore on the other. The drugstore had just closed for the day and the owner was dropping steel barricades down over the windows. Unlike DeMarco and his Georgetown neighbors, merchants in this neighborhood had no aesthetic pretensions about the heavy-gauge sheet metal covering their display windows.

DeMarco drove by Billy and parked half a block away on the same side of the street. He couldn't see Billy sitting inside his car but if he got out DeMarco would be able to watch him in his side-view mirrors.

At exactly ten o'clock Billy emerged from his car, looked around cautiously, and went to the bank machine. While he was punching his code into the ATM, two African American teenagers turned the corner on the opposite side of the street.

'Hey, money man,' one of them yelled, 'if you gettin' some green, get some for me.'

Billy's head jerked in the direction of the two teenagers and DeMarco could see he was strung tighter than Willie Nelson's guitar. Realizing immediately that the boys didn't pose a threat,

174

Billy completed his transaction at the ATM. He counted the money issued from the machine but didn't put it immediately into his wallet. A rather dangerous oversight in this neighborhood, DeMarco thought.

DeMarco was distracted momentarily by the two kids. To celebrate Billy's reaction to their wit they did a handshake routine so complicated it qualified as choreography, then continued down the street in DeMarco's direction, joking with each other. They were directly across the street from where DeMarco was parked when a dark-colored sedan pulled around the corner and stopped next to the ATM.

A man stepped from the sedan, keeping the car between him and Billy, and said something to Billy. Billy nodded his head and held up the cash in his hand. The man smiled — then raised the pistol he had been holding next to his right leg and shot Billy in the chest.

Billy Mattis slammed backward into the wall of the bank. He stood for a second looking down in amazement at his bleeding chest then slowly slumped to a sitting position at the base of the ATM. His hands folded neatly into his lap as he collapsed. The shooter ran over to Billy, took the cash he was still holding, and ran back to his car. He revved the engine and came roaring down the street in DeMarco's direction.

DeMarco didn't make a conscious decision to do what he did next. He just did it. It was an automatic reaction, devoid of any consideration of the consequences. He started the engine of Sammy's finely tuned machine and pulled the nose of the station wagon away from the curb and directly into the path of the oncoming car. The impact of the collision knocked DeMarco across to the passenger's side of the station wagon and his head banged hard against the window frame.

DeMarco shook the pain away and looked over at the shooter's car. It was stalled and the driver appeared to be unconscious. His head was pressing down on the horn ring, and DeMarco found the blaring of the horn strangely comforting.

DeMarco's brain finally caught up with his reflexes. He scrambled to find Sammy's gun, the one Sammy had said was hidden beneath the driver's seat. His hand flapped madly trying to locate the weapon and it seemed a small eternity before he struck hard metal. With the .38 in his hand, he slid out the passenger-side door of the station wagon and crouched behind the right front fender of the car for protection. Sammy had said the safety on the gun was off, which was a good thing since DeMarco didn't know where the safety was.

DeMarco could see the shooter was starting to recover from the collision. He sat up slowly, dazed and disoriented. Blood trickled down the left side of his face from a cut over his left eyebrow. A motion across the street caught DeMarco's eye. It was the teenagers, huddled behind a Dumpster.

He yelled at the teenagers, 'Call 911! Get the hell out of here and go get the cops.' Neither of them moved. Damn kids.

The shooter opened his door and slowly exited his car. He staggered and almost fell but recovered his balance. He was a thin-faced man about DeMarco's height, wearing a lightweight beige suit and an open-collared white dress shirt. His hair was jet black with a deep widow's peak, heavily oiled, and combed straight back from a hollow-cheeked, acne-scarred face. There was a large teardrop-shaped mole next to the man's right eye.

The mole was distinctive and DeMarco realized he knew the man. His name was John Palmeri and his father had been an associate of DeMarco's dad. But unlike Joe DeMarco, John Palmeri had followed his father into the family enterprise. At age sixteen or seventeen, the last time DeMarco had seen him, Palmeri was on his way to a juvenile facility for hijacking a car. And now here he was, some twenty years later, in southeast D.C., killing a Secret Service agent. What the hell was going on?

DeMarco could see that Palmeri was unsteady on his feet and looking as if he might pass out any second from the blow to his head. He watched in morbid fascination as a drop of blood rolled slowly down the side of Palmeri's face and fell to his shirt, making a small stain over his heart. Dangling down at the side of Palmeri's right leg was a revolver that looked two feet long.

DeMarco said, 'John, drop the gun. Please.' DeMarco's heart was pumping so much adrenaline it felt as if an electric current was passing through his body.

Palmeri didn't seem to hear DeMarco and

177

continued to stand, weaving from side to side. It occurred to DeMarco that maybe Palmeri didn't realize he was armed since he was crouched behind Sammy's car. To get his attention, DeMarco stood fully erect and pointed Sammy's gun at Palmeri like he knew what he was doing.

As DeMarco stood up, Palmeri looked in his direction. There was no sign of recognition. He blinked several times as if trying to clear his vision and get DeMarco into clear focus — then he started to raise his gun. DeMarco was sure Palmeri didn't realize how *slowly* he was moving.

'John, drop the gun, goddamnit!' DeMarco screamed.

Palmeri looked at him, eyes glassy, and continued to raise his weapon.

Why the hell didn't he drop the gun?

But he didn't. DeMarco thought he might have yelled again but later he wasn't sure because at that moment Palmeri fired and a bullet ricocheted off the front bumper of Sammy's car. The shot would have hit DeMarco in the gut or groin had the car not been there.

DeMarco fired back immediately. He wasn't trying to kill Palmeri. He jerked the hair trigger of Sammy's gun out of sheer fright when the killer's bullet zinged off Sammy's car.

DeMarco shot John Palmeri through the heart, completely by accident.

DeMarco stood there, frozen in disbelief at what had just happened. He waited a moment to see if Palmeri would get up, knowing he wouldn't, then walked slowly toward him, still pointing Sammy's gun at the man's prone form.

DeMarco's hand, the one holding the gun, was shaking as if he was afflicted with palsy.

Palmeri's black eyes were wide open, staring skyward at a God who had already forgotten him. His white shirt was absorbing blood like a blotter, the stain spreading geometrically, creating a perfect circle for his soul to pass through.

In his peripheral vision DeMarco noticed movement. The teenagers had stepped out from behind the Dumpster.

'Go call the cops,' he called to them, but there was little force behind his words.

Instead of doing what he asked, the boys started across the street toward him. Their finely tuned urban survival instincts had already concluded that DeMarco did not pose a threat.

'Man, you smoked him,' one of them said.

Still looking down at the body, DeMarco repeated softly, 'Go call the cops.' He didn't know what to do with the gun in his hand. He wanted to drop it but was afraid it might discharge and blow a hole through his leg. Finally he just put it down on the hood of Sammy's car.

'Is the motherfucker dead?' the same kid said.

DeMarco nodded and looked over at them. The kids appeared to be about fourteen years old. The one who had been doing all the talking was a friendly youngster with a lopsided grin. He was wearing a Chicago Bulls baseball cap with the bill pointed backward, a Michael Jordan sleeveless T-shirt, and baggy shorts that reached his knees. On his feet were high-top tennis shoes that seemed designed for walking on the moon.

179

The other boy was dressed almost identically, except he favored the New York Knicks.

DeMarco took his cell phone out of his pocket and flipped it to the kid wearing the Bulls cap. 'Call the cops,' he said.

The two boys glanced at each other uncertainly. Calling the police was not appealing in any circumstance.

'Why don't you call 'em?' the Knicks fan said.

'Because I need to check on that guy by the bank machine,' DeMarco said, and started walking toward Billy. He didn't walk fast. He already knew Billy was beyond help. 'And don't touch anything,' he yelled to the boys over his shoulder.

'We know that, whitey,' the Bulls fan said. 'Bet we been at more crime scenes than you have.'

DeMarco was certain they had been.

DeMarco gazed down sadly at Billy Mattis. Unlike Palmeri's, Billy's eyes were closed and he seemed oddly at peace. If it hadn't been for the small red-black hole in his chest he would have looked like a man who had just picked a peculiar place to nap.

Although certain he was dead, DeMarco knelt and checked for a pulse in Billy's throat. With his own pulse racing the way it was, DeMarco wasn't sure that he would have felt the last small surges of Billy's brave heart. You poor, poor bastard, he thought. How does a guy who looks like Mickey Mantle end up dying like this?

DeMarco refused to think about what Billy's death would do to his wife.

Returning to Sammy's car he asked the boys if

they had called the police.

'Yeah,' the Bulls fan said. 'Five-0 on the way.'

He tossed DeMarco's cell phone back to him. DeMarco almost dropped it.

'I can't wait till the cops get here,' the kid said. 'They won't fuckin' believe it, two dead white guys, and another one blowin' smoke out his nine.'

'They probably won't believe it, Ritchie,' the other kid said, looking worried. 'They'll probably arrest you and me.'

'They're not going to arrest you,' DeMarco said. 'I'm staying right here. I'll tell them what happened.' What the hell was he going to tell them?

He leaned against the fender of Sammy's now battered station wagon and lit a cigarette. The Bulls fan, the kid named Ritchie, bummed one from him. The other kid seemed uncertain, then asked for one too. DeMarco thought about lecturing them on the deleterious effects of tobacco on their young bodies but realized how absurd the speech would sound in present circumstances. He asked the other kid his name. Jamal, the kid said.

DeMarco knew he had acted in self-defense but wasn't sure the police were going to believe him. He could be in real trouble here — criminal, go-to-jail, spend-all-your-money-on-a-lawyer trouble — and that frankly bothered him a hell of a lot more than the death of the thug who had killed Billy Mattis. It occurred to him then that he needed Ritchie and Jamal as favorable witnesses and gave them each another cigarette.

He also knew he might be in a whole different kind of trouble, much more serious than the police. His old schoolyard playmate had obviously progressed beyond car theft, and had climbed the corporate ladder. Jesus, could the damn Mob have been involved in the assassination attempt?

The cops didn't arrive for almost twenty minutes, giving credence to complaints from area residents about the slow response time of law enforcement in minority neighborhoods. When they did arrive, they didn't seem particularly upset to find two dead bodies on the street, but like Ritchie had said, they were surprised to see the victims were white. The lack of visible emotion by either the police or the two teenagers made DeMarco recall a line from Larry McMurtry's *Lonesome Dove*: 'By God, life's cheap up here on the . . . Canadien.'

In retrospect, it was a good thing the police had dawdled as that gave DeMarco time to figure out the pack of lies he planned to tell them.

25

'Did you know either Mr Mattis or Mr Robinson?' the detective asked him. The detective needed a shave and had dark circles under his muddy brown eyes. He was a walking portrait of a man who worked double shifts in a live-fire zone.

'Who?' DeMarco said, thinking, *Who the hell is Robinson?*

Seeing the confusion on DeMarco's face the detective clarified sarcastically, 'Mattis was the guy killed next to the bank machine. Robinson was the guy you killed, cowboy. You blew away a Mr David Robinson of Waycross, Georgia. Now did you know either of the victims?'

DeMarco was surprised the detective didn't mention that Mattis was a Secret Service agent. Mattis must not have had his government ID on him, and the tired detective obviously hadn't made the connection between the dead man slumped at the base of the ATM and the agent in the video of the assassination attempt.

'No, I didn't,' DeMarco said.

It was two in the morning by the time he left the police station. The police might have kept him indefinitely were it not for Ritchie and Jamal. The boys were excellent witnesses. Neither was confused or hysterical, and they were both able to accurately and independently

183

tell the same story. By the time they finished, the detective was convinced that Mr Robinson of Waycross, Georgia, had indeed shot Billy Mattis in cold blood and stolen his money, that DeMarco had rammed his car into Robinson's to keep him from fleeing the scene, and that DeMarco had fired only in self-defense when fired upon.

The police should have treated him like a hero — but they didn't. Their sensitive, cynical noses smelled the aroma of rat when DeMarco explained how little ol' white him, a semi-rich guy from Georgetown, just happened to be parked in southeast D.C. while Billy Mattis was being shot.

He had decided from the beginning not to tell them he had been following Billy. The story he did tell was relatively straightforward and certainly sounded more credible than the truth itself.

It was obvious, he said, that Billy was killed for the cash he took from the ATM and it was just a coincidence that he had been there. He had been drinking (true — a couple of beers at the Greek deli), had wandered into the neighborhood by mistake because he wasn't familiar with the area (half true), and had stopped to call a friend to tell her he would be late meeting her (not true at all, but one and a half out of three wasn't bad).

The detective suspected DeMarco was lying but he couldn't shake him, and thanks to Ritchie and Jamal he couldn't debate the facts. And DeMarco was a lawyer. He told the cops he'd sue their asses off if they didn't quit picking on him. In the end they kept Sammy Wix's gun and gave DeMarco a steely-eyed warning not to leave town.

★ ★ ★

As he pried the battered fender of Sammy's car away from the front tire, DeMarco realized that in spite of the hour he wanted to talk to someone. He had just killed a man. He felt compelled to relive aloud the experience and justify everything he had done. And he wanted to explore the lack of emotion he was feeling after killing John Palmeri. He had taken the life of another human being and knew he should be feeling something — remorse, regret, sadness, something. But he didn't. There was a numb spot at the core of his being, and he wanted someone to stick a pin in him to see if his soul would twitch.

He knew even Emma must sleep, but when she answered the door at three in the morning she didn't look as though she had been rousted from her bed. She was wearing a beaded sleeveless top and leather pants that looked quite good on her. Behind her, in her foyer, DeMarco could see a cello case, and on the back of Emma's hand was an ink mark, the type they stamp on your hand after you pay the cover charge to get into a club. Emma and her cello player had been clubbing.

She opened her mouth to make a caustic remark but before she could speak DeMarco said, 'I killed a man tonight.'

Emma's reaction was to raise an eyebrow. 'I

guess you better come in then,' she said.

She told DeMarco to go sit in the living room then disappeared to the back of her home for a few moments. When she came back she poured him three fingers of bourbon over ice then listened without interrupting as he told her what had happened. DeMarco hadn't shaved since early morning and Emma couldn't help but think he looked rather brutal. If he had been pointing a gun at her across the hood of a car she damn well wouldn't have resisted. Well, maybe she would have, but most people wouldn't have.

When DeMarco finished, Emma asked, 'Who was the shooter?'

DeMarco told her. 'He was using the name David Robinson. His driver's license said he was from Waycross, Georgia. Maybe in the morning you can get on the horn and find out about him.'

'Sure,' Emma said.

They sat in silence for a while before Emma said, 'You realize, of course, that Billy wasn't the victim of a random cash-machine rip-off. Those two phone calls Estep made this morning? I think one was to get permission to take Billy out and the other was to line up this good fella, Palmeri.'

'Yeah,' DeMarco said. 'Someone paid Palmeri to pop Billy. Estep, and whoever else is involved in this, probably this guy Taylor, decided Billy had become a liability. He was unraveling. The little scene at the restaurant this morning. So Estep told Billy to go to an ATM at the corner of such-and-such street, meet this guy after dark, and when he gets there give him some money.'

'What reason would he give Billy for meeting the hit man?' Emma asked.

'Hell, I don't know. Estep made up a plausible lie and Billy, dumb innocent that he was, went along with it. It would have been a nice, neat scenario if I hadn't been there. They would have found Billy on the ground in a bad neighborhood next to a cash machine, the receipt stuck in his hand, the money gone. An easy-to-explain killing. In D.C. the odds of it happening are better than getting hit by a bus.'

'And you did them a favor when you eliminated the shooter,' Emma added.

Standing with his back to Emma, he poured more whiskey into his glass then said softly, 'I got Billy killed, Emma.'

'What are you talking about?'

DeMarco turned to face her. 'I squeezed him just like the Speaker wanted and he buckled under the pressure. That's what got him killed.'

'That may be, Joe, but Billy got killed because he was mixed up in something bad.'

'Yeah, but you and I both know he was somehow roped into this thing. Billy Mattis was a white hat that someone bent in the wrong direction. And his poor wife, Emma. By now she knows he's dead and she's crying and she'll never stop. There must have been something I could have done differently.'

'Billy should have come clean with us when he had the chance,' Emma said. End of discussion. With Emma things were black and white — gray areas of ambiguity were for lesser mortals.

'Yeah, I suppose,' DeMarco said. 'What

187

happened with Billy also explains what Estep was up to tonight.'

'What do you mean?'

'While I was waiting for the cops tonight, I called Mike. He was following Estep. He said Estep went to a bar over on K Street about an hour before Billy was killed. Mike said that while he was there he made a total ass of himself. Loud, obnoxious, drinking like a fish, hitting on all the women, even the ones with dates. At one point he buys the house a round and ten minutes later he gets into a fight with some guy. The bartender threw him out about midnight.'

'Ah,' Emma said. 'He gave himself a twenty-person alibi.'

DeMarco nodded. 'Mike also said that while he was in the bar, Estep said that tomorrow, make that today, he's getting the hell out of D.C. and heading back to Georgia. That's why he bought the drinks, to celebrate leaving.'

'Do you want Mike to follow him down there?' Emma asked.

'No way. I think these people are killers. I'm gonna make Banks go to the FBI and if he doesn't go, I'm leaking this mess to the press.'

'I doubt it will be that simple, Joe.'

'Yes it will,' DeMarco said. He emptied his drink and set his glass down. 'It's late,' DeMarco said. 'I . . . I better let you get some sleep.'

'Is something else bothering you, Joe?'

DeMarco hesitated. 'Emma, how many people have you killed?'

'Really, Joe. You don't expect me to answer that, do you?'

188

'No, I guess not. But how did you feel about it? Did it bother you when you killed someone?'

Her answer surprised him. 'It always bothered me,' she said. Maybe there were shades of gray in Emma's life.

'Then why don't I feel worse than I do?' DeMarco said. 'I took a man's life tonight, a man I knew as a kid. I should be feeling some remorse. But I don't. I used to wonder how my father could do it, how he could live with himself after killing someone. Maybe he didn't feel anything either.'

Emma shook her head. 'Joe, you're tired and you're in shock. You are not a sociopath. You are not your father.'

'I've got to get going,' DeMarco said and stood up.

'Just stay here tonight. It's late and you've been drinking.'

'I can't,' DeMarco said. 'I have to catch the first shuttle to New York in the morning.'

'New York? What for?'

26

The old man heard the doorbell ring. He pushed himself out of his chair with a grunt and moved slowly toward the door. He could see a man standing on his porch through the mesh of the screen door, the sunlight behind the man making it difficult to see his features. *Probably some damn salesman*, the old man thought, *some pain in the ass who had ignored the* NO SOLICITA-TION *sign*. He was a couple of feet from the door when he stopped abruptly and his mouth dropped open in shock. He almost crossed himself, but pride prevented his hand from moving.

'Gino? Is that you?' the old man said, ashamed of the tremor in his voice.

'No, Mr Taliaferro, it's not Gino. It's his son. Joe.'

The old man barked a laugh. 'Goddamn! You scared the shit outta me. Thought it was a fuckin' ghost. It's a good thing I got cancer 'stead of heart trouble.'

'Can I come in, Mr Taliaferro?' DeMarco asked.

'Come in?' Carmine Taliaferro said, still confused by the appearance of a dead man on his porch. 'Yeah, sure. You can come in,' he said, unlatching the screen door. 'Come in, come in.'

The old capo had lost a lot of weight since DeMarco had last seen him at his father's

190

funeral. The Carmine Taliaferro he remembered had always been heavy — too much of his wife's good pasta, he used to joke — but the man standing before him was almost skeletal. Carmine's eyes were the same though: inside the jolly, fat-man's face had been the coldest eyes young Joey DeMarco had ever seen. The cancer had not changed his eyes; they had always belonged to a corpse.

Taliaferro was wearing a short-sleeved blue shirt, open at the collar, and a pair of gray pants from an old suit. The pants were shiny in the seat and the cuffs dragged on the floor. On his feet were maroon slippers. The thin wisps of white hair remaining on his liver-spotted skull stood on end as if energized by static electricity. It was hard to believe this had once been the most feared man in Queens.

'I'm retired now, you know,' Taliaferro said as DeMarco followed him down a dimly lit hallway.

'I figured as much when I didn't see the bodyguards.'

Taliaferro laughed. 'Yeah. Nobody's gonna waste a bullet on me now. All they gotta do is wait a couple months.'

They entered a living room filled with old-fashioned, heavy dark furniture. On the fireplace mantel and end tables were black-and-white pictures of Taliaferro's extended family. The television in the corner was a Sony with a nineteen-inch screen and the once beige rug on the floor was almost threadbare. DeMarco noticed a small rip in the upholstery of the couch where he was directed to sit.

The house where Taliaferro lived was a modest three-bedroom affair in a middle-class section of the borough and most of his neighbors were blue-collar working stiffs. Taliaferro had lived in the house fifty years, and like most elderly people, couldn't see the point of changing anything in it at this point in his life. DeMarco knew he was worth millions.

Taliaferro dropped into a brown leather recliner. There was a green oxygen tank near the chair. 'I'd offer you a coffee,' he said, 'but my wife's at the church. Lighting fuckin' candles for me, like God can't see in the dark.'

'That's okay, Mr Taliaferro. I don't want any coffee.'

Taliaferro studied DeMarco's face. 'No, but you want somethin'. I know, after all this time, you ain't here 'cause you're worried about my health. So whaddaya want, Gino's kid?'

DeMarco nodded, glad the old bastard had decided to skip the stroll down memory lane.

'I want to know — '

'I kept track of you,' Taliaferro said. 'I know you work down there for the Congress, but you're nothin' special. My butcher makes more money than you. You coulda hadda good life, you wanted it, but you didn't want nothing to do with us, did you?'

'No, and I still don't.'

Taliaferro barked his harsh laugh. 'Just like your old man. Won't give a fuckin' inch, even when you're the guy who wants the favor.'

'I may be doing you the favor,' DeMarco said, hoping he was wrong.

'That'll be the day. So whadda you want?'

'I want to know about John Palmeri.'

'Palmeri! That rat fuck! Why you wanna know about him?'

Taliaferro's vehemence surprised DeMarco. Palmeri had obviously fallen out of favor. That was good.

'I want to know who he's working for these days,' DeMarco said.

'If I knew that he wouldn't be workin',' Taliaferro said. 'Palmeri turned state's evidence, oh, six, seven years ago. He put three of my people in jail. You remember Schmidt, that skinny kraut who used to keep the books for me?'

DeMarco nodded.

'Him and two others. Schmidt died in the slam. I would have gone with them but Palmeri didn't know enough to get to me. That fuck! They made the shit-head disappear.'

'Who did?'

'You know, the feds. Put him in witness protection and a good thing for him they did. If they hadn't, well . . . '

Taliaferro didn't complete the sentence. Even on death's doorstep he wasn't going to say anything to incriminate himself.

'Palmeri's been using the name David Robinson,' DeMarco said, 'and he's been living in Waycross, Georgia.'

'Georgia? He was down there all this time?'

'I don't know how long he was down there. I was hoping you could tell me.'

'Georgia. No wonder we couldn't find him.

That's like livin' on the fuckin' moon,' Taliaferro said. 'So why you wanna know about Palmeri?'

DeMarco hesitated. That Palmeri had killed Billy Mattis could mean many things, but one of the things it could mean was that the Mob was somehow involved in the assassination attempt. If that was the case, and they found out DeMarco was poking into it, he could soon be as dead as Billy Mattis.

But DeMarco knew something Oliver Stone didn't. Guys like Carmine Taliaferro didn't even kill cops, much less presidents. Crime families were under so much heat these days they'd never do something that stupid — or that big. The Mob didn't think big. They were about loan sharking and prostitution and stealing crates off the backs of trucks. And drugs, of course. But all their operations were petty, nothing on a grand scale; it was just when added together that they amounted to something. But assassinating a president, no matter what problem the White House was causing them, was not something they would do. At least DeMarco didn't think so; God help him if he was wrong.

'Palmeri killed a Secret Service agent in Washington, a man I knew,' DeMarco said. 'I'm trying to find out why.'

'Secret Service? What an idiot. And you're tryin' to find Palmeri because this agent was a friend or something?'

'No, I'm not trying to find him, Mr Taliaferro. Palmeri's dead.' DeMarco paused. 'I killed him,' he said. He hadn't wanted to tell Taliaferro that but knew he'd find out anyway.

'You! Mr Fuckin' Civil Service! You killed Johnny Palmeri? If it wasn't so early I'd pour us a drink.'

DeMarco said nothing.

'So why'd ya kill him?' Taliaferro asked, the laughter fading from his dead-man's eyes.

'I didn't have a choice,' DeMarco said. DeMarco knew Taliaferro would get a copy of the police report, maybe even have someone talk to the cops who had interrogated DeMarco, but he wouldn't find out any more than DeMarco had told the police.

'No choice,' he said. 'You don't say.'

DeMarco ignored the disbelief in Taliaferro's tone. 'So are you going to help me or not?' he asked.

'How can I help you? I told you, he ratted us.'

DeMarco didn't say anything; he just stared back at the old man.

'And anyway, why should I help you? Because of all the favors you've done for me over the years? Because you think I owe you something for your old man?'

'No, not because you owe me anything,' DeMarco said. 'Because it's the right thing to do.'

Taliaferro laughed. Right thing to do. What bullshit. He sat there a moment studying DeMarco's face, waiting for him to beg, knowing he wouldn't. 'All right, I'll make some calls. Leave a number where I can reach you.'

As DeMarco was leaving, the old man laughed and said to his back, 'So Gino's kid finally made his bones.'

27

On the flight back to D.C., DeMarco scanned a copy of *The Washington Post* to see if Billy's death had made the papers. He had expected it to be front-page news and was surprised that it wasn't. He flipped through the paper and finally found the story on page two of the Metro section. The paper only said that a man had been killed by an armed robber while getting cash from a bank machine and that a bystander had intervened and shot the robber. The victim's name was being withheld, pending notification of his next of kin.

DeMarco understood what had happened. Billy had been killed about ten last night and the detectives were questioning DeMarco and the two teenagers until almost two a.m. By the time Billy's wife had been notified and had identified the body, it would have been early morning, maybe later.

Sometime today, however, Billy's name would be released and enterprising journalists would connect the name of the dead man with the Secret Service agent guarding the President at Chattooga River. It had been eleven days since Harold Edwards's body had been found and in that time the press had pretty much accepted the FBI's position that Edwards had acted alone. But now that Billy Mattis had been killed, DeMarco was guessing that a herd of journalists would stampede over to the Hoover Building and ask if Billy's death was related to the assassination attempt. The FBI would probably say no — but the conspiracy theories would begin to bloom.

The good news was that DeMarco was fairly certain by the tone of the article that he wouldn't likely be hearing from the police again. By now six other murders had already occurred in southeast D.C. and the weary detectives manning that bloody sector had no time to waste on an innocent, if mysterious, bystander.

★   ★   ★

The light on his answering machine was blinking when DeMarco entered his home. Four of the five messages were from General Banks, all conveying the same sentiment: get your ass over to my office and tell me what happened to Mattis. DeMarco thought of calling Banks back but decided not to. He'd let Banks stew for a while; it was his fault DeMarco was in this mess.

The fifth message was from Carmine Taliaferro. DeMarco checked his watch: it was just four hours since he had talked to the dying mobster. Taliaferro's message was short: 'I got what you wanted, you fuckin' ingrate.'

★   ★   ★

'Palmeri was working for this jamoke down there in Waycross,' Taliaferro said. 'Guy by the name of Junior Custis. Custis controls a percentage of the

197

rackets there — the usual stuff, gambling, hookers, that sorta thing. Small-timer. Anyway, my guy tells me that this Custis used Palmeri for heavy lifting.'

'Like what?' DeMarco asked.

'What I gotta do, spell it out for you?'

'You mean to tell me the Justice Department put a mob killer into the witness protection program, and then lets him keep on killing?'

Taliaferro laughed. 'Hell, it was the only trade the man knew. And maybe Justice didn't know what he was up to. Palmeri married a gal down there who owns a motel. He was always livin' off some broad, even when he worked for us. Anyway, he helped her out around the place, so he had a visible source of income.'

'But the local cops must have known about Palmeri's connection to Custis.'

'Maybe, but if they tried to do a records check on him they'd've run up against a wall. Justice don't tell the FBI who's in their program — FBI's got too many leaks — and they sure as hell don't tell the local cops. As long as Palmeri wasn't arrested for anything, which he wasn't, and if he was careful, which my guy says he was, then Uncle's right hand, as usual, don't know what the left hand's doin'.'

'Your guy have any idea why Palmeri would have killed a Secret Service agent?'

'No. Didn't make any sense to him. Did this agent work down there, maybe trying to bust up Custis's operation?'

'No,' DeMarco said, 'he wasn't that kind of agent.'

198

'Well my guy also says Palmeri didn't work exclusively for Custis. He freelanced.'

'So when he killed this Secret Service agent, he may or may not have been working for Custis?'

'My guy says no way he was working for Custis. Somebody else hired him to pop your boy.'

My guy, your boy. Jesus, DeMarco thought. 'Can you find out who?'

'I tried. My guy says Palmeri was always careful when he set something up. The funny thing is he hardly ever left the area and when he did, he never went north, not to any big cities. Probably afraid of being recognized. Whenever he did a job outta Waycross, it was always someplace else in the South — Mississippi, Texas, shit-kicker places like that. Nobody can figure out what that prick was doing in D.C.'

That meant somebody had paid him a lot, DeMarco thought. 'Thanks for your help, Mr Taliaferro,' he said. 'I appreciate it.'

'Maybe you can return the favor someday.'

'Don't count on it.'

Taliaferro laughed. 'I wished I was gonna be around awhile longer to see how you turn out. You can't run from your own blood, Gino's kid.'

* * *

A plump gray-haired woman, concern etched into her normally pleasant features, answered the doorbell. DeMarco displayed his congressional get-him-in-anywhere security pass, pompously

199

stated he was 'from the government,' and said he needed to speak with Mrs Mattis.

There was a chance Billy might have confided in his wife. Darcy Mattis would be alone now, with no one to protect her. There would be a hole in the place where her heart used to be. Her mind would be numb, thinking if she didn't think at all, if she simply didn't acknowledge the news she had been given, it would all go away and her handsome Billy would come home again. And DeMarco, prick that he was, was going to question her in this vulnerable condition.

The woman looked briefly at DeMarco's ID, then up at his hard face. 'Oh, couldn't you come back? Please. She's in a terrible state.'

'And who are you, ma'am?' DeMarco asked. He needed to make sure the woman wasn't a Secret Service nursemaid.

'I'm her next-door neighbor. Dottie Parker. When the police came this morning — five o'clock it was — they came to my house first. They asked if I was a good friend and would I mind staying with her after they told her the news. I said sure, but . . . '

Now that DeMarco knew she was just a decent citizen, and therefore someone he could run roughshod over, he said, 'Ma'am, I need to talk to her right away. It's important. A government matter.'

Flustered, Dottie Parker — decent, compassionate Dottie Parker — said, 'Oh, sure. Oh, sure. I'm sorry. She's out back, sitting on the patio. I tried to get her to come in and have some tea but she won't budge.'

DeMarco found Darcy Mattis sitting in a folding aluminum chair, wearing jeans and a brown cardigan sweater over a white T-shirt. Her blonde hair was pulled back into a ponytail. The sweater was two sizes too large for her. The weather was overcast and a bit cool for the season, but not chilly enough to warrant a sweater. DeMarco assumed the sweater was her husband's, something that would have retained the warmth and smell of him, something to wrap too big about her the way his arms used to do.

He couldn't help but think of how she and Billy had looked the last time he had seen them together. They had reminded him then of Hansel and Gretel, hugging in the dank fen of Foggy Bottom, searching for bread crumbs the monsters had swallowed. And now the monsters had swallowed Billy.

Without waiting to be asked DeMarco pulled a chair close to her and sat down. She didn't turn her head in his direction until his chair scraped the patio concrete. Her eyes were red-rimmed and ravaged.

'Mrs Mattis,' DeMarco said softly, 'do you remember me?'

She nodded her head slowly. 'You were here the other night. You made Billy mad.'

'I'm very sorry about what happened to your husband, Mrs Mattis. He was a fine man. I wouldn't be here, intruding at such a time, if it wasn't important.'

Seeming not to hear him, she said, 'Did you

know that bastard killed him for a hundred dollars?'

'No,' DeMarco said. He had no intention of telling her he had watched her husband die.

'He never used that bank-machine card. Never. He only had one in case of emergencies, like when he was traveling and needed to get something I forgot to pack, but he never used it around here. Why in God's name did he stop at that machine last night?'

'I don't know, Mrs Mattis,' DeMarco said.

'He fought in wars and he didn't die. He dies getting money out of a cash machine. God's a joker.'

Tears leaked from the corners of her eyes and spilled down the contours of her pretty face.

'Mrs Mattis, I need to ask you a couple of questions. It concerns — '

'You thought Billy knew something about what happened at Chattooga River, the day the President was shot.'

'That's right,' DeMarco said. 'I don't think Billy did anything wrong,' he lied, 'but I think he knew something and was afraid to talk about it.'

'Billy wasn't afraid of anything!' Darcy Mattis said. A spark of anger flared in her tear-bleached blue eyes, but the spark died quickly and she went back to staring, dull-eyed, at memories only she could see.

'Do you know a man named Dale Estep?' DeMarco asked.

'No.'

'What about a Maxwell Taylor from Folkston, Georgia?'

'No. Billy never talked about anyone from down home except his mother. Billy didn't like his home-town. He only took me there once the whole time we were married.'

She withdrew inside herself momentarily, perhaps thinking of all the other things she would never do again with her husband.

'Did Billy's habits or patterns change at all during the last two months?' DeMarco asked.

'I don't know what you mean.'

'Had he been doing anything recently you thought was unusual or abnormal for him? Did his routine change in any way?' How many different ways could he say it?

She nodded her head. 'He came home late a lot back in June. He hardly ever stayed past his shift when he was in town.'

'Did he tell you what he was doing?'

'All he'd say was that he was usin' the computers at work. Evenings were the best time to use 'em, he said. Less people on the system.'

'Did he tell you what he was using the computers for?'

'No. That's all he ever told me — that he was using the computers — and he only told me that because I was gettin' mad at him for staying late so much. I couldn't understand it. Billy and I told each other everything. He never kept anything from me but the last couple months he was so . . . inside himself.' Stifling a sob, she added, 'God forgive me, I thought he was having an affair.'

'But he wouldn't tell you what was bothering him?'

'No.'

'When did this moodiness start?'

'I don't know exactly.'

'Was it about the time he was assigned to the President's security detail?'

She looked at DeMarco in surprise. 'Yeah, I guess it was. I thought he'd be real happy about the assignment, and at first he was, then he acted like he'd been cursed. I figured it was just the responsibility of the job.'

'But he wouldn't tell you what was bothering him?'

'No, I just told you. Why are you askin' all these questions, anyway? What do you bastards think Billy did?'

DeMarco ignored her question and said, 'Mrs Mattis, if he wouldn't confide in you, is there anyone else he might have talked to if something was troubling him?'

'No,' she said. She hesitated. 'Well, maybe his mom. Billy and his mom were real close.'

DeMarco remembered Mattis's phone bill and the large number of calls he had made to his mother in June.

'Would Billy have confided in Mr Donnelly?' DeMarco said.

'Who?' she said.

'Patrick Donnelly, head of the Secret Service.'

'No. I doubt he even knew who Billy was.'

'I was told Mr Donnelly personally arranged to have Billy assigned to the President's security team.'

She shrugged her shoulders. 'Maybe he did. Billy was real surprised he got the assignment.

He figured it was because of his record, but he said there were a lot of men senior to him who could have been picked. I don't know why he was picked but I know he wasn't friends with Mr Donnelly.'

DeMarco was trying to think of something else to ask when she said, 'We were thinking about adopting a baby, you know. I couldn't have children and Billy wanted a little boy. Wanted a boy to go fishin' with.'

She hugged herself and the tears came again, rolling slowly down her cheeks and falling like unanswered prayers into her lap. DeMarco couldn't do this anymore. He stood up and gave her shoulder a clumsy pat, and said, 'I'm sorry, Mrs Mattis. I'm so very sorry.'

He left her sitting there, huddled in her husband's sweater, knowing nothing would ever make her warm again.

28

DeMarco stepped into Banks's office and before he even closed the door, Banks screamed, 'What the fuck happened to Mattis? What'd you do?'

DeMarco told him, he told him everything. He discussed the odd connection between Dale Estep and Billy Mattis, Estep's military record and his skill with a rifle, and the tenuous link to a rich man in Georgia. He spoke of how Mattis had been set up by Estep and killed by John Palmeri.

'This guy Estep,' Banks said. 'Ex-military was the first thing I thought when the FBI said the shooter hid in that blind for two or three days. But what's his connection to Edwards? Did he help him?'

'I don't know,' DeMarco said.

DeMarco rose from his chair, walked over to a window, and looked in the direction of the White House. The papers had said the President was back at work, putting in half days as he continued to convalesce. DeMarco turned back to face Banks who was still contemplating what DeMarco had just told him.

'General, it's possible Harold Edwards had nothing to do with the shooting.'

'What are you talking about?'

'General, just because Edwards turned up with a tag on his toe saying 'I did it,' doesn't mean we should forget everything else we know. We know about the warning letter — the FBI doesn't — and we know that Mattis probably wrote that letter. And now we know his death wasn't a random act of violence.'

'So what?' Banks said.

'I talked to Mattis's wife before coming here. She said before the assassination attempt her husband was staying late at work using the Service's computers. It didn't mean anything to me at the time but now it does. I think Billy may have been trying to find — or was being forced to find — someone like Harold Edwards. Someone already identified in the Secret Service's files as being a threat to the President. I think it's possible that Billy found the perfect patsy, that Estep stole the weapons from the Fort Meade armory because Edwards previously served there, and that Estep was the shooter. After the assassination attempt, they killed Edwards — maybe Estep or maybe the guy who shot Billy — and then planted all this evidence at his house.'

'That's a lot of goddamn maybes,' Banks said.

'Yes, sir, it is,' DeMarco said. 'And that's why you have to talk to the FBI. They need all the facts. They need to be told about the warning letter and Estep and this man Taylor. If Edwards had nothing to do with the shooting there's a good chance the people who really tried to kill the President will try again.'

Banks didn't respond. He took off his wire-rimmed glasses and polished the lenses. He looked oddly vulnerable without his glasses, DeMarco thought, like an ancient eagle with weak eyes.

DeMarco knew that Banks had only asked him to investigate Mattis because he felt guilty about not acting on the warning letter as he should have. He'd never been certain that Mattis was involved in the assassination attempt, and even with everything DeMarco had just told him, he was still reluctant to expose the fact that he'd kept the letter from the FBI. Coming forward at this point could be more than just embarrassing for Banks — it could be political suicide.

Banks put his glasses back on, looked at DeMarco, his expression unreadable. He stared at DeMarco a moment longer, then he rotated his chair and looked at the photo of the World Trade Center behind his desk.

'Goddamnit,' Banks said, 'you're right. Let's get this over with.'

29

When DeMarco saw Patrick Donnelly sitting at the conference table in Simon Wall's office, he knew he and Banks were going to get their asses kicked. Banks had not invited Donnelly to his meeting with the attorney general, which meant the attorney general had. And DeMarco could tell that Donnelly, Simon Wall, and the third man in the room, FBI Director Kevin Collier, were quite good pals. As DeMarco and Banks entered Wall's office they were treated to the tail end of a pretentious conversation about the cost of country club memberships. Bretton Woods, it appeared, had raised its greens fees while simultaneously lowering its standards. The white man's burden was heavy indeed.

As soon as Banks saw Donnelly he said, 'What are you doing here, Mr Donnelly?'

Before Donnelly could respond Simon Wall said, 'I invited him, General.' Wall spoke in the soothing, nonconfrontational tone of a hostage negotiator trying to keep a volatile situation under control. 'When you called and said you wanted to discuss the assassination attempt, I thought we might benefit from Pat's, ah, experience.'

Simon Wall had sleek brown hair and oversize dark-framed glasses that magnified liquid brown eyes. Before he became attorney general he had been the Party's chief fund-raiser and there was talk about his viability as a vice-presidential candidate in the next election. Wall was a political hybrid who had evolved to survive in any environment. Like a beast with both gills and lungs he could live on land or sea, and if the air supply was suddenly cut off, he could hold his breath longer than any other species.

'A better question is what's he doing here?' Donnelly said, scowling and pointing at DeMarco. DeMarco was again struck by the incongruity of Donnelly's cruel, blue-jowled features atop his short form. He looked like a doll somebody had stuck the wrong head on.

Banks's head snapped toward Donnelly. 'I'm the one who called this meeting, mister,' he said, 'and I don't have to explain whom I invited or why.'

The attorney general, still playing the mediator, said, 'Pat, I'm sure the general had a good reason for bringing Mr DeMarco to this conference.' Looking at DeMarco, he added, 'I'm also sure Mr DeMarco can be relied upon to keep whatever he hears to himself. Isn't that right, Mr DeMarco?'

'Yes, sir,' DeMarco said. And three bags full. It bothered him that Wall even knew his name. He had tried to convince Banks that he wasn't needed for this meeting but Banks had insisted that he come. DeMarco was taking a big risk. He should have talked to the Speaker before talking to Banks, and he certainly should have told Mahoney about this meeting with the AG. There's an old civil service adage: it's better to ask first for permission than to have to beg later for forgiveness. DeMarco had violated a fundamental tenet of bureaucracy and he hoped he didn't pay for it with his job.

DeMarco and Banks joined the other men at a large circular conference table.

'Why don't you start, General,' Simon Wall said. 'When you called, you said the FBI might be overlooking some important information and you wanted to be sure Kevin and I had the benefit of your, ah, insights.'

'I may be wrong,' Banks said, 'but I think there's a possibility that Edwards was not the assassin or if he was, that he didn't act alone.'

Kevin Collier was a stocky man in his fifties. He had protruding eyes and a pugnacious face, and reminded DeMarco of one of those feisty little dogs with the pushed-in snouts. Collier wasn't as politically astute as Simon Wall but he was smart enough to know the FBI's arrest record was less important than whom he played golf with.

'General, forgive me, but the evidence against Harold Edwards is simply overwhelming,' Collier said. 'I mean, hell, the man left a note in his own handwriting saying he did it.' With a false chuckle, Collier added, 'What else do you want him to do, sir? Come back from the dead and confess?'

Banks ignored Collier's attempt at levity and said gruffly to DeMarco, 'Tell 'em what we got.'

DeMarco didn't like being thrust into the role of briefer but he cleared his throat and complied. 'Prior to the shooting, the general received a letter that could have only been written by a

Secret Service agent. The letter was on Secret Service stationery and was delivered in the Homeland Security pouch. It said — '

'Here we go,' Donnelly muttered and looked over at Kevin Collier.

It was apparent that Donnelly had already discussed the warning note with Wall and Collier, and DeMarco could easily imagine the spin he'd put on it. So could General Banks.

Banks's head spun toward Donnelly, his eyes blazing. 'Do you have something to say, Mr Donnelly?'

'Nope,' Donnelly said, and shook his head in an I-give-up gesture. 'If you want to continue to believe there was any truth to that letter, there's nothing I can do to stop you.'

Before Banks could say anything else, the attorney general said, 'General, why don't we let Mr DeMarco continue with his, ah, summary.'

And continue DeMarco did. He was doing fine until he made the mistake of saying that both he and Banks thought Mattis appeared nervous on the video of the shooting.

'Why don't we talk about that for just a moment, General,' Kevin Collier said. 'Because Mattis dropped his sunglasses before the first shot, my technicians naturally looked at him particularly hard when they examined the video. For example they timed how fast he moved to stand in front of the President's body and found that he moved faster than any other man in that detail. He was also the first agent to fire at the bluff to distract the shooter. There is absolutely no *scientific* evidence that Mattis acted or reacted in any way that was questionable.'

'Mr Collier,' Banks said, 'I may not have timed Mattis's movements with a stopwatch but I know men — and I know that Mattis looked different than the other men in the detail. That man was unusually nervous that morning *before* the first shot was ever fired.'

'That may be, General,' Collier said, 'but in addition to the lack of anything empirical on the video, Mr Donnelly polygraphed all his agents, including Mattis.'

'Billy Mattis denied being given a polygraph,' DeMarco said.

'You talked to Mattis?' Donnelly said, sounding genuinely surprised. 'What in hell gave you the right to do that?'

Before DeMarco could respond, Banks said, 'I gave him the right. Keep going, DeMarco.'

Later, DeMarco realized that Donnelly — a better inside puncher than either he or Banks — had just vectored the discussion away from whether or not he had lied about giving Mattis a polygraph.

But DeMarco kept going, as Banks had ordered. He explained how he had questioned Billy first on the National Mall and again at his home. 'He looked guilty,' he said. 'It was obvious he knew about the warning letter and was somehow involved in the assassination attempt.'

Donnelly laughed. Guffawed, to be accurate. 'He *looked* guilty! That's your idea of evidence. He *looked* guilty!'

DeMarco said you had to be there, which sounded incredibly lame even to him.

Donnelly snorted and said, 'If you ever presented a case like this in a courtroom they'd disbar you.'

Before DeMarco could answer, Banks said, 'Donnelly, I want you to quit interrupting this meeting. And that's an order, goddamnit!'

A direct order from a superior meant something to a man who had served a lifetime in uniform; it meant nothing to a civilian bureaucrat of Donnelly's standing.

Once again Wall stepped in to placate Banks. 'I must agree with the general, Pat. Let's allow Mr DeMarco to finish.'

But when DeMarco talked about how he had discovered Dale Estep and Maxwell Taylor by following Billy and listening in on his phone conversations, Donnelly couldn't restrain himself. 'Would you like to tell us, DeMarco, how you obtained these phone numbers without a warrant?'

'No,' DeMarco said.

Things did not improve as he proceeded. He described how he had followed Billy Mattis and watched him die, and was then forced to shoot Billy's killer.

'When I heard about you killing that guy Robinson,' Donnelly said, 'my first thought was that the apple doesn't fall far from the tree.'

'What the hell's that mean?' Banks said, not understanding the reference to DeMarco's father.

Before Donnelly could respond, Wall said, 'Let's get back on track, gentlemen. I don't see how Mattis's death has anything to do with — '

214

'It has *everything* to do with it, Mr Wall,' DeMarco said. It was obvious, he said, that Billy was waiting for his killer at the ATM and he was certain that Estep had arranged the meeting. He even told them what Billy's wife had said, that Billy never used his bank card in Washington. He concluded by saying, 'Why would Mattis hang around a bar until dark, then go to a cash machine he never used, in a part of town he had no reason to be in?'

'You know,' Collier said, 'this is exactly the sort of fuzzy, addle-brained thinking that gives birth to conspiracy theories. If I didn't know better, DeMarco, I'd say you worked for the damn *Enquirer*. The *facts* are that Billy Mattis went to an ATM and a man robbed him and killed him. Unfortunate, but rather common. Why Mattis went to that particular bank machine could have any number of rational explanations. He may have been on his way to see a friend that lived on that end of town and decided to stop because that particular ATM was convenient. Whatever the reason, we have no evidence to support, or even suggest, that Mattis was killed because he had a part in the assassination attempt. And to imply so, sir, is simply irresponsible!'

DeMarco felt his face flushing red. He was getting sick of Collier pinning his ears to the wall. 'The man who killed Billy Mattis came from Waycross, Georgia,' he said, 'and the morning of Billy's death, Estep made a call to Waycross.'

'All that tells me is that Mr Estep made a

215

phone call to an unknown party in his home state,' Collier said. With an avuncular chuckle, he said to Banks, 'My young agents do this sort of thing all the time, General. They leap to unsubstantiated conclusions because in their minds they've already solved the crime. I teach them they need to let the *facts* form their opinion, and not let their opinions organize the facts.'

'One of the *facts*,' DeMarco said, 'is that Billy Mattis's killer was not some guy who made a habit of ripping people off at cash machines. His real name was John Palmeri not David Robinson, and he was a Mafia hit man in the Justice Department's witness protection program.'

DeMarco could tell by the look that Collier exchanged with Simon Wall that they knew exactly who Billy's killer was and were hoping this fact would not come to light. This was why Wall had interrupted Donnelly earlier when Donnelly had made the comment about apples falling not far from their trees. Even if Mattis's death had nothing to do with the assassination attempt, the last thing Wall wanted publicized was that criminals placed in the witness protection program continued to be criminals.

'How did you get that information?' Simon Wall asked, his voice suddenly cold.

'What difference does it make?' DeMarco answered. 'The point is that John Palmeri wasn't a local bandit. He was a contract killer and he was hired by someone to kill Billy Mattis.'

Neither Collier nor Wall said anything for a

moment, then Wall said, 'Well, we're obviously going to find out what this Palmeri person was doing here but at this point we have nothing that connects him in any way to Chattooga River.'

Before DeMarco could respond that Billy Mattis's *death* connected him to Chattooga River, Collier jumped in with: 'And the man you think hired Palmeri was this Dale Estep, this park ranger?'

'That's right,' DeMarco said.

'Park rangers aren't exactly in the same company with disgruntled postal workers, Kevin,' Donnelly said to Collier, 'but I understand they're a bad breed.'

Collier started to chuckle and DeMarco saw Banks's big hands grip the edge of the conference table. He seemed on the verge of reaching across the table and throttling Patrick Donnelly, but then he took a breath and sat back in his chair.

'Estep,' DeMarco said, 'is not just some park ranger. He was a sniper in Vietnam and was discharged because he was a nut.'

'You also said that he's been a model citizen for the past twenty years,' Collier responded.

DeMarco looked over at Banks for support. The general's face was now set harder than concrete as he looked from Donnelly to Wall to Collier. DeMarco had the impression that Banks's military mind had already accepted the fact that his position had been overrun; he was planning the next campaign.

But the ongoing assault continued.

'And this man Taylor,' Donnelly said. 'You said

217

the only thing you know about him is that he's rich and gives money to the President's campaign fund. Do you think you just might be a little light on motive here, DeMarco?'

'I haven't had a chance to thoroughly investigate Taylor,' DeMarco admitted. 'I thought that should be left to the FBI,' he added.

'Hell, you thought you were qualified to investigate everyone else, including one of my agents,' Donnelly said. 'Why not Taylor? Why didn't you have this Georgia peckerwood hauled in in handcuffs and goosed with a cattle prod?'

DeMarco ignored Donnelly and said to Collier, 'Let's talk about your suspect, Edwards, the guy you people think dug a shooting blind in the side of a mountain and snuck past a platoon of Secret Service and FBI agents. He was an overweight, unemployable loser who drank too much. How did he — '

'He was an expert marksman, an outdoorsman, a hunter, and on record for blaming the President for losing his job. Those *pesky* facts again, Mr DeMarco,' Collier said.

'Then let me give you another fact,' DeMarco said. 'Billy's wife said the month before the assassination attempt, Mattis was staying late at work to use the Service's computers. I think he was searching through records for the perfect fall guy and he found him.'

'That's bullshit,' Donnelly said.

'Do you have any proof of this?' Collier asked.

'No,' DeMarco said, 'but maybe the Service's IT people can tell what he was using the computers for. Maybe there's a hard-drive record of his queries.'

When he looked over at Donnelly to confirm this was possible, he realized he had made another mistake. If DeMarco was right, Donnelly's computer nerds would wipe out any trace of Billy Mattis's search.

'For the sake of argument,' Collier said to DeMarco, 'let's follow your logic, if we can call it that, all the way through. Let's assume that Billy Mattis, for whatever reason, was — '

'I think he was being blackmailed or coerced in some way by Estep and Taylor,' DeMarco said.

' — was trying to locate somebody like Harold Edwards in the Secret Service's files. How did the assassination weapon end up in Edwards's house — a weapon stolen, by the way, from the same Army Reserve unit that Edwards belonged to?'

'Estep could have stolen the rifle from the armory. Billy Mattis being in the Reserve could have helped him or briefed him on the security procedures at Fort Meade.'

'But you have no proof of this, is that right?' Collier said.

'That's right,' DeMarco said. He was getting damn tired of saying that.

'Okay,' Collier said, as if speaking to a mental defective, 'we'll just forget the lack of proof for a moment and proceed anyway. Estep steals the weapons from the armory, uses one of the stolen weapons to take a few shots at the President, then places the weapons in Edwards's house. Now have I got that right, Mr DeMarco?'

DeMarco nodded, not trusting himself to speak.

'Then tell me something, DeMarco: Where was Harold Edwards while all this was going on? Where was he when the shooting blind was being dug and during the time the President was at Chattooga River? None of his neighbors saw him during this period.'

'I've thought about that,' DeMarco said. 'I may be wrong but it's possible that Estep, probably with Palmeri's help, kidnapped him and stashed him someplace while Estep was carrying out the assassination attempt.'

'Oh, for Christ's sake!' Donnelly said.

'This is absolutely fascinating,' Collier said. 'And then what, DeMarco? He makes Edwards write a suicide note, and then kills Edwards in such a manner that it looks like suicide? Is that what you're saying?'

'That's right,' DeMarco said. 'That's exactly the way it could have happened.' He just wished he had one damn thing to back up what he was saying.

'So how do you explain the physical evidence, Mr DeMarco?' Collier said. 'Such as the receipt in Edwards's car that puts him near Chattooga River just prior to the assassination attempt?'

'Anyone could have put that receipt in his car.'

'And the suicide note written — conclusively, I might add — in Edwards's handwriting?'

'Estep held a gun to his head to make him write the note,' DeMarco said.

'And the gunshot residue on Edwards's hands, consistent with a self-inflicted wound?'

'I don't know,' DeMarco said. 'Maybe — '

'That's right,' Collier shouted. 'You don't know! You don't know a goddamn thing and you don't have proof for one thing you've said!'

'For God's sake, Collier!' DeMarco shouted back. 'Doesn't it strike you that your case against Edwards is just a little *too* perfect? Oswald at least hid in a damn theater. Somebody actually had to chase the man! Edwards was *gift wrapped* for you people.'

'At least our opinions are based on *evidence*, DeMarco, and not the firm conviction that someone *looked* guilty,' Collier said.

Shit, DeMarco thought, completely frustrated. Maybe he should have practiced telling his story in front of a mirror. Before he could think of something else to say, Banks stood up.

'I've had enough of this,' Banks said. 'Wall, I recognize that you guys have a strong case against Harold Edwards. It looks open-and-shut. And when the press asks you about Mattis's death, you're going to give them all the glib answers that Collier here has been spouting. But let me tell you something: I'm no fool and I'd suggest you damn well take me seriously when I say that you need to look harder at Billy Mattis and Dale Estep. I didn't do what I should have when this thing started, but don't you make the same mistake.'

'Wait a minute, General,' Simon Wall said. 'Of course I take you — '

But Banks wasn't finished.

'And one other thing,' he said as he pointed a finger at Patrick Donnelly. 'I think this little son

221

of a bitch is deliberately obstructing this investigation.'

Banks walked out of Simon Wall's office, leaving DeMarco standing alone, staring into the hooded eyes of Patrick Donnelly.

★ ★ ★

DeMarco caught up with Banks just as his limo was about to pull away from the curb. Banks's eyes, still blazing with rage and embarrassment, looked over at DeMarco as he entered the car. He may have been angrier at Simon Wall than Joe DeMarco, but DeMarco was a closer target.

Banks stared at DeMarco a few seconds longer, shook his head in a gesture of disgust, then said, 'Fuckin' D.C. politicians. I had fewer enemies in 'Nam.' Tapping on the window which separated him from his driver, he said, 'Jimmy, I know you got a flask in the glove compartment. Give it to me.'

'Sure, boss,' Jimmy said, his voice twanging like a twelve-string guitar.

Banks took a long swig from the flask then said to DeMarco, 'And that's the last time I'm taking any damn advice from you, buster. Those bastards just cleaned my clock.'

'They cleaned both our clocks, General. Donnelly outflanked us.'

'I know he did and I swear before I leave this town I'm gonna get that little shit fired. I haven't figured out how yet, but goddamnit, I swear I will.'

He took another long swallow from the flask,

hesitated, and reluctantly handed it to DeMarco. DeMarco tipped back the flask. Cheap bourbon singed his throat and he enjoyed it thoroughly.

'So now what, hotshot,' Banks said, contradicting himself. 'Any more bright ideas?'

'I don't know. Maybe . . . ' DeMarco started to say, then stopped and simply shook his head.

'That's what I thought,' Banks said. 'Jimmy, stop the damn car.' To DeMarco he said, 'Get the hell out of my limo. I should have known this was the kind of help I'd get from anyone associated with that boozer Mahoney.'

30

The Speaker stood next to DeMarco, looking into the stone eyes of Robert Taft. They were once again at the Taft Memorial, the midway point in Mahoney's lunchtime walk. Today Mahoney's exercise togs were white, making DeMarco think of Melville's whale.

DeMarco told Mahoney the whole story of the investigation, everything that had happened since the last time they had talked. He thought Mahoney was listening but it was difficult to tell. He had suspected for some time that the Speaker was like a damn horse — a big, broad-assed one, like a Percheron or Clydesdale — capable of sleeping while standing up with his eyes wide open.

When he spoke of how he'd had to kill John Palmeri, he'd expected some sort of reaction from Mahoney, but Mahoney had just nodded his head. It was as if Mahoney had always known the hard-looking man he employed was capable of such mayhem. This bothered DeMarco.

Of the meeting in Simon Wall's office, Mahoney grunted: 'Those pricks.' DeMarco couldn't tell if this sentiment had to do with the way that Wall, Collier, and Donnelly had treated him and Banks or if it was just Mahoney's opinion of the trio in general.

DeMarco drew his story to a close by saying, 'Sir, I'm pretty sure Mattis and Estep were involved in the shooting, I'm almost positive Estep hired Palmeri to kill Mattis, and I think Edwards is a red herring.'

Mahoney said nothing for a minute, then he sighed. 'Jesus, Joe. You're *pretty* sure, you're *almost* positive, and you *think*.'

Ignoring the Speaker's sarcasm, DeMarco said, 'Yes, sir, and that's why the FBI has to be made to do their job. They need to question Taylor and Estep, get search warrants for their damn houses, check out where Estep was at the time of the — '

'But even if they did find something, with that agent getting killed, there's no hard connection to Donnelly.'

'I suppose so,' DeMarco said. Mahoney was fixated on Patrick Donnelly and he seemed to think that Mattis was the link to Donnelly. What the hell did Donnelly have on him?

'What do you think Banks is gonna do?' Mahoney asked, tugging at the crotch of his running pants.

'I don't know, but I'm guessing he'll do nothing at this point. He was pissed when we left that meeting but I think that was mostly because of the way Wall treated him. But now he's done his part: he's turned over what he knows to the FBI and it's in their hands.'

'Shit,' Mahoney muttered.

'Sir, you need to wade in on this thing,' DeMarco said. 'Talk to Wall and Collier yourself. If that doesn't work, talk to the President. He's the one at risk here.'

Mahoney's eyes widened in mock amazement.

'I'm not involved in this. Why would I talk to anyone?'

Christ, DeMarco thought. Harold Edwards's suicide note and the evidence found in his house had given Donnelly the advantage — and Mahoney had already factored this into the political calculus.

'Then let me leak the warning letter to the *Post*,' DeMarco suggested. 'The press will love it, the FBI will be forced to investigate, and Donnelly will get a black eye for trying to cover it up.'

The Speaker shook his head again. 'You leak this to the press now and Andy Banks and the whole Secret Service gets a black eye too. It'd be one thing if you could prove what you're sayin', but you can't. All you've got, Joe, is a gutful of conjecture. And like it or not, that jackass Collier might be right: Edwards could have done this thing all on his own and Mattis didn't have anything to do with it.'

'Yeah, but we have to do something,' DeMarco said. 'If I am right, these guys — Estep and Taylor — tried to kill the President and they may try again.'

Mahoney sighed. 'Joe,' he said, 'the fact that someone tried to kill the President isn't the problem.'

'What?' DeMarco said.

'Someone's tried to kill every president since Lincoln went to the show. Hell, they even tried to kill Gerry Ford, that Squeaky woman, remember? What the hell did Gerry Ford ever do?'

He pardoned Nixon, DeMarco thought.

'No, the assassination attempt isn't the issue, not the main one anyway,' Mahoney said, warming to his own rhetoric. 'The real problem is that the guy that's supposed to *protect* the President is a corrupt little shit who may have helped the assassins. *That's* the fucking problem.'

'So get the FBI — '

'The FBI isn't going to go after Pat Donnelly, not based on anything you've found.'

DeMarco was stymied. He was trying desperately to think of something that would persuade Mahoney to use his influence to get the FBI to investigate Estep and Taylor, when the Speaker said, 'Maybe you oughta head on down to Georgia and check out this guy Taylor yourself. And that forest ranger fella too. There's gotta be a link to Donnelly.'

DeMarco wanted to scream: *Are you fucking nuts!* Instead he said, trying to sound calm, 'I really don't know what good that would do, sir.'

'Me either,' Mahoney admitted reasonably. 'But it's better than doin' nothing, and it's not like you got anything more pressin' to do. Am I right?'

'Yeah,' DeMarco said, 'but — '

'Good,' the Speaker said, and turned to leave.

'Wait a minute!' DeMarco said. 'I'm in over my head on this thing and I think you know it. I'm not a cop and these guys could be killers.'

The Speaker looked at DeMarco seriously and gravely nodded his magnificent head. DeMarco knew what was coming next. He'd seen this scene before: he was cannon fodder and the Speaker was the ol' general regretting the need to send his faithful trooper into harm's way. His face registering false concern for DeMarco's well-being, Mahoney put a meaty paw on DeMarco's shoulder and said, 'You be real careful down there, son.'

31

DeMarco pulled off Route 23 and looked out at the Okefenokee Swamp, at the alien vegetation, at the gnarled cypress trees dripping with curtains of blue Spanish moss. He didn't like what he saw and some latent sixth sense, usually dormant in a city dweller like himself, screamed in warning of things with claws and fangs lurking in the slow-moving black waters.

That morning he had reluctantly packed a bag and caught a flight to Jacksonville, Florida. At the Jacksonville airport he rented a Mustang convertible, put the top down, and drove the forty miles through an almost impenetrable curtain of heat to Folkston. Once there he located a Days Inn, where he was checked in by a bright-eyed girl with a nose ring and purple-tinted hair who contradicted DeMarco's preconceived stereotype of southern youth.

Inside his room, DeMarco had plopped down on the bed and browsed listlessly through a stack of pamphlets that told him more than he had ever wanted to know about southeast Georgia. The motel's brochures informed him that ten thousand luckless souls made their home in Charlton County and that the per capita income was about eleven grand. A major source of this financial bounty was lumber. Throughout the county were small lumber mills, paper plants, turpentine vendors, and every other endeavor which could eke a meager profit from a tree. DeMarco recalled that Maxwell Taylor reported to the IRS an annual income of more than three hundred grand, thirty times what his county cousins made.

He spent the afternoon taking a slow tour of the region surrounding Folkston, including Uptonville, Billy Mattis's hometown. While driving he was forced to conclude that Charlton County was not a completely unattractive locale. This begrudging admission on his part was supported by the fact that the other major industry in the region was tourism. One of the motel's pamphlets said that in excess of four hundred thousand people visited the great swamp each year to gaze at its birds and enjoy its alligator-infested waters.

He told himself as he drove about the county that he was getting the lay of the land, reconnoitering the enemy's turf, but the reality was that he was stalling. He eventually ended up on the rim of the swamp where he was now parked, pondering his fate and cursing the Speaker: he was in an area he knew nothing about, where he had no contacts or authority, and he was supposed to investigate two people who may have tried to kill the President of the United States. And one of those people was a military-trained sniper and possible psycho.

DeMarco's options were limited. There was no way he was going to obtain physical evidence linking Estep or Taylor to the assassination attempt, so that was out. He might be able to prove that during the time of the shooting Estep was not where he was supposed to be, but that also seemed unlikely. Mostly what he would try to do is find the link between Taylor, Estep, Mattis, and Donnelly. Something connected these four men; finding the connection was the problem. Emma's man Neil, with all his computers and magic black boxes, hadn't been able to find a link, so what chance would DeMarco have? The best he could do was talk to people and search public records.

And then there was motive. To date he had discovered no reason why Taylor or Estep would want to kill the President. Maybe he'd stumble over a motive here in Georgia — if Estep didn't kill him first. He vividly recalled Colonel Moore's story of the army soldier rising up out of the earth, his camouflaged faced mottled with insect bites.

DeMarco jerked in alarm when a flock of birds that had been roosting in a nearby tree suddenly erupted into flight, shrieking in terror, startled by some invisible predator.

★   ★   ★

After a poor night's sleep in his overly warm motel room, DeMarco made his way to a quaint country diner for breakfast. Most of the other patrons in the place wore blue jeans, work shirts, and baseball caps. One dapper gent, however, sported a white straw boater with a red, white, and blue hatband. Matching his skimmer, Folkston's only fashion plate wore a white linen suit, a white shirt with an open collar, and red

231

suspenders. Probably the mayor, DeMarco thought. He hadn't seen a man in a straw boater since a revival of *The Music Man* at the Kennedy Center three years ago.

DeMarco was dressed casually himself, not only because of the heat but because he sensed this was not an area where his dark Brooks Brothers suits and button-down collars would fit in. He was clad in a white Izod polo shirt, khaki Dockers, and Top-Siders without socks — the kind of outfit he might wear in Georgetown on a sunny Saturday morn. Looking around the room at the John Deere and Caterpillar baseball hats he wished he had worn socks. These were the kind of people, he suspected, who left their socks on when they made love; they certainly did not take them off when they wore shoes.

A cheery waitress — a lass in her late twenties with a stack of blonde hair piled atop dark roots and wearing a pink uniform short enough to show off good country legs — came over to where he was seated at the counter and said, 'Good mornin', shugga. Y'all want some coffee?'

Shugga? Ah, sugar. He liked that. Yes, that's what he wanted: a woman who called him shugga. And when he was old and fat and impotent, she'd call him big daddy and cheat on him with a greasy-haired, lanky type who wore a John Deere cap.

'Please,' he said, smiling back at the waitress.

'Well ain't that cute,' she said, wiggling an index finger at his chest as she poured his coffee.

'What?' DeMarco said. Cute was not a word normally applied to him.

'That little green gator there on your shirt. Did you buy that at one of them tourist shops over at the swamp?'

'Ah, no,' DeMarco said.

'Damn, that's cute,' she repeated. She turned and yelled to a waitress on the other side of the restaurant, 'Hey, Patty May, come over here an' look at the cute little gator this fella's got sewed on his shirt.'

DeMarco felt his face redden in embarrassment as people turned to look at him. So much for maintaining a low profile. He looked across the U-shaped counter and saw Emma and the man wearing the straw boater smile at each other, partners in enjoyment of DeMarco's humiliation.

Emma was dressed in a white sundress, white pumps, and a strand of pearls. The only things missing from her Southern-belle ensemble were a frilly, flowered hat and a matching parasol. Emma enjoyed getting into costume when the job required it, and DeMarco could tell that the man with the red suspenders was quite taken with her.

Since coming to Georgia was dangerous, DeMarco had decided not to come alone. Emma owned a gun and actually knew how to use it; DeMarco took great comfort in that. They had flown down together but agreed from the time they landed at Jacksonville that they would act like strangers, as there might be an advantage to having someone unknown to the opposition covering his back — an operational concept Emma had explained to him

233

The young waitress finally brought DeMarco his breakfast. Friendly was part of the service — speed was not. He had ordered bacon and eggs, and bacon and eggs were indeed on his plate — along with something white and runny that looked like Cream of Wheat with a glob of butter on top.

'What's that?' DeMarco said, pointing at the white, yucky stuff.

The waitress flashed her teeth at him. 'Why them's grits, you Yankee devil.'

Grits. He should have guessed. He wasn't going to eat them.

The waitress lowered long false eyelashes over smoky-gray bedroom eyes. 'Y'all gonna be in town long, darlin'?' she asked.

DeMarco liked darlin' almost as much as shugga. 'For a little while,' he said.

'And whatcha doin' down thisaway?'

It was time to go to work.

DeMarco had to have some reason for asking questions and poking about. He considered telling the truth, that he was a congressional investigator, but he didn't think that was the best way to get folks to open up. His cover story, albeit flimsy as gossamer wings, was that he was a freelance writer doing research on Billy Mattis, hometown boy, soldier, and Secret Service hero. He wished he had taken the time to obtain credentials to match his cover.

He told the waitress about his bogus mission. After she oohed how cool that was, he asked if she knew Billy.

'Yeah,' she said, 'but not real well, him bein' a

few years older than me.'

She said Billy must have been a real fine man, bein' in the Secret Service and all. Shame about him dyin'. And how 'bout Billy's mother, did she know her? Yeah, sorta. Knew she lived up Uptonville way, was a waitress there. What about Billy's father? For the first time DeMarco's leggy new friend became evasive. She asked to be excused to check on an order but DeMarco thought it was to give herself time to think.

DeMarco watched the waitress walk away, enjoying the view, then glanced over at Emma. She was still talking to the natty guy in the straw boater. DeMarco started to look away but at just that moment a man seated alone at a window table behind Emma turned and stared at DeMarco.

DeMarco couldn't exactly define the nature of the man's stare. It was intimidating while simultaneously being coldly indifferent. Then DeMarco realized it was like the look a pro boxer gives his opponent when they tap gloves before the bout starts: an unflinching look that promises a violent yet unemotional beating.

The man's skin was the color of burnished mahogany and he had a hatchet blade of a nose that dominated his face. His thick black hair was pulled back into a short ponytail. Maybe Hispanic, DeMarco thought, but more likely Native American. On his face, on the left side, was a thin white scar that zigzagged from his left eyebrow to the corner of his mouth.

The man stared impassively at DeMarco a few more seconds then his black eyes blinked slowly,

235

a single time, and he turned his head away and raised a coffee cup to his lips. The forearm and wrist of the arm holding the cup were corded with muscle.

The waitress returned to the counter and leaned close to DeMarco, close enough for him to smell floral shampoo and bacon grease in her hair. She said coyly that she had heard a few rumors about who Billy's daddy was, but she wasn't the type to go spreadin' gossip. *My ass*, thought DeMarco. He didn't press her but he was puzzled by her reticence. He recalled how he'd hit a similar brick wall when he had asked the high-school vice principal questions about Billy's sire.

DeMarco chatted with the waitress a bit longer, left an oversize tip, and started to leave when she said, 'Hey, shugga. You forgot your receipt.'

'I don't need a receipt,' he said.

'Yeah ya do,' she said, and winked as she pressed a slip of paper into his hand.

DeMarco glanced over to the table where the man with the ponytail had been seated and saw he was gone. He looked down at the receipt in his hand, read the name Cindy, the 'i' dotted with a heart, and a phone number — and the words 'If a man answers, hang up.'

This was a dangerous, dangerous place. He wanted to go home.

★ ★ ★

DeMarco parked his car where he had a clear view of the Okefenokee Swamp's ranger station.

236

At five p.m., three rangers came out the building. DeMarco had received a description of Estep from Emma's man Mike, and none of the rangers matched that description. Two of the rangers entered a mud-splattered Ford Explorer, the other a midsize Japanese sedan. The sedan followed the SUV out of the parking lot and DeMarco followed the sedan. Five minutes later their small caravan stopped, as he had hoped, at a local watering hole.

All three men were in their fifties with beer guts and broad butts. DeMarco had been to Yellowstone once, and these guys didn't look like the rangers he'd seen there. They didn't look as though they spent hours hiking through woods, blazing trails, and cutting fire-breaks. They weren't clean-cut and outdoorsy; they chain-smoked Marlboros, drank beer at an alarming rate, and made lewd remarks about the shape of the barmaid's ass. These guys matched DeMarco's stereo-type of corrupt New York City cops: sly-eyed, apple-stealing, on-the-take beat cops like those he remembered strolling the streets of Queens casually swinging their nightsticks. Hiring criteria for swamp tenders, he concluded, didn't match Yellowstone's standards.

DeMarco ordered a beer and took a seat at the bar where he was close enough to eavesdrop on the rangers' conversation. He was hoping to find an opportunity to talk to them so he could eventually turn the discussion to Dale Estep and find out what Estep had been doing in Washington. While he sat there, he thought back on the day he had just wasted.

After breakfast he'd visited the building housing Charlton County's records and checked Billy Mattis's birth certificate for information about his father. No daddy was listed. From there he went to property and business records, and searched for links between Taylor, Estep, Donnelly, and Mattis. After three hours he confirmed that Taylor owned just about everything in the region as Senator Maddox had told him, but the other three men were not listed as partners, lenders, or tenants.

He'd spent the afternoon at the *Charlton County Herald*. To his surprise, he discovered that the man with the straw boater he had seen talking to Emma was the editor. He fed the gentleman the same lie he'd told the waitress, about writing an article on Billy Mattis, and he kindly allowed DeMarco to use his ancient microfiche machine to look at back issues of the paper. The major revelation produced by his research was that Maxwell Taylor rarely made the news. Prior to 1970 there was an occasional mention of Taylor purchasing some piece of land or taking over a business, but after 1970 his name wasn't mentioned again. This seemed unusual considering the man's wealth and acquisitiveness. DeMarco noticed the editor of the paper had changed in 1969 and he couldn't help but wonder if the First Amendment had not been further amended in Charlton County. Regarding Dale Estep, all he learned was that Estep had historically won every contest involving a firearm and was the current county record holder for largemouth bass.

DeMarco turned his attention back to the three beer-swilling rangers. They were now bitching about their wives, all having apparently married local harpies with sharp, nagging tongues. He was about to leave his bar stool to ask the rangers some inane question — Gee, do you guys work at that big swamp over there? — but before he could, another man in a ranger's uniform entered the bar.

The man was also in his fifties, but unlike his co-workers there was no flesh hanging over his belt and he moved with the fluid grace of a jungle cat. He had high, hard cheekbones and deep furrows on either side of his mouth. His nose was long and straight and his hair was black with a deep widow's peak. He reminded DeMarco of that actor/playwright, the one married to the actress, Jessica Lange.

DeMarco was sure the man was Estep and his opinion was confirmed when one of the rangers at the table said, 'Yo, Dale, come over and have a brew with the hired help.' DeMarco turned on his bar stool so his face wasn't visible to Estep.

Estep ignored the man who had spoken and said to one of the other men, 'Charlie, didn't I tell you to barricade the north access road today?'

'Yeah, Dale, but — '

''But' my ass. I told you I wanted it done today, that there's a crew comin' in tonight, and I don't want a buncha damn tourists going through there in the morning.'

'Dale, I was plannin' on doing it today but we had that problem with the drains. I just didn't get around to it.'

'So in other words, you just fuckin' quit at five like you always do and came over here to suck down beer.'

'Well, I guess, but . . . '

DeMarco studied Estep's reflection in the mirror as he railed at Charlie. When Mike had described Estep, he had said the man had 'hunter's eyes.' DeMarco had not understood what he meant, but now he did. Estep's dark eyes were always moving, as if searching the brush for game, just waiting for his prey to panic and run squealing from its hiding place. There was something tangibly dangerous about Dale Estep.

'Charlie,' Estep said, 'get your fat ass out of that chair. You too, Harv. You two dumb shits come with me. I've got the barricades and detour signs in the truck. We're gonna go put 'em up now.'

'Ah, Dale, can't it wait until tomorrow? I'll get up early and — '

'Charlie, are you refusing to obey a direct order?'

'Nah, Dale, I'm just sayin' — '

'What would you do Charlie, you and your fat fuckin' wife and your fat fuckin' kids, if you actually had to work for a living? Do you wanna find out?'

Estep stared at Charlie until he lowered his eyes like a whipped pup, then said, 'Let's go. Both of you.'

The two men rose and started to follow Estep from the bar when the third man said, 'Hey, Charlie, how am I supposed to get home? You drove today.'

Before Charlie could respond, Estep said, 'Just sit there and get drunk, Junior — like you do every night. I'll bring Charlie back in a couple of hours when the job's done.'

After Estep and the two rangers left the bar, the one called Junior sat for a while drinking before he walked over to a pool table and began to rack the balls. DeMarco let him take a few shots then asked if he'd like to play a game.

Junior looked at DeMarco, taking in his clothes and up-north accent, and said, 'You ain't some kind of Yankee pool hustler, now are you?'

'Nah,' DeMarco said. 'Just a guy who likes to play once in a while.' Actually, DeMarco was a pretty fair pool player but he had already decided to let ol' Junior win a few games.

'Well in that case,' Junior said, 'let's make it interesting. Say two bucks a game?'

It turned out DeMarco didn't have to let Junior win; the bastard played like Minnesota Fats. While Junior was whipping him at eight ball, DeMarco said, 'Sounded like that guy wasn't too happy with your friend Charlie.'

'Fuckin' Dale,' Junior said. 'He was up in Washington for two goddamn months sittin' on his ass and then he comes back here and tries to work us to death.'

'Really?' DeMarco said. 'I'm from D.C. What was he doing up there?'

'Nine ball, corner pocket. Oh, he was takin' these classes the Department of Interior puts on. Environmental shit, land management, that kind of crap. Five ball, side pocket.'

'Sounds interesting. Suppose you guys are

always going to school to keep up on environmental regulations and things like that.'

'Yeah, right,' the ranger said. 'None of us ever gets to go to any damn schools, and this is the first time Dale's ever gone to one. Hell, Dale hardly went to school when he was a kid. All he did was hunt. And goddamn Florida land developers care more about the environment than he does. What he did up north was sit on his ass all day and chase city tail all night. Didn't even bring back a damn book. Rack 'em up, city boy. That's eight bucks you owe me.'

While DeMarco was setting up the next game, he said, 'You said he was a hunter. What do you hunt around here?'

'I don't hunt nothin', but Dale, he'll kill anything with hide or feathers. Bastard just loves to kill things.'

'What does he hunt with? Bow and arrow? Rifle?'

'Rifle. And can that sumbitch shoot!'

'Is that right,' DeMarco said.

'Yeah, like one time we had to go out and kill this fox that had rabies and while we're trackin' the fox, I see this flyin' squirrel jump from one of the trees. I like them little flyin' squirrels. Fuckers can glide damn near a hundred yards. Anyway, I say, 'Hey, Dale, look at that little fucker,' and goddamn Dale raises that rifle, barely looks, and blows that squirrel right out of the sky. That sumbitch can shoot the eye of a June bug at three hundred yards. But goddamn, why kill a little flyin' squirrel? Crazy bastard.'

DeMarco realized this line of questioning,

though mildly interesting, was of little value. Colonel Moore had already confirmed that Estep was a crazy bastard who could shoot. DeMarco thought he'd see if Junior knew Billy Mattis and if maybe he could tell him who Billy's relatives were. He was trying to think of a way to steer the conversation in that direction when he noticed the pickup with Dale and the other two rangers pull into the parking lot of the tavern. Crap. Estep had said they'd be gone two hours.

DeMarco looked at his watch, said, 'Oh, shit, look at the time,' and pulled out a ten and dropped it on the pool table. He shook Junior's hand and started to leave but Junior said, 'Hey, wait up. You got some change comin'.'

'That's okay. Gotta go,' DeMarco said.

'Nah, just hold up,' Junior said. 'I got some ones in my wallet.'

Shit. Before he could get away Estep entered the bar. DeMarco took his change from Junior, shook his hand again, and told him what a pleasure it had been getting his ass kicked in four straight games.

Estep's eyes tracked him as he walked from the bar.

32

DeMarco lay on the bed in his hotel room, a towel still damp from his shower wrapped around his waist. The air-conditioning, now working when he didn't need it, was giving him a chill but he was too lazy to get up from the bed and turn it off.

He was speaking on the phone to a lady named Becky Townsend who worked at the Department of Interior. DeMarco had dated Becky a few times after his divorce but she could see that his heart wasn't really in it. She liked him though, and had hopes that he would one day heal. She was more than happy to do him a favor.

DeMarco asked Becky to find out if Dale Estep had indeed registered for any classes sponsored by the Department of Interior. He told her that he also wanted to know if Estep had *really* attended the classes, and in particular wanted to know if he was in class the day the President was shot. He didn't actually say 'the day the President was shot'; he just gave her the date. When Becky asked why he wanted to know all this, DeMarco said he suspected Estep had misused government funds and hadn't really gone to school.

'Crimes in low places, Becks,' he said casually. 'I think this redneck may have pulled a scam on our Uncle Sammy.'

'Wow,' Becky said. 'Hookey-gate.'

'Go ahead and snicker, but yours truly is diligently rootin' out corruption in Guv'ment.' He hung up, promising her a souvenir from the Deep South — maybe a plastic statue of George Wallace in a wheelchair. Becky didn't find that amusing.

He slipped into shorts, a T-shirt, and flip-flops and walked over to Emma's room. Since their plan was not to be seen together he looked around carefully, feeling foolish as he did so, to make sure no one was watching when he knocked on Emma's door. While DeMarco had been searching records, Emma's job had been to look at real estate in the area. DeMarco thought such an activity would provide a lead-in to asking folks about Maxwell Taylor as he owned almost all the real estate.

Emma took her time answering the door, and after she let DeMarco in he noted she moved slowly and deliberately back to the only chair in the room. Since there was no place else to sit, DeMarco flopped down on the bed.

A baseball game was playing on the television set. This was odd as Emma had stated on more than one occasion that her idea of hell was to be strapped to a chair and condemned to watch a no-hitter for eternity.

'Who's winning, Emma?' DeMarco asked. The Atlanta Braves were playing the Dodgers. DeMarco disliked Ted Turner almost as much as he disliked the owner of the Orioles — he was glad Jane Fonda had left him — and he hoped LA was kicking the crap out of Turner's Braves.

245

'I have no idea,' Emma said, speaking the same way she had moved earlier: slowly, precisely, deliberately. She fumbled for the television's remote control, pushed a button, and changed the channel; she pushed another button and increased the volume to a deafening level; she finally pushed the button that turned the television off.

She was drunk, DeMarco realized. Glassy-eyed, shit-faced drunk. He had never seen Emma even the slightest bit tipsy, and here she was smashed to the eyeballs and trying not to let DeMarco see it.

'So how was your day?' DeMarco asked.

'Interesting,' she said after several beats.

'Are you going to tell me what you learned?'

Emma paused, burped silently, and said, 'Excuse me. I learned what we already knew: that Taylor owns everything in the county. I stopped at three or four real estate offices to find out what was for sale, and every one of them told me the same thing: if I wanted to buy land I'd have to talk to Max Taylor. But they wouldn't tell me squat about Taylor himself. Seems he scares the hell out of people for some reason.'

'Any connection to any of the others?'

'Nothing I could find.'

'So the day was a total bust.'

'Not quite,' she said. She reached for a water glass on the small table next to her chair and knocked it over. 'Whoops,' she said. She rose with some difficulty and walked stiff-legged to the bathroom to refill the glass, bouncing one shoulder off the door frame as she entered the bathroom.

DeMarco couldn't stand it anymore. He laughed and said, 'Emma, you're smashed! How much have you had to drink?'

'A lot. I'm so drunk there's two of you, and Lord knows, one of you is bad enough.'

Emma returned to her chair, collapsed into it, and said, 'I was standing in front of a hardware store dressed in my Scarlett O outfit, jawboning with these crackers, when this gal, gal about my age, comes out of the store and finds a ticket on the windshield of her pickup. She goes berserk. Starts cussing like you wouldn't believe, rips the ticket off her windshield, and throws it in the gutter. Then she yells inside the store to somebody 'You tell that son of a bitch Max Taylor the day he kisses my fat ass, I'll pay that ticket.' Then she drives off.

'So I ask the crackers who the lady is and they tell me she's Hattie McCormack, hell on wheels. Stay away from that old bitch, they said. I find out she has five acres on the outskirts of this hellhole and grows her own tobacco, so I go out there and spin my real estate line. Well Hattie takes a likin' to me, charmer that I am. She invites me in and offers me some honest-to-God homemade white lightning. Joe, that stuff must have been two hundred proof. The hangover I'm going to have tomorrow may kill me. Anyway, we sat out there on her porch, drinking her booze, and talked. She was a kick, an American original. I had a ball talking to her.'

'Obviously,' DeMarco said. 'When are you going to get to the part about Taylor?'

'Oh yeah, Taylor. According to her, Mr Taylor

not only owns all the land around here, he also owns the government.'

'The government?'

'Yes. The sheriff, judges, city councilmen. All those guys. She claims he even gets a share of the taxes. That's why the ticket pissed her off; she said Taylor had the meters installed because he gets a kickback from the fees and fines.'

'Why isn't she afraid of Taylor like everyone else around here?'

'I asked her that, and she said she's too damn mean to be afraid of anyone. But she also said that if Taylor knew she was talking to me, he'd send the 'Injun' to see her.'

'The Injun?'

'Some guy who works for Taylor, I guess.'

DeMarco knew there was more than one Native American in the area, but he immediately knew the 'Injun' was the man with the ponytail he had seen in the diner that morning.

'Anyway,' Emma said, 'this Taylor's a piece of work. Hattie says he spends most days just touring the county. Drives around checking on things like a general doing a command inspection. Tells folks to clean up a mess if he sees one; checks on what's playing in the movie houses and what kind of books are being sold in stores.'

'Books?'

'Yep. Mr Taylor doesn't approve of girlie magazines or X-rated pictures or anything he considers pornographic. Guy's a character. He even checks on what they teach in the schools. Sees something he doesn't like and a teacher's liable to get her liberal ass fired.'

'He sounds like a dictator,' DeMarco said.

'Indeed, but Hattie admitted it wasn't all bad. There's no crime here because Taylor's judges throw away the key if you commit one. And Taylor's donated a lot of money for various things: ball fields, a swimming pool, sports equipment, that sort of thing. He even has a scholarship fund set up for the underprivileged.'

'So he's a benevolent dictator.'

DeMarco thought about what Emma had said and concluded that even if Hattie McCormack was right about Taylor, the information had no bearing on the assassination attempt or any connection to Patrick Donnelly. There wasn't anything particularly newsworthy about the richest citizen in a small rural area having undue influence over city and county officials. Rich men have owned politicians for centuries. The possibility of Taylor getting a direct kickback from taxes seemed far-fetched, but even if he was, so what?

DeMarco noticed Emma's head had dropped and her aristocratic chin was resting on her chest. She was about to pass out. DeMarco rose from the bed where he'd been reclining, put a hand under her arm, and helped her from the chair to the bed.

'What do you think you're doing?' Emma mumbled, but she didn't resist.

DeMarco gently lowered her to the bed, pulled off her shoes, and placed a pillow under her head.

As DeMarco was opening the door to leave

the room, Emma said, 'Oh, I forgot to tell you. Hattie said in April or May a man who wasn't from here asked her all kinds of questions about Taylor too.'

'Who was it?'

'She couldn't remember his name, she was as drunk as I was, but she said he was a handsome, honey-tongued son of a bitch.'

And then Emma began to snore.

33

Jillian Mattis's house was on the outskirts of Uptonville, a burg a few miles north of Folkston. It was a boxy, one-story affair in need of a new roof and a coat of paint. On one side of the house was a small vegetable garden where the main crop was a short, flowering weed. Behind the house was a barn with a swaybacked roof, listing walls, and a paddock for horses, though DeMarco could see no sign of livestock.

The woman who came to the door in response to his knock was tall, well proportioned, and handsome. She had striking blue eyes which were squinting as she peered through the screen door at DeMarco, trying to adjust to the contrast between the bright sunlight outside and the dark interior of the house. She was wearing a faded gray housedress that a million washings ago had contained a lilac-colored floral pattern. Her thick auburn hair was streaked with gray strands, and her eyes bore the look of a lifetime of wanting and never getting. If she had dyed the gray out of her hair and applied a little makeup she would have been a stunning woman, but DeMarco sensed she was beyond caring about the way she looked.

She left the screen door shut and said, 'Can I help you?' She spoke in a listless monotone.

'I'm looking for Jillian Mattis,' DeMarco said.

'I'm Jillian. What can I do for you?'

251

DeMarco was surprised. The woman appeared to be only in her mid-forties and Billy was thirty-two when he died. She must have been a teenager when she bore him.

'My name's Joe DeMarco, Mrs Mattis,' DeMarco said. 'I work for the United States Congress.'

DeMarco decided on the spot not to use his false writer persona. His instincts told him that she would resent some mercenary scribbler trying to make a buck off the tragedy of her son's death.

'Congress?'

'I'm sorry about what happened to your son, ma'am. You have my deepest sympathy.'

'Thank you,' she said. She was looking at him but not seeing him.

'I know you're in mourning, Mrs Mattis, but I was wondering if you would talk to me about Billy.'

DeMarco could see the woman was almost paralyzed with grief, barely able to carry on a conversation, but he needed to know why her son had called her so many times the month before the assassination attempt. He also wanted to know who Billy's father was. By now he suspected it might be Dale Estep. Estep was just a few years older than Jillian, and since he was crazier than a shit-house rat, DeMarco could also understand why the locals would be reluctant to discuss Billy's paternity. Dale being Billy's father also explained other things, like why a man like Billy might cooperate with him in the assassination attempt. The problem with this theory was that if all of DeMarco's other theories were correct, then Estep had arranged the murder of his own child.

'Why do you want to talk about Billy?' Jillian said.

'As you probably know, ma'am, your son was guarding the President the day someone tried to assassinate him. There are still some unanswered questions about the assassination attempt.'

'I thought . . . I thought a man already confessed to shooting the President.'

'Yes, ma'am. Harold Edwards. But there are still some outstanding issues.'

'Like what?'

'Mrs Mattis, do you know a man named Patrick Donnelly?'

This is where she was supposed to say: Why, gosh yes — he was Billy's mentor, pal, godfather, or some such thing. Instead she said nothing. She was looking behind DeMarco. He turned to follow her line of sight and saw a tire swing hanging from the limb of a dying elm. She was seeing a young Billy Mattis, blond hair flying, a grin on his face, as he tried to swing to the moon.

'Mrs Mattis,' DeMarco said, 'do you know a man named Patrick Donnelly?'

'I'm sorry,' Jillian Mattis said, apologizing for her mental lapse. 'No, I don't know him. Who is he?'

'He's the director of the Secret Service, Billy's boss.'

'Oh,' Jillian Mattis said.

'What about Maxwell Taylor, Mrs Mattis.

253

What's his relationship to Billy?'

Jillian Mattis suddenly gave DeMarco her full attention, her son's death momentarily forgotten.

'Max?' she said.

'Yes, ma'am.'

'You need to leave now.'

The woman seemed scared to death. 'Mrs Mattis, this is important,' DeMarco said. 'Let me come in and talk to you. Please.'

Jillian Mattis shook her head.

'What about Dale Estep, Mrs Mattis? Is he — '

'You need to leave,' Jillian Mattis said. She hissed the words, almost a whisper, as if afraid of being overheard. 'My son is dead, and he's never comin' back, and I don't need any more pain in my life.'

She shut the door in DeMarco's face.

★ ★ ★

Fuck Mahoney, DeMarco thought as he drove back toward his motel in Folkston. He was ashamed of himself for badgering Jillian Mattis. The damn FBI — with their badges and their warrants and their white-coated techies — they should be down here hassling people, not him.

DeMarco continued to sulk as he drove. He was wasting his time and he knew it. He was not going to find a connection between Donnelly, Taylor, and Billy Mattis in the back issues of a county newspaper. And how could Billy's mother lead him to any real evidence that Estep

254

and Taylor had tried to kill the President?

DeMarco knew what he should do next — he just didn't want to do it. Had this been a normal assignment, something involving a politician on Capitol Hill, he would at this point vigorously stir the pot and watch for something foul to float to the surface. He would question all the people involved and make sure everybody knew everybody else was being questioned. He would imply that one of the participants was talking to the authorities, turning on the others. He would browbeat the miscreants, lie about evidence that didn't exist, claim that an arrest was imminent. He would, in other words, do anything necessary to cause a precipitous reaction.

Yes, if this case had involved a leak on some politician's staff or the shenanigans of a wayward bureaucrat, that's exactly what he would do. He also knew exactly what his opponents would do in return. They would try to intimidate him by puffing out their chests and flashing their power ties. They would try to frighten him with tales of their awesome, terrible clout. They might try to bribe him; they would certainly threaten to get him fired. Their worst threat, their very worst, was that they would call their retained lawyers and sue his ass into poverty.

But Estep and Taylor, if they were involved — he always had to add 'if they were involved' — would not bribe him or intimidate him or sue him. They would kill him.

Yes, DeMarco knew what he should do next — he just didn't want to do it.

Back at his motel, he called Emma's room but

255

didn't get an answer. That morning his badly hungover friend had said she was going back out to Hattie McCormack's tobacco and moonshine farm. She wanted to question Hattie some more, but this time in a sober condition. DeMarco was puzzled that she wasn't back yet; she should have been by now.

DeMarco stared out the window of his motel room at the small swimming pool. He didn't want to talk to Taylor until he had talked to Emma. Or to state it differently, Emma provided an excuse for him to delay meeting with Taylor. So since he could think of nothing better to do, he decided to go down to the pool, drink a couple of beers, and act like a tourist. Hell, he was a tourist.

Arriving at the pool, beer in one hand, bath towel in the other, he discovered two small boys polluting the waters. They were nine or ten years old and wore baggy bathing suits covered with pictures of cartoon characters. They were running around the perimeter of the pool, squirting each other with magnum-sized water pistols, screaming at the top of their lungs.

DeMarco didn't exactly dislike children, he just wasn't certain how to act around them. The fact that they looked like short people didn't mean they were people. A caterpillar may be a butterfly in transition, but it isn't a butterfly.

DeMarco stood back from the pool and studied the boys. Frowning, he tried to guess the distance a sixty-pound kid curled into the shape of a cannonball could splash water. When he was certain he had it figured out, he placed the motel lounge chair twice that distance from the pool. He tried to relax but then one boy started shrieking because the other kid was trying to drown him. He watched anxiously for a bit, eventually realizing — somewhat to his disappointment — that neither child had the upper-body strength to hold the slippery head of the other under water the required length of time.

DeMarco took off his T-shirt, opened his beer, and settled back into the lounge chair. He took a couple of sips of beer then closed his eyes. He was determined to relax and not dwell on the futility of his current mission. He sat there only a minute when he felt someone staring at him, then realized he could no longer hear the two boys yelling. Opening one eye he saw the boys standing a foot away from his lounge chair. The water pistols hung menacingly at their sides.

They both had flattops, piggy blue eyes, and a sprinkling of freckles across stubby, runny noses. Brothers. Some woman had been twice cursed.

'Mister,' one of them said, 'you ever seen an alligator?'

'Yeah,' DeMarco said. *Go away, you little shit.* 'I saw one in a zoo once.'

'We saw one in the *swamp*. A big one. Its mouth was open and it had lots of teeth.' The kid opened his mouth and showed DeMarco his teeth. His brother nodded earnestly in agreement.

'Is that right,' DeMarco said.

'Yeah,' the boy said, his face very serious. 'Mister, do you think them alligators from the swamp can get all the way over here to the motel and crawl into the swimmin' pool?'

DeMarco was faced with a great moral dilemma. Should he tell the boys that chances were indeed high that a ten-foot alligator was coiled, chameleonlike, at the bottom of the clear swimming pool? This might make them go away, on the other hand he might give them bed-wetting nightmares of huge reptiles slithering over the transom of their motel-room door. What did they really want, DeMarco wondered — the thrill of danger close at hand, an imaginary beast to hunt with their water pistols, or assurance from a kindly adult that they were safe?

DeMarco opened his mouth to answer, but before he could speak, a woman's voice said, 'Bobby. Randy. Are you kids bothering that nice man?'

'No, Mom,' the two boys said in chorus. Little liars.

DeMarco turned toward the sound of the voice and saw a woman who looked absolutely delicious moving toward him in a very small lime-green bikini. She had light-brown hair streaked blond by the sun, eyes as clear and blue as the water in the swimming pool, and like the boys, a sprinkling of freckles across a pert nose. She was yummy.

'Have these monsters been bothering you?' she asked DeMarco, stroking the seal-wet head of one of the boys. She had a delightful smile.

'Not at all,' DeMarco said, smiling back. Lying to this woman was apparently contagious.

'They've been asking me about alligators.'

'Don't I know it,' she said, feigning exasperation. 'Ever since we went on that swamp-boat ride yesterday, they've been driving me nuts about alligators and snakes.' Taking each child by the hand, she said, 'Come on, you devils. You've been out here in the sun long enough. Let's go inside and get cleaned up.'

She smiled at DeMarco again. Her nose crinkled up cutely when she smiled. 'We'll let you enjoy the pool in peace,' she said. 'Bye now.'

As she walked away DeMarco enjoyed the view of her lithe body moving gracefully in the tiny bathing suit, her hair swinging rhythmically across her back with each step. The only blemish in this enchanting scene was the armed midgets clutching her hands.

★ ★ ★

DeMarco must have fallen asleep because the next thing he knew someone was kicking the lounge chair. He looked up into the sun and saw a man in a dark-blue uniform wearing a Smokey the Bear hat and mirrored sunglasses. Sunlight reflected off the badge on the man's chest. From DeMarco's reclining position, he seemed enormous, all beer gut and meaty, freckled forearms.

'Your name DeMarco?' the man said.

DeMarco sat up, trying to shake the fog of sleep from his mind.

'Yeah,' he said. 'What can I do for you?'

'Mr Taylor wants to talk to you.'

Well. It looked as though he'd stirred the pot

without even trying. DeMarco stood up, not liking the cop looming over him. Upon standing he realized that the man wasn't as tall as he had originally thought but was still not someone he'd like to arm wrestle.

DeMarco squinted at the badge on the man's chest: Charlton County Sheriff's Office.

'Mr Taylor wants to see me, Sheriff, so he sent you over here to arrest me?'

'Deputy,' the man said. 'Deputy Sheriff Pat Haskell.'

'Glad to meet you, Deputy, but why did Mr Taylor send you?'

The deputy's mouth tightened in irritation. He was used to more respect than DeMarco was giving him.

'The sheriff's just doin' Mr Taylor a favor. Mr Taylor said he wanted to talk to you, so my boss had me track you down.'

Great. Taylor had enough pull to use the sheriff's office as a messenger service.

'And if I don't want to talk to Mr Taylor, Deputy?'

'You know, you're kinda prickly, partner. I'm just passin' on a message. If you want to follow me, I'll lead you out to Taylor's place. If you don't wanna go, suit yourself.'

DeMarco stared into the deputy's mirrored sunglasses. 'Give me a minute to change clothes. I'll meet you in the parking lot.'

34

DeMarco followed the deputy's car up a long gravel driveway and parked in the shade of a weeping willow next to two late-model pickup trucks. Considering what he knew about Taylor's income and his influence in the region, the man's home was a surprise. DeMarco had been expecting a mansion, but Taylor's house was a simple two-story white house with green shutters and green trim. It was large and handsome and well made but no grander than several other homes DeMarco had seen in the area.

A swing was creaking on the broad front porch and the screen door at the main entrance was banging gently in time to a slight, much welcome breeze. The deputy rapped lightly on the screen door and a large black woman wearing a white apron over a black housedress appeared.

'Why how you doin', Deputy Pat?' she said. 'You here to see Mr Taylor?'

'No, Tilly, but this fella is. Mr Taylor asked me to bring him by.'

Tilly nodded at DeMarco. 'If you'll just wait here a minute, mister, I'll go tell Mr Taylor you're here. What's your name?'

'Joe DeMarco.'

'I'll be right back, Mr DeMarco.'

After the maid left, the deputy tipped his hat to DeMarco. 'I'll be seein' you around, partner,' he said. It sounded like a threat.

DeMarco fidgeted on the front porch until the maid returned. He wasn't sure what approach he should take with Taylor: go straight at him or beat around the bush. The maid returned to the front door before he had made up his mind.

'You go on down the hall to the first door on the right,' she said. 'Mr Taylor's there in his office.'

Entering the room, DeMarco saw a young woman and an older man he assumed was Taylor standing together next to a large hand-painted wooden globe. The globe was three feet in diameter and rested in a mahogany floor stand. With one hand the man was pointing at a spot on the globe saying, 'You see, Honey, that's where they all came from.' His other hand rested lightly on the woman's hip.

Voluptuous. It was the first word that came to DeMarco's mind. She was the most voluptuous woman he had ever seen. She was barefoot and wearing a light cotton dress that revealed more than it hid. The material barely contained her full breasts and wide hips, and you could see the dark outline of large nipples and the shape of strong thighs through the thin material. The top three buttons of the dress were undone showing a natural cleavage not requiring a bra for accent or support. Her legs and arms were tanned to the perfect shade of gold that was promised on the Coppertone bottle, and tousled blonde hair hung to her shoulder blades. The hair framed a flawless face with perfect features, and one absolutely devoid of any sign of intelligence. She was Daisy Mae, a Southern breeding machine

— and she was no more than fifteen years old.

DeMarco finally tore his eyes away from the girl and was embarrassed to find Taylor studying him. DeMarco could tell Taylor was amused by his reaction to the girl.

Taylor was in his sixties. He was tall, six three or six four, with a lanky, muscular frame. He was wearing new work boots, jeans, and a plaid shirt with the sleeves rolled up. He had a gaunt face, with deep furrows on either side of his mouth. His hair was full and white, and beneath bushy white eyebrows were deep-set dark eyes that glowed with the stern intensity of a country preacher's sermon. Standing next to the blond child-woman, all Taylor needed was a flowing white beard to resemble a harsh God who had evicted Adam from the garden while keeping Eve for Himself.

Taylor left the girl by the globe and walked over to a large desk made from the same wood as the globe stand. The girl glanced at DeMarco then ignored him, and began spinning the globe as if it were a large toy top. She seemed mesmerized by the blending colors as the world swirled beneath her slim fingers.

'Take a seat,' Taylor said, pointing DeMarco to a chair in front of the desk. It was an order, not a polite offering. To the girl he said, 'Honey, be a little darlin' and go fetch Morgan.' The girl acted as though she hadn't heard him and continued to turn the globe.

'Honey, I'm talkin' to you,' Taylor said.

Without looking at him, she said, 'Don't like Morgan, Uncle Max.'

263

Uncle Max? She was his niece?

Taylor smiled slightly, either amused by her childish pout or by her attitude toward this person Morgan. 'Morgan won't bother you, Honey. Now get a move on it.' He spoke softly but his impatience was beginning to show. Taylor was a man used to having his orders obeyed instantly.

The girl looked at the spinning globe a final time and reluctantly turned away from it. Taylor's eyes followed her, enjoying the motion of her full hips and the play of muscles in her bare calves as she walked slowly from the room. His lust was transparent, and considering the girl's age, sickening.

Whatever pleasant thoughts he had been having disappeared when he looked back at DeMarco. 'Bob Storch over at the newspaper said you were askin' about me. I thought I'd better see what you're up to.'

All DeMarco had done was ask the newspaper editor if he knew Taylor — the editor had said no — but that one question had apparently been reason enough for the editor to alert Taylor. The man had an early-warning system better than NORAD.

'I'm a writer, Mr Taylor. I freelance for magazines. I read about Billy Mattis, how he lived his life, how he died, and I thought he'd be a good subject for an article. I'm here doing research.'

'You got identification?' Taylor demanded.

Shit. DeMarco took out his driver's license and handed it to Taylor. Taylor looked at it, then took a pen from his desk and wrote down the information from DeMarco's license.

'Go on,' Taylor said.

'That's it. I'm just a guy doing some research for a story.'

Taylor was still holding DeMarco's license. He stared at DeMarco as he tapped the laminated card on the surface of his desk. 'So why were you askin' about me?'

'Did you know Billy Mattis, Mr Taylor?'

Annoyance flared in Taylor's eyes and he opened his mouth to snap out an angry response; DeMarco was asking questions instead of answering them. But then Taylor restrained himself, the effort noticeable, and his lips twitched in an insincere half smile.

'Sure I knew him. I've lived here all my life and know damn near everyone in the county. If memory serves, Billy was a hell of a shortstop for the high-school team. Probably could have gone to college on a scholarship but he decided to go into the military. Now answer the question I asked you. Why are you askin' around about me?'

DeMarco shrugged. 'Your name just came up. Somebody said they thought you and Billy were related.'

'Who told you that?' Taylor said, his eyes blazing.

'I don't really recall, Mr Taylor. It may have been Billy's wife.'

'You talked to Billy's wife?'

'Sure,' DeMarco said. 'So is it true that you and Billy are related?'

'No it's not true and I don't appreciate you

265

asking questions about me behind my back, mister.'

'Mr Taylor, I don't know what you're getting so upset about. I'm just trying to write a nice piece about a local hero. I would think — '

'I don't give a shit what you think. My experience is you damn journalists never have anything good to say about anybody. But we're gettin' off the point here. I don't like strangers asking questions about me. I won't put up with . . . '

Taylor stopped speaking and looked over DeMarco's head. At the same time DeMarco heard the sound of a boot scraping the hardwood floor behind him. He turned to see who was there and saw the man from the diner, the one with the ponytail and the lightning scar on his cheek. He was wearing scuffed cowboy boots, black jeans, and a gray sleeveless T-shirt that showed off a weight lifter's hard biceps. He looked at DeMarco just as he had that first time in the diner — his face expressionless, his eyes unemotional yet intimidating.

DeMarco exercised. He was in relatively good shape and the man standing behind him was only slightly taller than him and at most twenty pounds heavier. Yet DeMarco had the same feeling he had when he once shook hands with the starting middle linebacker for the Washington Redskins. The linebacker hadn't been much taller or heavier than DeMarco either, but DeMarco had known immediately that the linebacker was of a stronger, more violent species, one which would rule the earth if it came down to unarmed combat.

DeMarco looked back at Taylor. Taylor could see that DeMarco didn't like having Morgan at his back and his lips twisted into a thin smile with all the warmth of a winter's eve. 'This fella's from Washington, D.C., Morgan,' Taylor said, speaking to Morgan but looking at DeMarco. 'Says he's a writer. He thinks that gives him the right to go around asking questions about people behind their — '

'Mr Taylor, I wasn't — '

'Shut up,' Taylor said. 'Don't ever interrupt me when I'm talking.'

There was an arrogance about Taylor that was palpable. It was the kind of arrogance DeMarco had observed all too often in powerful politicians: men so accustomed to being catered to, so confident of their authority, so used to unquestioning obedience, that they come to believe they are untouchable.

'You need to understand something, mister,' Taylor said. 'You're not in Washington goddamn D.C. right now, and I won't tolerate you sneakin' around this community.'

DeMarco guessed a real writer would go into First Amendment orbit at this point, explaining he had the right to do anything he damn well pleased.

'You won't tolerate it?' DeMarco said.

'That's right. I won't. In fact, I think you better leave town tomorrow. That would be the smart thing for you to do.'

'Are you threatening me, Mr Taylor?' DeMarco said. Talk about a dumb question.

Taylor smiled at him; his teeth were like small tombstones.

267

'Can I have my driver's license back?' DeMarco said.

Taylor tossed it to him.

DeMarco rose from the chair and turned to leave the room but Morgan was blocking his exit. He didn't budge when DeMarco said, 'Excuse me.' He just stood there, staring impassively into DeMarco's eyes, the same way he had stared at DeMarco in the diner. DeMarco apparently wasn't leaving until Taylor dismissed him.

DeMarco didn't scare easily but Morgan . . . he raised the short hairs on his neck. DeMarco sensed that there wasn't anything *inside* the man.

DeMarco turned back to face Taylor. Taylor's dark eyes were shining with satisfaction. He had made his point. DeMarco was on his turf, playing by his rules. The sheriff's office was a limousine service that brought people to him. This was not, as he had said, Washington goddamn D.C.

'I want you out of Charlton County tomorrow,' Taylor said. 'Do you understand?'

DeMarco nodded.

'Let him by, Morgan,' Taylor said.

Morgan let DeMarco squeeze by. He executed the move like a boxer circling an opponent, shuffling slightly to his right, his hands ready, his eyes locked onto DeMarco's.

★   ★   ★

DeMarco pulled his rented Mustang out of Taylor's driveway and then stopped at the side of the road. The sky looked threatening and he decided to put up the convertible's top in case it started to rain. He latched down the top and was about to start the car again when he looked over at Taylor's house and saw the girl, Honey. She had just come out the front door and was taking a seat in the porch swing.

She put her legs up on the porch railing and with the short dress she was wearing, her shapely, tanned legs were exposed to the tops of her thighs. DeMarco stared a minute, then shook his head in self-disgust. She was a teenager; you had to draw the line somewhere. He began to turn the key in the ignition when he saw Morgan walk around the side of the house. Morgan also saw the girl sitting on the porch.

Morgan moved slowly toward the girl, placing his feet carefully so as not to make any noise. He reminded DeMarco of a panther closing in on its prey. Morgan stopped less than three feet from her, his body hidden by a large rhododendron, then he stood there, still as a statue, and stared at the girl. They stayed that way for a few minutes — DeMarco watching Morgan, Morgan watching the girl — then the girl sensed Morgan's presence. She jumped up from the swing, pointed a child's accusing finger at Morgan, and ran into the house. Morgan didn't move after the girl left, but continued to stand motionless, almost invisible in the shadows and foliage surrounding the porch.

He was still standing there when DeMarco drove away.

35

Emma was not in her room, she didn't answer her cell phone, and she had left no messages for DeMarco. She should have returned from visiting Hattie McCormack hours ago. Where the hell was she?

Since Emma wasn't available to discuss strategy, he called Becky, his friend at the Department of Interior, to see if she had completed her homework assignment. She had. She confirmed what DeMarco had suspected: that Estep had been registered for a series of classes sponsored by the Department of Interior and his attendance in class had been sporadic. However, since this was voluntary adult education, no one took roll call or kept track of the days he had missed. Regarding the day DeMarco cared most about, Becky hadn't been able to confirm if Estep had been there or not. Once again, no hard data; just another bit of inconclusive circumstantial evidence further indicating that Estep *could* have been involved in the shooting as DeMarco suspected.

Becky finished telling him what she had discovered about Estep then launched into a breathless account of her day battling political villains on Capitol Hill. DeMarco envied her optimism. He wondered, with a twinge of self-pity, what had happened to his own optimism. He didn't want the call to end but before long she claimed to have some power broker blinking on her other line.

By six p.m. DeMarco's annoyance at Emma's absence had changed to concern. He called the operator to obtain a phone number and address for Hattie McCormack. She was unlisted. Next he called the local hospital to see if anyone fitting Emma's description had been admitted and fortunately drew a blank.

Not knowing what to do next, he decided to get something to eat. He left the motel and drove around until he found a restaurant that was almost empty. He wanted to think and he didn't want to be surrounded by people. He went into the restaurant and took a seat at the bar in the lounge.

Before his butt hit the bar stool, the bartender came rushing over to serve him.

'What can I get for ya, podna,' the bartender said. He was a scrawny old guy who hopped around behind the bar like an organ-grinder's monkey, baring stained teeth obsequiously in his desire to please. He was nattily dressed in a white shirt with a Western string tie and blue jeans — Georgia black-tie apparel, DeMarco opined in his sour mood.

'A draft beer and a cheeseburger, please.'

'You betcha.'

While waiting for his dinner he used his cell phone to call the motel. Emma still wasn't back. He thought a moment and dialed the number of a guy he knew who worked at the IRS. The guy owed him. DeMarco cajoled, pleaded, and finally had to bribe his friend with a case of Canadian

271

beer before he agreed to go back to his office and look up the address on Hattie McCormack's tax returns. DeMarco wasn't sure a woman who made her own booze paid taxes, but it was the only way he could think of to get her address.

The bartender brought his beer. As he sipped it, he thought back on his meeting with Taylor. Taylor could have schmoozed him, been nice and friendly, and answered his questions with glib lies. Was he related to Billy? No, just an old family friend. There was no reason for Taylor to get high-handed with him. DeMarco concluded that Taylor couldn't even pretend to be humble if it was in his own best interest.

The bartender asked if DeMarco wanted a refill.

DeMarco knew no one would talk to him about Taylor, but maybe he could find out something more about Morgan or Estep.

'Sure,' DeMarco said, 'and pour one for yourself. You know what they say: you start drinking alone, you gotta go to those meetings.'

Although there was no one else in the bar, the bartender looked around, checking to make sure he wouldn't be caught nipping on the job. 'Well, maybe I'll just have a wee one to be sociable.' He poured three fingers of Jack Daniel's.

'I saw a guy today.' DeMarco said. 'Looked Indian. Had a ponytail and this scar.' DeMarco traced a scar with his finger from his left eye to his mouth. 'Got any idea who he is?'

'Why you askin'?' the bartender said, suddenly less sociable.

'He just looked familiar. The way he was built,

I wondered if he used to play ball or something.'

The bartender showed his teeth. 'Play ball, that's a good one.'

'So you know him?'

'Oh, yeah. His name's Morgan, but if he played any ball it was on a jailhouse team.'

'Jail?'

'Yeah, he did a little time. Was raised wrong, I guess you'd say.'

'Is that right,' DeMarco said.

'Don't know who his father was, but his mother was crazy as a bedbug.'

'Why do you say that?'

'She just was, livin' out there on the edge of the swamp in a shack with no 'lectricity. She'd come into town every once in a while to get supplies and she'd walk down the street mutterin' to herself, lookin' at people all odd. She was scary. She'd bring Morgan into town with her when he was young and he was always filthy. She treated him like an animal.'

'Didn't he go to school?'

'Not till his teens. One day he showed up in Folkston by himself. Someone asked him where his mother was and the only thing he'd say was that she was gone. That's all, just gone. The sheriff went out to where they lived to look for her but she'd disappeared like Morgan said. No one knows what happened to her.'

The bartender ignited a cigarette and took a sip of his bourbon. 'Anyway, the sheriff gets the reverend to take Morgan in and he makes the boy go to school to see if they can teach him to read and write. I understand he went for a while but then they sent him upstate, to a reform school. He was botherin' the girls.'

'Bothering them how?' DeMarco asked.

The bartender shrugged. 'Don't know. I was working over in Florida about that time so I wasn't here when it happened. But he musta done something more than pull their pigtails.'

DeMarco could see Morgan, hiding behind the rhododendron, spying on the girl on Taylor's porch.

'What happened after that?' DeMarco asked.

'Oh, when he gets out of jail, he's full grown and he's got that lightnin' scar on his face. And he'd been lifting them dumbbells in jail too, cuz he came back harder than an ol'-time blacksmith.'

'What's he do around here?'

The bartender finished his drink in one swallow. 'Hey, thanks for the drink, podna,' he said, 'but I'd better go see if your dinner's ready.'

DeMarco's cell phone rang while he was eating. It was his pal at the IRS and he had Hattie McCormack's address. DeMarco got directions from the bartender then called the motel one last time to see if Emma had returned. She hadn't.

★   ★   ★

DeMarco was just a block from the restaurant, driving in the direction of Hattie McCormack's farm, when he checked his rearview mirror and saw a red pickup truck tailgating him. The pickup passed, swerved in front of him, and stopped abruptly. DeMarco had to slam on his

274

brakes to avoid a collision; he stopped with his front bumper just touching the rear bumper of the pickup.

The driver's-side door of the pickup opened. It was Morgan.

Morgan walked slowly toward DeMarco's car, his dark face unreadable. DeMarco opened the door to get out of his car but before he could completely exit the Mustang, Morgan lunged forward, grabbed a handful of his shirt, and pulled him from the vehicle. Morgan then spun him around, grabbed his left wrist, and forced DeMarco's left arm up behind his back so that his hand was between his shoulder blades. The pain in DeMarco's left shoulder was instantaneous and excruciating, and Morgan had executed the move so quickly that DeMarco had had no time to react.

With his arm pinned behind his back, Morgan marched DeMarco over to the passenger-side window of the pickup. Taylor was seated in the pickup; the window was rolled down. He was dressed as he had been earlier in the day, in a plaid work shirt and jeans, except now a red baseball cap sat atop his head. His gaunt, old-time prophet's face was livid with anger.

Morgan released DeMarco when they were next to the pickup but DeMarco was furious and he spun around to confront Morgan. Before he could complete the spin, Morgan simply slammed him in the back with his palm, driving him up against the truck. My God, but the man was quick.

'What's your damn game, mister?' Taylor said

'What in the hell are you talking about?' DeMarco said.

Morgan took his hand off DeMarco's back allowing him to step away from the truck. Now he was standing slightly behind DeMarco, on his right-hand side. His breathing was normal, his face was expressionless. He was as relaxed as a man waiting for a bus.

'I called Washington, you jackass,' Taylor said. 'You're not a writer. You're a damn lawyer up there and you work for Congress. Now I want to know what the hell you're doing here and why you're asking questions about me.'

Who had he talked to, DeMarco wondered? Donnelly? Maddox? Billy's wife? It had to be Donnelly. But how much had Donnelly told him?

'What I'm doing here is confidential, Taylor. Now — '

'Goddamnit, don't you dare play games with me!' Taylor screamed. 'Morgan, make this idiot understand I'm serious.'

Morgan grabbed DeMarco's right shoulder, spun him partially around, and hit him in the solar plexus. The blow was so hard that it felt as if his belly had been driven into his backbone. DeMarco doubled over, clutched his gut, and tried to keep from puking while simultaneously trying to get his lungs to readmit air.

'You havin' a problem here, Mr Taylor?' DeMarco heard a voice say. 'This fella hit your truck?'

DeMarco looked up. Thank God. To his relief he saw a Charlton County sheriff's cruiser and a young deputy standing near the hood of Taylor's

276

pickup. The deputy could see the condition DeMarco was in: bent over, holding his stomach, his face contorted with pain.

Taylor hadn't seen the deputy drive up. Now he glanced over at him in irritation and said, 'No, he didn't hit anything. Take off, Gary. This is private.'

The deputy hesitated. He looked at DeMarco and said, 'If you say so, Mr Taylor. Just wanted to make sure everything was okay.'

Jesus Christ, thought DeMarco. *What's wrong with these people?*

'It is. Now take off,' Taylor said.

The deputy gave DeMarco another guilty glance and drove away.

DeMarco was still hunched over from Morgan's blow. He thought of coming up out of his crouch, spinning, and hitting Morgan in the balls. As if Morgan could read his mind — or the subtle change in DeMarco's position — he stepped back a pace. He was ready for DeMarco, balanced lightly on his feet, palms turned slightly forward. DeMarco knew he'd never get to Morgan in time — so he decided to threaten Taylor instead.

'Taylor,' he said, his breathing labored, 'if this son of a bitch hits me one more time he better kill me because I'll get federal marshals down here and have you both arrested.'

Taylor's response was an arrogant smile. 'That'll be the damn day,' he said, then he looked over DeMarco's shoulder and nodded to Morgan.

Morgan's right hand whipped out and

encircled DeMarco's neck from behind and his fingers dug into DeMarco's throat. DeMarco tried to pull free but Morgan just jerked on his neck, with one hand, upsetting his balance. DeMarco reached up with both hands to break Morgan's grip on his throat which gave Morgan the chance to grab his left wrist and he again pinned DeMarco's left arm behind his back. With only his right hand, DeMarco was unable to pry Morgan's fingers loose from his throat; Morgan's fingers were talons embedded into his skin.

Morgan increased the pressure on DeMarco's throat and the upward pressure on his left arm until he stopped struggling.

'Now I'm gonna find out what you're doing down here,' Taylor said. 'And if I have to have Morgan rip your arm out of the socket, by God, I will.'

Morgan released the pressure on his throat slightly so DeMarco could speak — and breathe.

'Taylor, I'm not talking to you until this bastard lets go of me,' DeMarco said, his voice strained, the pain in his shoulder joint almost unbearable. He didn't know what he was going to say if Morgan released him, but he needed to get out of this arm hold to have a chance to defend himself.

Taylor looked into DeMarco's eyes: he could see pain and anger, but not the fear he was looking for. 'I can see I'm just not gettin' through to you, boy. Morgan, just bust his goddamn arm.'

Fuck! DeMarco tried again to pry Morgan's fingers from his throat and to twist free of his

278

grip, but it was impossible. Morgan was just too strong and he could feel the soft things in his shoulder — the muscles and tendons and ligaments — start to yield and pull away from the bone.

'Max, did you have an accident? Can I help?'

Morgan reduced the pressure on DeMarco's arm and throat but continued to restrain him. DeMarco looked over to see a middle-aged woman in a Cadillac. She was speaking to Taylor while staring at DeMarco, a concerned look on her plump face.

'Goddamnit,' muttered Taylor, 'this town's gettin' more crowded than Atlanta.' To the woman he said, 'Thank you, Ellen, but everything's fine here. You just go on about your business.'

'Call the state po — ' DeMarco said. Morgan's fingers dug in again; it felt as if his trachea was being crushed.

The woman looked nervously over at Taylor. 'Are you sure everything's okay, Max? If I can help, you know I'll be glad to.'

Taylor's patience snapped. 'Goddamnit, Ellen! I said everything's all right. Now get the hell out of here!'

The woman flushed red with embarrassment. 'Sorry, Max, sorry,' she muttered and drove away so fast she burned rubber.

Taylor looked over at DeMarco then turned his head and looked up the street. There was another car coming in their direction.

'Shit,' Taylor muttered. 'Come on, Morgan,' he said, 'get in the truck.'

Morgan's grip immediately relaxed and DeMarco collapsed to his knees. As Morgan passed him he looked down at DeMarco. He said nothing and his face was expressionless, but DeMarco could read in the Indian's eyes his amusement at DeMarco's condition and his contempt for his weakness.

From the pickup window, Taylor pointed a finger down at DeMarco and his lips parted to speak, but then his hand dropped and he grunted to Morgan, 'Take off.'

As the red pickup drove away, DeMarco rose slowly and unsteadily to his feet, his breathing still labored from the damage caused by Morgan's fingers to his throat. He grimaced as he gently rotated his left arm. It was painful but fortunately his shoulder wasn't dislocated. Not by much, it wasn't.

He was lucky Morgan hadn't killed him as the good citizens of Folkston went about their business.

★ ★ ★

It took DeMarco more than an hour to find Hattie McCormack's farm and by the time he did it was dark. Partly it took so long because many of the roads weren't marked and he had to backtrack several times to pick up landmarks the bartender had given him for directions. The other reason the trip took a while was that he was being extremely careful to make sure he wasn't being followed.

He came at last to a dented mailbox that had

280

'H. McCormack' hand painted in uneven letters on the side. He drove up the single-lane dirt road and saw Emma's rental car parked in front of a small cabin.

DeMarco parked his Mustang near Emma's car and walked up and knocked on the cabin door. There were no lights on inside and no one answered his knock. He walked around and looked in all the windows, and quickly concluded the place was empty.

Emma must have gone someplace with Hattie. She said the first time she saw Hattie, Hattie was ripping a traffic ticket off the windshield of her pickup. There was no pickup near the house or a garage where one could be stored.

DeMarco looked at his watch: nine thirty p.m. He sat in his car until his back started to ache. He left the car to sit in one of the two rocking chairs on Hattie's porch but a few minutes later retreated back to the car when the mosquitoes began to make a banquet of him. He rolled up the car windows to keep the mosquitoes out but couldn't turn on the air-conditioning because he was low on gas. Within minutes the car became a sauna with bucket seats and DeMarco's back started to cramp up again. Jesus, but he was sick of this damn place.

His shoulder was also throbbing. He was shamed by how easily Morgan had manhandled him, though logic told him he had no reason to be. Morgan was just quicker and stronger than him — and less human. But he was still ashamed. Joe DeMarco, a tough kid raised on

281

the mean streets of New York, the son of Gino DeMarco, and he'd been slapped around like a ninety-pound weakling.

Which also led to the realization that there was no way that Morgan would have knocked his father around like that. Gino DeMarco would have put the barrel of his gun between Morgan's black eyes the minute the man approached him — and he'd have killed him the instant he sensed a threat.

Enough of this. He wasn't his old man. He didn't want to be and he wasn't going to be. But he had to wonder: What would he have done if he had been armed?

At ten p.m. he said to hell with it. He didn't have any idea when Emma would get back and it made no sense to sit in his car all night waiting for her. He would return to the motel, sleep a few hours, then get up at dawn and drive back out here. If Emma still hadn't shown up he'd contact the state police and get them to put out an APB on Hattie's truck. He wasn't going to bother calling the Charlton County authorities; it was obvious from what he had seen earlier that they would be no help if Taylor was involved in Emma's disappearance.

But there was someone who could help. DeMarco punched numbers into his cell phone.

'Mary Pat, it's Joe DeMarco. Is he there?'

'Joey! It's so good to hear your voice. How are you?'

DeMarco absolutely loved Mahoney's wife. If there was a kinder, more decent person on the face of this cruel planet, he didn't know who it could be. And she qualified for sainthood being married to Mahoney.

'I'm fine, Mary Pat. But I need to talk to him. It's impor — '

'Did you call that pretty young lady whose number I gave you, Joe? Bridgett, over at Senator Remmick's office?'

'Uh, I tried, Mary Pat. We didn't connect.'

'You're a terrible liar, Joseph. You'd think you'd be better considering who you work for. Wait a minute. I'll get him.'

'It's about time you called,' Mahoney grumbled. 'What's going on?'

'Emma's missing and a thug who works for Taylor beat the shit out of me.'

'You hurt bad?'

'Just my pride.'

'Pride heals.'

Not really, DeMarco thought.

'So what's happening?' Mahoney said, DeMarco's bruises already forgotten.

DeMarco told him.

'So other than findin' out that Taylor's some small-town big shot, which you pretty much knew before you went down there, you don't have squat connecting him to the assassination attempt or Donnelly or anything else.'

'I found out he's paranoid and goddamn dangerous. And I'm pretty sure he knows Donnelly. He called D.C. today to find out about me and it had to be Donnelly he talked to.'

'Yeah, but *why* would Donnelly help him? And what's Taylor's motive for tryin' to kill the President?'

283

'I don't know.'

'Shit, Joe, you gotta do better than this.'

'Right now I have to find Emma.'

'Emma can take care of herself. I'll bet you Taylor's guy couldn't beat her up.'

Now that hurt.

'She's still missing and if Taylor's involved, I'm not going to get any help from the locals finding her. I may need you to call someone down here, the governor or the attorney general.'

Mahoney didn't respond.

'And one other thing,' DeMarco said. 'If you don't hear from me tomorrow, you definitely better call someone.'

'Ah, you'll be all right. I'll talk to you tomorrow.'

Mahoney. What a peach.

★　★　★

DeMarco approached his motel room door with a feeling of relief and immediately had the unflattering self-image of a field mouse returning to its burrow after venturing out into the dark, owl-infested night. Home, sweet, home it wasn't but compared to Hattie McCormack's pitch-black, mosquito-infested tobacco patch, the Days Inn was paradise.

He opened the door, reaching for the light switch as the door was still swinging open. He remembered his finger touching the switch, thought he remembered flipping it up, but in less time than it took for electricity to become light the world disappeared in a flash of pain.

36

DeMarco didn't know where he was and for some reason his eyes wouldn't open so he could find out. He knew he was lying on his back on something hard, and the hard thing was moving and the motion was making him ill. He shook his head to clear away the cobwebs. That was a mistake. The back of his head began to throb. With his eyes still shut he reached back and touched the spot from which the pain emanated and felt a soft lump.

A voice said, 'Can't hurt too much, bucko. I sapped you damn near perfect — didn't even break the skin.' Adrenaline surged through DeMarco like an electric current and his eyes popped open in alarm. Dale Estep was smiling at him.

Estep was dressed in army camouflage fatigues and wore a shapeless hat that was also a mottled, camouflage green. His arms were moving oddly. Finally, DeMarco's brain engaged. Estep was paddling a canoe and the hard surface he was lying on was the bottom of the canoe. DeMarco's head was resting on the bow seat.

DeMarco started to sit up but Estep took the oar and poked him in the center of the chest. At that moment, DeMarco noticed the holstered pistol on Estep's right hip and a long hunting knife in a scabbard on his right calf. 'Relax, bucko,' Estep said. 'I don't want you rockin' the boat.'

DeMarco checked the luminous hands of his wrist-watch: it was one a.m. He'd been unconscious for more than an hour. He looked over the gunwale of the canoe at his surroundings: it was a moonless night but he could make out the silhouettes of a few cypress trees and hazy curtains of Spanish moss hanging from the lower branches. They were in the damn swamp!

'What the hell do you think you're doing, Estep?' DeMarco asked. He may have been scared but he was also angry. He was damn tired of getting pushed around by these hicks.

'So you do know me,' Estep said.

Fucked up again, DeMarco thought. He tried a different question. 'Where are we going?'

'Due west, bucko, right into the middle of my favorite swamp.'

'Why?'

'Well, I like the Okefen at night. Night's when things kill each other. Strong things kill weak things; fast things kill slow things. You hear things screamin' *all* the time out here at night. One more screamin' thing won't make any difference.'

'What in the hell are you talking about?' DeMarco said, fearing he already knew the answer.

'Uncle Max asked me to have a little talk with you, bucko. Said he wanted me to find out what you were up to. Thought I'd take you someplace where we could chew the fat and not be disturbed. Uncle Max said when he talked to you earlier, all sorts of people kept droppin' by.

286

No chance of that where we're going.'

Why did Estep keep calling Taylor 'Uncle Max'? Billy had called him Uncle Max too. So had Honey, the young girl he had seen at Taylor's place.

'You and Taylor are insane,' DeMarco said. 'I'm from Washington, Estep. I work for the United States government. People know I'm down here.'

'Now that's one of the things we're going to talk about: who knows you're down here and what they know.'

'Estep,' DeMarco said, 'I'm working with the FBI. If I turn up missing, you're the first guy the Bureau will come looking for.'

Estep stopped paddling and smiled at DeMarco — then he swung the oar at DeMarco's head. DeMarco was able to get his arms up in time to block the blow, but the wood cracking against his left forearm hurt like hell.

'Shit,' DeMarco said, rubbing his arm.

'It's not nice to lie to me, bucko. See, I already know you're not working with the FBI. The FBI thinks you're a looney. The only one you've been working with lately is some secretary named Banks. You and this Banks fella think me and Cousin Billy tried to kill the President.'

DeMarco now had no doubt it was Donnelly who had talked to Taylor. The little son of a bitch.

'Estep,' DeMarco said, 'if you have a brain in your head, you'll turn this canoe around and take me back to Folkston.'

Acting as if DeMarco hadn't spoken, Estep

287

said, 'You see, bucko, Uncle Max believes he knows how you tied me and him in with Billy. He heard all about you tailing Billy and listening to his phone calls. Shame on you.'

That goddamn Donnelly must have told Taylor everything DeMarco had said during their meeting with the attorney general.

'Now what Uncle Max needs to know,' Estep continued in his lazy drawl, 'are the names of everybody you've talked to about all this, what you told 'em, and what it was that made you decide to come down here to Georgia.' Estep smiled, his teeth luminous in the night. 'So we might be talkin' quite a while.'

Unless he did something, DeMarco was a dead man. This lunatic intended to take him into the swamp, torture him, and kill him.

DeMarco studied his captor. Estep was in his fifties but he was also a combat veteran and he was armed. At least he didn't look as strong as Morgan; given a chance DeMarco might be able to overpower Estep and take away his damn gun. The problem was the position he was in: flat on his back in the unstable canoe. By the time DeMarco pulled himself to a sitting position and lunged to the rear of the boat, Estep would easily be able to pull the gun and shoot him, or just do as he had done earlier and smack him with the oar.

Off the port side of the canoe something heavy slapped the water and DeMarco jerked involuntarily.

Estep laughed. 'Big gator there, bucko. Damn big. Bet that baby was ten feet long. Just et something cruisin' on the surface. Muskrat, I'll bet. Think you're faster than a muskrat, bucko?'

DeMarco didn't say anything. A moment later the boat passed through a curtain of Spanish moss. As the moss went over his head and arms, DeMarco let out an unmanly yelp. He was so jumpy he was coming out of his skin. This was not his environment.

Estep laughed and said, 'Creepy feelin' shit, ain't it? Sometimes snakes nest in that stuff.'

DeMarco realized Estep had deliberately rowed the canoe into the moss to further unsettle him, and it had worked. He had to get a grip on himself.

'Why did you try to kill the President, Estep?' DeMarco asked.

Estep smiled. 'Now that's purely insultin', sayin' something like that. Gonna make you *squeal* for that, boy.' Estep rowed a few more strokes. 'It's gettin' late, son, so let's get started. Let's start at the beginnin'. Let's start with whatever that Banks fella told you that made you go after Cousin Billy.'

What the hell did he mean when he said he had insulted him, DeMarco wondered. Estep seemed to be telling him he wasn't involved in the assassination attempt and in the same breath he was admitting that he and Billy had worked together. Were he and Billy involved in some-thing completely unrelated to the assassination? And why did he keep referring to Billy as his cousin?

'I'm waitin',' Estep said. 'And I have to tell you, I'm not a patient man.'

DeMarco tried to think. There wasn't anything he could tell Estep that the man didn't already know but he needed to tell him something just to stall for time.

DeMarco took too long to make up his mind. 'Well, I guess I just gotta get your attention, bucko,' Estep said, shaking his head as though disappointed. 'You remind me of those gooks I interrogated over in 'Nam; they never figured you were serious till you cut a chunk off 'em.'

Cut a chunk off 'em! DeMarco tried to sit up again but Estep just jabbed him hard in the chest with the oar.

'Yeah,' Estep said, his tone conversational, 'I think we've gone far enough.' He reached underneath his seat and pulled out a green plastic garbage bag. Looking DeMarco in the eyes, he took the hunting knife from the scabbard on his calf and slit the garbage bag open. The stench of rotting meat poured out. Seeing the expression of disgust on DeMarco's face, Estep laughed and said, 'Ripe, ain't it?'

Sticking the knife into the sack, Estep stabbed what looked like a leg of mutton and flung it into the water, about ten feet from the canoe. Reaching down again, he stabbed another piece of meat and tossed it in. DeMarco watched the meat sink into the black water, then turned back to look at Estep, wondering what in the hell he was doing.

Estep grinned at him. 'I want you to hop in the water, bucko.'

'What?' DeMarco said.

'I said, I want you to hop in the water. Time

290

for you to go swimmin' with my friends.'

'Fuck you,' DeMarco said.

'Thought you might say that,' Estep said. He patted the holster on his hip and said, 'Now, friend, you don't have a lot of choices here. I can shoot you a couple times, someplace that won't kill you right off, then throw you in bleedin'. Or you can get in the water on your own and hope the gators go for that ripe meat before they go for you. If you got a third choice, I don't know what it is.

'You see, bucko, the way this works is if you talk real fast, answer all my questions right away, I'll keep the gators from you by throwin' this chum in the water. They like rotten a whole lot better than fresh. Usually. Now I got a whole sack of chum here but you don't want to dally. Now hop in.'

DeMarco had read that most alligators weren't maneaters and he figured Ranger Dale knew that too. Nonetheless, there was no way in hell DeMarco was getting out of the canoe.

'Look, Estep, I'll — '

'Too late for that now, bucko,' Estep said, and he stabbed DeMarco in the calf with his knife. DeMarco screamed in pain — one more screaming thing in the night, just as Estep had said. The knife had penetrated about two inches and the wound began to bleed heavily.

'Now unless you want me to do that again, I'd suggest you jump on in like I told you. And I sure hope your blood don't attract those gators.' Estep grinned and threw another piece of rancid meat into the water.

DeMarco rose slowly to a sitting position. As he did, Estep slid the knife into its scabbard and pulled the revolver from the holster on his hip. Casually wagging the gun at DeMarco, Estep said, 'Careful now, son. Stand up real, real slow. You try tippin' the boat and I'll gut shoot you. Swear to God.'

DeMarco struggled to his knees and slowly rose to his feet. He stood with his legs apart, moving his arms slightly to maintain his balance and keep the canoe from rocking. He looked out into the swamp; he was surrounded by darkness. He couldn't see anything in the water near the canoe but he didn't know what was below the surface. Then he looked down into Estep's eyes. Hunter's eyes.

'Go on, son,' Estep said softly. 'Just hop on in. The water's warm.'

The next thing DeMarco did was not an act of bravery, but one of simple vindictiveness. Estep was going to kill him and he knew it. He was going to shoot him or knife him or let the alligators rip him apart. DeMarco decided then that he wasn't going to suffer alone. He jumped up and came down as hard as he could on the starboard gunwale of the canoe, tipping the boat over.

Estep was caught by surprise. He squeezed off a shot, but even as good as he was with a gun, he was already off balance and falling toward the water when he fired. The bullet tugged at DeMarco's shirt but missed his flesh.

As soon as DeMarco hit the water he dove and swam as fast as he could away from Estep

292

— and the garbage bag which was now spilling its rotten contents into the water. At one point something hard and scaly brushed against his leg, the one bleeding from the knife wound. DeMarco involuntarily opened his mouth to scream and his mouth immediately filled with fetid swamp water. He broke the surface, coughing. Estep heard him cough and fired a shot in his direction. The bullet slapped the water next to his head.

DeMarco sucked air into his lungs, dove, and swam, kicking with his legs, using a breaststroke. He couldn't see where he was going and was surprised when his right hand struck something hard and slippery. His left hand, then his head, struck similar objects. DeMarco realized immediately that he was tangled in the root-ball of a tree. There were at least a dozen roots, each about two inches in diameter penetrating the water and he was on the outer edge of the root-ball.

He stopped swimming, forcing himself to be calm, and grasped the roots and began to pull himself upward. He kept pulling on the partially submerged tree roots until his head was above water and he could feel the trunk of a good-sized tree. He put both arms around the slippery trunk and pulled himself up, his feet struggling for purchase on the tree roots. One shoe came off as he climbed which helped him get some traction, so he kicked off his other shoe. He kept pulling himself upward until he was finally standing on the exposed roots of the tree, holding tightly to the trunk. He swung around the tree so the trunk was between him and Estep's last position, then looked back to where he thought the overturned canoe was. He couldn't see Estep in the dark, but he could hear him. Estep was laughing.

'You got me that time, boy. I thought you was a broke dick, and you surprised me. Goes to show what can happen when a man gets overconfident. But them gators are gonna get you, bucko. They can *smell* that blood comin' from your leg. They're gonna chew your nuts right off.'

DeMarco tried to pull himself higher up the tree, but the trunk was too slippery. He didn't like standing with his feet in the water, on top of the root-ball, the blood running from his leg down into the water, but he didn't have a choice. And where he was, was a hell of a lot better than being in the water swimming.

DeMarco didn't know what he was going to do next. Estep would eventually right the canoe then all he had to do was wait until daylight to find him. He wished he could see what was near him. He could be just a few yards away from land where there might be bushes to hide in. But he wasn't willing, not yet, to jump back into the water and go swimming in the dark.

With perfect timing, Estep said, 'I'm gonna get you, son. I could survive in this swamp buck naked but you don't know what the hell to do. And when I get you, I'm gonna make you suffer like God's worst enemy.'

Sound carried oddly in the swamp. DeMarco didn't know how far he was from Estep but he doubted he was more than thirty or forty yards away. Estep then uttered a muffled curse. It sounded to DeMarco like he was struggling to flip the canoe back over. The next thing he heard was a grunt but not the kind of grunt a man makes when he's trying to move something. This sounded as if Estep had been hit in the gut and had had the wind knocked out of him.

Then he heard Estep scream.

That scream was the worst sound DeMarco had ever heard coming from another human being: the sound of unbearable pain combined with heart-stopping terror. DeMarco thought of what Estep had said about the swamp, about strong things killing weak things, fast things eating slow things. Of things screaming in the dark.

Estep screamed again, but not as loudly as the first time, then all DeMarco heard was black water churning as the alligators ripped him apart.

And then there was silence.

★   ★   ★

DeMarco stood on the root-ball for four hours, clinging to the trunk of the tree. Every time something touched him — a drop of moisture, a falling leaf, the water lapping up against his feet — he had to bite his lower lip to keep from crying out. DeMarco was a city boy and this wasn't his natural habitat. His imagination was spinning in overdrive with thoughts of water moccasins crawling down the tree trunk toward him, of poisonous insects stinging him, of leeches sucking his blood. Mostly he was worried that an alligator was going to rear up at any moment and grasp his bleeding leg in its jaws and pull him into the water.

During those four hours, when he wasn't thinking about getting bit or stung or eaten, he thought about the wound in his leg. He remembered that just before Estep stabbed him, he had stuck the knife into the rotten meat. DeMarco wondered what long-named organisms were swimming through his bloodstream toward his vital organs.

His one consolation was that the knife wound had stopped bleeding; Estep had hit muscle but no major blood vessels. The wound was throbbing and it felt like his leg was starting to swell, but at least DeMarco's blood wasn't continuing to pour into the water.

While DeMarco clung to that tree in the dark he even prayed. He had long ago stopped going to church and when asked his faith would joke that he was a retired Catholic. But now he asked for divine help. And since he had not been a steady churchgoer, and knew God knew it, he didn't ask for much. He didn't ask God to save him outright, to miraculously transport him to dry land, or to make the alligator extinct. All he asked of the Lord was to make the sun come up. He wasn't asking for much at all, DeMarco figured. Just for something He did every day of the year.

Never in his life had he wanted to see a sunrise so badly.

Dawn finally broke and in the first pink light

of morning DeMarco saw the most wondrous thing: the overturned canoe was only a few feet from the tree he was in. He reached down and pulled the sodden sock off his right foot, then carefully moved around the trunk of the tree until he was as close to the canoe as he could get. He reached out with his bare foot until he could touch the canoe, and being careful not to push it away, drew it slowly toward him with his toes.

When it was close enough, he squatted down on the root-ball and started to put his hand in the water to turn the canoe over. He hesitated, thinking about an alligator turning him into Captain Hook, then realizing he had no choice, shoved his hand beneath the water, grasped the gunwale of the canoe, and flipped it over. As he eased himself gently into the canoe, he felt safe for the first time in hours.

Now that he had a canoe, he needed a paddle. He looked around but in the dim light he couldn't see the oar that Estep had been using. It had to be floating somewhere nearby. There was no current and there had been no wind to speak of during the night. He decided to wait until it became lighter to see if he could locate the oar. It would be hard enough paddling out of the swamp with an oar; without one it would be impossible.

Half an hour later it became fully light, and twenty yards from him, caught in the roots of another tree, was the oar. Somebody up there loved a fool. Forcing himself not to think about the alligators in the water, he used his hands to paddle the canoe over to the oar and retrieved it.

He looked around for some sign of Estep but saw nothing on or in the water. Not even Estep's camouflage hat floated on the surface. DeMarco hoped the bastard was in Hell in very small pieces.

He sat in the canoe a minute, the oar across his knees, doing nothing. He had paddled a canoe before — there was a place on the Potomac where you could rent them — and was certain he could make it out of the swamp. His problem was that he didn't know which way was out.

Then he remembered that last night Estep had said they were heading due west. Due west was good. DeMarco was no Eagle Scout but he knew the sun rose in the east — the opposite of west. He pointed the canoe in that direction, squinting into the lovely bright light, and started to paddle.

⋆ ⋆ ⋆

At the best of times, DeMarco would not have described himself as a wilderness buff; his idea of 'roughing it' was a cabana on the beach with slow room service. With the dull ache persisting in his leg from the knife wound and the constant buzz of insects in his ears, he would have placed the Okefenokee right near Death Valley on his list of favorite getaways.

The wildlife was interesting though. He spotted several kingfishers and one bird he thought was a blue heron, balanced on one thin leg, looking as if it were posing for Audubon. At one point a snapping turtle appeared off his starboard side and he flicked water at it with the paddle until it dived. He wasn't being playful; he just didn't want anything nearby that might lure alligators toward the unstable canoe.

For the first half hour, he was in an open stretch of waterway surrounded by marsh grass and wildflowers. He knew from reading the tourist brochures in the motel that the grassy stuff was growing on peat — or maybe it was peat. Hell, who cared? He also knew from his motel room literature that the name Okefenokee meant 'trembling earth' because when one walked on peat — Lord knows why one would want to — it moved underfoot.

He felt relatively comfortable in the open area, but ahead of him he could see the waterway becoming a narrow lane with large trees on either side. He didn't want to enter the tree-banked passage but he needed to keep going east, and east was toward the mouth of the green funnel. Soon he was no longer able to move in a straight line as he had to keep detouring around tree trunks.

The swamp was becoming claustrophobic, with the suffocating humidity and the oppressive sensation of dense vegetation closing in on him. Blue Spanish moss hung down from the limbs of cypress trees like thick organic cobwebs, intensifying the sensation that he was being cocooned. The plants in this section of the swamp were alien in appearance and had names like purple bladderwort and climbing heath.

And mimsy were the borogroves, and the mome raths outgrabe.

The fucking place was giving him the willies and he could hear himself breathing more rapidly. He began to paddle faster, while at the same time telling himself not to panic, to quit acting like a kid afraid of the dark. *Calm down, calm down*, he told himself, muttering the words like a mantra.

He was relieved when the boat finally emerged from the tunnel of cypress trees and he entered another open area. Relief soon turned again to panic. He had been paddling almost three hours. He knew from the timing of last night's events that he should have been less than an hour from dry land. He thought he was still heading east but somehow he must have gotten off course, winding between the cypress trees. He realized later he was following the sun, and as the sun moved from east to west, it was traveling in an arc. Should've joined the Scouts.

He didn't know what he was going to do next. He was lost and getting more lost. He knew the Okefenokee Swamp covered more than six hundred square miles and he could paddle around in circles until he starved to death. Once again some deity — DeMarco was beginning to worship all of them — came to his aid.

He came out from behind a small stand of magnolia trees and saw, a hundred yards from him, a flat-bottomed boat and two kids fishing. He had never before loved the sight of children as he did at that moment.

'Hey, there!' he yelled. 'You boys!'

300

The kids looked over at DeMarco in panic. They probably weren't supposed to be fishing in the swamp.

'Yeah,' one of them said, his voice leery, probably wondering if he and his buddy could outrun DeMarco in their boat.

'Heh, heh,' DeMarco said. 'I'm a tourist. I'm lost. Which way's the highway that takes you to Folkston?'

They looked at DeMarco as though he was deranged, then one of them said, 'Thataway. About a quarter mile.' He pointed in a direction that was ninety degrees from the direction DeMarco had been heading.

When DeMarco reached the highway he held the canoe down to sink it — he didn't want somebody finding Estep's boat too soon — then walked up to the main highway. He realized he looked a sight. His clothes were wrinkled and dirty, his hair was plastered to his scalp, and his pants were torn where Estep had stabbed him. And he was barefoot.

He didn't know which direction Folkston was, so he flipped a mental coin and started walking. A car came by and he stuck out his thumb. Naturally, since he looked like a serial killer, the driver didn't stop. He thumbed at two more cars before a man driving a battered Toyota stopped for him.

As DeMarco started to get into the car he saw the driver look down suspiciously at his bare feet.

'Heh, heh,' DeMarco said, looking sheepish. 'Met myself this gal last night and she took me back to her place. She didn't tell me she was married. Lucky the only thing I lost was my shoes.'

The driver smiled broadly and said, 'Yeah, I been *there* before. Where ya headed?'

37

Emma was still missing when DeMarco returned to the motel.

He wanted to get out of Charlton County and he wanted to get out now. It wouldn't be long before Max Taylor would wonder why Dale Estep hadn't reported in, and then Taylor and his friend Morgan would come looking for DeMarco. DeMarco didn't want to be found sitting in a room with no back door. He changed clothes, thankful he'd had the foresight to bring a second pair of shoes, and threw his suitcase into the trunk of the Mustang and peeled out of the motel parking lot.

Since he knew the way this time it only took him half an hour to get to Hattie McCormack's place. Emma's car was still parked in front of Hattie's house and the house was empty. He knew he had to find Emma but driving around the county looking for her seemed futile. And he couldn't ask the Charlton County sheriff's office for help; not only were they under Taylor's control but Taylor could have them out looking for him. He'd drive to Waycross, call the Speaker again, and get state or federal authorities involved. And Mahoney had damn well better help.

DeMarco took a slip of paper from his wallet and wrote: 'Emma, I hope to hell you get this message. I almost got killed last night. I'm stopping at Jillian Mattis's house to ask her a question then I'm getting out of this county as fast as I can to get some help. Call me on my cell as soon as you read this.' He put the note under the windshield wiper of Emma's car.

Emma had to be alive, DeMarco told himself. She was too tough and too smart to kill, and he was certain she had been in situations more dangerous than this during her career. A bunch of Georgia yokels didn't stand a chance against her — at least he hoped so.

★ ★ ★

It was early evening and the light was starting to fade when DeMarco arrived at Jillian Mattis's house in Uptonville. Uptonville was on the way to Waycross and DeMarco was going to try one last time to find the links between Taylor and Donnelly and Billy Mattis. Jillian Mattis was the only hope he had left.

He knocked on the screen door but no one answered. The inner door was open and through the wire mesh of the screen he could see Jillian sitting on a sofa in a darkened living room. DeMarco let himself in and walked over to where she was seated and said, 'Mrs Mattis, I need to talk to you.'

Jillian had a glass in her hand and DeMarco could see a half-empty bottle of bourbon on the end table next to the sofa. Her fine features were distorted from alcohol and grief. Her thick, gray-streaked auburn hair was tangled and she had on the same shapeless, faded gray housedress she had worn the day DeMarco met her.

Jillian didn't acknowledge DeMarco's presence even though he was standing directly in front of her. She sipped from the whiskey glass, then reached up and absentmindedly began to twist a tendril of hair in a tight coil around her finger. DeMarco touched her shoulder gently to get her attention and said, 'I'm sorry about Billy, Mrs Mattis, but I have to talk to you.'

Without looking at him, Jillian said listlessly, 'You're that fella was here the other day. What's your name again?'

'It's Joe DeMarco, Mrs Mattis. I'm an investigator who works for Congress. I'm investigating the assassination attempt on the President, ma'am. And your son's death.'

Jillian nodded but DeMarco wasn't sure she had understood him.

She sighed and said, 'Well, you'll just have to excuse my manners, Mr DeMarco.'

'What?' DeMarco said.

'For not offering you a drink. I'm afraid I'm gonna need everything in that bottle there to see me through the night. And I really don't care who you work for; I'd just appreciate you leavin'. I don't want to talk. I want to get drunk and cry and mourn my baby.'

DeMarco nodded sympathetically but he didn't leave. He pulled a chair close to the couch and sat down facing her, his knees almost touching hers. 'I'm sorry, Mrs Mattis, but we have to talk.'

He waited for Jillian Mattis to acknowledge his

statement but she didn't. She just sat staring off into that place where her mind was, twisting a lock of hair.

'Mrs Mattis,' DeMarco said, 'I think Max Taylor was responsible for your son's death.'

Jillian Mattis made eye contact with DeMarco for the first time since he had entered the house. There was a look of shock on her face combined with numb confusion, like an accident victim moments after the crash.

'What did you say?' Jillian said.

'I said I think Taylor had your son killed, ma'am. I'm sorry to tell you this, but I think Taylor and Dale Estep — '

'Dale's a snake with feet,' Jillian said.

'Yes. And he and Taylor forced Billy to help them plan the assassination attempt on the President. Your son gave them information about the President's schedule and security arrangements. Billy also used the Secret Service's files to locate a man they could frame for the shooting.'

Jillian shook her head violently. 'You're a damn liar,' she said. 'Billy would never do something like that and you're a bastard for saying so.'

'I'm telling you the truth, Mrs Mattis,' DeMarco said softly.

He quickly told her the whole story: about the warning note, and how he and Emma had followed Billy and questioned him, and how Billy had reacted, calling Taylor and running to Estep. At first Jillian just shook her head, emphasizing her refusal to accept what DeMarco was saying, but by the time he finished she sat with her eyes closed, her head hanging, deflated by the strength of DeMarco's conviction.

'Mrs Mattis, I need you to tell me anything you know about all this. It's important; you must see that. Taylor might try to kill the President again.'

Jillian responded in a soft voice, a voice that was almost musical, like a whispered lullaby. 'He was so beautiful, my Billy. You should have seen him, mister, when he was young. Sweetest little boy God ever made. Curly blond hair, soft as a kitten's fur. And an angel's smile. Didn't have a mean streak in him.'

'I'm sure he didn't, Mrs Mattis. I know he was a fine man, a genuine hero. He didn't want to help them but Taylor and Estep made him.' DeMarco didn't know this for a fact but it was the only thing that made sense.

Jillian tried to say something but she couldn't form the words. Then her face contorted into a mask of tragedy. She opened her mouth to scream but no sound came out, and two tears spilled from her eyes leaving parallel trails through the stricken landscape of her features. To regain control, she hugged her arms to her chest and began to rock her upper body gently back and forth.

'God, how I hate him,' she said.

'Who Mrs Mattis?'

'That bastard, Max. He ruined my life, then he ruined Billy's.'

He didn't know what she was talking about.

'I've seen Billy's phone records, Mrs Mattis,' DeMarco said. 'The month before the assassination attempt he called you more than a dozen times. What did you talk about? Why did he call so much?'

Still rocking, she said, 'He was trying to get me to move up north, to Virginia, to live with him and Darcy. Said he was worried about me and wanted me to move away from here. I told him I couldn't. I told Billy I didn't want to live in a big city and be a burden to him and his wife. But Billy was just *frantic* to get me to move. That's why he called so much; he was trying to get me to change my mind. I couldn't understand why he was so insistent but now I guess I do.'

'What do you mean?'

'Max must have told Billy he'd . . . he'd hurt me if Billy didn't do what he wanted. The only way Billy would have done what you said, was if Max had threatened me or Billy's wife. Billy wouldn't have been afraid for himself. He probably thought he could protect me if I came to live with him.'

It was nice to know Billy's motive but it didn't help all that much. DeMarco still didn't understand the links between the players in this bizarre game.

'The last time I was here, I mentioned a man named Patrick Donnelly. You said you didn't know him.'

'That's right. I never heard of him. Who is he again?'

'Head of the Secret Service, Billy's boss. He's involved in all this somehow.'

She shrugged and said, 'Well I don't know him.'

308

'How did Billy get a job with the Secret Service in the first place?' DeMarco asked.

'His daddy helped him. The bastard.'

'His daddy? You mean Estep?'

'Dale? No, I don't mean Dale. I mean Max. Max is Billy's daddy, mister.'

DeMarco sat back in the chair in shock. It was hard enough to believe Taylor was Billy's father and even harder to believe he had had his own son killed, but Jillian Mattis wasn't through with her revelations.

'He's Dale's daddy too,' she said.

'What? You mean Taylor — '

'I mean Max Taylor's a damn king in these parts!' she said, her voice rising to a shriek. 'He owns everything. Everything! And if he sees something he wants, he just takes it. And you know what Max wants most? Pretty young girls, that's what.'

She didn't seem particularly drunk, but she wasn't making sense.

'Mrs Mattis, do you mean — '

'And if she's young and poor like I was, then she can't move away when Max starts sniffin' after her. And if she's got a man, God help him, Max just sends Morgan after the poor bastard.'

'Did Taylor rape you, Mrs Mattis?' DeMarco asked. 'Is that what you're saying?'

Jillian Mattis's eyes flared like a match igniting, and then just as quickly went cold again. 'I was fifteen when Max took an interest in me. He was almost forty at the time. Would you call that rape?'

'Wasn't there anyone who tried to stop him?'

Jillian Mattis shook her head at the stupidity of DeMarco's question. 'My daddy told Mr Taylor he'd sure *appreciate* it if he'd stay away from me, me bein' so young and all. And Daddy was as firm as you can be when you're talkin' to the man who owns the mill you work at. Well, Max didn't have Morgan then but he had a man named Cooper, who was just like Morgan. Cooper shot Daddy's dog to make his point.' Jillian laughed, a metallic sound devoid of humor. 'Truth is, I think Daddy was more upset about that dog than he was about me. I was sixteen when I had Billy and by the time I turned seventeen Max was tired of me. He set me up in this little house and I've been here ever since.'

Her lips twisted into a bitter smile. 'I've had a lot of truck drivers in my bed,' she said, 'men just passin' through, because no one in these parts was going to have anything to do with me. Max didn't want me anymore but he didn't want anyone else to have me either.'

DeMarco couldn't begin to imagine the emptiness of Jillian Mattis's life: a life that had effectively ended when she was fifteen years old, trapped forever in this stifling backwater, waiting tables, used and discarded by a man so powerful that other suitors were too frightened to approach her.

'Did Billy know Maxwell Taylor was his father?'

'Yeah. So did everyone else in the damn county but Billy wasn't allowed to talk about it. Max was proud of the children he'd sired, like a damn stud bull, but he didn't want anyone having legal claim to him. He let Billy call him Uncle Max, but that's as far as he'd go toward acknowledging his son.'

'Was Dale Estep's mother taken against her will also?'

'I don't know. Max was young when Dale was born; he wasn't rich and powerful then. But I do know that Dale turned out just like his daddy. He was bad enough as a boy, but when he came back from that war he was crazy — and meaner than a copperhead. Dale's the heir to Max Taylor's throne.'

DeMarco didn't bother to tell her that the only thing Dale Estep would inherit was a swampy half acre of hell. 'Have there been other women, Mrs Mattis? I mean young girls like you were at the time?'

'Will you quit callin' me Mrs Mattis!' she said. 'There ain't no Mr Mattis. My name's Jillian.'

'What about other women, Jillian?'

'You've met Max. What do you think?'

She still hadn't answered his question. 'I saw a young girl at Taylor's house the other day,' DeMarco said. 'He called her Honey. Do you have any idea who she is?'

'Max calls us all Honey. But yeah, I know that poor simple child. Her name's Cissy Parks. Max will *burn* for what he's doing to that girl.'

'And for what he did to you, Jillian.'

'No, you don't understand. Cissy's his own daughter.'

'Ah, Christ,' DeMarco said, his stomach tightening in a spasm of revulsion.

'Max took a shine to Cissy's mamma fifteen,

311

sixteen years ago, and got her pregnant. When Cissy gets to the same age, he goes after her. Even Max has never stooped this low before. The older he gets, the crazier he gets. Crazy and evil. And like I said, the child's simple. I doubt she even knows what's happening to her.'

This was something DeMarco could use. Taylor was committing statutory rape and incest. Maybe he could get somebody that wasn't local to investigate the matter. If Jillian would come forward, and if there were other women like her, they could put the bastard away until he was dead.

DeMarco realized he had gotten sidetracked by the news that Taylor was Billy's father. 'Jillian, you said Taylor arranged Billy's job with the Secret Service. How did he do that?'

'When Billy got out of the army he got it into his head that he wanted to join the FBI. He also wanted to get away from here. Well, I'd never asked Max for any favors before but I went to see him about Billy. I asked him, him being so rich, if there was anything he could do to help Billy get a job with the FBI.'

She glanced over at a photograph of Billy on the television set. He was wearing an army uniform, his chest decorated with rows of medals, and he looked about twelve years old. DeMarco was again struck by the handsome purity of Billy Mattis — Lancelot in olive drab. He should never have been dragged into this sordid mess.

'Max said he didn't know anybody in the FBI but he knew a fella in the Secret Service. He told

Billy to send in an application and a couple weeks later he had a job. I don't know who Max talked to.'

DeMarco did, but he still didn't understand why Taylor had a special relationship with Donnelly.

DeMarco looked at his watch. He needed to get going; the longer he stayed, the greater the chance that Max Taylor or his pet police force would find him. But there was something else he had to know.

'I can't believe nobody's ever tried to stop him, Jillian. I can't accept that the people here just allow him to drag a young girl to his bed like he's some kind of feudal lord.'

Jillian looked at DeMarco in disgust. 'You don't get it. I didn't say nobody ever tried to stop him. My daddy did, and he got a dead dog for his trouble and the message that it coulda been him. Another fella, fella named John Chism, he tried to get the state attorney's office interested. They sent this lawyer down from the capital. Well, Max paid off the lawyer and after the lawyer left, Morgan beat John so bad it put him in a wheelchair. Handsome man, he was. Drools down his chin now while he sits in that chair.

''Nother time,' she continued, 'a young man named Tom Hendricks shot at Max with a pistol 'cause Max was sniffin' around Tommy's wife. They'd only been married a year, them kids, neither of 'em over seventeen.'

'What happened to Tommy Hendricks, Jillian?'

'Max's sheriff arrested him and Max's judge

tried him, and Tommy was sentenced to twenty-five years in prison for attempted murder. He's been in prison now for, let's see, twelve years. His wife divorced him and moved away after Max finished with her. Are you starting to get the idea now, mister?'

DeMarco nodded. One last question and he was gone.

'Jillian, you know Taylor as well as anybody. Do you have any idea why he'd want to assassinate the President?'

She shrugged. 'Coulda been anything.'

'What do you mean?'

'Max's folks were so poor he didn't own shoes until he was five or six, and people here treated his family like the white trash they were. But Max had pride. He hated everybody in this county by the time he left to join the army. Well, when he came back from Texas, or wherever he was, he had money. A lotta money. He started buyin' things, and gettin' richer and richer, but he didn't so much want to be rich as he wanted to get back at everybody for the way they treated him when he was young.

'He wanted to make everybody bow and scrape and kiss his ass. He wanted to control everything, and eventually he did. When you get that kind of power over people, mister, and everything you want gets done your way, well after a while you start thinking it's your God-given right to have it *all* your way. If somebody around here does something that makes Max mad, he fires them or has his police arrest them, and if that don't work, there's Morgan.

'Anyway, I can see the President doin' something, God knows what, that riles Max. Maybe he raised taxes or said something in a speech. Hell, who knows? And Max, he's so crazy with power and pride that he just gets it into his head to kill him. He thinks he's, he's . . . oh shit, what's the word?'

'Invincible,' DeMarco said.

'Yeah, that's it. He thinks nothing can get to him. He's the King of Charlton County.'

DeMarco thought about what Jillian had said, but it didn't feel right. As arrogant as Taylor was, he still couldn't imagine him trying to kill the President because he'd simply raised taxes or caused a problem with one of Taylor's investments. There had to be something more.

They sat quietly in the darkened living room for a few minutes, Jillian slowly sipping whiskey, her finger again twisting the lock of hair. DeMarco was trying to think of something to say, some comfort to give her before he left, when she said, 'Do you think you can get Max for what he did to my Billy?'

'Yes, Jillian,' he said, 'I'm going to get him.'

'Well if you don't, I'm gonna. I'm gonna get a shotgun and blow his damn head off.'

'Now that's a real nasty thing to say, Honey. Ain't it, Morgan?'

DeMarco closed his eyes momentarily, hoping he was dreaming, then looked over to see Taylor and Morgan standing in Jillian Mattis's doorway.

38

Jillian jumped up from the couch spilling the whiskey glass from her lap. 'Oh my God, Lord Jesus,' she said when she saw the two men. Morgan was standing in the doorway behind Taylor, his body blocking out the weak light remaining in the evening sky. He didn't say anything and his dark face was as wooden as always, but his presence permeated the room like the smell of rotting flesh.

'Honey, you know nothing happens around here without me knowin' about it,' Taylor said to Jillian. 'When Morgan said this fella's car was parked here at your place . . . well, Honey, I just can't tell you how disappointed I was.'

Jillian stood there, too frightened to answer, both hands pressed against her lips as though trying to push back the words Taylor had heard.

Pointing a finger at DeMarco, he said, 'And you. What happened to Dale?'

'I don't know anyone named Dale,' DeMarco said.

'I'm so damn sick of you lyin' to me, mister,' Taylor said. 'I'm gonna find out everything you know, and after I find out, you just might disappear.'

DeMarco sat back in the chair and crossed his legs in an attempt to appear relaxed. 'After your boy roughed me up, Taylor,' he said, 'I made some calls. The governor knows I'm here and so does the federal marshals' office in Savannah. If something happens to me they'll be coming after you.'

Taylor grinned and said, 'I think you're bullshittin', mister. Not that it matters though because I think you're gonna have an unfortunate accident — with a whole buncha witnesses to say exactly how accidental it was. I'll betcha I can arrange that. What do you wanna bet? But we're gettin' ahead of ourselves here. The first thing we have to do is see what Honey told you.'

'I didn't tell him anything, Max,' Jillian said. 'I swear.'

DeMarco could see that her whole body was trembling, she was so frightened of Taylor.

'Honey,' Taylor said, 'this man's havin' a bad influence on you. You should know better than to lie to me. It angers me somethin' fierce.'

'Please, Max . . . ' Jillian said.

Taylor walked over to Jillian and took her chin gently in his hand and raised her face so he could look into her eyes. Speaking slowly and softly, as if he was trying to reason with a naughty child, he said, 'Honey, I'm so upset with you right now I'm thinkin' of giving you to Morgan.'

'Oh, God no, Max. I promise — '

'Yeah,' Taylor said, 'I didn't think you'd like that, Honey. You're gettin' a bit long in the tooth but Morgan don't care. Morgan don't care if a woman's young or old, fat or skinny. Hell, he don't care if you're bald and toothless, as long as you're female. It's all the same to ol' Morgan.'

DeMarco looked over at Morgan. His face was

as impassive as ever but there was a sick, wet gleam in his black eyes.

DeMarco stood up. 'Leave the woman alone, Taylor,' he said. 'I'll tell you what we talked about. You don't have to take it out on her.'

Still looking into Jillian's terrified eyes, Taylor said, 'Morgan, I wanna talk to Honey here without this jackass interruptin'. Give him a little love tap, will ya, so I don't have to listen to him until I'm ready.'

Fuck! DeMarco turned toward Morgan but the man moved so fast he was a blur in the half-light of the darkened room. As Morgan's right fist moved toward his head, DeMarco raised his arms and partially blocked the blow, but partially wasn't good enough. He didn't actually feel the impact of Morgan's fist; the universe just swallowed him whole.

★   ★   ★

DeMarco came to in the small barn behind Jillian Mattis's house. The only light in the building came from a Coleman lantern hanging from a support post. He could see two stalls where horses could be kept in the winter, and on the wall near the double doors was a collection of bridles and a worn saddle. Tools — a rake, two shovels, and a rusty pitchfork — hung on hooks near the door. The walls of the building leaned drastically and there were large gaps between the warped wooden siding, which allowed in the night air and the too-sweet smell of some native plant.

318

DeMarco was lying facedown on a straw-covered dirt floor and around his neck was a metal collar welded to a heavy chain. The chain was maybe eight feet in length and was attached to a metal stake driven deep into the earthen floor.

Morgan was in the barn, standing, leaning casually with his shoulder resting on the wall that contained the double doors. A baseball cap shaded his eyes. Sitting on the floor a few feet from him was Jillian Mattis. One of her eyes was swollen and her lower lip was cut and bleeding. The collar of her dress was torn, exposing one pale shoulder, and two raw-looking, red circular marks were visible on the bare skin of her collarbone. The marks looked like burns made with a cigarette. She appeared to be in shock, her eyes wide open but seeing nothing. She was hiding in a locked closet within her mind.

DeMarco tried to get up — actually all he did was move his head — and a white-hot lance of pain pierced his skull. He cried out and immediately collapsed back into the dirt and straw. Morgan had broken something with his 'love tap.' DeMarco didn't know the medical term for his condition — he was suffering from a concussion or skull fracture, or a combination of the two — but whatever the exact nomenclature, it was serious. It felt as if his head was being squeezed in a vise.

He must have passed out again briefly because the next time he opened his eyes, Morgan was squatting on his haunches near him. Morgan's face was a dark blur to DeMarco, the pain in his head almost blinding him. Taylor's man sat there quietly watching DeMarco for a while, his black eyes unblinking and unfeeling. Suddenly he reached out and pulled DeMarco violently to a sitting position and propped him up against the nearest wall. The rough movement made him nauseous and the pain was a jackhammer trying to crack through the thin bone of his skull.

Morgan stood, looked down at DeMarco, and nodded in satisfaction for some reason. He walked back to where Jillian Mattis was sitting, grabbed her under one arm, and dragged her over to where DeMarco was propped against the wall, stopping about two feet from him. He checked to make sure DeMarco was conscious and watching, making eye contact briefly. Morgan's eyes had the luster of Lucifer's wings.

Morgan pulled Jillian Mattis up until she was on her knees, took hold of her hair with one large hand, and unzipped his pants with his other hand. DeMarco attempted to speak, to make some sort of protest, but his mouth was so dry he couldn't force the words from his throat. He knew he had to do something to help her. He couldn't just sit there, no matter what condition he was in, and watch this. Ignoring the pain in his head he struggled to get to his feet — to do what, he didn't know — but before he was halfway up Morgan's right leg whipped out and the point of his cowboy boot caught DeMarco square on the chin. He fell onto his side, vomited into the dirt, and passed out.

DeMarco was unconscious for only two or three minutes. When he regained consciousness he could hear Jillian gagging, then heard a grunt of release from Morgan. He looked up at the two of them and immediately closed his eyes in shame. He didn't know what he could have done differently, but he knew his presence had added to Jillian's degradation.

Morgan threw Jillian roughly to one side and rearranged his clothes. She stayed where she had landed, facedown in the straw, sobbing quietly. Morgan studied her briefly, his face an obsidian mask devoid of emotion.

Morgan looked down at DeMarco, then began to search the floor of the barn with his eyes. Seeing what he wanted, he walked over and picked up something lying in the straw. He walked slowly back to where DeMarco was lying and reached down and grabbed the chain where it connected to the collar around DeMarco's neck. With one hand, he once again jerked DeMarco into a sitting position and braced DeMarco's back against the wall of the barn.

Morgan squatted down in front of DeMarco. In his right hand was the object he'd picked up from the floor of the barn: a small stick, two feet long, no more than half an inch in diameter. He sat there for a few seconds on his haunches, studying DeMarco, then he began to tap the stick against his left palm.

Morgan suddenly flicked his right hand toward DeMarco's face and the stick hit DeMarco's forehead in the exact spot where Morgan's fist had hit him earlier. It wasn't a hard blow but DeMarco cried out in agony. Morgan didn't do anything more for several seconds except study DeMarco patiently, like a sadistic child trying to decide which wing to pull off a moth.

Again his hand flicked out, and again the stick hit the bruised area on DeMarco's left temple. DeMarco tried to block the blow with his hands but his reactions were ridiculously slow, and Morgan just swatted his hands aside. Morgan then began tapping the stick against the side of DeMarco's head with the unrelenting regularity of a metronome, one light blow every three or four seconds. Tap. Tap. Tap. While he hit him he gripped DeMarco's wrists in one of his strong hands to keep DeMarco from defending himself.

Through a blanket of pain DeMarco could hear a sound he didn't recognize at first, then he realized he was the one making the sound. When he was very young, maybe seven or eight, he saw a puppy run over by a car. The animal's hindquarters had been crushed, and as the puppy dragged itself along the pavement, trying to crawl away from its own death, it made a sound just like the one DeMarco was making now.

'Damn it all, Morgan, what the hell are you doing!' DeMarco heard Maxwell Taylor say. Morgan stopped tapping the stick against DeMarco's head and stood up and Taylor took Morgan's place, squatting in front of DeMarco.

'For Christ's sake, Morgan, I told you to just give this fool a little tap. Look at him! You damn near caved in the side of his head. The bastard's no good to me in this condition.'

Taylor studied DeMarco a few more minutes

then said, 'Honey, go on up to the house and bring back a pitcher of water and a bottle of aspirin. Go on now, get up. You're not hurt that bad.'

Jillian got slowly to her feet and started walking toward her house in a halting, stiff-legged gait.

'You make it quick now, Honey, ya hear,' Taylor called after her. 'If I have to send Morgan to fetch you, you'll regret it.'

Pulling a handkerchief from his pocket, Taylor carefully wiped off DeMarco's face. 'I'm going to let you sleep through the night, son, and hope like hell you don't go into a coma. Now you might be wondering why I'm bein' so solicitous of your health. Well the fact of the matter is, I have to ask you a few questions and I'm afraid I ask questions kinda hard. In your present state you just might die on me before I get all the answers I need.'

Jillian reappeared with water and aspirin. Taylor gently braced DeMarco's head with his hand, placed two aspirin in his mouth, then held the water pitcher up to his parched lips so DeMarco could drink. When he choked getting down the aspirin, Taylor made little clicks of concern with his tongue.

Standing, Taylor stretched and yawned. 'Morgan,' he said, 'I don't feel like driving back to Folkston tonight. I'm goin' on up to the house and watch a little TV, then I'm gonna sleep in Honey's bed. You and the woman stay out here in the barn and keep an eye on this fool. Hopefully he'll be well enough to talk come first light.'

DeMarco tried to stay awake after Taylor left but he couldn't keep his eyes open. He was disgusted at his own helplessness. He wanted to curl up into a fetal position and sleep until he was healed — and so he did.

He woke once during the night, his head still throbbing, but not with its earlier intensity. He moved his hand in the dark until he could feel the water pitcher and aspirin bottle, and took some more aspirin.

He thought he woke one other time before dawn, although he couldn't be sure it wasn't a dream. He had a vague memory of a shape moving rhythmically in one of the stalls, and he heard the grunting of a beast and the moaning of a smaller creature in pain.

39

DeMarco could see the first streaks of pink-and-gray daylight through the gaps in the walls of the barn. His head still ached but the blinding pain of the previous night was gone. He took three more aspirin and finished the rest of the water in the pitcher.

As his eyes adjusted to the morning light he saw Morgan sitting with his back against the barn's double doors, his muscular body motionless, his arms folded across his chest like an executioner in repose. His eyes were open, looking at DeMarco. DeMarco looked away from Morgan and searched for Jillian Mattis. She was lying a few feet from Morgan, on her side, in one of the horse stalls. She seemed to be sleeping; he hoped she was sleeping.

DeMarco had to relieve himself. He had endured enough indignities in the last few hours and didn't need to add to his humiliation by pissing his pants. He stood up slowly, bracing one hand against the wall of the barn for balance. He waited for the pain to bring him back to his knees but it looked as though the aspirin and a few hours of rest had improved his condition. He walked to the end of the chain, as far as he could from the spot where he had been lying, and urinated. When he finished he walked slowly back, sat back down on the floor, and leaned against the wall.

For the first time he took stock of his situation. The chain attached to the collar on his neck was rusty but the links were solid and heavy. It would take a welder's torch to separate them. He could feel a padlock securing the metal collar to his neck but he couldn't see it. He checked his pockets with as little motion as possible but he had nothing to use for a lock pick. His cell phone was gone and the only exit he could see were the doors Morgan was leaning against.

Morgan was the real problem. Even if he could find some way to free himself of the chain and collar, he knew he wouldn't be able to get by the man unless he could find a weapon, something to club the son of a bitch to death.

DeMarco looked over at Morgan again and Morgan stared back. The white scar against his dark face was vivid, a neon brand in the morning light. DeMarco inhaled sharply when he noticed Morgan had a small stick in his hand, probably the same one he'd used last night. He was tapping the stick idly against his thigh as he looked back at DeMarco, and DeMarco knew that in his current condition if Morgan decided to torment him again the only thing he could do was endure it. To his relief, Morgan remained seated then closed his eyes and appeared to fall into a light sleep.

DeMarco thought briefly of Mahoney. It was almost thirty-six hours since DeMarco had called him from Hattie McCormack's farm. He wondered if Mahoney had become sufficiently worried to call out the cavalry. He doubted it, but even if he had, where would they look?

An hour later the sun was completely above the horizon. DeMarco saw Jillian Mattis stir, then sit up looking confused. Her torn dress exposed her left shoulder and yesterday's burn marks were vivid red blotches against her skin. The left side of her face was swollen, giving her head a lopsided look, and the bruise on her cheek was an ugly yellow-purple circle. The auburn hair DeMarco had admired the day before was plastered against her skull and hung in dirty, clotted strands to her shoulders. Every inch of her exposed skin was smudged and raw from being dragged about the straw-covered floor. DeMarco had calculated Jillian's age at forty-eight, but one night with Morgan had aged her twenty years.

Jillian came fully awake at that moment, and when she did, and when she saw Morgan, she suddenly remembered where she was. She immediately scooted backward into the horse stall until her back was pressed against the wall of the barn. She hugged her knees to her chest and began to make a soft keening sound, like an animal with its paw caught in a trap. DeMarco flashed back to the dream he had during the night, of the beast in the dark pinning its prey to the ground.

The barn doors opened. Taylor looked well rested and as if he'd just stepped from the shower. Drops of moisture twinkled in his white hair. He came over to where DeMarco was sitting, looked down at him, and smiled.

The smile had all the warmth of the silk lining in a casket.

'So how we doin' on this fine mornin', Mr DeMarco?' Taylor asked. When DeMarco didn't respond, he said, 'Well you look pretty good to me, son. A little sleep does a body wonders, don't it?'

Jerking his thumb in the direction of Jillian, he said, 'I'm afraid Honey over there looks like hell. It's going to take more than a good night's sleep to make her right again. Do you see the pain you've caused that poor woman?'

DeMarco knew Taylor was right. Jillian Mattis had suffered beyond description because of his visit. He had fucked up everything. Emma was missing, possibly dead, and Jillian Mattis had been tortured and raped. As for himself, he was chained to a stake in the ground and would be dead before long. And all for nothing.

Squatting down in front of him, Taylor took hold of the rusty chain affixed to the collar on DeMarco's neck. 'You know what this is?' he said. 'It's a bit of *penal* history. When I lived in Texas I got this chain and collar from an ol' boy that worked at the Huntsville penitentiary in the fifties. They knew how to treat criminals back in those days. And today, this chain's *still* serving a useful purpose, half a century later. Not too many things around you can say that about, is there?'

Taylor gave the chain a small tug, jerking DeMarco's head toward him. 'But I'm gettin' off the point. We have a little chore in front of us this morning, son. What we have to do is find out what you know and who else knows it. Honey told me what she knew last night and as you can see, the tellin' just plumb wore her out.'

'Why did your sons try to assassinate the President?' DeMarco asked. His voice was weak and his words were slurred, reminding him of the way people talked after having a stroke.

Taylor shook his head and chuckled; his dark eyes shined with mirth. 'Assassinate the President! I'm a God fearin' American, mister, not some pinko nut!'

'I know Estep and Billy were involved,' DeMarco persisted.

Taylor started to answer, then wagged a finger playfully at DeMarco. 'Shame on you. You're tryin' to distract me from my chores.'

Rising to his feet, Taylor rubbed his hands together, brushing off the rust that had transferred from the chain to his palms. 'Now, sir,' he said, 'what I need to know is real simple.' He held up a finger for each question. 'One, I need to know all the people you've told this silly story of yours to besides Honey over there, and two, I need to know what evidence you have to back it up. Now did you get those two questions? Well if you didn't, that's okay, because I'm gonna repeat 'em several times before we're through.'

DeMarco knew Taylor was going to kill him whether he answered his questions or not. He had to invent something to tell Taylor, something Taylor would have to verify and keep DeMarco alive while he did. He had to come up with something to gain some time. He had to.

Taylor winked and said, 'I can see the wheels

329

of your small Yankee brain a spinnin', son. It's no use. I'm gonna get to the truth.'

Taylor walked over to a milking stool a few feet from DeMarco and sat down. He paused as if to collect his thoughts, like a professor about to address a class of one.

'You probably thought you were in pain last night, didn't you,' Taylor said, 'with your noggin hurtin' like it was? That wasn't real pain, son. The human body, you see, is like an onion — and as you peel away each layer the pain intensifies, until you reach the core, that sweet place in the very middle where every nerve ending is particularly fine and tender. That headache you had last night was the outer layer of the onion, son. Just the outer layer.'

DeMarco realized he had been holding his breath the entire time Taylor had been speaking, and as he exhaled he could smell the sour odor of his own fear. He knew it wouldn't take long for Taylor to reduce him to the groveling, semi-deranged condition of Jillian Mattis. Morgan had proven that last night with his tapping stick.

Sounding more in control than he felt, DeMarco said, 'Taylor, I'll be happy to tell you what I know. And when I do, you'll realize that killing me is the biggest mistake you could make.'

Taylor shook his head as though DeMarco was a poor pupil who continuously gave the wrong answer. Even a class of one could have a dunce.

'Now, son, I doubt that,' Taylor said. 'See I can always tell the truth when I hear it and I didn't

330

hear it in your voice just now. I didn't see it in your eyes. I'm tellin' you, boy, I'm a human lie detector!'

Taylor smiled at DeMarco, his eyes radiating arrogance. 'You gotta know a man as rich as I am, a man with powerful friends in powerful places, can avoid trouble if he's properly forewarned. In fact, I sometimes think there isn't anything I can't do when I set my mind to it.'

Taylor, DeMarco realized, was a psychotic control freak, a man who had bought an entire county so he could completely dominate his environment. He didn't want the material trappings of wealth; he wanted the unbridled power that wealth could bring when totally focused on a small, rural backwater. He controlled the lives of a few thousand humble people and was able to indulge his every desire. He was the King of Charlton County, as Jillian had said, and he thought he'd live forever.

DeMarco still didn't know why Taylor had tried to assassinate the President but suspected it was just as Jillian had said. The President had somehow annoyed Taylor or endangered his lifestyle, and Taylor in turn had set about to remove the source of his annoyance, totally undaunted by the power of the highest office in the land.

Taylor stood up from the milk stool and winked at DeMarco. 'Well, sir,' he said, 'it's time to begin. It's time to remove a layer from that onion.' Turning to Morgan he said, 'Morgan, go on out to the truck, will ya? There's a pair of bolt cutters in the toolbox; bring 'em here. Ah hell,

331

bring the whole damn box.'

Jesus help me, DeMarco prayed.

Morgan left the barn without a word. Did that bastard ever talk, DeMarco wondered. He had yet to hear him speak.

'Now tell me, son. Did anyone else come down here with you?' Taylor asked.

At that moment, DeMarco saw Jillian Mattis emerge from the horse stall where she had been sitting while Taylor had been lecturing DeMarco. She looked at the double doors that Morgan had exited through, then over at Taylor and DeMarco. Taylor's back was to her.

'Listen to me, Taylor,' DeMarco said. He needed to keep Taylor focused on him.

Jillian scampered quickly to the wall near the barn doors, her bare feet silent on the packed earth, and grabbed the rusty pitchfork that was hanging there. She glanced again at the double doors, and then with a shriek that contained the grief of every mother who had ever lost a son, she charged across the barn at Taylor. Holding the pitchfork with both hands high over her head she looked like Neptune's daughter, straw clinging to her hair like dry seaweed, the pitchfork a trident of revenge.

Taylor swung around at the noise but before he could evade her, Jillian plunged the four sharp tines of the pitchfork into his chest with all the strength she had. For a minute they were frozen in place — Jillian pressing the pitchfork into Taylor's chest, her face primitive in its rage, and Taylor, wide-eyed in pain and disbelief, amazed that this pitiful creature who he had abused for so long had finally struck back.

Taylor fell at last, onto his back, only a few feet from DeMarco. As he fell the pitchfork was wrenched from Jillian's hands and remained upright in Taylor's chest. He turned his head toward DeMarco, his mouth open in a silent scream, his eyes no longer arrogant but begging for help. DeMarco didn't move; he just sat there listening to the air bubbling out of Taylor's wound, making a liquid, gurgling sound. And then the sound stopped and Taylor was still.

DeMarco looked up at Jillian Mattis, still standing where she had been when she thrust the pitchfork into Taylor. There was a small smile on her face.

'Jillian,' DeMarco hissed, 'run and bar the doors!' Morgan had to have heard her shriek.

Jillian just stood there, the small smile still on her lips, but now with an aspect of lunacy.

'Jillian!' DeMarco hissed again, but the woman didn't move.

DeMarco looked at Taylor's body. He was wearing a light jacket to ward off the morning chill. The jacket gaped open and DeMarco could see he had a pistol in a holster on his hip. Thank God for the Second Amendment. DeMarco tried to reach the gun, but the chain around his neck wasn't long enough by a foot. He grasped the sleeve of Taylor's jacket, which he could reach, and began pulling, trying to draw the body closer to him. The gun was still inches from DeMarco's straining fingers when Morgan burst through the barn doors.

DeMarco tugged fiercely on Taylor's arm. He

maneuvered Taylor close enough to finally touch the gun with his fingertips but before he could clear the gun from its holster, Morgan saw what he was doing. Morgan moved across the barn in three quick strides and pulled the body out of DeMarco's reach with a single strong yank on one of Taylor's legs. DeMarco still couldn't believe how incredibly fast the man was.

Morgan looked down at Taylor, and an expression — the only one DeMarco had ever seen him display — flitted across his face. The skin rippled as though something live was moving beneath it and for just an instant the rage and grief he felt at losing the only person who had ever cared for him was there for DeMarco to see. Then as quickly as it had come the expression was gone, and Morgan's features froze back into an inhuman, merciless mask.

Morgan turned toward Jillian Mattis. He realized she was the one who had stabbed Taylor with the pitchfork. She looked back at him defiantly. Her whole life had been one of degradation and shame, but for one instant she was the picture of pride — ragged and ravaged, but finally triumphant.

Morgan walked slowly toward her. She didn't back up as he approached but held her ground, continuing to stare straight into Morgan's lifeless eyes. He stopped in front of her, then reached out slowly, almost tenderly, and grasped Jillian's face between his two huge hands. He paused a moment, nodded to her as though acknowledging her courage, then twisted his hands viciously. The snap of her neck breaking sounded like a rifle shot in the empty barn.

Jillian's death shocked DeMarco into motion. He lunged to the end of the chain and the metal collar dug painfully into his neck as he tried to reach Taylor's body to get the gun. It was hopeless; the body was at least two feet beyond his grasp. Morgan watched in amusement as he lay on the floor, stretched out, straining against the chain.

DeMarco quickly got to his feet and backed away. As he moved backward, his eyes frantically scanned the area around him looking for a weapon. He already knew, though, that within the radius of the chain there was nothing but straw. With his back against the wall of the barn and his fists clenched, he waited for Morgan to come and kill him.

Morgan's lips twitched in an approximation of a smile and he began walking toward DeMarco.

At that moment, Emma walked into the barn. She quickly took in the carnage around her: Taylor prone, the pitchfork standing upright in his chest; Jillian Mattis, bruised from abuse, her neck and limbs twisted at awkward angles. Finally, she saw DeMarco, chained like an animal, his back against the wall waiting for Morgan.

Emma pulled a pistol from a shoulder holster, aimed it at Morgan, and said, 'Stop right there.'

Morgan glanced over his shoulder at Emma, then he surprised both her and DeMarco. Instead of stopping as any sane person would have, he ignored Emma and the gun in her hand and lunged at DeMarco, grabbing him and spinning him around so that DeMarco's body provided a shield. Then he put his hands on the sides of DeMarco's face.

'Drop the gun,' Morgan said to Emma, 'or I'll break his neck.'

It was the first time DeMarco had heard Morgan speak; his voice was a deep baritone, raw and raspy from disuse.

Emma smiled in response to Morgan's threat. DeMarco had never seen anything so wonderfully evil as that smile.

'Drop the gun,' Morgan repeated, 'or I'll do him like I did the bitch.'

'Don't do it, Emma,' DeMarco yelled. 'He's strong and he's faster than hell. He'll kill both of us.'

DeMarco was afraid to move knowing Morgan could snap his neck just as easily as he had Jillian's. He also knew what Morgan was thinking: with his speed, he could kill DeMarco, distract Emma by flinging DeMarco's body in her direction, then charge her, hoping Emma would miss with the pistol. With his speed he might be able to pull it off and unless Emma was using hollow-points, it would take more than one bullet to stop him.

Looking into Morgan's eyes, Emma said to DeMarco, 'Do you trust me, Joe?' and she began to lower the gun down to her side.

'No!' DeMarco screamed.

As Emma lowered her gun, Morgan's hands began to increase the pressure on DeMarco's face. Morgan was going to snap his neck in the next second.

'Don't drop the gun, Emma!' DeMarco shouted.

'Of course not,' Emma said, then she raised the pistol in one fluid motion and fired.

Nothing happened for an instant, then DeMarco felt the hands on his face relax and something warm and wet spill onto the back of his neck. Then Morgan fell, his weight driving DeMarco to the ground, his body landing heavily on top of him.

Emma quickly moved to DeMarco and pulled Morgan off him with a grunt. 'Christ, he's heavy,' she said.

DeMarco sat up and wiped the blood off his neck, then turned to look at Morgan. Emma's bullet had gone through his right eye.

'Jesus Christ!' DeMarco said. 'You could have killed me.'

'Don't be silly. It was an easy shot.'

'Easy, my ass! You could have blown my head off!'

'You're welcome, Joe,' Emma said.

DeMarco took a deep breath. 'Yeah, sorry. Thanks. Now please get this fucking collar off me.'

40

'Where the hell have you been?' DeMarco asked.

Emma ignored the question as she applied Taylor's combination bolt cutter/torture tool to the padlock on the metal collar. She grunted as the lock snapped, then replied, 'Jail.'

'Motherfucker,' DeMarco said as he tore the collar off his neck and flung it violently against the wall of the barn. 'How did you end up in jail?'

'Well — '

'Never mind; save it for later. Right now we need to get out of this county.'

DeMarco looked around the barn. The pitchfork was still sticking straight up from Taylor's body. His eyes were wide open, still astounded, staring into the maw of hell. Morgan lay like a toppled statue, a bloody socket where his eye had been. And Jillian Mattis — neck bent, limbs akimbo — made him think of a soiled, broken doll discarded by a careless child.

DeMarco refused to think about his role in Jillian's death. There would be time for guilt later.

'If we call the sheriff and report this,' DeMarco said, 'we'll never leave here.'

'After what happened to me, I'm inclined to agree with you,' Emma said, apparently referring to her recent incarceration.

Fleeing the scene of a homicide was not a decision DeMarco made lightly but he didn't see

338

that they had a choice. He discussed it with Emma and they decided to make it look as though Taylor and Morgan had killed each other. DeMarco pulled the pitchfork from Taylor's chest, wiped Jillian's prints off it, and placed the fork in Morgan's hand. Emma took Taylor's pistol and fired a bullet into a mound of hay, then put the weapon into Taylor's hand. Although the type of bullets they used was different, Taylor's gun was a .38 caliber, the same as Emma's.

DeMarco figured the local cops would walk into the barn and correctly conclude that Morgan — psychotic son of a bitch that they all knew he was — had raped Jillian Mattis and broken her neck. Based on the way DeMarco and Emma had arranged the evidence, they would then incorrectly reason that honorable Maxwell Taylor, county patriarch and exlover of Jillian Mattis, had tried to avenge her. Alas, Morgan stabbed Taylor with the pitchfork, and Taylor, with his dying breath, plugged Morgan through the head.

If the sheriff's office had the services of a top-of-the-line forensic specialist, their simple subterfuge would be uncovered but DeMarco reasoned they had two things in their favor: Taylor's lack of popularity and the absence of an immediate successor to his throne. People in the county would be relieved to have the despot gone and without someone in authority pressing the local cops to solve the case, DeMarco was betting they'd do a slipshod investigation. At least he hoped so.

His biggest concern was that someone other than Morgan had seen his car parked in front of Jillian Mattis's house, but there was nothing he could do about that. No plan is without flaws; there are no perfect crimes.

Emma and DeMarco rechecked their work in the barn then DeMarco entered Jillian's house and wiped it free of his fingerprints. At the last minute he remembered he had forgotten to wipe his prints off the chain and collar and went back into the barn to finish the job. Exiting the barn, he looked one last time at Jillian Mattis and silently begged her to forgive him.

As they walked toward their cars, DeMarco stumbled and almost fell.

'You okay, Joe?' Emma asked.

'Yeah.'

'You're limping.'

DeMarco nodded. The knife wound in his leg where Estep had stabbed him was throbbing. He wanted to pull up his pant leg and look at it but he was afraid of what he might see.

Emma took hold of DeMarco's arm to stop him and turned him so she could look at his face. She studied DeMarco's pupils as though she knew what she was doing and touched the lump on his head tenderly. 'We better get you to a hospital and have that hard head of yours checked out,' Emma said.

'No, we need to get out of here before the sheriff drives by and sees our cars. I'll find a hospital in Waycross if I need one.'

'Okay, but try not to pass out at the wheel on the way there,' Emma said.

There was no chance of that happening, DeMarco thought. He feared if he slept the dead would invade his dreams: a grinning Dale Estep draped in blue Spanish moss; Taylor smiling arrogantly as air hissed from the holes in his chest; and Morgan, Cyclops's twin, blood running hot out of his eye socket. But he knew it wasn't the ghouls that would keep him awake in nights to come, it was the innocents: Billy Mattis and his mother. He'd hear the snap of Jillian's neck breaking until the end of time.

★ ★ ★

The doctor at the clinic in Waycross asked what had caused the wound in DeMarco's leg. DeMarco told him he had cut it on a piece of sheet metal. 'Doin' some work around the house, ya know? Threw all the junk in a heap, then tripped over it.'

The doctor took in the condition of DeMarco's clothes and the bruise on his head, then gave him a look to let him know he wasn't stupid. Fortunately — at least from DeMarco's perspective — two ambulances bearing the carnage of a three-car pileup distracted the doctor and without further comment he gave DeMarco a tetanus shot and a prescription for painkillers.

He found Emma in the emergency room waiting area reading a magazine on gardening. He couldn't imagine her being interested in an activity where one couldn't occasionally draw blood.

They drove their two rental cars to a drugstore

for DeMarco to fill his prescription, then to a grocery store for DeMarco to buy a six-pack, contrary to his physician's orders. DeMarco took his beer to Emma's car, popped the top on a can, and drank. It was an ordinary Bud in a can — and he had never tasted anything so wonderful.

'Better watch the booze,' Emma said, 'with that head injury and those pills.'

DeMarco ignored her advice, took another swallow, and told her about his night in the Okefenokee Swamp. 'What a way to go' was Emma's only comment about Estep's demise.

'Now you wanna tell me why you were loafing in a jail cell while Estep and Taylor were trying to kill me?' DeMarco said.

Emma took the can of beer from DeMarco's hand, took a sip, and handed the can back to him. 'I went to see Hattie again, as you know. Among other things, Hattie told me how Taylor was using the Okefenokee Swamp as his own private reserve: poaching alligators for hides, harvesting the lumber, taking rich men gator hunting. That kind of thing.'

'Interesting, but what does this have to do with you getting arrested?'

'I'm getting to that.'

DeMarco nodded. 'Was Estep helping Taylor?'

'Of course,' Emma said.

DeMarco lit a cigarette and swallowed more beer. It felt so good to be alive and able to enjoy all his life-shortening vices. 'How in the hell did Taylor and Estep get away with it?' he asked.

'For one thing, everyone who worked at the

342

swamp really worked for Taylor and — '

'I knew those rangers weren't spotted-owl fans.'

' — and Hattie thought he was bribing someone back in Washington responsible for the swamp. Maybe at the Department of Interior. And the other thing he'd do is change the swamp boundary.'

'Change the boundary?'

'Think about it. He owns all the land adjacent to the swamp. How the hell can anybody tell where public land stops and private land begins? Estep would change the boundary markers every few years, bring in crews to harvest timber or whatever, then move the boundary back and start someplace else. According to Hattie, Taylor's been doing this for almost thirty years. He had himself this huge, tax-free estate, and would use state and federal money to replant trees or clean up whatever mess he made. Hell of a scheme.'

DeMarco shook his head in amazement.

'But that's not how he made his *real* money,' Emma said. 'According to Hattie, that damn swamp gets thousands of tourists every year.'

'More like four hundred thousand. I saw that in one of the brochures at the motel.'

'Well aren't you smart. Anyway, Taylor was raking it in big-time from the tourists. He was not only getting a legitimate share of the tourist trade from his businesses — he owned the motel where we stayed in Folkston, by the way — but he was also taking a slice of the gate at the swamp.'

'A slice of the gate?'

'Yeah. Ten folks pay the entrance fee; they

343

pocket the cash from three and the books show only seven went in. Same thing with the crap they sell in the souvenir shops.'

'Can we prove any of this?'

'I would imagine. An accountant could take a look at the books and put some of it together, and I'm sure if squeezed properly, Estep's ranger friends will talk.'

'So how did you end up in jail?'

'Hattie wanted to show me where the boundary used to be and a couple of places where Taylor currently had crews working on federal land. We drove down to a fence line that said 'No Trespassing,' and she convinced me to crawl under it with her. Like an idiot, I did. Couple of lumberjacks see us, tell us to get lost, and Hattie gives 'em a ration of shit. The lumberjacks call the sheriff's office, and Hattie gives the deputies a ration of shit. So they threw us in jail.'

'Why the hell didn't you call me so I could make bail for you?'

'They wouldn't let me. Prisoners' rights are not a hot social issue down here. They decided to teach Hattie a lesson for shooting her mouth off — she'd given 'em problems before — so they just let us sit in jail for two days. I'm lucky I didn't end up on a chain gang. Anyway, when I got out I saw your note and went right to Jillian Mattis's place.'

DeMarco shared with Emma what he learned from Jillian Mattis, the sad tale of the Honeys.

'My God what a horror story,' Emma said.

Indeed it was. Taylor had dominated the

county since the late 1960s. He used the money he had mysteriously obtained in 1964 to gain economic control, then used his influence to take over the legal system and the media. And with power came the abuse of power — a symbiotic relationship DeMarco had seen all too often in the nation's capital. Taylor indulged his lust for teenage flesh and when any whim was opposed, and he couldn't get what he wanted by threats or economic pressure, he turned to Morgan or Estep for assistance.

DeMarco also thought about Taylor's lifelong plunder of the Okefenokee Swamp, and reflected that the money was probably not as important to Taylor as his ability to treat the swamp as his personal property. It was *his* swamp, not the government's. It was the moat surrounding King Max's castle.

'We still have three mysteries, Emma,' DeMarco said.

'Only three?'

'One, where did Taylor and Donnelly get their money in 1964? Two, what's the damn connection between Taylor and Donnelly? And three, why in the hell did Taylor try to kill the President?'

'He didn't try to kill the President, Joe. Haven't you figured that out by now?'

'What?' DeMarco said.

'You remember Hattie saying something about a man questioning her, a honey-tongued, handsome son of a bitch?'

DeMarco sat a moment.

'Oh, shit,' he whispered.

41

DeMarco's head hurt — in fact, his whole body ached — and the whiny, high-pitched voice of Philip Montgomery's daughter was an auger piercing his skull. He was sitting with the woman in the kitchen of the late author's Atlanta estate. Outside the kitchen window was a rose garden where a sprinkler ran, creating small rainbows as the late-afternoon sun struck water-drop prisms.

DeMarco had called Mahoney before flying to Atlanta. He left a brief message, telling his boss that Emma was fine, that Taylor was no longer a problem, and that he had a few things sorted out. He was glad that Mahoney hadn't been available to speak to him; he'd let the callous bastard stew over the meaning of the message until he got back to Washington.

Janice Montgomery was a disgruntled woman in her thirties dressed in baggy jeans and a black T-shirt. Her short hair was mousy brown, her doughy face devoid of makeup, and her thin lips locked in a line of perpetual disapproval. One of the many things she disapproved of was her father.

'He was a complete bastard,' she said. 'He cheated on my mother the whole time they were married. And when my brother committed suicide, the son of a bitch gave the most moving eulogy the world has ever heard. I still see it quoted in magazines. The truth was that he hardly knew his own son and had no idea how depressed Peter always was, living in the great man's shadow, unable to measure up to his famous name. Philip Montgomery spent more time with his agent than he did with his family.'

This bitter tirade had started when DeMarco told Janice Montgomery how sorry he was about her father's death and how much he had admired his work. Though he was just trying to be cordial and establish a relationship with Montgomery's dour daughter, he truly had admired the man's writing.

Montgomery wrote fiction, but fiction based on harsh reality and obtained by completely immersing himself in his subject. He lived in India for almost a year before writing a nine-hundred-page novel similar to James Clavell's *Shogun*. He put into historical and social perspective the Indian class system and described a poverty so great that it was beyond the average American's comprehension.

For another book he spent four months in Cambodia with a group of peasants who had survived the killing fields and were so emotionally traumatized that they were like zombies. From this experience came *Silent Cries*, a novel that even the most apathetic could not read without becoming enraged at the plight of a people the world had abandoned. For a short time after the book was published, charitable donations to that part of the world tripled.

He loved to travel — maybe to get away from his family — and almost everything he had written had been set in a foreign country, lending his novels an exotic touch that would have been absent in more familiar surroundings. Montgomery's apparent passion for the down-trodden, as much as his literary brilliance, made him one of the most popular writers in the twenty-first century — but clearly his daughter was not a fan.

DeMarco had arrived at Montgomery's house half an hour earlier and introduced himself as a member of Congress doing a follow-up investigation on the assassination attempt. He had said that as a matter of routine 'we' needed to know what Montgomery was working on before his death. His daughter's first reaction had been to slam the door in his face.

'I'm getting every dime of his royalties from this point on and if I can sell the rights to whatever he was writing before his death, I'll do that too. I'm not showing you shit.'

DeMarco explained he had no intention of removing anything from the premises, or even of making copies, but she was obdurate. He tried to be gentle with her, thinking she might still be mourning her father, but when he couldn't move her he abandoned the compassionate approach.

Threatening to serve her with a warrant, then bagging everything in the house as evidence — virtually guaranteeing she wouldn't be able to sell the rights to Montgomery's last work for a decade — finally got him through the front door and into the kitchen.

He didn't know what to say about her feelings toward her father, and frankly with his head hurting the way it did, he didn't really care.

'I'm sorry to hear he was so, uh, callous toward you, Ms Montgomery, but do you think I could — '

'And this crap with the President,' she said. 'Their famous reunions. Maybe when Daddy's drinking buddy became President, maybe then they cleaned up their act. But when they were younger they'd tell their wives they were going hunting and spend a week getting shit faced, trying to fuck anything in a skirt. They were just a couple of gray-haired frat rats, both of them. They made me sick.'

'Uh, Ms Montgomery,' DeMarco said, 'do you think I could see your father's papers now, whatever you have that might give us some idea what he was doing the last few months?' He was so tired of listening to this woman complain.

'There aren't any papers, not in the sense you probably mean. There's no rough draft or plot outline. When my father was researching his books, he'd jot down facts in a spiral-bound notebook like the type kids use for school. He had an incredible memory. After he did his research he'd take long walks for a few weeks, mixing everything he'd learned around in his head. Then he'd sit down and just write his books. He was a prick but he was also a genius.'

'Could I see the notebooks, please?' DeMarco asked.

'Yeah,' she said, heaving herself up from the kitchen chair with a groan you'd expect from a woman twice her age.

As they were walking toward her father's study, DeMarco asked, 'Do you have any idea

349

what he was working on?'

'Me?' she said, followed by a bitter laugh. 'My father didn't confide in me. He just used me like he did my mother. I was his free cook and cleaning lady when he was in town.'

So why the hell did you live with him? DeMarco wanted to ask but didn't.

'All I know,' she continued, 'is that he was working on something here in the States, which surprised me. He was packing for a trip back in April and when I asked where he was going, he said 'Out in me own backyard, m'dear' in this idiotic W. C. Fields accent. He said there was a 'delicious pile of shit' just a few miles away, but he didn't explain what he was talking about. It never occurred to him to involve me in his work; I was just his daughter.'

They entered Philip Montgomery's den and DeMarco took a moment to take in the photos and plaques of a life of incredible achievement. While he was looking at a picture of Montgomery accepting the Pulitzer Prize, his daughter walked over to an antique rolltop desk and picked up a spiral-bound notebook with a red cover and handed it to him.

'I have to change the water in the garden,' she said. 'I'll be back in a moment. I'm going to take you at your word that you won't take anything.'

DeMarco nodded, no longer listening to her. Montgomery had doodled on the cover of the red notebook, mostly spirals and stars and geometric figures, but in one corner was a crude picture of a castle and a man wearing a crown. DeMarco took a seat at Montgomery's desk and flipped open the notebook. The only thing written on the first page, in capital letters and underlined, was THE SWAMP KING. DeMarco was surprised to see only about twenty pages filled with writing, mostly cryptic phrases, names, and numbers. There were no long narrative sections. There was enough there, however, to confirm what Emma had suspected.

Philip Montgomery had somehow gotten wind of the situation in Charlton County. DeMarco could imagine someone living there writing a letter to the author, telling him he didn't have to go to Asia to uncover a tale of despotism, tragedy, and repression. He could also imagine Montgomery, probably not initially believing it but intrigued by the possibility, eventually journeying to southeast Georgia to investigate. DeMarco couldn't tell from Montgomery's notes if he was going to write a nonfiction account or a novel as he usually did. He was guessing a novel. With a novel Montgomery would reach a broader audience and with his talent, truth couched as fiction would be even more effective than straightforward reporting.

If Montgomery's book had been published, Taylor would have been finished.

DeMarco also concluded that Montgomery was a better researcher than he was. His notes contained things DeMarco had not even suspected. Some of the figures suggested that Montgomery had been able to calculate how much Taylor was making off Charlton County taxes and his illegal use of the Okefenokee Swamp. Compared to most white-collar crimes and Wall Street scandals, the numbers weren't mind-boggling — only a few hundred thousand a year — but then Max Taylor didn't need much to maintain his rural lifestyle. There was one note in the book that didn't make sense to DeMarco. The notation read: $$$$ — Guerrero — Dallas?????

Simple phrases told everything else: 'feudal lord,' 'pocket police force,' 'strong-arm enforcement.' One line simply said, 'the Honeys, God help 'em.' Estep's name was mentioned, so was Hattie McCormack's and a dozen others DeMarco didn't recognize. Unfortunately there was no mention of Patrick Donnelly, nor was there any indication that Montgomery had figured out the original source of Taylor's income.

It had never occurred to DeMarco — or anyone else — that the real target of the assassination attempt had been Philip Montgomery. The sequence of shots at Chattooga River had made it seem clear that the intended victim was the President because after killing Montgomery with the first shot, Estep had taken two more shots in an evident attempt to kill the President.

That the President had been wounded, DeMarco now realized, was deliberate. Estep was too good with a rifle to have missed the President three times. The final shot Estep had taken — the shot that passed between Mattis's legs and hit the agent lying on the President — was the kind of sick, playful thing Estep would do. Estep had shown DeMarco just how playful he could be that night in the swamp.

Taylor must have learned — just the way he had learned about DeMarco — that Montgomery was researching a book about Charlton County and his despotic hold over the region. Taylor would have been afraid of Montgomery. State and federal authorities might ignore complaints from poor county residents, and if they did investigate they could be bribed or frightened, but no one was going to bribe or frighten Philip Montgomery, best-selling author and confidant to the President.

Taylor also knew that if he simply killed Montgomery, the police might wonder if the motive wasn't related to whatever Montgomery was writing about. So Taylor did something incredibly audacious: he made it appear as though Montgomery was killed accidentally during an attempt to assassinate the President. Taylor's great advantage in pulling off the murder, in addition to Estep's marksmanship, was Billy Mattis. Taylor could manipulate Billy into giving him the President's security arrange-ments, and Billy was someone who could also find a perfect fall guy to blame for the shooting. DeMarco wondered now how much of Taylor's hold over Billy was the threat to harm his mother and how much was because Taylor was his father.

Now DeMarco knew everything except for the link to Patrick Donnelly.

42

'You were right,' DeMarco said into the phone. 'Montgomery knew everything Taylor was up to. The man was a helluva researcher.'

'But nothing in his notes connected Taylor to Donnelly?' Emma said.

'No. There was one weird ... Hang on a second, Em. Emma, they're calling for my row to board. I gotta go.'

'You started to say something,' Emma said. 'About something weird.'

'Oh, yeah,' DeMarco said. 'There was a notation in the notebook that didn't seem to fit. There were a buncha dollar signs, followed by the name Guerrero, followed by Dallas, then a buncha question marks. Anyway, I couldn't figure out how it tied to what Taylor was doing. Emma, I gotta go. I don't want to miss this flight.'

'Dallas?' Emma said. There was a pause then she said, 'Oh, Christ!'

'What?' DeMarco said, irritated. Goddamnit, if he missed this flight there wasn't another one to D.C. for three hours.

'Joe, when did Taylor and Donnelly get rich?'

'Early '64. What's that have to do with — '

'And what happened the year before? November of 1963, specifically?'

DeMarco thought for a second, then said, 'Oh, come on, Emma. Kennedy? You've got to be kidding.'

'Change your reservation, Joe. Neil and I will meet you in Dallas.'

43

Mahoney had a migraine. The curtains were drawn and the lights were out in his office. There was a light on in the hallway outside his office and it provided enough illumination for DeMarco to see Mahoney's silhouette but not the expression on his face. He didn't have to see the expression to know his boss was unhappy.

'So they never were after the President?' the Speaker said.

'No,' DeMarco said.

'But you have no more proof that they killed Montgomery than you did when you were convinced they were trying to kill the President?'

'No, sir,' DeMarco said. 'But it all fits — and I found a hell of a motive.'

'Humph,' Mahoney said.

'And everyone involved is dead?' Mahoney said. 'Estep, Mattis, Taylor, all of 'em?'

And Harold Edwards and John Palmeri and Morgan and Jillian Mattis. A lot of people had died and DeMarco had killed two of them.

'Yeah,' DeMarco said. 'All except Donnelly and I don't think — '

'And the link between Taylor and Donnelly, you can't prove that either?'

'No way,' DeMarco said. 'Just two reports related to a forty-year-old accident.'

'But if Donnelly and Taylor really did what you think, coverin' that thing up . . . My God.'

356

'We don't have any proof. All we've got is the timing and Emma's gut feeling.'

'And Montgomery's.'

DeMarco shook his head. 'Texas is a dead end, boss.'

'Damn it all,' Mahoney said. He put down the ice bag he'd been holding to his forehead and his hand reached out from the shadows and grasped the bottle on his desk. It never occurred to him that bourbon might contribute to his headaches; if it did occur to him, he would drink anyway.

'I feel bad about Mattis,' DeMarco said as Mahoney poured his drink. 'He was a victim in this whole thing from the beginning.'

'Fuck him,' Mahoney said, his voice rumbling. 'His job was to protect the President and he didn't do it.'

Sitting in the dark as Mahoney was, DeMarco felt as if he was talking to a bear in its cave. A wounded bear.

'But the President was never the target,' DeMarco argued. 'And he was afraid for his mother. If you'd seen this guy Morgan you would have understood why.'

'Fuck him anyway,' Mahoney said.

Mahoney sat there glumly for a moment then said, 'Do you know why I wanted to get him, Joe? Donnelly, I mean.'

DeMarco shrugged. 'I assumed he had something on you.'

'Nah. You remember Marge Carter, what happened to her five years ago.'

'Yeah,' DeMarco said.

Margaret Carter had been a Republican

357

representative from Mississippi. Even though she'd been a member of the opposition Mahoney had liked her and found it possible to work with her. Five years ago an article, complete with grainy, long-range photos, had appeared in a tabloid. The photos showed Carter, who was married, in a compromising position with her lover — a gentleman of color. She lost her seat in the House and her marriage. And her husband, who was by all reports a complete bastard, gained custody of their two children.

'Those photos in that scandal rag were taken by agents working for Donnelly. I know that for a fact. He was pissed at Marge because she cut some of his budget in committee. That little bastard ruined a woman because he was mad about a budget mark, and he used his agency to do it.'

And all this time DeMarco had thought the Speaker's animus against Donnelly had been personal. The man continued to surprise him.

'We can still go to the media with this,' DeMarco said. 'I've got more than enough to feed *60 Minutes*, and by the time they're done the FBI would be forced to investigate Donnelly.'

DeMarco saw Mahoney shake his head.

'Going public now would be bad for the country,' Mahoney said.

'What are you talking about?'

'You go to *60 Minutes* with this and Mike Wallace or Morley, one of those guys, they'd make Donnelly look guilty as hell but — '

'He is guilty. Maybe he wasn't directly involved in the assassination attempt but he did everything he could to obstruct the investigation.'

'I know, but there isn't enough to send him to jail, so after *60 Minutes* gets done with him Congress'd be forced to hold a buncha damn hearings. We'd be holdin' fuckin' hearings for the next two years. And the Secret Service and the FBI and Homeland Security, they'd all get black eyes. They'd — '

'They deserve black eyes.'

'No they don't, Joe. Not the career civil servants, not the agents, not the men and women who really do the work. Clucks like Donnelly and Simon Wall and Kevin Collier, they deserve it but the agents don't.'

Mahoney, champion of the little guy. DeMarco could not believe him sometimes.

'Yeah,' Mahoney said, 'if all this went public, this whole incredible fuckup — Secret Service agents helpin' assassins, Donnelly trying to cover it up, the FBI pinning it on the wrong guy ... I mean ... Hell, Joe, Donnelly would lose his job, sure, but then we'd waste more time running the Secret Service up the flagpole than it would ever be worth. Nah, no media. If I can't put Donnelly in jail then I just want his ass fired. So that's what I'm gonna tell the President to do.'

'You think he will?'

'Oh, yeah. I'll explain it to him. I'll talk slow. And anyway, the President won't want this to go public either.'

'Why the hell not? They killed his best friend.'

Trying to follow the workings of John Mahoney's mind was like driving a winding road at night with the headlights off.

'Joe, think about it,' Mahoney said. 'That lad in the White House has gotten a lotta mileage outta this thing. For a guy who dodged the draft, getting shot the way he did is as good as a combat wound. Hell, the man's still wearing a damn sling and his doctor told me all he needs now is a bandage! No, the President doesn't want it known he wasn't the intended victim. He's up twenty points in the polls.'

Mahoney rubbed his hands together — a fat white-haired spider spinning its web.

'Yeah, the President will fire Donnelly and that's when his troubles are really gonna start.'

'Oh?'

'Without his position to hide behind, without access to the government's lawyers, Lil' Pat's gonna start havin' all kinds of legal problems. Old ladies are gonna slip on his sidewalk. He's gonna rear-end a family with spinal cords as brittle as eggshells. Ex-agents are gonna sue him for discrimination and sexual harassment and any other damn thing I can think of. The mother-fucker's gonna spend the rest of his life in a courtroom and every damn dime he has to his name.'

John Mahoney was not a man you wanted for an enemy.

'But none of that will be as bad for him as getting fired. Without his job, that little fuck is nothing. His job defines him; it's his whole life. That's why he's never retired, no matter how much money he has. He loves walking around with his agents, meeting with the President, having the local cops kiss his ass whenever he comes to their town. And since 9/11, he's had a new lease on life, investigating every poor bastard in the country with an Arabic name. Yeah, if he loses his job he'll be just another short old guy waitin' in line at the pharmacy window.

'Who knows,' Mahoney said, ever the optimist, 'maybe he'll commit suicide.'

Mahoney turned on the light on his desk. He looked terrible. He looked his age.

'So you go see him today, Joe. Tell him everything you've got on him. Embellish as much as you want. Just make sure he understands he's in shit up to his eyeballs.'

'Maybe he'll resign after I talk to him.'

'No, he won't do that. But after you soften him up, when he gets the call from the President, he'll go without a fuss.'

'You're sure about that?'

'He's a weak man, Joe. He proved that in Texas in '63. And his actions before and after the assassination attempt prove it. You lay it out for him and he'll stew on it — and when he gets the call, he'll go.'

Mahoney opened a drawer in his desk and rooted around inside it with a thick hand.

'Damn, I'm outta cigars. No wonder my head hurts the way it does.'

44

DeMarco sat with Emma in the bar of the Georgetown Four Seasons, sipping a cobalt-blue martini. They were there because Emma liked the piano player, a man she claimed sounded like Tony Bennett, though DeMarco had never heard him sing.

'Are you sure you want to be here for this meeting, Emma?' DeMarco said. 'If this guy finds out who you are, he could turn your life upside down.'

'Let him,' Emma said. 'I have nothing to hide.' Then she said something that made DeMarco choke on his drink: 'My life's an open book.'

Donnelly arrived at that moment accompanied by four of his agents, all strapping six-footers who towered over their boss. Donnelly, DeMarco realized, loved to travel with a contingent of bodyguards as if he was an ancient rock star and needed his guards to beat back the autograph seekers.

Donnelly saw Emma and DeMarco and pointed at their table for his agents' benefit. The agents glared at them, then spread out, taking up positions around the room. They stood out like cactus plants in a rain forest, holding no drinks, grim expressions on their faces, the ever present earpieces in their ears.

Donnelly walked over to DeMarco, his face a

thundercloud. 'Who's this?' he said, pointing at Emma.

'She's — '

'I'm Emma,' Emma said, smiling brightly. 'Now sit down, you little shit.'

'Lady, I don't know who the hell you think you are but I run the Secret Service. I can — '

'Pardon me,' Emma said. She stood and walked over to the piano player, chatted with him briefly, then put a large bill into his tip bowl. Donnelly, confused and not knowing what else to do, took a seat. As Emma walked back toward their table, the pianist began to play 'As Time Goes By.'

'I love that song,' Emma said, resuming her seat. 'Now let's talk about you, little man.'

'I want to see some ID from you, you bitch,' Donnelly said. 'Right — '

'In 1963,' Emma said, 'you were twenty-five years old and working at the Secret Service's Los Angeles field office. On November 23rd of that year you were sent to Dallas to help investigate the Kennedy assassination. You didn't fly — I've heard you don't like to fly — and you drove from LA to Dallas in an agency car.'

'So what?' Donnelly said. He was still angry but there was a tone of uncertainty in his voice that hadn't been there a moment ago.

'Your car broke down in Odessa and you called the Texas highway patrol and told them to send a car to get you. The highway patrolman who gave you a lift to Dallas was a young man named Maxwell Taylor.'

Donnelly inhaled sharply. He started to say

something but Emma kept going.

'On I-20, thirty miles east of Abilene, a hundred and sixty miles from Dallas, you and Patrolman Maxwell Taylor came upon a one-car accident. A car driven by one Ivan Antonio Guerrero had overturned. The front of the car was badly damaged, a dead deer was found on the side of the road, and Mr Guerrero was dead. Do you have any recollection of this event, Mr Donnelly?'

'What the hell does this — '

'You and Maxwell Taylor became suddenly and mysteriously rich in the winter of 1964. Taylor quit his job with the highway patrol three weeks after you two good Samaritans happened upon that accident.'

'I inherited — ' Donnelly said.

'Ivan Antonio Guerrero was a Cuban national,' Emma said, 'and there is no documented explanation for why he was in Texas in November of 1963. But I have to wonder, Mr Donnelly, what would the Warren Commission have concluded had they known that in Mr Guerrero's car was four million dollars in cash?'

'Four million?' Donnelly said. 'What in the hell are you talking about?' Donnelly was trying to act as if he was completely lost by Emma's narrative but he was too nervous to bring off the lie.

'That's right. Four million. You were financially reborn in 1964, Mr Donnelly. You paid taxes on two million dollars that year and claimed you'd inherited the money. I guess you felt the need to come up with a cover story to

364

explain your newfound wealth. Coincidently, Maxwell Taylor started to buy acres of real estate at the same time you supposedly inherited, but unlike you he gave no accounting for the source of his capital. So I did the math, Mr Donnelly. I multiplied your two million dollar bogus inheritance by two and deduced that the amount of money you found in Guerrero's car was four million, assuming you and Taylor split it down the middle.'

Fat Neil had previously been unable to find any connection between Taylor and Donnelly, but he had discovered that Taylor had been a highway patrolman in Texas in 1963. It occurred to Emma, when she heard about the strange notation in Montgomery's notebook, that a Secret Service agent assigned to the Los Angeles field office in 1963 just might have been sent to Dallas after Kennedy's assassination to assist with the investigation.

Emma, Neil, and DeMarco had spent four days in Texas looking through boxes and boxes of old records. They'd pushed and prodded and bribed and lied to people to get access to those records. And they finally found what they were looking for: a documented link between Taylor and Donnelly. On November 23, 1963, Texas highway patrolman Maxwell Taylor gave young Secret Service Agent Patrick Donnelly a ride from Odessa to Dallas. This simple fact would never have surfaced had Taylor not reported Guerrero's accident. Why he'd reported the accident was not clear.

There was no mention of Patrick Donnelly in

Montgomery's notes, but Emma assumed that Montgomery had tried to determine the source of Taylor's wealth and had traced Taylor's career back to Texas in 1963. He would have learned either from the same records that Emma and Neil had found or from other sources, such as acquaintances of Taylor's during his time in Texas, that Taylor quit his job with the state patrol three weeks after coming upon a car accident involving a Cuban national. If Montgomery found the same report, the one that mentioned that a Secret Service agent was traveling with Taylor when they found Guerrero's body, he would have made the same assumption that Emma did: that the Secret Service agent was in Texas at that time because of the Kennedy assassination.

That Guerrero had cash on him, and that Taylor and Donnelly, two young men who had been poor all their lives, had decided on the spot, as they stood over a bloody corpse on a bleak Texas highway, to split the money and tell nobody, was pure speculation. But it made sense to Emma as it had made sense to Philip Montgomery.

'Who was Ivan Guerrero,' Emma said to Donnelly, 'this Cuban national with a load of money in his car? A second gunman fleeing with the money he'd been paid? Or maybe he was just a bagman, and the money in the car was for Oswald and whoever helped him. Or maybe he wasn't even connected to Kennedy.'

'Oswald acted alone,' Donnelly muttered — but by now all the belligerence had leaked out of him like air escaping a punctured tire.

'Well I guess we'll never really know, Mr Donnelly. Thanks to your greed.'

'I'm leaving,' Donnelly said. 'This is all nonsense and you can't prove a damn thing you've said.' To DeMarco that statement sounded more like a question, and he noticed Donnelly had made no effort to rise from his chair.

'I *can* prove you had a large amount of unexplained income in 1964, Mr Donnelly,' Emma said.

'I inherited that money, goddamnit.'

'From who, Mr Donnelly? Never mind, we'll let the FBI ask you that question.'

'The FBI isn't going to ask me shit,' Donnelly said. 'I run the — '

'But the most important thing I can prove, based on a report filed in Texas in 1963, is that you and Max Taylor knew each other.' Emma leaned across the small table until her face was almost touching Donnelly's. 'That I can prove, you little bastard.'

'We met once. It doesn't mean a — '

'You assigned Mattis to the President's security detail when Taylor ordered you to,' Emma said. 'You may not have known that he planned to kill the President but after the assassination attempt you did everything you possibly could to hinder the investigation. And why? Because Taylor has been holding over your head — over the head of the director of the Secret Service — what you and he did in November of 1963. The last thing in the world

367

you ever wanted discovered was your connection to Maxwell Taylor.'

'You can't prove any of this,' Donnelly said again, maybe for the third time.

And he was right. They couldn't. There was no record of any communications between Taylor and Donnelly; both men were too careful for this. There was no way they could prove Donnelly and Taylor had found a large amount of cash in Guerrero's car. They couldn't even use the IRS to squeeze Donnelly; he'd paid his taxes regardless of the source of the money. But none of that mattered.

'Proof is for judges, Mr Donnelly,' Emma said, 'but journalists don't require proof to make your life a living hell. We have a string of coincidence and strong circumstantial evidence that will be more than enough for Stone Phillips to stand up on *Dateline* and make you look like an accomplice to robbery, murder, and conspiracy while saying with every other breath that you're not an official suspect. And the FBI will be forced to dig harder. Who knows what they might find at Taylor's house linking the two of you. And your friends in Congress, not that you have any, will invite you to televised hearings. You're going to have to explain why you lied about giving lie detector tests to Secret Service agents and why you didn't investigate the link between Dale Estep and Billy Mattis. You'll be asked repeatedly, and for the rest of your life, about your ties to a madman in Georgia and your role in the attempt to murder the man you were sworn to protect.'

Mahoney had told DeMarco not to tell Donnelly that Montgomery was the real target of the assassination. It's one thing to conspire to kill an author; it's a whole other thing to conspire to kill a President.

Donnelly's face had turned ashen. DeMarco was guessing that he was probably a heartbeat away from a stroke.

'No,' Donnelly said. He rose from his chair on shaky legs. 'No,' he said again, louder this time. 'You can't get to me. Nobody can get to me. I run the Secret Service.'

He left the table walking slowly at first, trying to maintain his dignity, but before long he was walking as fast as his short legs could move. His bodyguards had to run to catch up to him.

'Well that was fun,' Emma said.

45

The Speaker was torturing a pigeon.

He and DeMarco were sitting next to each other on the steps of the Capitol looking west toward the Washington Monument. The sky was cloudless and there was just enough wind to make the flags around the monument fly in picture-perfect fashion.

Mahoney, who had bought a bag of unshelled peanuts from a street vendor, had dropped a peanut on the ground only a couple of inches from one of his oversized feet. A few yards away stood a pigeon with tail feathers that looked as if they'd been caught in a lawn mower. The pigeon had just waddled in toward the peanut, then waddled away, then waddled back in again. The bird was a study in indecision, its small brain trying to decide if a single nut was worth coming within stomping range of the huge white-haired animal that smelled of fermented grain.

'You actually went to his retirement ceremony?' DeMarco said.

'Hell, yes. And I took Andy Banks with me.'

'Banks went with you?'

'Yeah, I had to explain things to him, make sure he understood why we were doin' what we were doin' and why he needed to keep quiet about it. He didn't like it at first, straight arrow like him, but he figured out pretty quick that I was right — and that it's better having me and the President on his side than not. He's actually a pretty good guy. I'm glad he's in that job.

'Anyway, I had a ball at that damn ceremony. Wouldn't have missed it for the world. The little shit was so popular that only about twenty people were there; the bosses probably made their secretaries go. The neat thing was they held it in an auditorium that seated three hundred. That was a *nice* touch on somebody's part.'

'If he was fired, why hold a retirement ceremony?'

'Woulda looked funny if we hadn't. The press might have asked why a guy as important as him wasn't given a send-off.'

Mahoney dropped another peanut next to his foot, doubling the pigeon's temptation. The pigeon flapped its wings madly, loose feathers flying; the bird's way of protesting Mahoney's cruelty.

'Yeah, the President got up, said about three sentences, and then he gave Donnelly a pin and a cheap watch and the kinda little plaque they give postal workers for luggin' the mail.'

A third peanut slipped from Mahoney's paw. The pigeon was now insane, darting back and forth on its little pigeon feet — toward the peanuts, away from the peanuts, toward the peanuts. Mahoney was oblivious to the bird's anguish.

'Banks just glared at Donnelly the whole time he was there, like he was trying to laser the skin off his face with those eyes of his. But not me. I walked up to him while people were eatin' this shitty little cake they got him. He was just standing there by himself, lookin' damn near catatonic. Anyway, I leaned down and said, 'This was for Marge Carter, you little fuck.' And you know what he said? He said, 'Who?' I almost belted him, Joe.'

The pigeon was now moving sideways toward the peanut pile, a crab with feathers, apparently thinking this maneuver rendered it invisible. It had just entered the shadow created by the creature's body, the peanuts only inches away.

'But right at the end, when everyone's ready to leave, this woman comes up and screams at him, right in front of the journalists. 'I'm gonna tell 'em all what you did, you bastard,' she says. Naturally Donnelly doesn't know what the fuck she's talking about. How could he, he never met her. But the journalists surrounded her right away.'

'Who was the woman?' DeMarco asked.

'The beginning of Donnelly's legal troubles,' Mahoney said with a wink.

Then Mahoney whooped a laugh and slapped a knee to punctuate his joy — and the pigeon exploded into the sky like it had a bottle rocket up its ass. Its ragged feathers almost hit Mahoney's square chin.

'Jesus!' Mahoney said. 'Crazy fuckin' bird. What's its problem?'

'So that poor bastard Edwards is going to go down in history as an assassin, and nobody will ever know about the link that may have existed between Kennedy and a dead Cuban,' DeMarco said.

Mahoney waved a hand, removing this small

obstacle. 'Nah, I wrote up a memo last night. I'll have it put over in Archives, not to be opened for fifty, sixty years. Can't you just see it when people read it? I wish I could be there to see the fuss it'll cause.'

Given his luck, DeMarco thought, he probably would be.

Mahoney stood up and dusted off the back of his pants.

'I gotta get goin'. It's my anniversary, did I tell you?'

'No,' DeMarco said.

'Yeah, we've been married, Mary Pat and me, almost forty years now. Can you believe it?'

DeMarco decided to remain silent.

'How 'bout you, Joe? What's a handsome young fella got planned for a perfect Friday night?'

'I'm meeting a woman I know. She works over at Interior.'

'Good for you. It's about damn time you got back in circulation. Get yourself laid, get drunk, have a good time.'

'Actually she's gonna help me pick out some furniture,' DeMarco said.